Quintspinner

Quintspinner

A Pirate's Quest

by

Dianne Greenlay

iUniverse, Inc.
New York Bloomington

iUniverse books may be ordered through booksellers or by contacting:

iUniverse
1663 Liberty Drive
Bloomington, IN 47403
www.iuniverse.com
1-800-Authors (1-800-288-4677)

Because of the dynamic nature of the Internet, any Web addresses or links contained in this book may have changed since publication and may no longer be valid. The views expressed in this work are solely those of the author and do not necessarily reflect the views of the publisher, and the publisher hereby disclaims any responsibility for them.

ISBN: 978-1-4502-3397-2 (sc)
ISBN: 978-1-4502-3398-9 (hc)
ISBN: 978-1-4502-3399-6 (ebook)

Library of Congress Control Number: 2010909960

Printed in the United States of America

iUniverse rev. date: 06/30/2010

To my children,
because you are loved.
Ooh-ah.

Acknowledgments

No book is the result solely of an author's efforts and therefore I wish to offer my gratitude to the many people who assisted me upon this journey:

To the wonderful Shaunavon Library staff who fulfilled my numerous requests for reference materials, without which this book would not have been written;

To my many teachers over the years, whose lofty standards ensured that I became fluent in at least my mother tongue;

To Diana Gabaldon, historical author extraordinaire, for her encouragement and excellent advice to me during a blue pencil session at the Surrey International Writer's Conference;

To the very knowledgeable and engaging staffs of the many marine exhibitions and nautical museums of Nova Scotia, Canada. The information that they had at their fingertips was amazing, immeasurable, and full of unexpected bits of historical entertainment;

To the crew of the tall ship *Silva*, in Halifax, Nova Scotia, for allowing me to hoist sail aboard their ship, or should I say, *attempt* to hoist sail—it was the hardest physical thing that I've ever done;

To my husband, Mike, who tirelessly edited page after page of manuscript, and whose input kept me grounded when I tended to float with my head in the clouds;

To Kim Laidlaw, a good friend who gave me something to prove;

To Hazel Lavoy, whose attention to detail, meticulous eye, and critiquing abilities were phenomenal;

To Norman Lavoy, Shirley Nordlund, and Cathy Smith, for getting caught up in the story and never flagging in their enthusiasm for it;

To Catherine Millard and Deb Widmer, who were there for me from the beginning, sharing their belief in the value of this story at crucial times when my own faltered;

And to my children, Michael, Tobishan, Sheridan, Byron, Clayton, and Brianne, whose teenage escapades provided plenty of fuel to fire up my already overactive imagination, and who taught me that there's always somethin' what comes from somethin' ....

I would also like to note that all errors contained within are my own and, although I spent a good deal of time researching particulars, the characters and events are products of my imagination and are entirely fictional (except, of course, for those that are entirely true). Enjoy.

Love with care—then what you will, do.

– St. Augustine
Algeria, 4th century

There's always somethin' what comes from somethin'.

– Mrs. Hanley
London, England, 1717

Prologue

He would have retched, had his mouth not already been open in a strangled scream. He hoped the thickness of the stone walls would prevent the others from hearing him. It would not do for a man of his ranking to be caught in such a compromising position. Performing such a compromising act. It was revolting to him yet had to be done.

Sitting erect on a chair in front of the fireplace's bed of embers, he swiped at a bead of sweat that ran down his cheek and into his carefully groomed beard. His legs, powerfully built from past years of required training, nonetheless shook uncontrollably. Exhaling a long steadying breath, he began. It was time.

The tip of the iron rod glowed crimson and sizzled as it seared into his flesh, melting skin then muscle. He pressed it deeper into his own upper chest. Hot tendrils of smoke curled up into his nostrils.

The brand would make the difference. He was certain of that.

He was alone in the bed chamber and had secured its great wooden door shut against any intrusion. This was not a procedure for the uninitiated to witness. He had had to do it on his own. He had considered taking a stiff drink beforehand to help numb the anticipated pain but had wisely decided against it. There could be no room for error.

It had to be perfect in its placement.

Perfect in its outline.

Was it any wonder he'd had no results with the ring before this? The bejeweled circle sat just above the middle knuckle on his little finger and could be pushed down no further. It was too small for him to wear it properly.

And he'd not been born with the mark.

Without one, it was said, the power of the ring's verdurous emerald stones would be minimal. Ineffectual. Obtainable, to be sure, but not without months, maybe years of practice. But now ....

He could hardly wait for his burnt flesh to heal.

Deeper in the bowels of London, tucked down a narrow cobbled alleyway, the sharp bouquet of smoldering herbs permeated a shuttered room. Its lone occupant sat at a table, inhaling the vapors as they rose from her infusion dish. As she peered at the flame of the lone candle burning in a holder beside her clay dish, its tip flickered and danced, probing the darkness of the room.

She owned only one item of any value—its real worth was known to only a few—and she manipulated it with her fingers, breathing slowly and deeply, willing the visions to visit. There were many things that she wanted to know. Things that had been asked of her by others. Things she needed to know for herself. The visions would come—they always did. The visions would tell her.

Something pushed into the edge of her thoughts. An intrusion. An unbidden presence challenged. She tilted her head. No, not challenging. *Seeking.* A faint pulsing energy ... growing stronger. She caught her breath and began to tremble. *A Spinner?* Why now? Had the time truly come to prepare a successor?

The suddenness of the first vision's arrival made her gasp. This time there were horrific flashes—terrifying and grotesque clips of violence and pain—and she whimpered as they slammed through her mind. It was not the first time that the visions had touched her with fear but now they announced that the inevitable would soon be forced upon her.

Chapter One

William would never forget the last day of his life as he knew it.

He was being attacked for the first time that morning. The rough grip clutching him dug into his shoulder and shook him hard. His heart bolted into a sudden pounding frenzy.

"William! Wake now!" The voice was shrill and pierced his sleep. His eyes shot open and focused on the face hovering above him.

His mother. Even in the dim pre-dawn light, he could see a deep furrow of worry lacing her eyebrows together. Her lips were pressed into a narrow frown and he couldn't quite read the emotion fueling her painful grasp on him.

Worry or anger? It didn't matter. Whatever it was, it wasn't going to be good.

"C'mon lad! Up with you. Your father and brother didna' return from the pub last evening–still drunk as mice in the dregs of a brandy barrel, I 'spect–but that's no relief to Millie, will it be, with her bag near ready to burst, nor to those of us needin' kindling to have kept the flame tucked overnight. Sometimes I curse the day John Robert discovered his dammed drink!"

His confusion at being woken well before sun up was quickly replaced with alarm. Not home? Neither one? William wearily struggled to sit up on his straw-filled mat. A tangled lock of sandy colored hair swung down into his face and he tucked it behind his ear. He recognized his mother's angry use of his father's proper names.

"Bring us wood and dung as fast as you can, lad, and I'll set to save what embers I can. Your sister will start the milkin'. Quickly! Off with you now!"

He could hear the strain in her voice. His Da' not home? Nor Johnny? His mother's worry was well placed then. His father would never have left the evening milking undone. At the very least his older brother, John, would have been sent back to help do the chores. And no wood for the overnight or morning fire!

He quickly slid both feet into the boots lying on the floor beside him. The worn leather had molded to his feet like a second layer of calloused skin. Throwing his woolen tunic on overtop of his night shirt and trousers, he quickly lashed it around his waist, and called out.

"Lucas! C'mon boy, let's have a look." From a woven floor pad, the grizzled hound lifted his head in response to his name, but the relative warmth of the house called more strongly to his arthritic joints than his master's voice, and he merely yawned and laid his head back down upon his front paws. "Fine then, you old fart! Stay here while I go looking." Lucas simply closed his eyes and exhaled a contented sigh. William didn't blame him. The dog was nearly as old as William was now and the past winter's ache had settled and stayed in his bones. Being allowed to stay inside was a special treat. Giving his dog a fond scratch between the animal's ears, William pulled the tunic's hood up over his own head, and stepped through the hut's doorway into the chill of the damp air.

An urgent lowing greeted him as he strode the few steps it took to reach the livestock shed's doorway. Running footsteps from behind told him that Abbey was already on her way to milk the cow. For a heartbeat William felt a pang of guilt for his little sister. The cow's bag would be swollen hard and the animal would be more miserable and uncooperative than usual. Millie was calmer with a female's handling of her teats at the best of times, it seemed to him.

Probably comes from having the same kind of equipment, and knowing how to handle 'em without harm.

William trotted silently further down the rutted path, its surface having been torn into parallel troughs by years of foot traffic and cart wheels. Anything useful as kindling had long since been picked clean near the buildings. His keen eyes gradually adjusted to the dim pre-dawn light. He preferred to find branches and twigs to burn, rather than to have to return with an armful of dung from the cowshed. Although the manure burned slowly and gave off decent warmth, its smoke was thick and noxious.

He was closer to the village than to his home by the time he came across anything worth picking up. Skirting around the edges of the underbrush that lined both sides of the path, he gathered a small armful of dried twigs. They would burn up in no time, he knew. He continued to scour the bushes deeper into the underbrush in hopes of discovering a few decently sized branches.

Just a bit more and I'll have enough to make the porridge fire, anyway.

He realized it was the wrong time of year to be finding much dead wood. Everything was leafed out and no limbs on the trees or bushes were dry enough to have been shaken down by wind passing through the thickets and forest.

Scrambling out of the underbrush, he clutched the twigs and a few skinny branches to his chest. Reaching the road once more, he stumbled in one of the ruts and pitched forward onto his knees, dropping his kindling. An intense bolt of pain shot through his leg as his kneecap cracked against an exposed cobble rock. William ground his teeth together in quiet agony.

Goddamn these ruts! Where in the hell are Johnny and Da' anyway?

Still on his hands and knees, he lifted his head and glanced down the road. Something off to the side glowed eerily white, lying in an area of dark trampled grasses. He squinted in the semi-light and cursed the rut again for being the cause of his knee pain. *Damned stupid stumble–*

William strained his eyes on the strange discoloration ahead, his knee pain immediately forgotten.

What the hell is that?

Chapter Two

A branch! A large friggin' branch!

He struggled to his feet and fixing his gaze on it, lurched towards it. Living at the edge of the forest as his family did, William knew the different woods on sight, and he also knew their properties—which smelled sweetest when burning, which was strongest for fences, and which wood was flexible enough for bows. Even so, in this dim predawn gray, he could not place from which kind of tree it was. The shape was unlike anything that he was familiar with. He kept his eye on the precious branch as he hurried onward. Upon reaching it, he bent down and froze in mid-reach.

Not a branch.

Wood, yes to be sure, but it was the splintered remains of a broken club, its shattered end darkly stained. William's nostrils flared as the faint metallic scent wafted up from the dark patch of grass.

'Heme' they had called it in the slaughter shed. "It's the heme 'o the blood what gives the smell," his father had once told the boys. Johnny had declared that he smelled only the pigs' shit, but William had been blessed with a sense of smell more keen than most, and to him the warm blood smelled vaguely like the hot metal in the blacksmith's shop.

"You're part wolf, I swear," his father had declared. "Ya' see and smell things the rest of us can't. Whatever use that will come to though, I can't declare."

William held the broken club to his nose and sniffed. It was the heme alright. Alarmed, he threw it down and it landed with a soft wet thud onto a saturated piece of cloth lying in the crushed grass. William bent closer and peered at the spot. His stomach lurched.

Da's cap!

Wet with the heavy morning dew. Wet with blood. It laid in the grasses as though already part of the earth.

Oh Jesus! It can't be! His heart hammered in his chest as cold panic washed over him. *Oh God! Wha–what happened?* His father was a large man. Determined. Stronger than most. *What could possibly have gotten the best of him?*

William dropped onto his hands and knees, oblivious to the shrieking pain in his knee. His stomach was heaving. The burn of the bile in his empty stomach filled his mouth and his shoulders hunched high under his ears as he heaved, choking and spitting.

Then suddenly, horribly, his eyes came to rest on a calloused pale hand protruding from the tangled roots of the hawthorn bush beside him, the broken wrist bent at an odd angle, the entire arm awash with blood.

Oh Christ Almighty!

William strangled a cry in his throat and his stomach heaved anew. The dry heaves tore at his insides and he gasped for breath. The curl of the fingers, the shape of the broad thumb, so much like his own–

Dear God! Let him be alive!

Jerking his head up from the sight of his grisly find, William scanned the area around him. His breath came in ragged gasps. *Am I alone? Oh God! Lucas! I need you here, boy! Who did this? A club? It wasn't an animal! Bandits? Are the attackers still around?*

Self-preservation instincts took over. Seeing no one and hearing only his own blood roar in a frantic whoosh in his ears, William reached out for the protruding fingers.

"Da'?" he whispered in the semi-darkness. Clasping the cold finger, he shook it as though to wake its owner. The hand was already stiffening in death.

"Da'!" William's silent scream was punctuated by the whoosh in his head. His breath came in burning gulps as he reached out and parted the bushes. His eyes travelled from the hand, up the bloodied forearm, to the body, then upward to the face. His vision blurred with hot tears. *Oh Da' –*

The words died in his throat. The sightless blue eyes were not his father's.

The roaring inside his head increased to a high pitched squeal. He felt his thoughts spinning, spinning, as he sank mercifully into blackness. The void sucked him down into nothingness, away from the terror of his discovery.

His head dropped with a soft thump onto the cold chest of his brother's stiffening corpse.

William never felt the rough hands that pulled him from the bush, nor felt the coils of rope splitting his skin as the strands were tightened, cutting into his wrists and ankles, binding them together.

Chapter Three

To the girl on the stool, the scream was at once both ear-shattering and guttural. The hairs on her arms and the back of her neck stood on end and her heart pounded furiously against her chest wall. The woman on the low bed beside her moaned and writhed in agony, gripped in a contraction beyond her control.

"Tess!" The woman hissed, the contraction slowly ebbing away. Her eyes clenched shut in fear and pain.

"I'm here," Tess responded and shifted her weight forward on the stool, gently wiping the woman's brow. In spite of the fire burning in the hearth, cold rivulets of her own sweat trickled down between Tess's shoulder blades.

Being the daughter of the much sought after London physician, Dr. Charles Thomas Willoughby, Tess had heard similar cries of distress coming from the many pregnant patients her father attended to. She had, on several occasions, accompanied him into the bed chambers of these laboring women for their deliveries, handing him whatever linens, medical potions, and tools that he required. However, this time, the screams burst forth from her mother, and it was horrifyingly different.

Elizabeth Willoughby lay on the cot, her nightshift pasted with sweat to her chest. A thin sheet draped her lower body. As her eyes slowly opened, she fixed Tess in a glassy stare. She breathed a series of shallow gasps behind chattering teeth.

"C'mon, Mum," Tess encouraged, in a voice that she hoped did not relay her own fear. "Squeeze my hand and bite down on this linen when the next pain comes—"

Another wrenching scream cut Tess off as her mother's body tensed then arched with the fury of the contraction.

Something is very wrong!

Tess again mopped the sweat from her mother's forehead, and wiped a sliver of drool which slid down from the corner of her mother's mouth. She tried to keep her voice low and soothing.

"Cassie's gone to find Father! Father went to tend to a mishap down on the docks but they'll be back any minute."

Cassie would be able to find Dr Willoughby as quickly as anyone, but being labeled a "nigger servant", she might have been subject to interference by any number of London's citizens. Tess fervently hoped that Cassie had been able to make her way to the waterfront unimpeded.

"Any minute now, they'll be here–do you hear me? Elizabeth Willoughby, answer me!" she scolded, but her mother did not respond. Not even to the use of her formal name.

"Packing, Tess." Her mother's cracked whisper was barely audible. *What did she say?*

"Packing? But you've not had the child yet, Mum–" Tess stopped short as her mother weakly pulled back the sheet covering her abdomen. Tess's eyes widened in fright. A dark spreading stain was seeping along the bedding between her mother's legs.

"Oh my God, *Mum!*" Tess shrieked and sprang to her feet. She raced across the room to the barrel that held the cleaned battings of raw cotton. Jamming an armful of the yellow fluff between her mother's thighs she pressed with both hands.

"Father says steady pressure is the key to stopping any bleeding," she gasped. "You'll be alright, you'll see, Mum!'

What is keeping Father? He should have been back by now! How long can bleeding like this continue? Tess sent up a silent prayer. *Please, God, don't let her die! Don't let them die!*

She felt stiff with building panic. She wasn't sure if it was being fuelled by her mother's impending doom or the thought of bearing the brunt of her father's quick temper. She adjusted her pressure on the cotton wad and felt a small hard knob push back into the palm of her hand.

What is that?

Sweat dripped freely from the tip of Tess's nose and chin now; droplets slid from her forehead and burned her eyes as she blinked fiercely to clear the sting.

It feels like a –it can't be! Please, Dear God, don't let it be!

Tess pulled the edge of the sodden cotton bundle back and quickly felt for the knob again.

There it is! A heel! Slippery with warm blood and birth fluids, it was definitely a tiny foot.

Dear Mary in Heaven, the baby is coming the wrong way!

A sanguineous effluence announced another contraction's arrival, but this time her mother was silent.

"Mum?" Tess anxiously scanned her mother's face. No reply.

"Mum!" It was Tess's turn to scream. "Don't you leave me! Father's coming! This baby needs you! Stay with me!"

What to do? What to do? Her thoughts crashed and collided with each other. *Get the baby out!* a voice inside her instructed. It sounded vaguely detached yet familiar and comforting.

Tess positioned herself with one hand on her mother's swollen belly and began pushing towards her mother's feet. With her other hand, she grabbed the baby's foot and gently pulled. Another nub protruded from the birth canal, announcing the arrival of the second foot. Her mother's swollen torso hardened again and again. Tess lost count of the contractions before the baby's tiny body finally emerged with one horrible bloody gush.

A boy! I have a brother! Tess had not thought of the child in terms of a sibling until this moment.

"God, spare him!" she pleaded in audible prayer. As if in answer, the baby's head emerged with the next contraction. The tiny boy laid ominously still in Tess's hands, his face and body quickly deepening to a dusky purple.

Too long! It took too long!

Frantically Tess swiped the mucous from her new brother's face then grasped and squeezed his rib cage with her hands.

"Breathe!" she screamed into the still blue face. The shock of her scream had its desired effect. At once, the curled up arms and legs flew open and the baby sucked in a gurgling breath, then emitted a high pitched squeal of indignant newborn rage. Tess had never heard a more beautiful sound. A sob of relief escaped from her chest. *He's alive!*

"Tess!" a voice roared. "What in God's name have you done?"

The angry words thundered from the doorway. Tess gasped, nearly dropping the infant in her panic. Reflexively clutching the screaming bundle to her chest, she whirled around to meet her accuser. Her father's imposing frame charged into the room.

Chapter Four

A foul musky rot.

William's semiconscious brain attempted to sort the two scents out. A soft sniffing sound and a quick brush of fur against his chin startled William into full wakefulness. Darkness engulfed him, his surroundings unfamiliar and threatening. He tried to remember where he was. Not on his own sleeping mat, tucked under his warm woolen bedding, that was for sure. *How did I get here?* He lay still for a few seconds, the sour taste of vomit still strong in his mouth. For a moment, his own blue eyes fluttered open but he could see only dim outlines in the lantern lit darkness.

Lanterns! At once all of his senses screamed high alert.

Many more strong odors filled his nostrils. Pitch. Rot. Animal dung. Shit and sweat. He closed his eyes to mere slits and took stock of his predicament. He was lying on his side, rough plank flooring beneath him, his wrists and ankles bound. *My knee is aching like a sonofabitch. What–*

A low rumble of voices cut his thought off short. The odor of unwashed flesh grew stronger with the approach of another lantern. He mentally separated it out from another, less prevalent stench, but one which seemed to lie in an invisible ribbon at floor level. Old rotted meat. Kerosene. Something fermenting.

He could hear the soft swoosh of his own blood in his ears again and nausea returned. His shoulders had begun to ache fiercely as well, though he could not feel his wrists or his hands.

How long have I been lying here, and where is here?

He could feel in his cheek, really, more than he could hear the vibration of the creaking floor planks that he was lying upon. Was that the faint calling of gulls? He couldn't be sure. *Am I near the shoreline then? Am I in a waterfront shop somewhere?* He thought of the smell of rotting meat. *A butcher shop? Or is it rotting fish? Definitely near the wharf then.* As he slowly recalled his thoughts, panic and confusion rose again.

Johnny! Is Da' dead too? They would have fought to the death to save one another. He struggled to hold back tears. *And Mum —she'll be worried out of her mind! All three of us gone; Da' and Johnny aren't ever comin' back!*

William *had* to get home, back to her. *What will happen to her and Abbey? And Lucas.* William couldn't remember a single day in his life without his beloved dog.

The lantern light was moving closer. William fought to keep his breathing slow and even. The lantern hovered close, just above his face. A booted foot thudded him forcefully in his mid thigh. William did not move.

"Get this one loose and movin' about, 'afore he shits himself, too," a gravelly voice commanded.

"Yessir!"

More voices. Younger than the gravelly one, William guessed. He strained his memory to recognize any of them as belonging to any of the merchants that his father had done business with. He could not place a single one.

William felt hands grab him and haul him to his feet. At least he thought he was standing on them. His feet were really too numb to tell. With eyes wide open now, he saw the glint of metal in the lantern light, as a dagger blade flashed in front of his face. With one quick slash from his captor, his wrists were cut free, and with a second, his feet.

"What's yer name, lad?" the gravelly voice asked. William tried to speak but his tongue felt furry and thick.

"Answer me now, piss-pants," Gravelly Voice commanded, "or I'll flog it outta' ya'!"

William was suddenly aware of a cool wetness in the crotch of his trousers. The pungent smell of urine rose above the cornucopia of so many other strange smells. For a moment his fear was squelched by a stab of hot shame in the realization that he had indeed pissed himself.

He licked his dry lips and croaked, "William."

"William, eh? That's a fine name fer a tar. Welcome aboard the *HMS Argus*, Piss-Pants William. Follow Mr. Smith, here. "He'll get ya' something to eat and show ya' to yer work station and yer hammock, in that order. Yer duties start this evenin' before tomorrow's first light. Mr.

Smith, Piss-Pants William is yer charge fer today. We're doin' one on one fer all the new recruits in case they get any frisky ideas.

"Wait! Duties? I don't understand–" William began to protest, but Gravelly Voice had moved on, kicking at the next unfortunate body lying in bondage a few feet away.

Smith tugged at William's sleeve. "C'mon," he said quietly, "Ya' wanna' eat or not?" William stared at the one called Mr. Smith. Brown eyes stared back at him from a face that was laced with a network of fine scars over high cheekbones and forehead. The boy's hair appeared to be a coppery brown in the dim light of the lanterns; it was tied back in a braided plait that reached just past his thin shoulders. Smith was a head taller and appeared to be somewhat older. William guessed Smith was probably around John's age–*Johnny!* His mind filled with an unspeakable sorrow. He pushed the ache aside, trying to make sense of this living nightmare.

"Wha–what is this place? I don't understand what's happened–"

Smith turned and looked at him. "How old are ya' anyway?" He peered closer. William could see a faint scar running across Smith's cheek from his ear to the corner of his mouth. "You've not even many whiskers, do ya'?"

Pride forced the truth from William. "I'm sixteen. Nearly seventeen."

"Sixteen? Hah!" Smith snorted, "Not a boy anymore, but a helluva' long ways out from being the eighteen that the friggin' Navy Proclamation states we must be before volunteerin'...."

The Navy? What the hell? "But I didn't volunteer!" William protested, "I–"

"Ya' did as far as the Navy's concerned."

"But I didn't! I'm not doing this!" William hissed, "I'll leave–"

The sting of Smith's sharp slap across William's mouth caught him in mid sentence. "See here, now," Smith whispered menacingly, "there is no leavin' this hell hole, 'cept overboard in a tarp with a stitch through yer nose. Ya' hear? Leaving alive is *not* a choice ya' have. We're already near a day out to sea."

William took in this new information in stunned silence. Feeling was beginning to return to his feet and he stumbled painfully along as though walking in oversize wooden clogs.

So I'm on a ship! And in its belly at that. He followed behind Smith, as they made their way through a narrow pathway lined on each side with boxes and barrels of all sizes piled to shoulder height. By now William's eyes had adjusted to the low light and he caught a brief glance of a small flash of movement at the base of a barrel. *Rat! And judging from the smell, more than one.* He shuddered to think that the sniff and brush of something soft against his face that had awoken him a few minutes earlier had likely been one of its cousins.

Filthy damn creatures.

A rat bite almost always brought on the fevers, William knew. Problem was, most rats snuck up on a lad when he was lying down, asleep. He had not suffered a bite from one himself, but had heard of the livery owner and all who worked there routinely getting bitten. One of the livery boys had even died of the fevers last winter. William had not known the boy personally, but he had seen him once, when William had accompanied his Da' into town for supplies. He remembered the lad, a scrawny, shy boy, small even for his age of ten, forking old bedding out of the stalls into a wagon. Talk had been last winter that he had died a fitful death, his vision clouded with demons, such as the fevers often brought on, and him yelling out till his last hours.

Would the demons have followed the boy into the afterlife? William hoped that when it was his time, his death would be quick, and not drawn out in the unseen horrors that seemed to afflict all who died a feverish end.

Smith stopped at a long narrow wooden table. "Sit. Cook'll get us some chowder." He planted himself on a low wooden bench and motioned for William to do the same. "So, you'll work as yer told, ya' see," he continued, "or you'll die." It was a simple statement. Smith shrugged as though to emphasize such inevitability.

William stared at Smith in frank astonishment. *Has he been reading my thoughts?*

William's eyes, wide in surprise, did not escape Smith's notice, and the corner of his scar-licked mouth pulled into a thin, sad smile. "Ya' survived the pressin', didn'cha? Many don't."

Pressing? Christ! So that's what happened! William had heard that press gangs roamed the countryside near every port in Great Britain, physically abducting nearly all men and older boys that they came across, to be recruits for His Majesty's Royal Navy. Physical force was almost always used by the "gangers", as no man who neither had a family nor made his living on land went voluntarily. Being "pressed" into service meant suddenly disappearing, leaving family behind with a good chance of never returning to see them again.

William thought again of John. Of his father's cap ground into the bloodied grass. Of his mother and Abbey begging at the neighbors' door–*Stop it! You can't help them now!*

"So, who are ya'?" Smith peered at William, holding him in his gaze.

"William."

Smith continued to stare, waiting for William to go on.

"William Taylor," William added. "Me Da's a farmer ...." William's voice trailed away. *Da's dead. John's dead. And somebody's gonna' pay* .... William could feel his chest tighten and his cheeks grew hot. He clenched his teeth and pinched his thigh, focusing on the pain. *Don't cry! Don't you dare cry, you milksop! Stay hard. Keep your wits about you,* he scolded himself.

Smith leaned in on his elbows and announced, "Well, Mr. Taylor, glad to have ya' on board." He extended his hand and shook William's. "Samuel Smith, makin' yer acquaintance." Glancing over his shoulder, he squinted into the ship's murky semi-darkness and cocking a thumb back towards the other sailors, he continued in a low whisper. "And I'll tell ya' now, they don't see no point in feedin' a body what won't haul and scrub, ya' see," he explained quietly.

"Work, or die, Mr. Taylor," he sat back and nodded. "That's yer only choice now."

Chapter Five

The child would live. At least for now. The fate of his newly post-partum wife was not so certain, but in his experience, the doctor knew that she stood a chance if the bleeding could be controlled.

In tending to his wife's hemorrhage, Dr. Willoughby immediately demanded that Tess and Cassie chew copious amounts of tobacco leaves, spitting the soggy cuds out into a bowl, while the bulk of the noxious stuff simmered in a cauldron over the room's fire. Mixing the tobacco with fresh cotton, he packed the bundle into his wife's birth canal, and added more steeped tobacco juice and leaves as they cooled, to the vaginal poultice.

"Broken tobacco slows the bleed and the cotton clots any blood that does escape," he explained. Both girls felt nauseous and in an effort to ward off the impending headache that would surely follow their own absorption of the tobacco juices, they sipped a warm cup of tea laced with laudanum. Light headed then, and full of silliness, they took to their beds early, each giggling at the other's brown stained teeth and lips.

"We look like the old corner Crone!" Cassie exclaimed, smirking at her reflection in a silver-backed looking glass. Tess smiled too, although the mention of the old woman gave her the shivers.

The corner Crone was a beggar woman renowned for her eerily accurate prophesies and gift of second sight. It was said that she had not been burned as a witch because her advice was frequently but confidentially sought by high ranking city officials and men of power. Dr. Willoughby, however, had only open contempt for the woman and her herbal potions.

"Have you actually seen her, Cassie?" Tess asked.

"Oh yes, I was on an errand and had to go almost down to the waterfront, when I turned a corner and there she was, all dressed in a shabby brown robe, her hood all up and around her head and face," Cassie recalled and pulled her nightshirt up over her head, clasping it under her chin, to simulate just such a hood. "Her hand was all knarled and fingers all curled, but there was a ring on one of her fingers. It caught my eye because it sparkled as though it had some gems or the like in it catching the sun."

Cassie's eyes widened as she recalled the details, then her eyebrows knitted together in a frown. "Come to think of it, that ring actually didn't sparkle so much as it *glowed*, just like the glow of a fire's ember, only it was as pure a blue as I've ever seen. I remember wondering how a beggar would come to have such a thing, let alone keep it from being stolen off her ...."

"Did she say anything?" Tess pressed.

"No. Mind, I'd not gotten close to her, but I knew when I saw her, who she was."

"Let's seek her out one day. Soon."

Cassie turned to look at Tess in amazement. "Are you mad? Why would you want to?"

"I don't know. I just want to. Maybe she'll tell our fortunes. Wouldn't that be exciting?" Tess flopped back onto her soft mattress.

"Tess, your father would whip you if he ever found out you went to her, let alone to that part of town. It wouldn't be good for his reputation as a doctor and respectable citizen to have his daughter consorting with the like."

"Well then," Tess retorted with a conspiratorial smile, "he mustn't ever know."

A faint high pitched squeal that ricocheted off the walls and echoed down the hallway abruptly interrupted their conversation.

"Charles the Third bellows, Madam, and I must go" Cassie groaned and gave a tired smile.

Tess held up a hand towards Cassie. "You go to bed." The squeal was more insistent. Tess rolled her eyes and sighed. "I'll tend to the little monster."

"No, it's my duty," Cassie responded and wrapped herself in her dressing gown.

"This one time, I'll go," Tess countered, "he's *my* brother, after all–" As soon as her words were out, a flicker of hurt flared in Cassie's eyes.

"No. I'll go," Cassie affirmed, the smile fading from her face, and she hastily left the bedroom, padding noiselessly down to the nursery.

Cassie was Tess's unofficial adopted sister. Cassie was also one of the family's servants. She was neither full kin nor indentured servant. She had been received as a young child, in partial payment for medical services that Tess's father had provided to a nobleman's family during an outbreak of fever.

The deadly fever and sickness had spread like wild fire through the man's house servant and serf populations, decimating both, including Cassie's parents, before ripping through the nobleman's own family. Cassie, spared but orphaned by the plague of disease, had been brought into the household by Dr. Willoughby himself. Not a supporter of slaves in his own household, the doctor nevertheless felt pity for the youngster and all other possible destinations for her seemed filled with only certain hardships.

Accurate birth records on servants and slaves were seldom kept, but by an estimation of his own making, based on the number and size of the child's teeth, Cassie had been perhaps only two years older than his six year old daughter, Tess. Dr. Willoughby had accepted his patient's desperate payment scheme, knowing that the man's fortune, like so many of the fever's victims, had nearly disappeared in less than a fortnight.

Now, at nearly eighteen, Cassie had grown into an attractive young woman. Her hair curled, rather than kinked, in loose waves reaching past her shoulders and nearly to her waist, onto golden brown skin.

Like a man's morning coffee with a dollop of sweet cream stirred in, was how Tess's mother had once described the color. Cassie's teeth, no longer gapping with the smile of a shy eight year old, were straight and white. This in itself made her stand out from most people, as darkly stained or missing teeth were the norm by adulthood. Elizabeth Willoughby, however, would not abide poor oral care within her household, demanding that everyone, servants included, polish their teeth and gums with a spit-rag before retiring each evening.

Although Cassie had grown up officially as her house servant, most times Tess considered Cassie to be a sister, a replacement for the blood sibling she'd never had. As children, the girls had been inseparable. Tess herself was blossoming into womanhood, and she and Cassie were often compared, her creamy complexion and own head full of thick, soft, copper colored ringlets to Cassie's darker palette.

"You two are like the sunrise, all gold and red, and the sunset, all soft shadows and tawny dark," Mrs. Hanley, the family's corpulent cook, had declared. "One's always sure to be followin' the other, too," she noted, nodding with a smile of satisfaction on her face, pleased with her philosophical observation. Mrs. Hanley often made such pronouncements about the goings-on around her, although Tess was quite certain that the jolly woman had never had real education of any kind, and was, in fact, like most of the household help, perfectly illiterate, not being able to read a single printed word.

She was, however, a treasure house of folk wisdom and often shared bits and pieces with the girls, of the folklore and mystic chronicles that were firmly entrenched in her beliefs. Many blustery winter nights had been spent with the three of them cuddled in front of the roaring kitchen fireplace, sipping on hot broths brewed from the various vegetations that the girls had helped to collect during the growing season.

"Ya' know," Mrs. Hanley had once said, her voice low enough that her words would not have carried beyond the closed doors of the kitchen, "there's a reason us three gets on so well." She had nodded her head, her plump cheeks and second chin shaking ever so slightly, as her eyes had sparkled with the excitement of sharing her secrets with the girls.

"Three's a strong number, ya' know," she had confided, looking at each girl, ensuring that she had their rapt attention. Looking back and forth from one to the other, she had leaned alternately toward each of them and continued in a quiet voice, "It's a thing of nature, three is. Three's the number that's important in the Church, fer them what studies and teaches there, but fer us all, three's the number of parts to a *family*. Mother, father and child. And three's involved in lot of things— sun, moon and stars, fer instance, land and water and air. And the Irish have their three leafed shamrock fer luck … but the Irish luck and magic, well … that's another story altogether." She'd shaken her head and given them a wink, and then rushed on. "Three makes a triangle, all sides and points," she'd whispered conspiratorially, "and everyone knows that 'third time's the charm'." She'd beamed at them and gathered them in her arms. "However, mostly three's fer things what wants to be together, like us!" she'd exclaimed happily.

Tess and Cassie had also spent many daytime hours in the warmth of Mrs. Hanley's kitchen, sipping hot tea and eating her freshly baked biscuits while seated at a table where Tess had painstakingly taught Cassie her letters and numbers. Most times, Mrs. Hanley observed the lessons none too tactfully, peering blatantly over the girls' shoulders.

"That's right," she would advise in an authoritative voice from behind, in apparent sagely assessment of Cassie's written words, "but be a bit cleaner with yer penmanship, won'cha now." And glancing sideways at each other, the girls would bite their cheeks to keep from laughing out loud at such a formal judgment of their work.

It was expected that Cassie would stay with the family until marriage or a further employment offer arose to change her destiny. Hers was an odd arrangement. The Willoughby's had raised her alongside their own daughter, as one of their own, although like their house servants, she had been given daily tasks to do. For such tasks, she had begun to receive small payments for herself on the occasion of her approximated sixteenth birthday. Nevertheless, no one ever discussed her leaving.

She had been dressed and schooled in the social graces as Tess had been, and Dr. Willoughby's approval was expected to be sought out by any prospective young men wishing to spend time in his adopted daughter's presence. Not that there were many. The socialites of upper class London may have secretly found the young woman to be attractive and intelligent, but her mixed parentage was still a negative factor in most of their eyes. Cassie did not care. Her life had been blessed with this family–people who treated her with respect and, yes, even loved her. She had no wish for change.

With them, she had learned all of life's basic skills. Her assistance in the kitchen with Mrs. Hanley had taught her how to cook, to start or bank a hearth fire, and to keep a living space clean and tight enough to discourage rodents, insects, and disease. The errands that she ran for Mrs. Willoughby introduced her to the finer things in life–soft linens and laces, teas, sweets–and gave her respected contact with the merchants involved in their procurement.

Dr. Willoughby's errands were more likely to be of an urgent nature– delivering letters and messages to colleagues and patients, picking up an assortment of medical supplies–he seemed to forever be running short of herbal mixtures, suturing supplies, surgical tools, and bandaging materials—and it was one of Cassie's duties to keep the shelves in the surgical room at the Willoughby's residence fully stocked. In between market visits there was the expected daily cleaning routine for her to perform as well as a thorough mopping up in between patients as required.

This last task was her least favorite, as Cassie did not have the stomach to sop up the jellied blood and small puddles of putrification and bits of flesh and bone that were invariably present after a surgery She admired Tess's fortitude and her ability to help her physician father when he required an extra pair of hands. The amputations and the birthing were the worst, she had decided, although the amputations were over quickly, while the birthings were hours, sometimes days of agony.

Cassie had also decided that she never wanted to put herself through that agony. Her lack of suitors was a blessing to her. Coupling with a man would only bring pain and a life of looking after yet one more person.

No, Cassie assured herself, *I have no wish for change in my life. I have enough.*

Chapter Six

Life with the newborn was unbearable. Charles Thomas Willoughby III was mostly a mewing brat, in Tess's opinion. He had only four stages of existence–sleeping, crying, eating, and pooping–and he rotated through them with the same regularity as the arrival of night and day. Tess's mother had remained weakened and bedridden for several weeks after the difficult birth, and a melancholy had settled deep within the woman.

The babe was small, with scrawny limbs that seemed soft and floppy, until he was startled, at which time he would throw his head back, his arms and legs shooting out in stiffened little sticks, making him look like a human starfish. The biggest things on her brother, Tess observed, were his eyes and his voice. Everything seemed to upset him, sending him into a high pitched screaming fit that grated on her nerves. The birth had been long and difficult, her father had explained, and such tumultuous births often left babies easily irritated.

At the time of the birth, he had checked the newborn over and quickly pronounced him to be 'unmarked'. The relief in his voice cut through Tess like a surgical scalpel. Her own birthmark–an acorn-shaped brown spot below her left earlobe from which a few delicately shaped teardrops trailed three finger widths long down her neck–had always been a source of shame to him.

"Ye've a gypsy's earring, ya' have," Mrs. Hanley had cheerfully explained to Tess when she was old enough to understand. "That's what it is, alright." Her eyes had narrowed and she whispered, "The Fates mark their Chosen ..." and she'd looked suspiciously over her shoulder as if expecting someone to jump out at her that very moment, before she continued, "but that's another story altogether." She had sighed and smiled at Tess. "Mark me words, little one, much of what ya' imagine will become a reality fer ya', if ya' wants it bad enough and ya' can put yer mind to it." She had nodded in her wisdomly way. "Yer meant fer great things, ya' are," and she had hugged Tess to her bosom, kissing the girl's head. "Great things."

Her father did not share Mrs. Hanley's optimism.

"Mrs. Hanley, this is a Christian household! I'll not have you speaking of gypsies and pagans within my home! Not while you are in my employ!"

He required Tess to wear high collars, powdering the mark over when she didn't, and her hair was nearly always fixed in a left sided plait. An overheard conversation between her parents and not meant for her ears, had brought Tess's sense of self worth into painful perspective a few years prior.

"Charles, she's past thirteen years of age," her mother had pointed out," and we must start making arrangements for possible suitors—"

"Elizabeth, have you forgotten that she is marked?" her father had asked irritably. "What reputable man would have her so?"

"The 'mark' as you call it, could possibly remain out of sight until after the marital legalities were completed, by which time it would be too late to matter."

"I am quite certain 'false pretenses' would be adequate grounds for annulment."

"She's *not* disfigured, Charles! It's just discolored skin—"

"People less educated would not interpret it so!" he had shouted. "Better that she had been marked by cowpox or measles than carry the mark of the Druids! It's pure superstition, but superstitious people talk! As do any who are in envy of our station in life." He had stabbed the air with his finger as if to mark his next thought. "At least a pox survivor would have some great worth in the work force." And with that, her mother had abruptly risen from her chair and swept from the room.

Out in the hallway, Tess had shrank back from sight, tucking into the darkness of the under-stairs cubby, hot tears of shame sliding silently down her cheeks, her hand softly covering the side of her neck.

Chapter Seven

The chowder, thin and oily, had an overpowering smell of fish to it. William hoped the smell of rotting fish that he had encountered earlier had not come from the cook's galley. Still, he had not eaten since the previous evening and the broth was warm. As he swallowed down the lumpy chowder, he studied the one called Samuel Smith, sitting across from him. Silky brown eyes stared calmly back at him.

Thin as he was, what flesh Smith did have, was well defined muscle; his hands seemed extraordinarily large, attached to the ends of such lanky forearms. William noticed that Smith's knuckles were swollen and covered in scars and scabs. *He's been in some scraps, alright.* In fact, the more William stared, the more he noticed that Smith seemed to be covered with scars everywhere. His upper arms were laced with a cobweb of silver strips that disappeared under the body of his shirt, and a long thin one on Smith's cheek seemed to pull up on the corner of his mouth, leaving him with a permanent half grin.

"How'd you get those scars?" William nodded towards Smith's arms. Smith glanced down at his own shoulders and shrugged.

"Kissed the gunner's daughter a time or two."

The gunner's daughter? A female? On a ship?

William himself had kissed only one girl. Maggie. They had been behind the slaughter shed the first time, and it had been at Maggie's instigation. He had sensed rather than felt someone behind him and when he had whirled around he had nearly knocked her over, she had been standing so close to him. He had reached out to steady her grabbing her by her upper arms. She'd fallen in towards his chest, and not by mistake he came to realize, as she'd quickly risen up on her toes, and turning her face up towards his, had pressed her moist lips to his.

He remembered his surprise and feeling a rush of pleasure as their tongues had met, and he'd returned the kiss fiercely, holding her tightly to him, his hands traveling up and down her body in new exploration. The warmth of her young breasts, the tautness of her nipples as they hardened in response to his palms cupping her breasts had made him aware of the hardening in his own crotch. He was breathless and he had pulled away to catch a snatch of air, before kissing her again.

A hunger for more—much more—of that pleasure was stronger than the guilt or the fear of getting caught, and he and Maggie had met on several occasions after that to enjoy their new intimacy. There had been many nights that William had listened to the grunts and gasps coming from his parents' bed, and his fantasies of his secret meetings with Maggie had brought him his own solitary pleasure, his low moans going unnoticed amid the sounds of his parents' coupling.

Maybe she had been worth it, this gunner's daughter. He could not imagine however, being scratched so deeply so as to be scarred like Smith.

William's puzzled look seemed to amuse Smith. "You'll have yer own set 'afore long I 'spect," he said, rising from the table, "near everyone does, sooner or later. Come on. You're a midshipman, but you'll also be helping Cook. Them barrels is the food stores fer this particular sailing an' Cook'll have ya' fetchin' from them, I've no doubt. I just hope that yer skills is considerable less than his," he cocked an eyebrow up and continued, "as it wouldn't do to have the men gettin' fat on flavor, or eatin' fer any other reason other than to stay alive." In spite of his fear of his strange surroundings, William smiled at Smith's description, and felt some of his tension drain away.

"You'll start at mid evenin' shift, so's the breakfast is ready by dawn." Smith pointed ahead of them deeper into the gloom. "Down there's the slings."

The 'slings' proved to be narrow strips of stained canvas strung in the fashion of hammocks that were hooked from the rafters of the deck flooring above their heads. Row after row of the grimy sheets swung from the ropes, in rhythm with the ship's sway. Most rows had two layers of the makeshift beds strung one above the other. A few were occupied, the sailors' arms and legs hanging over the edges, with the width of a sling being roughly only the space between a man's shoulder blades.

Thinner sailors obviously slept more securely and comfortably in these contraptions.

"When you're off shift, grab an empty one," Smith instructed. "Best to choose one what's highest up, but give her a shake just the same."

"A shake?"

"Fer dumpin' cooties and such off 'afore lyin' yer own noggin down amongst them." Smith saw William's face cloud in confusion. "It's to rid yer sling of the little buggers and chiggers what's fallen off from the lad who slept there 'afore ya;—do ya' not know even a single thing?" Smith asked exasperatedly.

"I've never sailed," William replied. "Never been on a stinkin' boat of any kind. I'm not a sailor. I'm—"

"You'll learn, and for yer sake, you'd best be a quick study. You're a lander fer now, but you'll be a sailor too. And probably will be for the rest of yer life." With an upward shrug of his eyebrows Smith added, "However short that may be."

Chapter Eight

William followed Smith through the innards of the ship, its unfamiliarity closing in on him like a poisonous fog. The two of them reached a ladder, which rose through an apparent hatch in the roof, up to the next level of the ship. "This here's the companionway to the main deck, so stay close," Smith instructed William.

The daylight was nearly blinding after coming from the darkened midlevel. The fresh sea air, however, was as sweet a thing as William could ever remember inhaling. Each breath was warm and clear, filling William's lungs with an unexpected sense of pleasure, washing the stew of below-deck stench from his nostrils and lungs.

He squinted into the sunlight, his eyes tearing up in response to the brightness of it all. Overhead, an airborne maze of riggings supported the white canvases of huge sails which boomed and snapped in response to the wind's prodding. The riggings were alive with sailors, all scurrying up, down, and sideways, as gracefully as hungry spiders inspecting a web. Beyond the sails, the vast blueness of the sky stretched to the horizon in all directions. Days with such a clear sky were precious few back on the coastline of Britain. William stared in amazement.

With his eyes having fully adjusted to the light of day, he looked around at his strange new world. The open deck was bustling with young men.

"Them right here are doin' drills," Smith pointed out, "and it's just such drills what's supposed to make our Brits such a formidable fightin' force." He nodded towards the other end of the open deck. "And them there are doin' the endless chores what keeps the Navy's fleet afloat."

Twenty or so crew members, some not much older than William himself, marched in unison along the back lines of the deck, handling their weapons in a perfectly choreographed routine, all moving as one body in a synchronized fashion. "Them boys there be the marines," Smith explained. "They'll be runnin' their drills every day and when they be done with that, it'll be a wee bit of trainin' fer the rest of us. Backups, sorta. Ever used a gun?"

William shook his head.

"No matter," Smith continued good-naturedly, "'cause they'd not be lettin' us landers have such a thing anyways. How's about a hanger?" he asked nodding towards a wicked looking blade gripped by one of the sailors. Again William shook his head, never taking his eyes from the marines' precise movements. "Ya' had any weapon use at all?"

"A skinning knife," William replied. "I had my own knife back home."

"Didcha' now?" Smith grinned as though he'd unearthed a secret. "A big one, was it?"

William shrugged his shoulders. "Big enough."

"But not a hanger. Could ya' do more with one than pick yer ear wax?"

William thought back to his chores at home. For a few moments he imagined himself back in the shed with his father and brother. Slaughtering a pig or goat had been easy enough but a cow or a wild deer had always required much more strength in wielding the blade. And then there was the memory of the smell of the heme, and the warmth of the slippery organs and entrails. William and John had usually managed to turn a day in the slaughter shed into a contest of skills between them. Skinning the carcass as quickly as possible yet carefully enough that the hide was removed intact was William's specialty. Such a hide could be sold to the tanners for far more than one that had any skinner lacerations through it.

John had always bested William in the carving up of the carcass, being older and stronger. However, the end of each day in the shed had seen the boys finishing up their brotherly competitions with several rounds of knife throwing. At this, they had been evenly matched. The main difference had been that John was right handed, and William had preferred to use his left.

His left hand however, bore a congenital peculiarity. His fourth and fifth fingers were webbed together from the middle knuckles to his hand, resulting in his remaining three fingers having developed the strength of a much more powerful grip.

"*Me granddad had a couplin' with a mermaid what he found washed up on the rocks along the shore, an' she infused him an' his future kin with her essence forevermore,*" his Da' had bragged in the pubs. The eloquence of his descriptive words and the outlandish story never failed to earn him a free drink from someone in the crowd. William's mother had different ideas.

A left hander was the sign of the Devil, his mother had declared, and she had determinedly insisted from the time he was small, that William learn to use his right hand. He had obligingly done so with a great deal of success but had also continued to use his left in most things, his coordination in both hands therefore becoming equally honed. His keen eyesight had allowed him to hit the target pole at the end of the shed nearly every time.

"Well do ya'? Eh?" Smith broke into William's thoughts with his question. "Do ya' know how to defend yerself?"

"I don't know," William answered truthfully. "Never had to."

Smith's eyes narrowed into dark dangerous slits and he hissed through his lopsided grin, "*That* opportunity will come about 'afore ya' even see it comin', I 'spect."

Chapter Nine

The marines were now repeating their drills and William's attention shifted to the other sailors around him. Several were on their hands and knees, wetting down and scrubbing the wooden planking with stiff brushes made of boar's bristle; some busied themselves with mops and rags, wetting and polishing. Still others hoisted and adjusted the huge sails, hollering back and forth to their airborne mates overhead, all the while pulling on the riggings strung intricately from each of the ship's two masts.

The sailors wore knee length breeches and most were deeply tanned and shirtless; those who sported upper garments wore nearly identical linen shirts, bleached in various shades of white, grime, and sweat. All of the men on deck were shoeless.

It was only then that William realized his own feet were bare. His footwear had been removed while he had lain unconscious. He glanced down at himself. Although the trousers were his own, he was embarrassed to see that he still wore his nightshirt which hung lopsidedly over the front of his pants. Attempting to tuck it in, William discovered that the large pocket sewn into the front of his trousers still contained something. The only thing in the world that was truly his. It was so trivial, yet here, having been wrenched away from anything familiar in his life, it was a desperate talisman, connecting him with his memories of home. His hand carved flute.

Where are my shoes? They left me my tunic? In the middle of his thoughts, William spied a young boy polishing the glass on the ship's cabin windows. The child appeared to be about seven or eight years old and was painfully thin. Smith noticed William staring and explained.

"That's young Tommy. He was brought on board only two sails ago. He be the powder monkey."

"The what? Whose son is he?" William was appalled that any father would let so young a son on board.

"He be the monkey. The one what delivers the powder to the gunners when we be in battle. An' he's no one's boy. Picked him off the street, they did."

"Stolen?"

"Nah. Rescued." Smith saw William's questioning look. "He'd a' died anyways, left on his own, he would. Starved or beaten dead by someone, just fer fun maybe. On board, he gets fed and beaten no more than he deserves."

"But his parents—"

"Probably don't have none. None what he knows of anyway. He don' even know his last name no more." Smith grinned and continued, "So's he just goes by Jones. Tommy Jones. That's 'cause one day he'll go back to Davy Jones, which is the only thing what'll take him back. Ya' see," he said thoughtfully, "Davy Jones's is likely to take us all to the depths sooner or later."

Their appearance on deck gave cause to the men to pause in their chores as they stared at the two arrivals. Some openly leered and shouted obscenities about what they would do with the boys' mothers. William had never been the centre of attention for anything. The only person who had ever stared at him for more than a few seconds at a time had been Maggie—dear, sweet Maggie—and William wished with all of his heart that he was back at his family's hut, back with his dull and repetitive daily tasks. He felt the eyes of the sailors boring into him.

I feel like a sow taken to town and put in the sale pen. You got your eyeful, you friggin' fish eaters, now go to hell!

As if reading his thoughts, Smith placed a hand on William's shoulder and yelled, "Ahoy! Listen up you slimy bastards! This be Cook's help and a lander, Mr. Taylor!" As if in response to this news, William heard low grumblings and words of acknowledgment coming from the crew members nearest to him. He glared back at them in defiance, his fingers curled into tight fists at his sides—a reflexive action in self defense, but it also hid the nervous shaking he felt.

"Back to work, ya' farkin' toads!" a voice louder than all the others bellowed, and the command was punctuated by the sharp crack of a whip on the wet decking. The voice belonged to a huge man, a man who towered over the rest and whose massive biceps rippled as he slowly and deliberately coiled up the strands of his whip.

"That's First Mate Rogers!" Smith gasped, his voice quivering, as the giant of a man advanced upon them. "Fer God's sake!" he pleaded in a whisper, "Taylor! Don't be lookin' him in the eye!"

Smith's warning came too late.

Chapter Ten

"What have we here?" the giant bellowed. William stared up at the mountain of flesh approaching him. He had never seen so large a man. With skin the color of darkened wood, and thick greasy strands of hair as black as coal streaming from underneath a red bandana, the First Mate towered over William. The giant's eyes were small and piggish, with irises so dark that they seemed one with the man's pupils. *The eyes of a demon!* William stood frozen to the spot in the shadow of the bulk before him, with only his nostrils twitching involuntarily at the foul body odor wafting from the man.

The giant scowled and his thick black eyebrows knitted together above his bridge of his nose. William stared, transfixed. The eyebrow hairs seemed to be moving of their own accord, shifting and undulating with the busyness of the lice which had taken up residence there. In fascinated disgust, William watched as small, wiggling specks fell from the giant's head and face, their tiny bodies plunging to certain death onto the deck below.

"Answer me ya' snot-nose or ye'll feel me lash lickin' ya', by God ya' will!" the giant roared, breaking William out of his trance.

"He's Mr. Taylor, Sir," Smith broke in. "He's new. Brought on just 'afore we sailed, Sir!"

The ebony eyes swiveled and fixed on Smith. The first mate's mouth pulled back in a frightening scowl, showing a few remaining stained and blackened teeth, listing in their sockets, separated by gaps, protruding from reddened, oozing gums. The man's tongue was swollen and blistered, and each exhalation carried out the fetid smell of rot. "D'yer thinks I'm talkin' to you? Or is this one here mute? Eh? Is that it? 'Cause we've one gimp aboard already and that'll be more than enough to care fer the shitpots!" He raised the fist clutching the whip's handle and let the coils slither to the deck. He drew his arm back and glanced at the length of rope as it followed his pull. "I bet my sweet one here could make him talk." In an instant William clenched his eyes shut and stifled a scream in his throat, as he prepared for the slash of the whip's knotted ends to slice open his shoulder's skin.

"Mr. Rogers!" A voice boomed out from the quarter deck. The big man's arm froze in mid swing. "I appreciate your enthusiasm, Sir," the voice continued, "but I hold it to be more prudent to get some work out of him before you strip the flesh off his bones, don't you agree, Mr. Rogers?"

William's eyes snapped open and he scanned the quarter deck for the source of the commanding voice. There, standing tall and imposing, at the railing, was a man, his hands clasped loosely behind his back, legs slightly astride. The blue jacket he wore was fastened up the front; its gold buttons glinted in the sun. His hair was neatly pulled back and hidden under the brim of a tricorn hat, it too, as blue as the man's eyes.

"Well, Mr. Rogers? What say you, Sir?"

The first mate scowled and his jaws clenched in defiance. "Aye, Cap'n," he grunted, but his gaze fixed on William like a snake about to strike its prey. "Aye, Sir, she'll wait a'right," and he slowly and methodically recoiled the whip, caressing the coils as he gathered them up in his calloused hands.

"Mr. Smith!" the captain continued, "Has your charge signed to wear the King's coat yet?"

"Not yet, Captain Crowell! We was just on our way, Sir!"

"See that it's done then. And, Mr. Smith, see that he is put to good use as soon as possible."

"Yessir!" Smith stood stiffly upright, his long gangly arms held straight at his sides.

"You, Sir," Captain Crowell nodded at William, "What's your name?"

"Uh, William Taylor ... Sir." It seemed natural, necessary even, to William, to address this man as 'Sir'.

"Do not fail me, Mr. Taylor, in any of your endeavors upon my ship, for I would not like to be shown to have been wrong in my immediate judgment of you, and Mr. Rogers to have been right." And with that,

Captain Crowell lifted his head and resumed his watch over his wooden domain from the raised sights of the quarterdeck.

"C'mon!" hissed Smith as he jerked roughly at William's sleeve. William could hear the anger shaking Smith's voice. "Do ya' have a death wish then?" Smith propelled William ahead of him with a hard shove. He herded William through the throngs of sailors, towards the officers' quarters and the log book awaiting William's mark. "There's no honor dyin' at the end of a cat-whip, boy! Ya' want pain? Ya' want to have yer own blood spillin' yer life down yer back? Do ya'?" Smith's eyes narrowed into a hard glare. "Well, save it fer the fightin' ahead! She's a small Navy ship, just a ten-gunner, this one, that's a fact, but Cap'n will not use her size or quickness to outrun troubles. He's not one to back down from anythin'. Ye'll see! Ye'll soon be fightin' fer King and country, boy, ya' see, and *that* at least, offers an honorable death!"

Smith's rant was cut off by a chorus of frightened, angry shouts which shot up through the companionway from the deck deep below them.

Chapter Eleven

"He's got the *pox*, I tell ya'!" one voice bellowed. A wild-eyed sailor's face burst through the hatch. "It's the pox!" he screamed.

All on deck stopped what they were doing and turned towards the commotion. William stared at the man. The whites of the sailor's eyes shone with intense fear, the same way one of his Da's cow's had done when it had been haltered in the slaughterhouse.

"Here now! What's that you are announcing?" Captain Crowell quickly strode down and over to the man. "Has the surgeon seen him?"

"No, Cap'n, Sir! I just seen him with me own eyes, I did! He's got the fever, Sir, an' he's all broke out in blisters and pus spots! Oh, Lord in Heaven, save our souls!" he continued to wail.

"Mr. Lawrence! You *will* cease and desist that caterwauling at once! Or I will unleash the fury of Mr. Roger's appetite upon your back, so help me God, I will. Do you hear me, Sir?"

"But it's *the pox*, Sir! We hafta' save us all! We have to—"

"Mr. Rogers!" the captain commanded, "Apply Moses' Law to this man at once. That will give Mr. Lawrence thirty-nine reasons to stop these lunatic ravings. Or at the very least he'll have something worthy to cry out about. Immediately if you please, Mr. Rogers! Mr. Nawthorne, have the man below in question examined by the Surgeon, and instruct the good doctor to then see me with due haste in my quarters."

William shrank back as several pairs of arms suddenly reached out and bound Mr. Lawrence's arms together, then hauled the man over to the foremast where he was quickly strung up with ropes to the rigging, spread out like a crucified figure. The crew gathered around as Mr. Rogers took his place behind the man's back.

"'Here's the cat, fresh fer ya'!" the first mate roared at the man, as he withdrew a shorter whip from a red bag which had been handed to him. This new whip was much shorter than the first, a tangle of ropes only about two feet long, but each strand ended in a hard, tight knot. Crewmen pushed and jostled for position around William until he was squeezed to the back of the throng. He could not see over the heads of the men in front of him but the whistle of the whip and the sharp crack of it as it slashed open fresh skin was outplayed only by the screams of the bound man as the knotted ends of leather tore open flesh. The man's terror was out of control, William realized, and that was going to make the flogging all the worse. Towering above the others, Mr. Rogers' face was in plain view. His lips were curled back in an unholy grin, and his eyes gleamed wildly. They were the eyes of a demon.

The sailor's screams grew weaker and faded out altogether by the fifteenth lash.

"Throw the water on him!" Mr. Rogers yelled. The salty sea water burning in his fresh slashes was enough to rouse the unfortunate man and the lashing began again in earnest. The crowd of men counted out each fresh blow in loud unison, for which William was grateful, as it partially obscured the man's continued shrieks. From the corner of his eye, William caught sight of a portly fellow emerging from the companionway. He turned to watch him scurry away into the captain's quarters.

Before the flogging finished, the paunchy surgeon and captain appeared back out on the deck. The surgeon waddled over to the edge of the gathered crowd and quickly spoke with two men standing on the outer edge. They in turn, left and followed the surgeon down the hatch, returning a few minutes later with a long lumpy roll carried between them. It was a heavy item, and the men staggered to the edge of the ship with it.

Something rolled in a hammock. William watched with curiosity. As the sailors attempted to lift the roll up, one end slipped from their grasp and William gasped as an arm weakly pushed up and out from inside the roll. Grabbing the limb, and stuffing it back inside the hammock wrapping, the sailors recovered their grip on it and heaved the package up and over the edge of the ship. It hit the water surface with a soft splash and the men returned to the foremast to watch the final counts of the whip.

William stood in stunned astonishment at what he had just witnessed. *That roll had a man in it. He was still alive! The poxed sailor? The surgeon was a part of it! He's supposed to help the sick! Is this whole thing the Captain's order?*

Once again William's heart pounded and his chest tightened in renewed terror of this hostile world. Life at home had been hard and he was no stranger to illness and death, but the casual violence with which all aboard this ship lived and died was overwhelming to him. *I'm living a nightmare and there's no escape!* He forced himself to breathe deeply. *You're still alive.*

Well then survive if you can, boy-o, survive if you can, a voice inside his head taunted.

Chapter Twelve

"See here, Tess," her father beckoned her over to his desk, where he stood hunched over his newest acquisition. It was a strange looking stand about a foot high, with several knobs, and a tube that her father stared down into. A small flat platform was secured several inches below the eye tube.

"Quickly! You've not seen anything like this!" he exclaimed.

Tess peered into the eyepiece and gasped. Fat little lines squirmed and undulated, curling and uncurling on the glassy surface.

"What are they?" she asked in wonderment. "What is this?"

"You are looking at the smallest of all animals in there. They've taken up residence in the pus from Mrs. Waddington's leg boil, they have. And this, my dear, is a microscope. It's a great invention for medicine, brought to England, by its inventor, Dr. Leeuwenhoek, a great man, from the Netherlands." Her father gently touched the contraption as though stroking a beloved pet.

"There's a whole world in here," he said softly, returning his attention to the eyepiece.

"Father, if you've no further need for my help presently, I'd like to go with Cassie when she goes for goods this afternoon."

"Hmmff— what?" Her father's concentration on the small squiggles within the contraption was absolute. Tess doubted that he had even heard her request, but it was going to be easier to deal with possible punishment, than to gain his permission at this point.

Until today Tess had only been outside the confines of her home in the accompaniment of her father when they had been en route to a patient's home. She marveled at the crowds of people in the marketplace, pushing and jostling amid the cries of the vendors as they competed to sell their wares. It all mingled into unintelligible babel.

"Stay close!" Cassie commanded. Tess clung to her sister-servant's arm and trotted alongside her, her own feet sliding and tripping over the cobblestones which were slickened to various degrees with dumped wash water, sputum, and manure. Within the hour, she and Cassie had their supplies purchased—writing paper and inks for Dr. Willoughby's study, that day's catch of fish, as well as greens and turnips for the evening meal, a supply of salt, more flour and eggs for the breakfast loaves. Tess had also made a spontaneous purchase—a bouquet of fresh flowers for her mother's bedroom. Maybe their fresh sweet scents and bright colors would bring a smile to her mother's face. It had been so long since Tess had seen her mother smile.

The girls' arms were thus fully laden when they turned down an alleyway as a shortcut back to their house. Licks of dark shadows on the stone walls stretched up on either side, while the smells of the rotting food from the marketplace mingled with the sharp stench of urine and feces. Heavy footfalls behind the girls echoed off the sides of the buildings. As the cadence increased, a chill ran down Tess's spine

"Eh, me pretties!" a hoarse voice called. "Whacha' got wigglin' there under all them petticoats?"

Tess glanced at Cassie out of the corner of her eye. Cassie was hugging her parcels to her chest, her mouth drawn tight in a thin line of determination. Eyes straight ahead, Cassie quickened her pace.

Is this what Cassie has to endure every time she goes to the market?

"Don't be shy now! Slow it down a bit and fer a penny or two we can all have a good time!"

How dare he speak to us like that! Tess trembled with a mixture of anger and fear. *If he knew what my father would do—*

Suddenly Tess felt the sting of a sharp slap on her buttocks. Stunned and indignant, she whirled around, catching her shoe in the crevasse between the street cobbles. In the blink of an eye, she lay sprawled on her back, her eggs and flowers instantly crushed beneath her.

A burly body landed on top of her with a heavy thud that knocked the air out of her. At once one of his hands groped and roughly kneaded her breast while the other hiked her skirts up and pushed between her legs. Struggling to breathe, Tess started to scream, but the sound was squelched when he lowered his face to hers in a spittle drenched, mead-smelling kiss. Gagging, she gasped for even a small breath.

You bastard! A white hot rage surged through her, burning away her fear. For a few heartbeats, she was filled with a murderous desire made stronger by her inability to move. Pinned to the ground, she struggled, helpless under the weight of the man, when a more familiar voice filled her thoughts.

Who would want her? Her father's question burst into her mind.

And her own voice responded: *I won't give in! Not to this man! Not here like this! I deserve better!*

Her rage at this stranger and the shame of somehow being undeserving in her father's eyes exploded inside of her. Unable to move her arms or legs beneath the man's crushing weight, Tess used what was left to her.

She bit.

With all of the strength that she could muster, she bit, chomping her teeth into the disgusting tongue he had shoved into her mouth; she felt the crunch of it as it tore. The stranger wrenched backward with a howl, and clambered to his feet, disappearing into the small crowd of onlookers that had gathered. Suddenly aware of the attack, two men in gentlemen's apparel bolted forth, jerking Tess to her feet before pursuing her attacker. She spat the bloodied lump of flesh out onto the street, then bent over and vomited.

"Cassie!" she gasped in between heaves.

A wrinkled hand shoved a small piece of rag into Tess's face. "She was chased down the alleyway, Miss." The voice, belonging to an older person, was low but clear. "Good men followed to see to her rescue. Stay here with me. It's not safe for ye alone." The wrinkled hand gently tucked an escaped wisp of hair behind Tess's ear as she crouched forward and retched again. The knarled fingers froze over her exposed birthmark. The voice gasped.

"Quintspinner!" The exclamation was soft but accusatory.

Tess wiped her mouth with the rag and straightened up. She stared at the humped beggar standing beside her. No, not a beggar ....

"What?" Tess asked. The fingertips still lightly touched her neck. Tess's gaze followed the arm back to the source of the voice. Hairs on her arms stood erect, their gooseflesh announcing her shock. Intense eyes as green as her own shone back at her from within the depth of a heavy brown hood pulled far forward.

"The Gods be heard, it's true then. A Quintspinner lives," the Crone quietly announced to no one but herself.

Chapter Thirteen

The Crone's fingertips remained in light contact, feathering over the skin of Tess's birthmark. Her touch seemed to produce a soft buzz on Tess's neck. Pulsating warmth, not unpleasant, spread down her neck but still Tess shrank from the woman's touch.

"Aye," the seer clucked to herself, "Her Soul knows the Touch, it does." Again the green eyes shone from the dark recess of the hood as though lit from a source within. She peered closer at the birthmark.

"Aye, a Spinner ye be, yet truly… a Quintspinner," she exhaled in an awed whisper.

"A what?" Tess once again felt the hairs on her arms and the back of her neck stand up.

"Lass, ye bear the mark of the Source. A silhouette of the acorn, seed of the most powerful tree and lasting life form of this land in which ye were born. And it trails five seedlings below it." She held Tess in her stare. "Five spinners will seek ye in your lifetime. May ye live to harness their power." She grasped Tess's hand in her own.

"You're crazy, old woman! Let me go!" Tess pulled her hand back but the woman held fast. Her grip was surprisingly strong and Tess's hand remained locked between the deformed digits.

A glint of gold shone from one of the twisted fingers.

That ring! That's the one that Cassie saw!

Tess stared at the ring, mesmerized. It was a wide golden band, with a centre band of silver. The silver band, in turn, was braided with strips of gold and inlaid with blue gems, each set into delicate swirls of miniature silver and gold waves. It glowed more brightly than the old woman's eyes.

The blue gems seem lit from within! That ring must be worth a fortune! How would she have come into possession of such a thing? Not even among any of her father's wealthy friends and acquaintances had Tess seen anyone who wore such a fine piece. Tess's thoughts reeled in her head.

"Where did you get this ring? Are you a common thief? Let go, or I'll yell for help!" Tess struggled to free her hand from the Crone's grip.

"I am no thief, but a Spinner, like yourself!" the Crone retorted, letting go of Tess's hand. "Ye've much to learn and—"

The old woman gasped and stopped in mid sentence to glance up above Tess's head. Tess turned and looked, seeing nothing. The Crone continued to stare into the air, cocking her head at an odd angle as though listening for something.

"Not much time," she shook her head, and continued, "and ye must be taught! Quickly! Follow me! We cannot stay here."

Something in the urgent tone of the old woman's command made Tess fearful but obedient.

"But what about Cassie?"

"She comes back, even as we speak. Ye must come now. Follow!"

"But—"

"Tess!" Cassie's voice rang out. "Tess! Are you alright?" Cassie ran out of an adjoining alleyway and embraced Tess in a fierce hug.

"I'm fine. Cassie! What happened to you?" Tess looked at the tear stained face of her sister-servant.

"I never should have brought you along! This is all my fault!' Cassie wailed.

The Crone reached for Cassie and wiped the tears away with another bit of rag. "Fault? Child, it was as it was expected to be. Now come. Both of ye. Hurry!"

Chapter Fourteen

Tess nervously cradled the hot cup of fragrant tea between her hands, finding the warmth of it in her palms soothing. Her eyes swept over the dark room's contents and came back to rest on the tiny woman perched across the wooden table from her. Cassie, too, sat at Tess's side, staring wide-eyed at their strange hostess. The woman seemed lost within her tunic's folds. Scrawny from malnutrition perhaps, yet her overall structure was diminutive, child-like. Even so, there was a quiet sense of power about her.

"Ye've no idea, do you lass?" the woman quietly asked Tess.

"About what?" Tess had dozens of questions of her own to ask and she hadn't the faintest understanding of the woman's question or where to start with her own.

"Do ye even know about the Source and the power of the Spinners for ones like us?" The Crone leaned forward until her nose nearly touched Tess's. Tess felt helplessly caught in the woman's gaze. "D'ye ever have thoughts that are not your own? Voices inside?" She tapped her own shrouded head and her blazing eyes searched Tess's face. "Ye've not paid attention to them, but ye will and ye'll be given what ye need to hear for the moment," she murmured.

"I–I don't know what you are talking about," Tess stammered. "What's a Spinner? Do you mean like a weaver woman? And that name you called me back in the market? How did you know those men would bring Cassie back here anyway and who were they–"

"A Spinner!" The Crone's voice boomed with authority and her hand shot out in front of the girls' faces, her fingers curling into a fist and presenting the ring on her fourth finger. Only the arthritic enlargement of the knuckle prevented it from slipping off her skeletal digit.

Cassie gasped. "That's the ring I saw before!"

Even in the shadowy darkness of the tiny room, the ring caught the faint candlelight and appeared to glow along its outer golden bands, while the inner silver one sparkled intermittently with the bluish glow of its imbedded gems.

The Crone stroked her ring with the fingers of her other hand and after rubbing it and warming it between her fingertips, slowly twisted the inner band. The braided band spun around her finger within the golden track, and Tess thought that she could hear a high pitched hum. It made a slight tickle in her ears.

"Do ye hear it, lass?" the woman asked and studied Tess's face. "Ye can, can't ye?" She cackled and nodded. "This be a spinner ring. And one who can learn its power be a Spinner. Not anyone who wears a spinner has the power right off, but the power can be learned, can be harnessed."

The tickle in Tess's ears was becoming uncomfortable. "What has this to do with us?" she demanded.

"The mark. The one ye carry on the left side of your neck. 'Tis your destiny. A spinner ring strengthens the wearer's intentions, be they good or bad, and when worn alongside another spinner ring by one who has practiced, the power grows.

"What others? What power?" The tickle inside her ears had become an annoying itch.

"A Spinner comes to know things, senses 'em before they happen. The power can be used to make healing happen, and it can be used to manifest desires. But some are born more apt than others. As ye have been. As I have been."

The Crone withdrew her hand and held the silver band still. Tess's itch stopped. The old woman lit a candle and stared into its flame for several minutes before speaking. When she began, she closed her eyes, though her lids fluttered. Her voice seemed stronger, much lower in pitch, as though belonging to another. Gooseflesh rose on the girls' arms as a voice more commanding, its inflection far different from the old woman's, flowed from her throat.

"The story of the Spinners began from the time when oceans rose, dividing up the land. An ancient brotherhood existed then. It is told that they were skilled in the powers of their minds. This thought-power was weak at first among initiates but always became more effective with practice. The practice was taught among them in many forms. Some called it chanting, some spoke of meditation, some of prayer.

"It is all the same. And it was, and is, made to happen with more powerful results if there is a focal point. Sometimes a flame was used, sometimes scented vapors, but a focal point such as a ring was always with the wearer. Always ready.

"The ancients foresaw that such gifts would come to be scorned by disbelievers; such abilities would fall out of practice and be forgotten and lost to most of mankind.

"Five spinner rings were forged for these visionaries, by masters of the craft, those whose skills have since been lost to us. No other rings other than those five have the ability to spin on themselves.

"Pieces were created from precious metals and gemstones from many different lands. Each band bore that ore of the earth which calls other metals to itself.

"The gemstones and design of each ring enhanced certain abilities and powers of the wearer, each one a spinner. As the piece spins, the power available to its wearer grows. The crystals are a gift to mankind and have inner vibrations made stronger by such motion.

"Five pieces were chosen to be made, each one in honor of the elements of earth, water, wind, fire, and finally, aether. The ancients called this last one Quintessence. It is the fifth element. Spirit. The force which connects and empowers all others."

The Crone's voice was, by now, so deep that it seemed not to belong to her at all. Her eyelids fluttered briefly before opening to reveal that her eyes had rolled far back into her head. Her eyelids closed once more, and she breathed deeply and slowly several times before continuing.

"Each of the five pieces enhances the five senses of the wearer–sight, hearing, taste, smell, and touch. The pieces were sent out in five different directions, representing north, south, east, west, and to the centre, or the unknown.

"It was prophesized that when the time was right, the energies of the Source would magnify, and the pieces would reappear to seek out each other. A Spinner would appear who could harness such power and bring the pieces together. It is said that when the pieces are once again together, it will signal the beginning of great changes for the Earth and mankind. Changes will occur, the speed of which has never before been seen.

"But this you must know—if such rings were to be worn by one with an impure heart, the power could be corrupted. There are those who will attempt to steal them from you for their own personal gain. But know this, too, that the powers stay strong only when the rings are *voluntarily given*." The woman inhaled a deep shuddering breath and her eyes flew open as she stabbed a bony finger at Tess and hissed, "The rings will seek you. Pay attention to your inner voice, Quintspinner." Her eyes narrowed and she continued in a hushed voice, "It is the only sense to trust."

Tess sat quietly on the stool, made speechless by the Crone's story. Cassie, however, spoke first.

"That's a fine story, it is. A fine yarn for scaring us. Spinner, indeed! Tess doesn't even have a ring, if you haven't noticed. And she's not bloody likely to find one in the marketplace, is she now?"

"She has the mark. They will come," the Crone said simply.

A sudden loud knock on the door made both girls jump. A wisp of fear flickered in the Crone's eyes and then it was gone, replaced by a look of grim expectancy.

Chapter Fifteen

"Into the back room with ye both!" she whispered. "Hide yourselves so as not to be found." The knock sounded again, this time louder and more impatiently. The Crone grabbed Tess by her arm. "Ye'll come to know things, Quintspinner. Do not doubt your inner voice. It will not fail ye, if ye choose to hear it."

The knock swelled into a fierce pounding. Tess and Cassie barely had time to slip behind the curtain into the small back room before the front door burst open admitting two strangers. In the murky back room the two young women crouched behind a narrow open-face cupboard. Its sway-backed shelves were laden with jars and small lumpy sacks. Other than a few hand tools leaning against the far wall, and a grimy straw mattress lying on the floor, the room was empty.

"Surely you have no reason to keep us waiting out in the filth of your street," one of the strangers began. His voice was deep and he spoke with the clipped words of an educated man. However," he sniffed with great distaste, "it may have been more pure of air than in here, after all." He sniffed again. "What is that particular scent?"

"Only tea, Sir. An' perhaps the blend of the herbs an' roots," the Crone offered.

"Yes, I suppose there's no accounting for peasants' fondness for things from the bog, disgusting as that may be ...." His voice trailed off and although Tess and Cassie dared not look out past the thin sheet separating the two rooms, they could hear the shuffle of the gentlemen's shoes and the click of heels on the floor as the visitors shifted their weight from foot to foot, obviously looking about the room.

The deep voice spoke again. "You are aware, I am sure, that each time in the past year, when I sought out your debatable services, it was on behalf of George Augustus, Prince of Wales."

"I've not forgotten nor misunderstood Your Sir's visits to me," The Crone replied.

"And do you recall your words to me during our last encounter, the one for which not even I, the Prince's own courtier, could dissuade him from seeking your dubious advice with regards to his newborn son's safety? I speak, of course, of the delicate matter that arose between the Prince and his father, His Majesty, King George. In fact, I speak specifically of the King's appointment of Lord Chamberlain, Duke of Newcastle, as one of the sponsors of the child."

"I am aware of that of which ye speak, Sir."

"It was a matter in which you advised that although the Prince greatly objected to this godparent arrangement, that such an appointment would result in no harm."

"I do recall my own words, Sir."

"But ... perhaps not even as great a seer as yourself," he sneered, his contempt for her plainly audible and barely in check, "is aware of the circumstances which have transpired from that appointment ...."

The Crone remained silent. Any reply from her now would only be construed as a hostile challenge by the courtier.

"At the child's christening, the Prince of Wales and the Lord Chamberlain publicly spoke words of disagreement to one another, leading his Lordship to mistakenly believe that the Prince had issued to him, a challenge to a duel. His Highness, King George became enraged by the Prince's participation in the argument and he has therefore banished the Prince and his wife from the royal residence within St. James Palace."

There was an audible gasp from the Crone.

"I see you may be taken aback by the news," the courtier chuckled, and then his voice became hard and full of malice. "They must now reside at Leicester House," he hissed, "but His Highness has decreed that their children are to be separated from them and left behind at St. James under the care of the King."

"Is the male child alive and thus far healthy?" the Crone interjected.

"Alive? Yes. Healthy? For the time being. But how long can a child thrive and flourish without the love and care that only his mother can provide to him? Hmm?" He took a step forward and slammed his fist upon the table. "Safe! You predicted him to be *safe!*" he shouted.

Tess's ears began to itch once more. *Can it be? She must be spinning the ring!*

Recovering his composure, the courtier cleared his throat and continued. "I see that you are in possession of a piece of jewelry fine enough in appearance so as to properly belong to the Prince himself. I believe that I might be able to obtain the Prince's forgiveness of you if I were to present him with such a gift from your miserable self—"

The high pitched hum in Tess's ears had changed in tone, from a pleasant harmonious sound to a shrill squeal that seemed to be stabbing somewhere inside her skull.

"Ye'll not come to have a spinner in your possession while there is breath in my body!" the Crone cried.

"As you wish, useless old woman!" the man growled. "I had heard it talked about, that your so called power of predictions was gained from a talisman of some sort. I just had no idea that it would have another, more worldly value to me!"

A heavy thud of a stool and that of a body hitting the floor together was mixed with a bitter shriek of agony from the Crone. Blindly grabbing a bag of roots off a shelf Tess sprang into the forward room, a defiant cry escaping from her throat. Swinging the bag overhead, she brought it crashing down upon the courtier's head. The man screamed in fear and shock as the skin on the back of his skull split open in a spray of blood. Cassie jumped past Tess, screeching with equal volume and slicing the air with a short handled pitch fork.

The unexpected onslaught was too much for the startled men. Clutching his head, the courtier lurched for the doorway, followed quickly and nearly overrun by his companion, the two of them disappearing into their waiting carriage. The carriage bolted away as the perfectly paired horses strained forward in their harnesses under the sting of the driver's whip.

Breathing hard, Tess and Cassie looked at one another in amazement at the success of their sudden attack. A low moan arose from the floor behind the table.

"Oh my God!" Cassie blurted, "The Crone! She's hurt!"

Tess knelt by the woman's body and was horrified to see a seeping blood stain widening on the floor around the woman's head. Blood seeped from both nostrils and joined another trickle oozing from one corner of her mouth. She attempted to speak but her lips spewed only bubbles of blood and saliva. The Crone motioned weakly that Tess should bend nearer. As she did, Tess's face hovered close to the dying woman's.

"The ring," the woman gurgled softly. "It must be yours now. Find it," she whispered.

"Find it? What do you mean?" Tess cried.

With great effort the Crone held her trembling hand close to Tess's face.

"Find it ... yours ..." she slurred and her hand dropped into Tess's lap. Tess looked down and screamed.

The Crone's fourth and fifth fingers were missing. Hacked from her hand. The wound had at first streamed dark blood but it no longer flowed, and the spilled blood was already clotting, as blood does when a heart no longer beats to push it through the vessels. The Crone's chest rose and fell one last time in a soft wet exhalation.

"Tess! We have to get out of here! They may come back!" Cassie shook Tess by her shoulder. Tess scrambled around on her hands and knees, sweeping the floor with her hands in obvious search of something.

"What are you doing? Didn't you hear me? We have to leave!" Cassie tugged hard on Tess's dress collar.

"Help me find them, Cassie!"

Find what?"

Her fingers! The ring! Hurry!"

Cassie dropped to her hands and knees and the two of them scanned the floor.

"They must have taken the fingers with them," Cassie said. "I don't see them anywhere!"

"Keep looking!" Tess commanded, but the room was small and it took only a minute longer to prove that Cassie was right. Neither fingers nor ring had been left behind on the floor.

"It's no use, Tess, we have to go! How are we ever going to explain this, if someone finds us here?"

"We can't just leave her like this," Tess sobbed, her panic dissolving into tears. She straightened the Crone's legs out and arranged the tattered skirt's hem neatly over the worn slipper tops. Reaching slowly up to the woman's face, Tess gently closed the eyelids with her fingertips. Finally, she placed the injured hand upon the woman's chest and reached to place the other over top of the gruesome wound. As Tess pried open the fingers of the second hand to spread them over the first, she gasped. Held tightly in the hand, even in death, were two fingers with the spinner ring still in place.

Chapter Sixteen

Their disappearance and late return home from the market was held secondary in importance to another household situation that was in full blown crisis when Tess and Cassie slipped in through the back door and entered the kitchen.

"Oh my heavens! Where have you girls been! The Doctor, he's been in a right state about ya' bein' gone and now he's beyond reason, what with his wee son an' all!" Mrs. Hanley scurried into the kitchen and gathering both girls to her ample bosom, pressed them to her in a fierce hug.

"Charley? What's wrong with him?" Tess wasn't sure if she felt more annoyance that her baby brother was the centre of her father's attention again, or relief that he had taken the attention away from their fateful day trip into the market.

"Ooh! It's just awful!" Mrs. Hanley fretted, and then with a quick look over her shoulder, she continued in a hushed voice. "Even from down here, we heard Mrs. Willoughby screamin' an' carryin' on somethin' frightful. The Doctor ran up to her room an' found her at the side of the wee lad's crib, pointin' at him an' callin' for her husband. An' that poor babe, well, he was takin' a fit. Oh, his eyes was rolled back just so, and his little body was shakin' so hard you'd have thought he was dyin'! And so Dr. Willoughby was callin' an' callin' fer ya' to come an' calm Mrs. Willoughby, so's he could tend to the babe. But of course ya' wasn't here, neither of ya', was ya'?" Her tone had changed from excited story teller to reproachful caretaker. "An' wherever it was that ya' was, it not bein' here, it couldn't have been at a worse time, what with the visitor arrivin' at the door an' all...."

"A fit? Is Charlie alright? What did father do? And who was the visitor?" Tess felt her heart fluttering with a fresh sense of panic.

"Ah, the Doctor was near as worked up as his wife, with their son lookin' like that, but no sooner did the fits pass, when a man arrived, dressed in fine clothes an' demandin' the doctor's presence to attend to himself. That's when Dr. Willoughby started yellin' fer ya' both again, but findin' neither one of ya' here, he grabbed his medical satchel and left in a hurry with the gentleman. Said he'd need to treat the gentleman at the gent's own residence, bein' as how he'd probably need to sedate him an' so thought it best that the fellow be treated in the comfort of his own bedchambers. Told me that when ya' returned, Cassie was to tend to young Charles an' yerself was to tend to the Missus, Tess." She shook her head and clucked her tongue. "An' me darlin's, I have never seen him in such a rage...."

Dr. Willoughby arrived back home shortly after the evening meal had finished. He summoned both girls to his study, where they found him sitting behind his great desk. He wore a look of outward calm, but his hands, curled into fists so tight that his knuckles were white, belied his emotions.

He cut directly to the heart of the matter. "Explain yourselves."

"It was my fault!" Cassie began but Tess quickly cut her off.

"There was no fault of either of us at all! We just went to the market to do the day's shopping–"

"Tess was attacked!" Cassie interjected.

"Attacked? How so? And by whom?"

"A man, a filthy foul-smelling man, knocked me to the ground, but I bit him and he got up and ran–," Tess admitted.

"And an old woman took us to her place for a cup of tea–," Cassie carried on.

"You went to a complete stranger's house? Unaccompanied at that?" Dr. Willoughby asked in frank astonishment. "What could you have possibly been thinking?"

"Father, it wasn't just anybody, it was ... the Crone," Tess ventured to say, hoping that such a detail would be in their favor. It was not.

"The Crone?" he roared and sprang up from his chair. "A filthy old woman idolized by the superstitious peasants?"

"She's not filthy!" Tess shouted back "She was a Spinner! She had the ring! And she knew things! And–," her voice close to breaking, she fought to control the tears that threatened to spill from her eyes, "—and those things got her killed! By someone connected to the Prince of Wales!"

Her father's eyes widened in disbelief. Tess continued on, her words tumbling out in a jumbled recount of the afternoon's attack on the Crone, and of their counterattack on the Crone's two assailants. Dr. Willoughby sunk back down into his chair, speechless.

"So we came directly back here. And we're sorry. We didn't mean to cause you any worry. And we thought that you might call the sheriff to report her murder," Tess finished.

Her father stared intently at them, his nostrils flaring and his cheeks flushing with color. He looked from girl to girl before speaking.

"How dare you!" Each word was weighted and delivered with controlled anger. "I cannot believe what I am hearing!"

"But Father! We only meant to go to the market—"

"It is quite one thing to fabricate such a story to hide your impetuous behaviors, no doubt an attempt to cover up some illicit meeting with unsuitable and unsavory young men, but to go so far as to implicate the entourage of the Prince of Wales ... well, I am stunned and shamed beyond words!"

"But Father!"

"Do *not* disrespect me any further with your lies and embellishments!" he shouted, slamming his fist down on the desk. "I will not have it! Do you hear me? As of this moment, you are both confined to your room until I say otherwise." He paused and stared at them both before continuing. "I have just come to an immediate decision, spurred on in no small part by your actions this afternoon and your mendacious behavior just now." His mouth pulled down at the corners, his lips forming a thin disapproving line. "We shall be leaving this residence. We shall be relocating at once."

Chapter Seventeen

"What?" Tess and Cassie simultaneously gasped.

"I have been offered an appointment. A position, by the Royal Family—the very one that you attempted to discredit with your fabrication. The offer has come just this very afternoon, actually." He waited for the effect of his words to sink in. "And as it is a posting for chief physician of a royal colony, it will mean a great deal more money and security for this family. I must admit that I had had some reservations about leaving London and embarking on such a bold adventure, but now," and his eyes narrowed to a glare, "now I see that I must remove you both from any further temptations to forge your own carnal relationships." He sighed and rubbed his eyes and forehead with his hand. "Perhaps Elizabeth was right. We have procrastinated far too long in this business of finding a suitable marriage partner for either of you."

"But Father!"

"Not another word out of either of you! I have decided! Now off to your rooms until the traveling plans have been concluded. I will call for you at such time. Pack up whatever you hold dear, but no more than two trunks apiece. Now go."

Sitting in the common drawing room between the girls' bedrooms, Tess and Cassie mulled over the news.

"Moving? Where will we be going to, do you think?" Cassie asked nervously. It was her unspoken worry that at some point she would cease to be considered a part of the family. She wondered now if she was included in the relocation plans. She replayed the doctor's words in her head, and then decided that yes, he had spoken of leaving right away, and had also mentioned marriage arrangements for them both. She hoped that meant continued inclusion for her.

Tess did not answer. She was lost in thoughts of her own. Her father's accusation that they had fabricated the afternoon's events to cover for a supposed scandalous liaison left her outraged. How could he mistrust them so much? Tess sprang to her feet and strode over to her dresser.

"I'll show him! Then he'll have to believe us!"

"What do you mean? Tess what are you going to do?" Cassie's voice was wary.

Tess spun around and stretched her left hand out. The spinner ring sparkled on her fifth finger; the tiny band fit perfectly there. "I'm going to show him this, Cassie. This is proof that things happened exactly as we said." And with that, she left the room, closing the door behind her before Cassie could object.

Her father was still in his study, poring over papers at his desk. He looked up in surprise as Tess entered the room.

"Are you contradicting a direct order that I gave you?" he frowned.

"Father, we are telling the truth about what happened this afternoon. It happened exactly as we told you. I have proof."

"You have witnesses willing to collaborate with your story of fantasy?"

"It was *not* fantasy!" Tess replied, her voice shaking with indignant anger. "Here is the ring!" She thrust her hand forward. Dr. Willoughby's face remained impassive and as smooth as a stone wall. Coming from around the back of his desk, he approached Tess and grabbed her hand to examine the ring. Silently he scrutinized it, and then met Tess's eyes with his own.

"Where did you get this?" His voice was cold.

"The Crone said I was to have it. Those were her last words to me before she died!" Tess felt relief flood over her. He could not dispute the ring.

Her father's next words stunned her.

"I can only assume that this is either a trinket given to you by whomever you had arranged to meet, or worse yet, you have stolen it from its rightful owner. Remove it at once and give it to me. I shall do what I can to redeem your reputation and prevent you from being hauled off to the public jail on charges of theft!"

"What? Stolen? How could you even consider that to be possible? It was given to me!"

"Remove it! Or I shall pull it from your hand!" he shouted, the fury building in his voice.

"I won't!" Tess shouted back, stamping her foot in defiance.

The slap to her cheek arrived so hard and fast that Tess had no time to brace herself. It sent her reeling to the floor, where she landed on her outstretched hand. She screamed as her finger bearing the ring crumpled under the full weight of her body.

"What on earth is happenin' here? Sir! What are ya' *doin'*?" Mrs. Hanley cried in bewilderment from the study's doorway. She rushed to Tess and was crouching beside her in an instant.

"Have you forgotten your position, Mrs. Hanley?" the doctor roared at her. "May I ask *you*, what it is that you are doing?"

Mrs. Hanley looked up from where she held a sobbing Tess. "The Missus sent me to find ya'. She said it's urgent. Wee Charles is gripped by the fits again."

Upon hearing this, the doctor bolted from the room and charged up the stairs towards his wife's room, leaving the two of them clutching one another in a dazed heap upon the floor. Mrs. Hanley cradled Tess in her arms and rocked her as though she were a small child.

"There, there," she soothed, "Let's have a look at ya'. Are ya' hurt?"

Tess's cheek was already beginning to swell in a raised fiery red hand print. "It's my hand!" she sobbed. "I think my finger's broken!" Indeed, the finger was visibly swollen and had immediately turned a dusky purple at the knuckle just above the ring.

"Come then, me darlin'," Mrs. Hanley encouraged as she helped Tess to her feet. "Let's get a poultice on that, an' yer cheek too. I've just the thing fer that back in the kitchen."

"I don't understand why he's so angry," Tess sobbed. "And I would never lie to him!" She walked alongside Mrs. Hanley, the woman's comforting warm arm across her shoulders offering a measure of safety.

"He hit me," Tess continued sniffling. "His own daughter ...."

Mrs. Hanley's mouth hardened in a scowl. "Yes he did."

"I hate him!" Tess snapped.

Mrs. Hanley stopped in her tracks and looked at Tess for a moment. "Tess, darlin' you've a right to feel hurt, but anger that turns to hate often takes up too much space in our heads. No room fer real thinkin' then." She was silent for a moment, then gently cupping Tess's chin in her hand she lifted Tess's tear stained face upwards. "This has happened fer a reason, me darlin' doncha' see? There's always somethin' what comes from somethin' ....

"An' there is somethin' that I am goin' to tell ya'. Somethin' that I was sworn not ever to say, but I believe it's needin' to be said now. Ya' needs to know." Tess looked at Mrs. Hanley's kind face and recognized a deep sadness etched in the lines there.

"I can poultice yer body's bruises, but poultice alone canna' treat the wounds of yer heart." The housekeeper sighed and then gently added, "Grief is the price we pay fer the gift of love."

Chapter Eighteen

Tess sat at the familiar oak table in the kitchen, with a poultice of comfrey leaves held softly against her cheek. Already her cheek felt stiff and achy, and the swelling was making it difficult to see out of her eye. Her left hand lay on the table, wrapped in a second poultice. Mrs. Hanley poured a cup of tea for each of them and then settled herself on the bench across the table from Tess.

"Ya' see, Tess, Dr. Willoughby is made distressed by the wee babe's condition. He and the Missus have waited for so long to have a child of their own, an' now that he's here an' less than perfect, it's breakin' their hearts, it is."

A child of their own? What does she mean? I'm their child, too! Just because he's a boy doesn't mean that he's more valuable!

Tess snapped, "And they think I'm less than perfect, too, don't they? Because I have this!" Tess flung her thick plait back off the side of her neck to reveal her birthmark. Mrs. Hanley seemed to hesitate.

"That's alright, you don't have to say anything," Tess continued. "I already overheard them talking about me. I know what you are trying to tell me. I've been their less-than-perfect daughter since I was born with this, this *thing* on my neck!"

"No, child, there's more." Mrs. Hanley took in a big breath of air and slowly exhaled it, as though using the time to decide what to say next. "Ya' *are* a perfect daughter. No one could ask fer one more beautiful an' smarter than you. But yer not ... yer not ... a child of their blood."

Tess sat completely still, not comprehending what she had just heard. Mrs. Hanley reached for Tess's right hand before continuing.

"Many years ago, I had a daughter, too. An' she meant the world to me. She was comin' up near twelve years old when one day she went along with me husband on an errand to the village. They was attacked by men wearin' the colors from the court of London but havin' the godless souls no better than highwaymen, and there was a struggle." Her voice choked as she recalled the painful memory.

"Me husband tried to defend our daughter, but he was outnumbered. He said afterwards they tied him to a tree an' made him watch as they each satisfied themselves with our baby girl." Mrs. Hanley paused and wiped the corners of her eyes with the back of her hand.

"They all raped her ... an' my poor Bennett couldna' do nothin' to stop them." Her voice cracked with pain. "It destroyed him, seein' her like that ...."

Tess gasped sharply as she imagined the horror of such a scene. Now it was her turn to hold Mrs. Hanley's hand, as she waited for the housekeeper to regain her composure.

"When they finished with her, they left them both, with him tied to the tree screamin' at them, and her lying all curled up, torn an' bleedin' on the ground."

"What happened to them?" Tess asked softly. "Your daughter and husband, I mean." She had never heard Mrs. Hanley talk about a husband or child before.

Mrs. Hanley stared out the kitchen window, tears slowly rolling down her cheeks and disappearing into the high stiff collar of her frayed work dress.

"Me Bennett, he was a broken man. He couldna' live with that memory inside his head, so ... one evenin', he went out to the barn after the supper meal an' dinna' come back to the house. I found him out there ... he'd hung himself from the barn rafter." Her voice was hoarse and barely a whisper.

"An' me Annabelle, my poor little darlin', some months after that, she birthed a child, a beautiful perfect baby girl with a headful of hair that blazed like the sun shinin' on a copper kettle. But her not being much more than a baby herself, she died on that birthin' bed, an' there was nothin' even Dr. Willoughby could do to save her ...." Mrs. Hanley's tears rolled down freely now, and she made no effort to staunch their flow.

"They both left me behind in this wicked world, with that perfect wee one that I'd no way of supportin'. Dr. Willoughby and his Missus agreed to take us both in, me an' the babe, which they took on as their own." She looked at Tess and smiled through her tears. "They even let me choose the wee girl's name."

"Tess. My perfect granddaughter."

Chapter Nineteen

William was still stunned at the casual tossing of the diseased sailor overboard.

"Maybe he was poxed, an' maybe he weren't" Smith reasoned. "If the Surgeon thought it was the real pox, then God have mercy on us all, we owe him our lives fer stoppin' it right then and there. See these?" He pointed at the pock mark scars on his own hands. "T'was only the cowpox when I was a wee mite, but it near killed me just the same. There's them what say ya' can only get one kind of the pox and if ya' survives, ya' won't be gettin' any of the others." Smith laughed out loud. "I'd probably be the only one what survived the real pox, and have to try sailin' this beauty all by myself, an' I'd end up dyin' anyways 'cause even a ship this size needs a crew, she does, an' I know bugger all about the steerin' and map readin'. I'm a lander, just like you."

"But that man was still alive!" William argued. "They killed him. They drowned him!"

"Better one man dies than the whole crew, doncha' think?" Smith countered reasonably. "Besides, a drownin' is only uncomfortable fer a few breaths, it seems, an' the real pox has a man gaspin' and fightin' fer every breath fer hours, sometimes days. It was out of kindness to him, what they done."

William shuddered at the thought of the cold waves sucking the man under, closing over his face, and wondered how long it would take to die that way. He had learned to swim a little bit in the river back home, but he doubted that anyone could stay afloat for long in the ocean. Besides he had heard that sailors mostly couldn't swim a single stroke. And from the smell of these men, most had not submerged their bodies in water anywhere in recent memory.

"C'mon, I'll show ya' more of the decks below," Smith offered. "Unless you've a hankerin' to mix with the blue jackets on the riggings up there, or these here marines an' their sorry gun drills?"

Going back into the dark belly of the ship was not something that William found desirous, but neither was staying topside with the crew full of hostile strangers. He followed Smith back down the companionway and shuffled past the table where they had eaten a short time ago.

"This here's the lower deck. We'll be eatin' with the other landers, mostly. There's a handful of us aboard, an' another what's still in sick bay, if he makes it. Apparently didn't come out of the pressin' as topnotch as the other lads, includin' yerself. Took a bad blow to the noggin. Surgeon says he'll be gimped if he does recover." Smith shrugged his shoulders. "Says he'll be good enough fer the shitpots anyhow."

"And they would be–?" William let his question hang in the air.

Smith grinned. "Not ours. That's what the pissdales alongside the railings is fer. The shitpots is fer the sick ones what can't haul their sorry asses up and over the railings, or out onto the bowsprit fer a piss, and them pots is also somethin' to shovel into when yer cleanin' up after the animals."

"Animals?" William felt trapped in this floating world that was getting stranger by the minute. "What animals?"

"Back here." Smith pointed up ahead. "There's a couple of goats fer milk an' breedin' an' some crates of birds what'll keep us in cacklefruit fer the journey. They're normally kept topside, but Cap'n is a stickler fer his marines' drills—wants the top deck space fer that—an' this sail's got enough room here. You'll be in charge of their care, I 'spect. You've had some experience with livestock?"

William heard the chickens' busy clucking and could already smell the acrid droppings which formed moderate sized mounds of gooey white and black excrement on the planks below the crates. Beyond the crates a small area was corralled off and inside the makeshift corral were three goats, bleating in unhappy protest. William stared in open amazement.

Two of the animals were suspended in hammocks which ran under their bellies and then attached to the overhead beam by ropes and hooks. Their hooves barely touched the flooring. The third was a small black kid. Laying in the straw bed at its nanny's feet it was nearly invisible in the below-deck darkness.

"What the hell?" William could not hide his confusion.

"Hmm?" Smith followed William's gaze. "Oh, that's so's they won't be breakin' their legs in the rough seas, rollin' over and fallin' down and such. They'll be let down, I 'spect, fer some of the time during calm sailin'." He continued on, pointing at a floor to ceiling wall of hay held in place by an expanse of fish net strung along the ship's side. "There's their grub an' the birds' is in them barrels over there." He bent over and picked up a foul smelling bucket by its handle, holding it out at arm's length. "Here's yer shitpot," he grinned. "There's a scoop hangin' on the nail there so's ya' won't have to use yer hands to do the collectin'." His grin widened. "Ya' see, the Navy's real civilized."

They continued on Smith's tour, stopping to meet Cook. He was a scowly fellow, bare-chested with his skin glistening in sweat, its sheen reflected in the dull orange glow of a single lantern. He wielded a large curved blade, and hacked furiously at a partial carcass on the thick wooden table in front of him. *He could use a lesson from John.* William caught himself silently judging Cook's sloppy technique. The man's arms were massively muscled, and as William's eyes travelled over his physique, he was surprised to see that Cook had only one full length leg. He rested the stump of his right thigh on a stool that looked as though it had been made with that specific purpose in mind.

"This here's William Taylor, Cook, Sir." Smith made the simple introduction. Cook glanced at the two of them for a split second in between his attacking slashes on the meaty slab on the table. From the looks of the deeply stained scars in its wooden surface, William guessed that this was a common occurrence. Cook at first grunted acknowledgement without changing his blade's rhythm, then spoke.

"The seas be calm enough today. Stir the embers a bit, Mr. Smith, won'cha? And let nary a spark fly."

Grabbing a poker, Smith reached into the midst of a small pile of embers which were barely glowing as they lay on the iron plate of the cooking hearth. He leaned forward and gently blew at their base, exciting them back into a fiery red dance.

"That'll do Mr. Smith. You and Mr. Taylor bring us a couple armfuls of taters and turnips from the stores, an' a bit of the greens too. It's a lamb stew we'll be havin' that'll make the lads' eyes bug an' their maws water with the thought of it, it will. They'll not forget this one!"

"They're still talking 'bout the last one" Smith nodded in agreement before commenting under his breath "An' none too kindly, if ya' take my meanin'." He grabbed William by the shoulder and tugged him out of earshot. "An' speakin' of butchery," he smiled, "we're off to see the Surgeon's workin' quarters."

Chapter Twenty

Sick bay was an area that contained four hammocks and two low wide tables. Only one hammock was occupied. William supposed that its occupant was the unfortunate pressing victim, as the man's skull and forehead were obscured in a thick blood-matted turban.

The fellow is still alive anyway. He watched as the injured man moaned and thrashed his arms about, the movements threatening to tip the poor fellow completely out of the narrow hammock. The patient appeared to be unattended at the moment, as the surgeon was nowhere in sight.

"Who looks after the ones in sick bay?" William inquired, his nose wrinkling with the onslaught of the repelling mixed odor of human waste, urine, sweat, and blood.

"You'll be the one, I 'spect. Seein' as how the last lander helpin' out here had a short sail with us," Smith explained. "He was the poor sod what took sick himself. The one with the pox."

Just then the man in the hammock flailed his arms in a wildly contorted circle, and the meager sling swung sharply back and forth, rocking high to one side, spilling the man's torso towards the floor. William lunged forward and grabbed for him, cushioning the fellow's bloodied head. The two of them landed with a hard crash, tangled together on the floor. William found himself cradling the man's skull and then realized that the foul crusted bandage had come off in his hands. Dropping it in disgust, he gaped at the disclosed wound. A skull depression high over the left ear was still fresh with splinters of bone protruding from a thick bed of clotted blood. William felt the man's gaze on him and he sucked a sharp intake of breath as his own eyes shifted down from the wound and locked in shock onto the familiar deep blue eyes staring back at him.

"Naaaagh–," the man pleaded, his tongue rattling in the back of his throat.

William's own throat had spasmed so tightly he thought he would choke. He managed to squeeze out only a ragged whisper.

"Da'...."

"Nice catch, fer a lander," Smith said, and extended a hand towards William. "C'mon. Back on yer feet."

William looked up at Smith, then back down at his father's face. "Help me get him up."

"Jus' leave him where he lies," Smith countered. "If'n he can't get up on his own, he's of no use to this crew an' they'll send him on."

"Send him–" William looked up in alarm. "They're not going to toss him overboard! I'll fight to my last breath before I let that happen!"

"Easy now!" Smith warned, "It's not me what decides an' makes the rules in this hell hole! ' Just like the one with the pox, it'd be a favor. A quick death is the best a man can hope fer, instead of lingerin' on, trapped inside a body what's ill or not listenin' to his own commandin' any more. I don' believe anyone would choose that over the other. Now c'mon, I tell ya', leave that useless–"

"I'm not leaving him!" William took a deep steadying breath before softly continuing. He stared up at Smith. "This is John Robert Taylor. My father."

It was Smith's turn to gape in astonishment. "Eh? What's that? What did ya' just say?"

"My Da'. I thought he'd been killed! By the pressors!" William rushed on with the details. "I found his cap and they killed my brother, John–"

"Naaagh–," his father uttered a high pitched moan. William suddenly realized with some relief that his father understood what was being said, even if he couldn't form words himself. He also felt suddenly sick to realize that his father had not known until this moment that Johnny was dead.

"Hush, Da'!" William scolded, and then turned to face Smith, fearful that his father's incapacitation would bring on the wrath of the crew. "Here! Help me get him up!"

Smith shook his head in exasperation, still surprised by William's introduction of the wounded man then sighed in resignation. Grasping William's outstretched hand, he pulled him to his feet. The two of them hoisted the elder Taylor up by the shoulders and propped him between them, staggering under his weight as he struggled to stay upright.

"Take a step or two now," William encouraged his father. His father only slumped more heavily on the support of the two of them.

"I'm tellin' ya'" Smith repeated, "They're gonna' dump him. Sure as hell they will. If he can't walk, he'll have to go. An' fer God's sakes, don't be tellin' anyone he's yer father, or they'll find some excuse to make both yer lives short but miserable."

"John Robert!" William pleaded, his voice cracking with desperation, "Do you hear what he says? I thought I'd lost you already! You're all I have left! Now walk, damn you! *Walk!* You got to *try!*"

And with that, John Robert stepped down hard, locking one knee back, and with enormous effort, he lifted his other leg forward in a first wobbly step.

Chapter Twenty-One

The next few weeks were a blur for William. Fear of the unknown was soon replaced by the dull comfort of routine. Each shift began with tending of the goats, whose milk sweetened the officers' breakfast porridge. Egg gathering from the crated hens followed.

Not so different from life back on land, in that respect, William reminisced as he cleared the planking of the animals' dung, scooping it into the shitpot and lugging the foul bucket up onto the main deck to empty it over the side of the ship.

He kept a small tin cup buried under the straw bedding in the goats' pen, and at each milking, secretly filled it with fresh milk for his father. When there appeared to be enough eggs at any one gathering so that one would not be missed, he would break one open and add it into the cup for extra nourishment, delivering this contraband to his father in sick bay. Once there, he carted the man's shitpot up to the main deck to empty, before returning to the galley to help Cook prepare each day's tedious meals for the nearly seventy crew and officers aboard the *HMS Argus*.

A thin porridge was standard fare for breakfast, along with a serving of either salted beef or pork and a thick slab of cheese. Noon and evening meals included boiled potatoes and turnips, and always, hard tack biscuits. William found the biscuits dry, tasteless, and loaded with weevils, which the experienced sailors just knocked out by tapping the biscuits on the tables. Some of the more squeamish preferred to eat biscuits only at the evening meal when the light was so poor that the insects were not readily noticed. Once or twice a week, if the seas had been calm enough for the crew to have been lucky with their fishing lines and nets, there would be fried fish or the occasional turtle served up as well.

"Flounder's too skinny fer the eatin' plates," Cook had declared, sorting through the various fish on his table. "But they've a better use in the barrels.

"Split the flounders open like this," he demonstrated, "and place the raw fish along the bottoms of the biscuit barrels. Leave them overnight, and then take them out." The weevils much preferred the juiciness of the soft fish flesh to that of the hard tack, and once they had had time enough to infest the fish strips, it fell to William to remove the bug infested fish slices, placing the hard tack back into fresh barrels.

The fish pieces in the barrels are disgusting. He could hardly bring himself to pick them up. They were practically moving on their own. The chickens, however, had no such compunctions about having weevils served to them and they fell to greedily pecking upon the loaded fish strips with a fierce, hungry intensity. Nothing ever went to waste aboard a ship.

Besides the food, monotonous but plentiful as it was, each crew member received his daily portion of grog–eight pints–and a large serving of straight rum at the end of his shift. Fresh water stored in barrels on board quickly went stale, and if consumed in any large amounts often made a sailor's guts cramp and bowels run. It was no wonder then, that men of the ships viewed water with a great deal of suspicion.

Grog, on the other hand was doled out quite freely. As Cook's helper, it fell into William's line of duty to mix up a steady supply of the stuff. Each man's mealtime portion consisted of a large ladle of the liquid which had been prepared by mixing together one measure of rum, three measures of hot water, lime juice while the supplies lasted, and enough sugar to make it palatable. William was amazed at the sailors' tolerance for the fiery liquids, as the taste was, at times, far less than pleasant.

Officers, on the other hand, were supplied with French brandy and a variety of wines with which to wash their mealtime fare down. William was expected to serve each shift of messmates at the narrow tables, as well as deliver food to the patient in sick bay. He felt himself fortunate to be in such a position as to easily slip a better cut of meat or an additional serving into the sick bay bowl.

One morning William was astonished to see his father sitting at the low table in sick bay. John Robert slowly rose to his feet and lurched over to William. Even the rocking of the boat, which was by now much more intense than on any of the previous mornings, did not seem to hinder his father's steps much. William grinned. He would have hugged his father out of sheer relief had a sharp voice not caught him off guard.

"You there, Shit Boy!" The pendulous stomach preceded the rest of him by a split second as the surgeon suddenly advanced towards them into the lantern light; he seemed to have come out of nowhere. "Take the Gimp here and be on your way!"

"The Gimp–?" William's inquiry was cut off.

"We know not his name. He has suffered a head wound of such kind that he has lost the capacity for speech and is slow of movement as well, except for the fits which now overtake him. But he'll unfortunately live, so perhaps he can be trained to do something useful to earn his existence on board. If you were to be relieved of the shitpots, your own two hands might be put to better use, seeing as how we did set sail desperately undermanned for such a voyage. I shall present such suggestion of duty allotment to Captain Crowell myself."

Dismissing them with a flutter of his fat hand, he turned and continued to muse out loud to himself. "What should happen if calamity of any kind were to befall us or the *Mary Jane* that sails alongside us, I can only imagine. Even the bravest among this crew are presently ill at ease, but the Captain appears not to notice. I myself feel compelled daily to squash such worries with a tot of the officers' good brandy, but this crew, bless them, have only their miserable grog with which to fortify their courage." And doing an about-face, he tottered back in the direction from which he had appeared.

Chapter Twenty-Two

It was less than a full shift later that Smith found William and delivered to him the news that the Gimp was officially on shitpot duty while William had been assigned the added chores of attending to repairs with the ship's carpenter, in between his continued duties in the cooking galley.

"It seems Cook's taken a bit of likin' to ya', an' he don't like many," Smith confided. "Ya' see, most cooks aren't cooks by choice," he explained. "They be a bluecoat or a marine what's been injured an' can't be a fighter no more. Take Cook's leg, fer instance. Without it, he canna' board another ship during battles nor even help too well with the loadin' of the guns, but a life at sea's the only thing he knows, ya' see, so he cooks. An' every day he's resentin' those who can go on fightin'. They remind him just by bein' whole, of what he's lost. And *that* makes him as miserable an' unpredictable as a freshly knackered bull."

With his father cleaning up after the animals, William adjusted his own chore schedule so that he gathered the eggs at the same time. John Robert's previous experience in animal care was apparent, and the three goats quickly showed a fondness for him. The shaggy billy was smelly and aggressive but he could do little harm from the confines of his sling. A well placed head butt from him had sent William sprawling forward on more than one occasion, but John Robert's touch seemed to please the scraggly animal, especially when it was a playful scratch along the goat's neck or around his ears.

The doe, too, welcomed John Robert with an excited bleat, and often stretched her neck out in an invitation to be rubbed. But it was the kid, a tiny she-goat, for whom John Robert reserved most of his attention. Not yet entirely weaned and needing to reach her mother's teats, the dark little doeling had not been put into a sling, and was allowed to frolic in the thin hay bed at her mother's feet.

William took to calling the kid 'Gerta' and his father grinned in agreement when William called to her. The little animal soon came to recognize her name, and would be waiting at the rungs of the goats' small corral, her inquisitive nose poking through the slats, her soft ears flapping sideways in an excited welcoming gesture. Her curiosity and frank interest in her keepers' movements were in sharp contrast to the attitudes of the humans on board.

Conversations with his father were still one sided, other than the few guttural grunts that Da' could manage, and it pained William to see his father struggle with most basic functions. Frequently, his father dropped the shitpot scoop, splashing the muck over the decking and on himself. Carrying the full pot up the companionway was a laborious task for him as well, and William could see that each step up the wooden ladder was an effort.

He's getting stronger, though, William frequently told himself, *and he doesn't fall as often. He's gonna' make it. We're both gonna' make it and one day soon, we'll be free of this goddamn ship! We just need to carry on for a bit longer, that's all. This voyage won't last forever. It's tolerable for a couple more weeks. I've heard the others say maybe one month more till we land. We can do this. We've been lucky to have had no trouble from anyone so far. It will be alright.* And it was.

Until the day the shitpot was lost overboard.

It was a very bad sign, Smith said. Nothing good could come from the loss of a bucket overboard, just horrible bad luck to the ship and all on board, the crew said. And three dozen lashes for the Gimp, for such inattentiveness, Captain Crowell said.

"But he can't help it!" William's terror at what was about to befall his father fueled a reckless courage within him. "Captain Crowell, Sir! Please! It fell from his hands as he was overcome with a fit, Sir! He didn't do it on purpose!"

Steely blue eyes locked onto William's own. "Do you dare address me on the Gimp's behalf, Mr. Taylor?" Captain Crowell asked.

"Yes, Sir, I do." William replied. "He has no speech–"

"And you feel compelled to be personal champion for all of the deformed and the demented and the shit-stained simpletons in life?"

His father was none of those! William felt his cheeks go hot with rage.

"It's the frigging Navy's fault!" he yelled. "It was the Navy's press gang's attack on him that robbed him of his speech! It was *your need* that destroyed his life!" William spat it out, all of his pent-up anger delivered with each word. The accusation left him breathless even as he heard the collective intake of breath from the stunned crew members.

They understood standing up for a fellow crew member – they lived their lives by such an unspoken creed – but to defy *the Captain*? And all for the lowly Gimp at that? Most shook their heads in disbelief, unable to decide if what they were seeing was a new level of raw courage and seaman's loyalty that would put the rest of them to shame, or a display of unbelievable stupidity.

Silence hung thickly in the air for the few seconds before Captain Crowell spoke. "Very well, then, Mr. Taylor. If you feel that the man is undeserving of and should somehow be relieved of his pronounced punishment, I will offer to you this fair exchange: your back for his own. And let this be a lesson for your impudent mouth, lest your apparent disrespect for my authority bring your short life to its conclusion. Mr. Rogers, the gunner's daughter for Mr. Taylor, if you please."

The gunner's daughter? William was bewildered as his arms were grabbed and he was dragged over to the nearest cannon. The linen shirt he wore was quickly stripped from his torso and he was forced to lay face forward over the cannon. Within seconds, his hands were lashed to his feet. *Kissing the gunner's daughter! Smith's scars!* At that moment, William understood, with great clarity, the meaning of the seaman's term.

Chapter Twenty-Three

The first crack of the whip sent a searing pain down the length of his back. William nearly fainted with the shock of its intensity. The second lash was worse. In spite of clenching his teeth together, William cried out with each slash of the whip across his shoulders and back. He lost count of the lashes and concentrated instead on keeping his head bent low, his eyes out of reach, he hoped, from the skin-splitting force of the whip's knotted ends. The pain was unbearable, as the lash landed again and again. William felt himself beginning to black out, and his screams became muffled and distant to his own ears.

Somewhere, from the hazy side of reality, angry voices rose and mixed together. William was doused with a bucket of cold sea water, the salt searing every exposed nerve ending in his fresh wounds. *Mother of God!* Merciful unconsciousness was going to be denied to him.

"There's the first dozen fer ya'!" Mr. Rogers shouted.

Smith's words came back to William. *Do ya' want to die at the end of a cat whip, boy? Well, do ya'?*

"I'll stand in fer the next shift." It was Smith's voice, alright, but William thought his mind must be making up the conversation at this point. Suddenly, the ropes were loosened from his hands and feet, and William was roughly pulled from the cannon. He crumpled to the deck and struggled to stay conscious. Raising his head, he stared dumbly at the scene in front of him.

Samuel Smith was now bent over and tied to the cannon in William's place, and Mr. Rogers drew the whip back for the first lash. Only a pained grunt escaped Smith's lips as the whip tore into his flesh.

"*What are you doing?*" William screamed.

"'He's takin' the lash on yer behalf, he is," the sailor next to William stated.

"*What?*"

"It's any man's option, if he chooses to stand in fer his mate." The sailor looked down at William, half in pity for his bleeding wounds, half in amusement at his confusion. "Ye'd probably not have survived much more, without a break, it bein' yer first time an' all ...." He saw slow understanding begin to show on William's face. "Ye've got another shift comin', anyhow. That's his twelve about done with now."

William struggled up onto his feet and staggered forward towards Smith.

No one knew for sure who arrived at the cannon's side first, but in the days and years to come when the story would be recounted for the amazed amusement of others who had not been there to witness it first hand, it would be told that there seemed to be a crush of bodies all vying for a spot at the cannon. William dropped to Smith's feet, intending to untie him, while at the same time, two others pulled Smith off the cannon and tried to lay themselves face first over it, each jostling and shoving the other out of the way.

"Goddamn ya', get the hell outta' the way, ya' scupperlout! I'm takin' the boy's next shift!"

"Naaagh!"

William jerked his head up. His mouth dropped open in astonishment. Right above him, his father and Cook pushed and punched at each other.

"By God above and the devil's twisted tail below, I swear I will break ya' in two, ya' damned dunderhead, see if I don't!" Cook roared, executing a wild swing of his fist toward John Robert's face. The momentum of the effort threw him off balance and as he fell, several pairs of hands snaked out to catch and right him back up on his leg, just as John Robert's slow motion punch arrived, connecting squarely with Cook's chin and sending him immediately backwards into the crowd again. Hoots of laughter exploded from the gathered group of crewmen. It was apparent that they were very much enjoying this unexpected change in entertainment.

John Robert threw himself towards Cook and the fisticuff continued, much to the glee of the gathered crew. Even the outraged shouts from First Mate Rogers to stop, were drowned out by the cheers and calls of the crew as they surrounded the two fighters—Cook hopping recklessly on his remaining leg, and John Robert swaying in slow motion on both of his.

As Mr. Rogers stepped forward, Cook reached out and snatched the whip from his hand, bringing it down instead with a crack across John Robert's shoulder. Spurred on by pain and anger, John Robert wrestled it from Cook's grasp and brought the handle smashing down across Cook's ribs. The two men struggled fiercely, each striking the other when he gained possession of the whip. With each blow landing, the crew grew more boisterous and raucous laughter rang out loudly above the general cheering.

"*Enough!*" The command was punctuated by a single gunshot into the air. The effect on the brawlers and spectators alike was immediate. Voices hushed as the men shuffled backwards, opening their circle to reveal John Robert and Cook bloodied and entangled, lying on the deck with limbs entwined and hands at each other's throat. All faces turned to look up and stare at the captain as he stood glaring down at them from the quarter deck, his pistol calmly raised and aimed in the direction of the men.

"It would seem, oddly enough, that enduring a lashing is the choice event of the morning. And therefore, as peculiar as that is to me, I will have the remaining twelve lashes divided equally among the four of you, without favorite." A slow smile spread across his face as a thought took hold. "In fact, I will have three lashes administered to each and every one of you present, so as to remove any feelings of a man being left out! Mr. Rogers, begin with the crew and leave those four until last."

Monitored under the watchful eye of the captain and his pistol, the crew lined up to receive their lashes without complaint. William was grateful that the captain had decided to leave the four of them until last. By that time, even Mr. Rogers' bulky arms were playing out and the force of the remaining lashes upon their backs was nothing more than a sharp slap.

"Told ya', didn't I?" Smith nodded to William as the Surgeon later applied a greasy salve to their whip wounds. "Now you've a set of yer own stripes."

"You didn't have to take my second set," William mumbled. It shamed him to have had Smith rescue him from the fury of Mr. Rogers' lash. "However, I hope to pay you back somehow."

"You'd have done the same, I'm sure," Smith replied. William was not so sure he would have.

"And I don't understand what Da' and Cook were doing—"

"Why, what's to wonder 'bout that?" Smith cut in. "Yer Da's yer Da', and he's the sort of Da' what would do most anythin' to save his son's ass, an' Cook's the sort of man who'd do anything to *have* yer ass ...." Smith laughed at William's shocked expression. "You're really a bloody lander, ain't ya'? Did ya' not notice the lack of ladies aboard?" William remained speechless.

"Just watch yerself," Smith chuckled, "if Cook be the one to offer to apply the grease to ya'!"

Chapter Twenty-Four

The injury to Tess's finger had made removal of the ring impossible. Even when the initial swelling had receded, the affected knuckle remained enlarged, as though determined that the ring should stay put. Before the family left their house for the final time, Dr. Willoughby had insisted that Tess wear long gloves to keep the ring hidden from public observation. Tess was still so numb from Mrs. Hanley's revelation to her that she barely noticed the passing sights of London, its lanes clogged with its inhabitants, as the carriages made their way along the cobblestone streets, down to the docks lined with waiting ships on the riverbanks of the River Thames.

Cassie, on the other hand could barely contain her excitement. She and Tess were in a smaller carriage of their own, while Mrs. Hanley sat in the grand and ornately decorated front carriage with the Willoughby's and their son. Elizabeth Willoughby's depression had deepened since the onset of the infant's seizures and Dr. Willoughby's countenance had not improved. Cassie was glad to have been able to ride in a carriage separate from them, although she was beginning to think that the other carriage may have held more cheerful company.

"We're going to be on a ship!" she exclaimed to Tess, in an effort to cheer her. "I can smell the sea already!"

"That's only that vile dead fish smell. No different than it was in the market the day we were there," Tess pouted. "That day we got into this stupid mess ...."

"What mess?" Cassie responded. "Honestly Tess, look at it this way. You now have the most astonishing ring anyone has ever seen, and we're going on an adventure together!"

"*You're* not the one who just found out that your whole life has been *a lie!* You think that a ring makes up for that?" Tess retorted loudly. As soon as the words were out of her mouth, she regretted her angry tone. It was not Cassie's fault. She herself had been the one to insist on going to the market with Cassie. She had been the one who had wished out loud to have been able to visit the Crone. A minute of uncomfortable silence passed before Cassie spoke up.

"Well, you can drown yourself in a lake of sorrow, if that's your choosing. *I* don't see it that way." Cassie's eyes met Tess's and she continued. "The fact *is* that you didn't *lose* the family that you thought you had–nothing's changed about your life that you've had with them so far–but don't you see that you have *gained* another family that you didn't even know you had. Now you have two! You've been doubly blessed."

A hot wash of angry shame flushed Tess's neck and cheeks. Cassie had not meant for her words to make Tess feel bad, but the sudden realization that Cassie was the one without *any* blood family, made Tess burn with the humiliation of her own self pity. She wished she had not confided her real bloodline to Cassie. Tess was no more a Willoughby than Cassie was and the even playing field made Tess feel unreasonably competitive.

At the docks, the wharves were thick with sea-going vessels, and the ships filling the harbor seemed massive. Tess and Cassie had never been so close to any before, and they watched in awe as the multiple pieces of cargo were hoisted and hauled up and over onto the ships' decks before disappearing down into their holds. Heavily muscled men pulled and strained at the ends of squealing ropes and creaking tackles, as the massive crates, trunks and barrels became airborne. Tess wondered about their contents. She hoped they contained everything she and her family would need to make their lives in the new lands hospitable. She and Cassie had not been allowed to pack much of a personal nature.

"There's my trunk!" Cassie squealed in delight as she pointed to it swinging over the side of a ship's railing. "And Mrs. Hanley's too!

Mrs. Hanley's larger trunk was readily identifiable. She had loaded hers with all of her worldly possessions, those things being one change of work clothes and one other dress that she reserved for church and special occasions. Other than the one she had donned for this momentous day, she owned no further garments. She had stuffed a smaller trunk with items of even greater value to her–an assortment of herbs and cooking spices, a personal supply of limes and sugar for her teas, and poultices secured in neat little bundles with linen strips, with which to treat a variety of ailments.

She had locked the greater trunk with a long thin iron key which she wore dangling from a finely braided strap of leather around her neck. Having secured her trunk in that fashion, she had proceeded to mark each of its four wooden sides with a bright red "H", in a stain made from the pressed berries and boiled juices of wild strawberries.

"Ya' dinna' think I knew me letters, did ya' now?" she had said with a husky note of pride in her voice. The red letter, she explained, not only identified the trunk as hers, but it was a symbol of wealth and good luck. "There was a Chinee' fellow what told me that." He'd been taken off a ship from the Orient and brought to England as an indentured servant, she explained further, but he had insisted upon retaining and wearing his red shoes from his home country. Not even beatings by his new master had been able to dissuade him from wearing them.

"Seems to me that they didn't bring him much luck, then," Tess had pointed out.

"Oh, but they did!" Mrs. Hanley countered, "'Cause one day word came back that the ship he'd been taken from was lost in a storm off the coast of some far away shore, an' there he was all safe an' sound on land." She nodded in satisfaction at her story's ending. "He outlived his master, too an' was able to set up his own spice wagon in the market place. He was the only one what could get the cinnamon an' the ginger. Made enough with that alone, he did, to send fer a lady to marry from his own country, too. Swore it was the red shoes, what brought the luck an' money to him."

"We must board now," Tess's father announced in passing, catching the three of them off guard and bringing Mrs. Hanley's story to an end. He strode back to the carriage in which his wife and son had waited throughout the loading process.

Tess's mother emerged from the carriage, looking frail and uncertain as she accepted help to dismount down its stairs. She held a linen handkerchief to her nose and mouth in a futile attempt to block out the nauseating smells of the harbor area. Mrs. Hanley hurried over to the carriage and plucked up the baby who was wrapped in his softly woven travel cradle. Still so small, weeks after his birth, the only thing that seemed to be growing on the child was his head. His elfin arms and legs became stiffer every passing week and their diminutive size accentuated his large face and skull. So far the child had slept deeply and had had no further fits.

Tess was glad of this as it seemed to her that his fits were always preceded by nerve wracking inconsolable screams from her tiny brother. *Not really my brother,* she reminded herself. *No blood relation at all.* She reached out and threaded her arm tightly through Mrs. Hanley's as they climbed up the steep gangplank to board their ship together. The smells of the wharf seemed to get stronger and Tess wished that she too, like her mother, had had a handkerchief to hold in front of her nose. A furious tickle started in her nose and she sneezed.

"Ah! A sneeze! Means yer goin' to travel," Mrs. Hanley snorted at the obvious truth. Tess sneezed again. Mrs. Hanley hugged Tess's arm and continued. "Now that's interestin'! Two sneezes means you're going to meet a stranger when you travel." Tess smiled a rheumy smile at her grandmother before emitting a third and more powerful sneeze.

"So what do three sneezes mean?" Cassie asked eagerly, knowing Mrs. Hanley's fondness for attributing mystical properties to numerical events.

Reaching up the sleeve of her dress, Mrs. Hanley withdrew a crumbled piece of linen and handed it to Tess.

"Three sneezes means you're coming down with the sniffles. Wipe yer nose an' cover yer mouth with this. Looks like I'll be needin' to brew a tonic fer ya' sooner than I expected."

Chapter Twenty-Five

Tess inwardly groaned. She had just finished a tour of their on-board quarters. Their accommodations aboard the ship were generous and richly supplied compared to the crews' area, but greatly lacking in the space and luxuries to which they were accustomed in their own home. Her parents would be staying in a cabin that was paneled in dark oak; its far wall let in dulled sunlight through a row of glass windows, slightly grimy with lantern-smoke.

Within this main cabin there was room only for the double bed equipped with a thickly stuffed mattress layered with soft blankets, and floor space for a travelling trunk. In one corner, a small writing desk was bolted in place to the floor. A tin wash basin sat upon the desk, securely cradled in a crater carved in the corner of the desk's surface, and a chamber pot was tucked away under the sleeping platform. The rest of the space under the bed would be used as storage for her father's more precious belongings—his dismantled microscope, his medical bag, a small bag of tins containing medicinal tinctures and powders, and two leather-bound medical reference books—all packed in a flat leather trunk.

A narrow door in the far wall of the cabin opened into an adjoining room. It was even smaller in size than the first. In this one, there was space only for a narrow sleeping mat upon the floor, although a second door opened directly from it out onto the deck, making the room accessible from two directions. A low bench had been built into an alcove in the wall. This was to be Mrs. Hanley's room for the trip, once it had been proven that her generously rounded bottom would fit through either of its narrow entrances.

Tess and Cassie shared a room on the other side of the Willoughby's cabin. To Tess it looked as though it had been a storage closet hastily converted to a sleeping area. One wall was lined top to bottom with shelving and the other was occupied with two sleeping hammocks, one strung above the other.

"Come out onto the deck. We're weighing anchor," her father ordered, his voice tinged with excitement.

"Away aloft!"

At this command from their captain, the crew responded immediately, taking their places in a well rehearsed drill. The handful of passengers had gathered along the upper railings to watch. Sailors heaved in unison to hoist the massive anchor aboard. The bollards, ropes as thick as a man's arm, were loosened from their knots around the docks' capstans and hauled aboard. The ship, thus free from her ties to the shore and with her sails unfurling in an orderly manner, began to glide out and away from the heavy timber docks. The river's harbor remained congested with ships of all sizes and types, and their own craft slipped slowly and carefully past the others, migrating towards the open sea.

Tess glanced up as shouts overhead drew her attention. Men had begun to climb up the vibrating lines, shimmying out along the yardarms high overhead. Loosened sails snapped sharply and the riggings hummed in the wind; the ship shuddered and gently rolled side to side in response to the sails' tugging dance with the lofty air currents. Lower winds snatched at the women's hair and threatened to lift the hem of their skirts up above their knees while seagulls boldly screeched and soared on the drafts above.

Even the birds are excited, Tess observed. *Why do I feel only dread?* Cassie and Mrs. Hanley stood on either side of her, with broad smiles blazoned across their faces, but try as she might, Tess could not drum up even one ounce of excitement towards the change in her family's circumstances. As the river exited into the sea's lap and shores slipped further from her view, the heaviness in her chest grew. She mentally ticked off her losses. Left behind forever were not only the home she had lived her entire life in—and a comfortable one it had been—but as well her few close friends and the majority of her books, along with most of her wardrobe. Her misery deepened. As if on cue, a faint high pitched squeal pierced her ears. Charley.

He's distressed too. At least we have that in common.

"Tess, your mother is ailing. Tend to your brother. Clean him and make sure he gets fed and is kept quiet." *Administer some laudanum in sweetened water to Charley* was her father's unspoken instruction. She shot a look of annoyance at him, but he continued to stand at the railing and had already engaged another well dressed gentleman in conversation. He expended no further attention towards her.

You're the one who wanted him, she fumed. *You're the one who should be looking after him.* She stripped off her long white gloves in the expectation of finding Charley's nappy dirty and wringing wet. Seeing the ring upon her finger, she stopped and spun it around in its track, admiring the brilliant blue stones as they glittered and shone in the sun's rays.

Quintspinner indeed. She'd gotten caught up in the drama of a dangerous situation and, unaccustomed to such excitement, she'd let her imagination get the best of her. A diaper full of poop from a squalling baby was just the thing to pull her back to reality. She scratched with absentminded annoyance at the tickle deep within her ear canals, and headed back to the cabins, stumbling along as the ship's flooring dropped and heaved beneath her feet as the ship continued to rock from side to side in the yet unfamiliar rhythm of the open water.

Chapter Twenty-Six

Rather than being seen as the cause of their misfortune, as William had expected to be, his entire lashing episode was treated as top notch entertainment by the crew of the *Argus*, and the sailors continued to hilariously replay the fight between the one legged Cook and the Gimp, enjoying the retelling with many a guffaw. The loss of the bucket overboard was not spoken of, however, except in hushed tones, as though the men thought that the mere mention of it would awaken the wraith of impending bad luck.

With each passing day, however, the seas grew rougher, and tension grew among the sailors as their chores became more difficult and dangerous, with progressively fiercer waves and winds tossing the ship about. Two crew members had been swept overboard in the course of trying to loosen some tangled rigging. The remaining crew became more irritable and tempers frequently flared as the crowded living conditions meant an absolute lack of personal privacy. Accusations of perceived wrongdoings flooded the Captain's ears and the resulting number of floggings seemed to surpass even Mr. Rogers's taste for blood.

William frequently overheard quiet grumblings of dissatisfaction and unease among the crew members as they gathered in turn for meals with their messmates. The rougher seas frayed everyone's nerves as all hands were ever on the ready for possible disaster to strike them. The tossing seas were the hardest on the top hands—so named for their duties as lookouts stationed on the very top yard arms of the fore and main masts—as they clung tightly from their bird's eye perches far above the main deck.

"They be our eye in the sky," Smith informed William. "They keep the watch fer any other ships other than our charge, the *Mary Jane*—see, ya' can just see her top sail over on the horizon there, when we sit on the crest of the wave—an' they'll be on storm watch, too."

Because of sailing shorthanded, chores for all were doubled up and shifts were longer than normal. William had already been assigned to assist in the galley as well as to carpenter duty, but the day came when the captain, upon learning of another of William's skills, assigned him an additional, more pleasant chore.

On a particularly cool but calm night, William and several other sailors sat on the main deck, wrapped in their tunics, preferring to relax and even sleep in the cool, fresh ocean breeze, rather than breathe in the rank air of the lower decks. A full moon shone down upon them, bathing the entire deck in a silvery wash. The sailors brought out their pipes and pouches of tobacco, as well as their daily tots of rum, and one of the men began to play an English reel on his fiddle. It was a lively tune and was soon accompanied by the rhythmical stomp of feet.

It was a tune that William recognized; he had sung it many times while working the fields in a time that seemed so long ago now. Memories of his former life flooded back, and he tucked his chin down and jammed his fists deep into the pockets of his tunic, determined to not let his misery show. His knuckles butted up against an object in the deep recesses.

His flute. His fingertips outlined its familiar hand-carved edges. He put it to his lips and blew. The clear notes melded with the fiddle and gave sweet harmony to the tune. Several of the crew looked on in amazement, smiling their approval. Soon voices rose up and men jumped to their feet, dancing with sheer abandonment, the voyage's tension melting away in them with each verse. Song after song was played, William keeping up as best he could with the impromptu recital.

Overhead, the full moon slowly traversed the sky, and by the time the men were done with the dance and the rum, the white orb had lost her nighttime beauty, diluted by the approaching sun's pink glow on the opposite horizon. William sunk gratefully into his hammock and for once fell immediately into a deep dreamless sleep. He was wakened a short time later by a vigorous shaking of his shoulder.

"Mr. Taylor! Captain Crowell wishes to speak with ya' in his quarters." William did not know the sailor speaking to him but the young sailor obviously knew William. William swung down from his hammock and blearily made his way to the captain's office.

"Mr. Taylor. We meet again. This time under much more favorable circumstances, which I'm sure pleases you as much as it does me." Captain Crowell motioned to William to have a seat in the chair across the table from where he sat. "Mr. Rogers has informed me that you are in the possession of a musical instrument and that you play it very capably."

"Yes, Sir," William replied cautiously, not knowing where this line of questioning was leading.

"Do you have any other traits that I should know about?" the captain asked casually.

"No, Sir." William thought his left handed abilities and accuracy with a knife were best kept to himself for now. And so far, no one had identified him with his father.

The captain's eyebrows shot up as though he had been expecting a confession of some kind. "Very well, young sir, I am hereby assigning you to participate in regular musical interludes for the crew. Saturday evenings and also once midweek, I think, should work out best. You will receive an extra portion of rum for your troubles. Is this to your satisfaction?"

"Yes, Sir." William lowered his eyes and nodded. An uncomfortable silence filled the room.

"Mr. Taylor, are you a god-fearing man?" William looked up but said nothing. Captain Crowell continued. "You might look upon such an assignment to be to your advantage." He waited to see William's reaction. William held the captain's gaze. "God provides the birds with food but He does not drop it into their nests, Mr. Taylor. Make what you can of your given opportunities."

William left the captain's room, pondering the meaning behind the cryptic words. He returned to his hammock and fell asleep once more, still mulling over the strange advice.

Chapter Twenty-Seven

HMS Argus was one of the smaller British Navy ships. Usually employed as a scout rather than one sent to engage in battle, she was presently sailing as an armed escort to the merchant ship, the *Mary Jane*. William learned of their intended destination as he sat alongside Mr. Lancaster, the ship's carpenter.

"Eh, Mr. Taylor, there'll be plenty of maintenance of her bottom side once we reach warmer waters of the West Indies. There's worms in the seas there—telodos they call 'em—what bore right through if the wood's not coated up proper like. We'll be careenin' her soon's we find a decent beach out of harm's way on which we'll run her aground and keel her over. Ever done a careenin'? 'Course you've not."

"Careening?" William had come to know that Mr. Lancaster not only didn't mind his questions, he seemed to welcome them as a chance to show off his extensive knowledge of the ship and all things associated with a sailor's life.

"There's all kinds of crusties and seaweed what attach themselves to the waterside of her hull. Slows her down, it does, so every three months or so, we'll run her up on a beach and at low tide, tip her over by winching with some rigging 'round trees and the like. Then we'll set about scrapin' and fixin' and pluggin' holes till she's clear of all of that. She's doubled planked, she is—pine, fer a sacrifice like to the sea worms, on the outside, and good white oak on her innards—but we don' want them slimy bastard worms to be drillin' through em' both, do we? No sir, we don't," he replied in answer to his own question. "We'll coat her up good with a thick coat of grease an' brimstone to repel the damn beasties, especially the worms, then tip her over on the other side an' do it all again."

Ships were never watertight, William discovered. In the deepest bowels of the *HMS Argus*, sea water constantly seeped in from small seams between the boards of the hull, or splashed in through the gun portals and down hatches, finally collecting on the lowest level of the ship, where sailors regularly manned the pumps in a mostly futile attempt to keep the ship's innards dry. The brackish bilge water had a horrid smell to it, and William was glad that manning the pumps was one task that was not his. Plugging the leaks, however, was.

"Mr. Taylor, it's time, ain't it?" Mr. Lancaster queried. William had come to know that the carpenter did not expect nor want, any reply to his questions from those around him, intending to always answer his own. "Yessir, it is. An' time fer what, ya' may ask. Well I'll tell ya'. We must plug off as many of the leaks as we can find with oakum."

"Oakum?" William wondered out loud.

"Oakum, boy. Bits of frayed hemp, the old riggings like, soaked in hot pitch and stuffed in her seams, inside an' out."

"How do we get the seams on her outside done?"

Mr. Lancaster had anticipated William's question and took obvious pleasure in answering. "Why, one of us hangs overboard in some Spanish riggin', doin' the pluggin'—uh, that'd be you—whilst the other stays along the railing up top, lowerin' down the hot oakum—and that'd be me." He grinned at William.

"Over the side—" William felt faint at the thought of dangling over the side, fathoms of the dark cold sea sucking and tugging at his legs as the ship coursed onwards through the frothing waves.

"Ya' don' want to be a lander forever, now do ya'?" Mr. Lancaster reasoned. "'Course ya' don't! Pluggin' her up will earn ya' much gratitude from the others, too," he winked, "if it means less time fer them needed on the pumps below with the stinkin' bilge. C'mon, now, I've already put an order in with Cook to be givin' us a couple of hot pots of pitch, an' I've sent Mr. Smith to round up the frayed riggings." He squinted and swiveled his head from side to side. "Ya' don't see him anywheres, do ya? 'Course ya' do!" He pointed straight ahead. "'Here he comes now with our—"

An anguished scream ripped through the air interrupting Mr. Lancaster in midsentence.

Chapter Twenty-Eight

"He's burnin'! Cook's burnin' alive! The pitch's tipped!" Panicked screams carried up onto the deck, but none so loud or anguished as the first.

At once the deck was covered in a swarm of bodies, crushing and jamming themselves down the companionway, as men grabbed buckets of water and wet rags, and slid or jumped down the steps, disappearing with them into the deck below.

"Oh my Holy Christ! Please let 'em put it out!" Smith pleaded out loud to himself. William saw fear in Smith's eyes and that same fear of an unknown danger set William's heart to hammering inside his chest again, his breaths shallow and tight.

"Wha—what's going on?" William yelled.

"The pitch's spilled! If it was hot enough to burn a man's flesh, it'll have started the planks an' timbers on fire! C'mon!"

"Where to? What are we doing?" William gasped. "Surely we're not going back down to the galley? If Cook's burned himself, there must be someone who can take care of him—"

"Oh, fer Chrissakes! You're bloody stupid!" Smith screamed at him in exasperation. "They don't give a rat's black arse about Cook! It's the powder! We need to wet the powder or we'll not have to worry about burnin' up or drownin' if she burns through! Don'cha understand? If even one spark burns through to the deck below it, an' hits the powder room, we'll all be blown outta' the shittin' sea!" With that, Smith whirled about on his feet, and grabbing up a wet mop, he raced towards the companionway. William followed in close pursuit.

The deck below was a scene of mass chaos. The previous dimness in which William had come to rely on to navigate his way around below deck had been replaced by a heavy impenetrable blackness. The far end of the lower deck was illuminated only by a menacing orange glow that flickered off the walls and upright timbers. The air, already thick and hot with oily black smoke, rolled over William, stinging his eyes and gagging him. Cries and shouts of the crew ahead of him were punctuated by the harsh coughing of heat-seared lungs. William tore the sleeve from his shirt and wrapped it over his nose and mouth, tying it at the back of his head. When he looked up again, he realized he had lost sight of Smith.

"This way!" Someone was tugging at his arm, but he could not be sure of whom it was. He followed the sailor ahead of him down another set of stairs, down into the deck below. The air here was not as heavy with smoke, but being so deep in the bowels of the ship, it was oxygen starved just the same. William gulped hungrily as his lungs sought more precious oxygen where none was forthcoming. A lantern lit the area ever so slightly.

"Bucket that water! Convoy those buckets, Sirs! Make haste! Fierce work now!" It was the voice of the Captain. William was sure that he recognized it. *He's down here with his men!* A bucket swung out of the dark, dangling from the end of a sailor's arm, smashing into William's arm, and soaking him with the bucket's sea water. William grabbed the bucket and blindly passed it across his body towards his other side. A pair of hands took it from him just as another bucket slammed again into his shoulder just as the first one had.

"Mr. Taylor, faster if you please! It's our powder supplies that require wetting, not you, Sir!" Captain Crowell shouted. *He knows me, even though I have my face covered like this!* William redoubled his efforts and passed the buckets on, over and over, until his shoulders ached from the effort. The putrid air by now had an ominous tarry odor to it. *The smoke is settling down here too! Dear Lord! Have they not put it out yet?* William detected the smell of wood fire and burning flesh mixed in with the burning pitch. Screams from overhead confirmed what his nose was telling him.

"Give me some sweat now lads, and show a leg! Wet the timbers overhead!" the Captain yelled. William hoisted the buckets to sailors in front of him. It was all he could do to pass the bucket forward. His arms felt heavy and limp. It seemed to William that the buckets were coming slower now, as though the convoy line was losing man power. Everyone around him was moving in a curiously slow motion dance. The yelling seemed to be stretched out into long piercing shrieks and grisly howls. Even the collapse of men around him seemed to be a slow motion nightmare, as William felt his own legs go soft beneath him. *Don't wanna' burn, don't wanna' … the ocean will be so cool…* he slurred to himself and the flooring planks rushed up to meet him.

Chapter Twenty-Nine

The stabbing pains in his head competed fiercely for his attention against the burning throb in his left ankle. As the fog in his head began to clear, William slowly became aware of the groans and voices around him. He struggled to prop himself up on his elbows, only to find himself sandwiched in between two bodies, which in turn, were part of a carpet of sailors, all laid out side by side, upon the plank flooring of the open main deck. Some, like he, were attempting to sit up; others moaned and writhed with the pain of their seared flesh; still others laid ominously still. Two soot stained sailors emerged from the companionway, a crew member's lifeless body swinging heavily between them. A third and forth carried up the lifeless bodies of the two full grown goats.

The air was still thick with the smell of burnt wood and raw wounds. William gingerly probed the gathering swelling around his ankle. Toes wiggled; nothing crunched. Not broken then. Carefully he got to his feet and gritted his teeth against the pain that shot through his ankle and foot when he attempted to put weight on it.

"'Here, wrap it up with these," a gruff voice commanded from behind, "then give a hand to them what needs a drink, won'cha." William recognized the voice as being the one he had first heard when his wrists and ankles had still been bound. The man, like so many of the others on board, was shirtless and showed a well built torso laced with scars—some thin, some thickened, and some consisting of large rippled patches. The man's head was wrapped in a grimy bandana from which a few strands of limp brown hair hung down. A cloudy grey film covered one eye, and he tilted his head at an odd angle as he spoke. "This be the good rum, not the grog, ya' understand. Help yerself as ya' need, too." He shoved a handful of cloth strips and small wooden shims at William, and then passed a ladle and a full bucket of rum over to him.

With his ankle wrapped and braced as best he could, William stumbled among the men, ladling out the dark clear liquid in liberal amounts to each of them. As medicine, familiar comfort, and painkiller, the rum soothed their pain, and diluted their worry and thirst.

Under the direction of the ship's surgeon, the injured were shuffled and sorted into sections according to the likelihood of their survival. Those remaining unconscious were sorted from the already dead by the surgeon's very own, very effective test—a finger tip, ear cartilage, or upper lip of the man in question was pinched firmly with pliers , or crushed, in several cases that William observed, until the man moved or moaned, or until blood seeped from around the pliers' tips. Most of the men had roused; only four remained unresponsive to the good surgeon's inquisition. Three of those looked unharmed, as though they had simply fallen asleep there on the floor. The mouth of the fourth victim however was stretched open in an eerie death grimace, stiffened in his last moments of life by what William imagined would have been the man's last scream. Blackened and burned beyond recognition from the waist up, the sailor's right leg ended in a familiar stump.

"It's the smoke's poison vapors what done them in," a familiar voice explained and a hand clapped William on the shoulder.

"Smith?" William whirled around to see a soot stained face grinning at him.

"Ya' got any more in that bucket fer the one what saved yer skinny arse?"

"Saved me? That was you?" William scooped a full ladle out and passed it to Smith, who gulped it down, then passed it back for a second round, downing that one too, without a word.

"One more, Willy Boy, won'cha?" Smith prodded William in the ribs with the empty ladle, and then drank down the third offer with as much vigor as his first.

"*You* saved me?" William asked again, his gratitude barely contained.

"Nope," Smith replied and with a satisfied belch, he smiled then wiped his mouth on the back of his hand. "Actually, it weren't me at all. I was just askin', in case that one there should be wantin' any!" and he pointed to a man sitting on a low bench. Both of the man's arms were raw, his forearms and hands blackened in places and already blistered where skin still clung.

William's heart lurched. His Da'.

"Hey! He burned rescuin' the Captain, not just you," Smith offered, seeing William's stricken face. He continued softly, "He pulled many of ya' outta' there, he did," and then summed the situation up. "Be glad fer him. This crew'll never abandon him now...."

William refilled the bucket from the large barrel into which a pouring spigot had been inserted and returned to his father.

"Da'?"

The man slowly lifted his blistered face to look at William. His eyebrows and lashes were gone, burned away William realized, and his eyes were beginning to swell shut.

"Da'?" William spoke again, not caring who heard him address his father. "Some rum?" William held the edge of the ladle to the man's blistered lips and gently tipped the liquid down his father's throat.

Chapter Thirty

"We'll be joining the Captain and his officers for tonight's evening meal," Tess's father informed his family. Mrs. Hanley, being the family's servant, had not been included in the invitation.

"Charles, I simply cannot," Tess's mother pleaded. "Give him my deepest regrets but I am in poor health tonight. Assure him that I shall endeavor to make his acquaintance as quickly as my countenance should allow it to be so." The boat's rocking motion had set all of their stomachs on edge, but none more so than hers. She had been unable to keep even weak tea down, and now spoke through gritted teeth, her eyes tightly closed as she lay upon their bed.

"Very well." He did not push the issue. "Shall I bring you something back? A warm biscuit with butter perhaps?"

She groaned at the suggestion. "I doubt that there will be anything offered that I would find palatable at the best of times, let alone now. No, I shall persist with Mrs. Hanley's tea. Go and enjoy yourself. I am quite certain that I will be here upon your return."

In fact, the supper meal spread out before them at the Captain's table was quite delectable. Tess stared at the gold rimmed plate set before her. A hot, thick slice of roasted beef and another of seasoned pork crowded the boiled potatoes next to them, the meat's salty juices creating a lake around the neatly arranged cooked greens. Biscuits were offered, with toppings of butter and sweet marmalade. All of the guests at the table washed the main course down with several glasses of rich red wine.

Just when Tess felt certain that she could not consume another mouthful, small bowls of warm buttered rice and currants were served with a generous sprinkling of cinnamon, ginger, and sugar on top. Cups of sweet tea completed the meal for the ladies, while the men's brandy snifters were replenished without end.

"I do not know of any time at which I have had a finer meal," declared Dr. Willoughby. Others at the table murmured in agreement. Tess studied the faces of those around the table. Besides themselves, there were three unfamiliar gentlemen, and four officers looking splendidly official in their white and blue uniforms. The gentleman with whom her father had spoken at the ship's railing earlier in the day was one of the men in attendance. He looked vaguely familiar and Tess thought that he was probably one of her father's wealthy clients she had seen at their house at one time or another. *Perhaps he is even another physician ....*

Something about him made her quite certain that she had seen him before. She noted the outline of his cheekbones, his hair thick and wavy, and his beard perfectly groomed; she blushed as his dark eyes met hers for a moment. He acknowledged her with just a brief hint of a smile before averting his gaze. His manners and posture suggested that he was a man who had been well educated. *Perhaps he is one of the gentlemen who helped me to my feet in the marketplace!* The more she thought about that possibility, the more certain she felt of the connection. *If he is, he could verify the attack on me!* Obviously, her father respected the man's views. *It probably wouldn't matter anyway, as he won't be able to provide any truthful evidence about the Crone and the ring ....*

"I thank you, Dr. Willoughby, for your kind compliments." The Captain was now on his feet, with his glass raised. "However, I would expect nothing less from our petty officer, Mr. Mertrand here, when we are to have guests aboard so esteemed, as to grace us with their presence at the insistence of His Royal Highness, King George. It is because of these circumstances that we are to experience meals on this voyage that are fit for a King!" Laughter erupted around the table as glasses were raised in a chorus of "To the King!"

Tess knew of her father's royal appointment as physician in a West Indies colony but she wondered if the handsome gentleman were also here on royal appointment. Perhaps he too, would be setting up a medical practice in Port Royal. She wondered how large the settlement was. Surely it would require the services of at least two physicians. She stole a sidelong glance at him again, and felt her face go hot as she realized that he had been openly staring at her, his eyes locked intensely upon her. She looked away and stared at Cassie who stood by her other side.

In preparation for the meal, both girls had worn their best dress. Although Dr. Willoughby had insisted, as always, that Tess's dress have a high collar, and that she wear her hair in a side plait pulled to the left side of her neck, Cassie had been allowed to pull her own thick black waves back and up into a beautiful French roll. The neckline of Cassie's dress plunged deeply enough to show the top of her bronzed cleavage peeking out from its laced edge. Tess felt dowdy and plain in comparison and her nose shone red tonight from having had to wipe it so often as her cold symptoms had set in, yet here was this gentleman staring and smiling at her.

Not Cassie. Her. She felt a small pleasant shiver of satisfaction run down her back.

Dr. Willoughby stayed standing and thanked the Captain once again for the evening. "I would like to thank you on behalf of myself and my two daughters who you see here with me tonight. May I present Tess," he nodded, and with just ever so slight of a hesitation, he continued, "And Cassie." Eyebrows rose in surprise and then furrowed in confusion at the two girls' differing appearances, but faces quickly and politely masked over. Extra-marital dalliances were common among the wealthy although not many had the power and such confidence to be so open about it. "And also on behalf of my lovely wife, Mrs. Willoughby, who sends her deepest regrets, for she has taken ill, and myself, I thank you once more and bid you good evening."

Chapter Thirty-One

Mrs. Hanley sat on an overturned bucket outside the door to the Willoughby's cabin. She rose to her feet with a great deal of effort from so low a perch and greeted the girls upon their return from supper. Dr. Willoughby and the dark-eyed gentleman had escorted them back to the cabin, with the intention of carrying on to the open railing to enjoy a cigar in the evening air.

"Good even' Doctor," Mrs. Hanley nodded, and then exclaimed, "Mr. Graham! How very good to be meetin' ya' again," and she curtseyed slightly.

"And you as well, Mrs. Hanley," the gentleman replied and tipped his hat towards her.

Mr. Graham! Even my grandmother knows him. I was right! He must have been to our house. That's where he seems so familiar from. Tess resolved to ask her grandmother about the man as soon as she could.

"You have been blessed with two very beautiful daughters, Sir," Mr. Graham stated and turned his disarming smile upon Tess and Cassie. "Two daughters, a wife, *and* a lovely housekeeper." He smiled at Mrs. Hanley, causing her to blush furiously in response to such an unexpected compliment. Returning his gaze to the doctor's face, he continued. "It must be a great burden on you to be solely responsible for the safekeeping of so many feminine virtues."

"A burden only recently, Sir, I can assure you," Dr. Willoughby chuckled, but his steely gray eyes sent a clear message to Tess. He considered the safe keeping of *hers* to be the problem. "Shall we continue our business discussion on the upper deck perhaps?" he suggested. "Mrs. Hanley, retrieve two cigars from my humidor, if you please."

Up on the quarterdeck Edward Graham stood next to Doctor Willoughby. He inhaled the last of his cigar which had by now burned down to a stub. "Charles," he began, his eyes scanning the dark horizon behind the ship where the seam between the sky and water was nearly invisible in the darkness. "I hope you know how valued your medical services have been and will continue to be to us, and how highly regarded you have become in certain circles because of your skills and your notable intelligence. I realize that we have had a relatively short acquaintance, you and I, going back only the past year, and your daughter I have only just met this evening." He stopped to glance at the doctor before continuing on.

"However, when we arrive in Port Royal I shall be in need of a wife to provide companionship and to run my substantial household. You will have your hands more than full with a wife of your own, another daughter, a servant and your son to look after ...." He paused and chose his next words carefully. "Therefore, I would be deeply honored if you would consider and grant my request for your daughter's hand in marriage."

Dr. Willoughby stood silently for a few moments, and Edward's heart beat wildly in his chest. He was afraid that he had overstepped the line of propriety. *Damn it! Too fast! Too soon! You should have waited*, he admonished himself.

The doctor turned and fixed Edward in his stare. "I am aware of the enormous value your influence has given my career. I am deeply grateful for this appointment, not only for the opportunities it will provide for me, but I am also hopeful that a change of residence as well as the increase in sunshine and warmth there will provide my wife's melancholy with a healing influence that all medicines so far have failed to achieve." He turned back towards the railing and looked out across the water.

"As for my daughter's hand in marriage, consider it granted. I am certain that you are a man of great means and influence and will be able to provide more than adequately for any woman of your choosing. You shall be married with my blessing and consent as soon as you are settled in the West Indies. Port Royal does have the appropriate clergy, I believe." He turned his head to look once more at the man standing beside him. "Only one question remains in my mind."

Edward Graham turned to look back at the doctor. "And that is?"

"Which of my daughters is it that you desire to wed? I shall have to break the joyous news to her in the morning."

Chapter Thirty-Two

"Who is he?" Tess tried to sound nonchalant. Mrs. Hanley attempted to keep the smile from showing on her face, but the dimples in her rosy cheeks gave her away.

"Who is who?" The housekeeper enjoyed such verbal games. She handed a steaming cup to Tess. "Here. Drink this. It'll put an end to the scratch in yer throat an' the drip in yer nose."

"Mr. Graham, of course!" Tess recognized that she was being baited, her interest in the man pulled out into the open.

"Ah. Mr. Graham. Let me think …." Mrs. Hanley put her index finger up to her pursed lips and knitting her brows together, looked as though she were deep in thought.

"You know him! You addressed him by name as soon as you saw him! Don't pretend that you can't remember him! Who is he? Why does he look familiar? What would he be doing on the ship with us? Is he a physician too? Is he married?" Although exasperated with Mrs. Hanley's withholding of his identity, Tess giggled with anticipation of the impending information.

"Caught yer eye now, did he?" Mrs. Hanley inquired coyly.

"He just looks familiar, that's all, and it's driving me crazy trying to figure out where I might have seen him," Tess replied casually.

A deeper furrow creased Mrs. Hanley's brow. "Well I can't rightly say where ya' might have seen the gentleman, as yerself an' Cassie was both wherever ya' said ya' was, on that day in the market, an' he turned up at the house with his footman, askin' fer the doctor's services. He an' Dr. Willoughby had both left just before ya' arrived home, but I know that he was definitely gone before ya' set foot back in my kitchen. Perhaps you're mistaken …?"

Gone from the house? Then where …? Something was niggling in the back of Tess's mind, some important detail flirting just beyond her conscious reach. "Why did he need a physician?" She wondered if he had been hurt as he pursued her attacker.

"Hmm … let me think …." This time Mrs. Hanley was searching her memory for real. "It was …." Her eyes brightened with the recall. "It was fer the doctor to see to Mr. Graham's head wound."

"Head wound?"

"Oh yes! A nasty one, it was. Right on the back of his noggin!"

The back? But my attacker would have been in front of him ….

"I heard Dr. Willoughby say that his skull bone had been broken. Smashed in when some common thief hit him from behind. Poor man had been attendin' to some important business of some royal nature, when he was set upon." She clucked her tongue in sympathy. "It's a wonder he survived such an attack! Dr. Willoughby said he thought Mr. Graham had probably been whacked on the head with a rock."

Or a bag of last year's beet roots! Tess felt a cold wash of panic envelop her. *Of course! The educated speech mannerisms.* She hadn't seen his face in the Crone's room, but the body build was the same. Not her rescuer. The Crone's attacker! A flash of the old woman's severed fingers swept into Tess's vision. She blinked hard to clear the thought away. *It was him!* Tess felt dizzy with fear. She hastily said goodnight to a bewildered Mrs. Hanley and joined Cassie in their tiny room, where she shared the news of her discovery.

"My God! Tess, we are imprisoned here on this ship with him! Remember what he said? He is one of the Prince of Wales' courtiers! That's the royal connection! He must have been appointed to work in some official capacity at Port Royal too!" Cassie's logic was undeniable.

"Do you think he recognized us?" Tess whispered fearfully.

Cassie hesitated for a moment before answering. "No. I don't think so. He has no reason to connect us with being there that day. He didn't see either one of us. We attacked them from behind. I think we're safe from him for now…."

Grateful for Cassie's presence and words of comforting logic, Tess wrapped her sister in her arms, the physical contact of the hug dissolving away the evening's petty jealousies.

Blood or not, Cassie *was* her sister.

Chapter Thirty-Three

"She looks very bad, nay?" Mr. Lancaster shook his head while poking at the charcoaled ends of the burnt planking of the walls and flooring. "Yessir, very bad indeed," he assured himself.

William looked around. He felt as though he were on the inside of a weeping blackened cocoon. The beams above his head and the planks beneath his feet were burned to varying degrees. Water trickled and dripped down from several spots along the ship's side, pools of it gathering with alarming speed in low spots in the flooring. He and the carpenter had had to tread carefully on the many charred planks to reach the burned area of the ship so as to avoid falling through to the deck below. William squatted down beside the carpenter and peered at the damaged section of wall. He reached out and tentatively felt around the burnt perimeter.

"What's this?" he spoke his thoughts out loud. "There're two layers of wood here?"

"Aye. You've a keen eye fer such, don'cha now?" Mr. Lancaster nodded his approval. He too, ran his hand over the charcoaled edges. "It looks bad, but see here? Like I told ya', this beauty's built with two layers." He ran a hand through his graying hair and sighed.

"Her outer wall's not yet breached, but will she survive a poundin' from the seas? That is the question, we ponder now. An' what do we think, Mr. Taylor?" He again shook his head and gave a sad sigh. "We think not, Mr. Taylor, we think not."

William tried to focus on Mr. Lancaster's assessment of their predicament but as the shock of the fire wore off, he felt compelled to find his father, needing to reassure himself of his father's safety and condition after the fire. John Robert had been among the injured waiting in turn to have the ship's surgeon tend to their burns, but William could not help feeling alarmed at not having seen him anywhere since the fire.

"Can it be repaired?" he asked, forcing his attention back to the damage.

"She could be saved, perhaps in a shipyard, but not here," Mr. Lancaster replied. "Not out in the open water." The carpenter was squatted down on his haunches and he had just reached forward to probe the wall again, when a loud crack followed by a deafening roar exploded around them and a massive object crashed down upon them through the weakened beams from the deck above.

Instinctively, William collapsed into a protective ball, and threw himself back and away from the object. It was over in a second. Recovering, William sprang to Mr. Lancaster's side, coughing and choking on the new cloud of soot and ash.

"Mr. Lancaster! *Sir!* Are you alright?" William yelled, desperately feeling through the dark cloud for the carpenter somewhere in front of him. His hands butted up against a smooth cold surface. Metal. *Oh Christ Almighty!* It was a cannon, its massive iron weight having been too much for the charred and weakened beams.

Scrambling now on his hands and knees, William frantically groped around and quickly felt a torso. "Mr. Lancaster!" he shouted. "For God's sake, can you hear me? Are you alright?"

"I'm here, Mr. Taylor," a trembling voice rose weakly through the settling ash and dust, "but I'm a' feared this monster's taken me foot fer itself, it has …."

The cannon had smashed down through the weakened hull, wedging itself and Mr. Lancaster's lower leg tightly into the hole it had made, the combination of the two filling the jagged hole completely, like a cork in a bottle. Nevertheless, sea water already slowly seeped in around its edges.

"Pull me clear!" Mr. Lancaster commanded. William grabbed the man under his arms and pulled. Nothing moved.

"Again! Harder!" It was a plea. William braced his feet against the cannon. "No!" Mr. Lancaster screamed. "Don't budge the cannon. Fer God's sake! Leave it pluggin' the hole! Pull me as you can!" William tried again without success.

"Go! Give warning! Leave me here!" he gasped. "Step to it! We must abandon ship! Board the *Mary Jane*! There's no time to lose!"

"But I can't just leave you here—"

"Go!" the carpenter screamed. You're wasting precious time!"

William scrambled up the companionway stairs shouting to all he saw.

"The cannon! It broke through the hull! We're sinking!"

"What's that?" Captain Crowell yelled down to William from the quarterdeck.

"The cannon! The sea's coming through the bottom! Mr. Lancaster says to abandon ship! The cannon's got him pinned below! I need help to free him!"

"*Abandon ship!*"

The order spread through the crew within seconds. Men rushed to and from the decks below, trampling over each other in a scramble to save what weapons and possessions they could reach. A topman scampered up the rigging to raise a flag of distress on the main mast. Marines lined up along the edge of the ship and fired three shots off in unison, waited five seconds and fired three more.

All prayed that the *Mary Jane* had noticed.

Chapter Thirty-Four

"She's turnin'!" the yell from the topman was clear. "Ship's hard alee, starboard side!"

William fought to get through the wall of bodies to gain entrance back down the companionway stairs but was pushed back by the larger men. "Help me!" he pleaded as the crew members rushed by. "Mr. Lancaster's trapped!" A firm grip on his shoulder caught him off guard and William spun around, finding himself face to face with his father, Gerta tucked firmly to his chest. John Robert shoved the small black kid into William's arms, and her scrawny legs kicked wildly. Her eyes were wide with fear. Before William could speak, his father pushed past him and disappeared down the companionway stairs. A thin rope encircled Gerta's neck like a collar and William quickly lashed the end of it to a piece of railing before pushing through the crowd with renewed vigor, following his father to the decks below.

William moved as quickly as he could through the darkened decks, amazed at his father's ability to move so quickly once again. The man was already far ahead of him. *He's really healing up.* The thought filled him with a moment of joy. He arrived at the side of the cannon in time to see his father positioned beside Mr. Lancaster.

"Pu-u-uhh!" his father yelled, his eyes pleading with William to understand.

"What?" William panicked. "I don't know what you want me to do!"

"Pu-u-uhh!" his father commanded again, this time with enough gestures that William understood that his father wanted him to pull on Mr. Lancaster. His father braced his shoulder against the cannon and gripped the ensnared limb with his own hands. William grabbed the trapped man under his arms once again.

"Na-a-ow!" John Robert heaved his weight against the cannon, rocking it momentarily out of its hole. Sea water exploded in and William pulled with all of his strength, falling onto his back as Mr. Lancaster's limb suddenly broke free of the cannon's massive weight before the weapon settled back into the hole.

"Gho-o!" his father screamed. "Na-a-ow!"

William struggled to his feet, his ankle sprain throbbing with renewed agony. With Mr. Lancaster's arm over his shoulders, William dragged him towards the hatch and up the stairs.

"Gho-o!" his father's voice urged him from behind.

The situation on the level above was total chaos. William looked over his shoulder but could not see his father. Mr. Lancaster was slowly slipping from his grasp and William felt his own legs begin to buckle under the man's weight.

"Help me!" William screamed, and a burly sailor grabbed Mr. Lancaster's other arm, propelling both William and the carpenter up the companionway and out through the hatch, sprawling onto the main deck.

Voices screeched and howled in a mixed jumble of commands, and legs rushed by in a blur from every direction, obscuring William's view of Mr. Lancaster. A heavy foot landed squarely on William's upper back, knocking the wind out of him as he lay momentarily splayed out on the deck. As he lay gasping for a full chest of air, he could see tiny goat legs from where he was. The poor beast had pressed herself against some rough rigging in absolute fear of the mayhem going on. William crawled over to her, heedless of scraping the skin on his knees open on the planking. Untying the small animal, he cradled her in his arms, and felt her heart beating wildly against her chest wall.

William scanned the area, frantic to catch sight of his father. There was no sign of either him or of Mr. Lancaster in the boiling mix of bodies before him.

"Load on, men! The *Mary Jane's* alongside!" With this new command, sailors began to swing from ropes on the *HMS Argus* over to the safety of the merchant ship's deck. William saw horizontal packages swinging wildly in the air, as they were propelled over to the other ship. Squinting at one, he recognized the face and shoulders protruding out of one end of it as that of Mr. Lancaster. William let out a whoosh of air as the carpenter landed on the *Mary Jane's* deck. He hadn't even realized that he'd been holding his breath. Quickly lashing the trembling goat to his own torso before taking his turn at a rope, William sent up a silent prayer. *Oh God! Let Da's arms be strong enough to carry him over this way!* Hanging on tightly to the rope, he hobbled a few steps forward then jumped and swung out between the two ships.

He landed with a thud on the deck of the *Mary Jane*, rolling sideways in an effort to cushion the tiny goat from injury. Staggering back up onto his feet, he looked back at the *Argus* just in time to see her begin her death roll as the incoming sea water changed her ballast, tipping her far over to her portside. The remaining men on board made desperate jumps across the widening chasm, with only three of them having stride enough to reach the *Mary Jane*. William watched helplessly as the others surely plunged to their deaths, disappearing into the churning sea between the ships. The *HMS Argus* followed them within minutes, expelling her remaining cargo into the choppy waters, littering the sea's swells with her remnants before slipping forever beneath the surface.

Word spread quickly that an unofficial roll call had revealed that thirty-five men had been lost. Clutching the goat like an oversized talisman to his chest, William limped through the crowd of transferred crew, most of whom were already milling amongst the merchant's ship crew. Some faces were familiar, some were not. His father's was not among them.

"Da'!" he called, his voice breaking. "*Da'! Where are you?*"

"Mr. Taylor!" The voice was strained but recognizably Mr. Lancaster's. "Over here! Calm down, boy. Who do yer seek?"

William stared at Mr. Lancaster's bloodied foot. It was crushed into an unrecognizable pulpy mass. "The one they call the Gimp! The one who saved you! Where is he?" William blinked hard to hold back the tears.

Mr. Lancaster's face softened and he grabbed William's hand with his own. "He's gone, lad," he said softly. "The cannon rolled back on him when he set me leg free. He never made it outta' the hold."

William stood still, stunned by what he was hearing.

"No, that can't be! He was right behind me! I heard his voice telling me to go! I heard him!"

Mr. Lancaster gently shook his head. "He sacrificed himself so's we could make it out. You an' me. He's gone now, gone down with the *Argus*." A tear slowly rolled down the craggy carpenter's face, and he brushed it brusquely away with the back of his hand. "The Gimp's gone."

At that moment William felt the crushing loss of everything that he had ever loved in his life. He slowly sank to his knees, bent under the weight of such sorrow, his body shuddering as he silently cried, his own tears running freely. As if sensing his grief, the little goat still tucked in his arms, timidly stretched her neck out, lifted her soft muzzle up to William's face, and began to ever so gently lick the tears as they fell.

Chapter Thirty-Five

Crewmen from both ships worked furiously side by side, to salvage what they could of the *HMS Argus's* remains. The heavy guns—all ten of the cannons—had been lost, along with most of the ammunition that the *Argus* had carried. The *Mary Jane's* two jolly boats were immediately dropped over her side into the roiling waters, manned with sailors who frantically retrieved barrels, bobbing boxes, and whatever floating items they could reach with the long gaffs. It was no small relief that a few *Argus* crew members had managed to stay afloat after her sinking, and they too were plucked from the ocean's deadly grasp.

William saw none of this. As he squatted down by Mr. Lancaster's side, his own grief was brought up short when his hand came to rest in a warm jellied puddle. The carpenter's mangled foot had continued to bleed heavily onto the decking. Letting go of the goat, William sprang up and stripped off the remains of his shirt. Twisting it into a crude tourniquet, he tied it around the carpenter's mid calf and twisted the ends into a knot.

"Help! We need the Surgeon!" he yelled, but his voice was drowned out by the continued chaos around him. William frantically scanned the deck for the Surgeon. He saw no one familiar to him but as he continued to yell for help, a large, neatly dressed man approached with purposeful strides and reaching the carpenter, quickly crouched down and examined the injury.

"Are you a surgeon?" William inquired. The man appeared to know just what and how to examine someone, as though he had done it all of his life. Mr. Lancaster groaned with the increasing pain of his wound. Ignoring William, the stranger stood and called out to two sailors who were struggling to skid a rescued trunk across the deck.

"Here! You two! Transport this man immediately to the surgical quarters! This leg must be squared off and the wound cauterized before he bleeds out! His life depends now upon your haste!" Leaving the trunk where it was, the men grabbed Mr. Lancaster and half dragged, half carried him down into the lower deck.

"Wait!" William cried out in challenge. "Where are you taking him? He needs the Surgeon!"

The stranger spun around to face William, assessing him with a disdainful glare. "I am a *physician*, trained in the practice and science of human medicine, and not just a *surgeon*, as you are so inclined to call the human butchers who masquerade as men of medicine aboard ships such as yours. Therefore, in the future, if you are to speak to me at all, you may address me as *Dr. Willoughby*."

The surgical area of the *Mary Jane* was an actual room, partitioned off from the rest of the second deck and secured by a door equipped with a heavy sliding bolt. The walls were lined with shelves and with cabinets whose doors were secured shut with hooks and locks. In the middle of the small room, there was a sturdy table upon which the sailors deposited Mr. Lancaster. William pushed his way into the room on the heels of the sailors. The doctor was already choosing his surgical tools from a shelf that had been built into the wall.

"Call my daughter in to assist," he instructed the men, "and heat the broad knife in the fire." Without so much as looking up, he thrust a small glass vial towards William. "Mix this in with a half mug of rum from the bottle in the first cupboard, and make sure he drinks it all. Then give him this leather thong to bite down upon, if he remains of present mind for the procedure." For the first time since William had entered into the room, the doctor looked up.

"You! By whose authority are you in here?"

Only half conscious and showing increasing signs of the extent of his blood loss, Mr. Lancaster spoke up in William's defense. "Leave the lad be, Sir. Don'cha know that without his help I'd have lost more than me foot? 'Course ya' don't." He spoke between teeth clenched against the pain. "He's me mate, he is."

Glancing from his patient to William, Dr. Willoughby snorted. "Very well, if you are to stay, be useful. Administer the rum and laudanum, immediately." William quickly poured the vial's contents and two glugs out of the rum bottle into a battered tin mug and offered it to Mr. Lancaster.

"Ya' won't be lettin' him take off more than what seems necessary, will ya' now?" Mr. Lancaster whispered. His eyes searched William's face. "'Course ya' won't" he murmured to himself as he tipped the cup back to drain the last few drops. Within minutes he closed his eyes, the powerful mixture having done its job.

"Father? You sent for me?" A young woman, her hair in a thick shank of auburn ringlets gathered loosely to one side, stood in the tiny doorway. William looked up and froze in an all-out stare. It had been weeks since he had seen a woman, let alone one of his own age group. Her eyes were as deeply green as the ocean and her pupils threatened to swallow him up in their intensity. Her eyes locked with his, as they momentarily assessed each other. Wisps of copper curls framed her face and a faint smattering of freckles splashed across her cheeks and nose. Her lips were full and pink and set in a determined line as she stared back at him. He stole only a glance at her thin figure before the doctor's voice sliced through the air.

"Tess, you will stand to my right, please, and hand me the tools. Men," he continued, instructing the sailors, "bind the patient's arms to the table and hold him down should he come to. And you," he nodded toward William, "will apply the cautery blade from the fire to the vessels to seal them as they are cut through." And with that, he set about to work with the curved blade of the amputation knife.

Soft skin, muscles, nerves and blood vessels were severed to the bone with just a few deft slices.

"Seal that," the doctor ordered," gesturing towards the sanguineous gush.

The smell of seared flesh in William's nostrils brought back the horror of the fire all over again. He swallowed hard to keep his stomach steady. The young woman stood by her father, showing no signs of discomfort or disgust as the doctor placed the bloodied tools into her hands.

Peering more closely at the injured limb, the doctor peeled back the tissues to reveal the shin bones, one larger, one thin, until he had exposed a hand's width of raw bone.

"The bone saw now, Tess." He thrust an outstretched hand towards her and she placed it in his grasp. With a few hard rasps of its blade, the bones were cut through, and Mr. Lancaster's lower leg and mangled foot tumbled to the floor. William's head filled with the rushing sound of his own blood, and he leaned heavily into the table to steady himself. The young woman stood beside him, showing no sign of emotion.

Her nearness was a welcome distraction. *She is beautiful. Shapely.* He inhaled a slow breathe to clear his head. Her scent struck him like a club. *She smells so good! And –*

To his horror he felt an unbidden stirring in his loins. *For Chrissakes! Settle down!* he scolded himself. *You'll impress no one with a telltale bone in your pants! Least of all her father! Especially while he's got a weapon in his hands that just sliced a man's leg off!* This last truth had its desired effect on his budding erection but William leaned a few seconds longer against the table edge just to be sure.

"Seal off the last of that, and we're nearly done," Dr. Willoughby ordered. William grabbed the knife handle from the edge of the embers and applied the glowing blade broadside to the bleeding stump. He winced as the skin and bloodied tissues crackled and hissed.

Satisfied that the bleeding was under control, the doctor pulled the retracted tissues back down and quickly laced the skin flaps tightly together with a dozen stitches. He finished the procedure by sprinkling the end of the raw stump liberally with flour before covering it with a layer of cotton lint and a cloth dressing.

"We are done." Dr. Willoughby looked at William. "Thoroughly cleanse these tools, and dispose of the droppings of flesh and bone." The doctor then beckoned to his daughter. "Tess, let us wash up."

Chapter Thirty-Six

The amputation had taken only minutes. Although the doctor's demeanor towards William and the sailors had been aggressive, his skill level was impressive. The stump wound had not bled through so far. William checked Mr. Lancaster's face for any signs of discomfort, but the carpenter remained unconscious, breathing in blowy, gurgling breaths. William looked up and caught the pair of deep green eyes staring at him again. A building fullness in his crotch warned him that the attraction he felt was about to rise again. *Goddamn it!* He clutched the knife in front of himself with both hands. *Why won't she quit looking at me?*

Tess? Is that what her father called her? She continued to stare. *Probably judging me to be of a status well beneath her, just like her father did.* William returned the stare, partly in defiance and partly in open admiration of the young woman.

Holding out one hand, he motioned for her to hand over the saw and amputation knife. A look of surprise flitted across her face and was quickly replaced by a hint of a smile. *Perfect teeth behind perfect lips.* A small bolt of heat shot through his fingers as her hand momentarily grazed his. The bloodied tools clattered onto the floorboards.

"Take more care or I'll have you whipped, boy!" Dr. Willoughby spun around at the noise.

"It was my fault, Father," his daughter quickly interjected. "I accidentally dropped them before he had a chance to take them from me."

William dropped down onto his knees and quickly grabbed for the tools with his left hand. Again, a soft gasp from *her*. William did not dare look up, but gripped the items tightly in his hand. He struggled to his feet, trying not to put full weight on his injured ankle which now throbbed anew. "I'll clean up, Sir, right away."

"What is your station?" The doctor's voice was commanding.

"My station, Sir?"

Dr. Willoughby sighed in exasperation. "Yes, your station. What is it that you do?"

"I cooked. And I helped Mr. Lancaster there, with the boat's repairs. And...." The doctor's glare was withering.

"And?" the doctor asked impatiently.

"And... I entertained the men in the evenings," William finished in a rushed breath.

The sudden silence in the room was nearly palpable.

A deep and disapproving frown on the doctor's face and the blush in his daughter's cheeks marked William's poor choice of words.

"Uh, I mean, that is to say, I entertained them with my instrument!" he flustered. "I mean, I was also one of the musicians—I play the flute...." William's voice trailed away in embarrassment.

The doctor locked William in his gaze for a moment while stifling a small smile. "Well it seems that you are rather skilled with your hands. What is your name, should I find the need to call upon you for assistance again?"

"William Taylor, Sir."

"Mr. Taylor. Very well then. Clean these quarters with haste and diligence as I've no doubt there will be others requiring our true medical care. May I present Miss Willoughby, my daughter. You will be working alongside of us both. Perhaps she could apply a wrap to that ankle of yours."

William nodded his head in introduction. *Miss Willoughby. Tess.* She was still smiling at him.

A loud crash from outside the cabin on the deck brought William out of his reverie. He bolted out the door, unheeding of his ankle pain as he recognized the panicked bleating mixed in with loud shouting and the heavy slaps of many feet.

The goat! His Da's goat! Out on the deck men were bunched up, their bodies creating a thick wall in front of William. He could hear the terrorized animal and realized from the laughter that the little she-goat was somehow the focus of it all. In a panic, he pushed and tore at the arms and bodies in front of him, working his way through the crowd. Tiny hoofed legs flailed helplessly in the air above the heads and shoulders of the men in the front of the gathered mass. *They're throwing her in the air!*

"Stop it, you *bloody bastards! Stop!*" William screamed, his voice only diluting in with the rest.

Amid the shouts and laughter, William realized the *Mary Jane's* sailors were jeering and hurling insults at something else. William listened. No, not something. *Someone.*

"Hey! You! Ya Lame Brain! They shoulda' left ya bobbin' in the sea! Christ! Ya' look like a sea monster anyhow! What's the matter, huh? Ya' son of a sea cook! Ya still got a water-logged brain? Ya want this goat? Let's see ya' come an' get her then! Over here, boys! Catch!"

"Na-o-ogh!"

William froze for just a heartbeat. In the next moment, he was crashing through the wall of bodies, a roar of outrage exploding from him, the bloodied surgical tools still in his grasp. Mindlessly, he slashed and hacked at those around him, slicing through the air with the amputation knife in one hand and the bone saw in the other, immediately clearing a path to the centre of the melee.

"*Da'?*" William gasped for breath, the pain in his ankle forgotten, blocked by the surge of hope coursing through him. William watched as the sodden, rumpled giant in the centre of the crowd grabbed Gerta from the hands of an equally large and fierce looking sailor. Clutching her to his chest, he slowly turned around in an awkward, swaying pirouette.

"We-e-um!" John Robert smiled his lopsided grin.

Initially caught off guard, the sailors had widened their circle, but they quickly recovered and like a pack of wolves sensing easy prey before them in the form of a disabled man with an armful of young goat and an unknown young man looking back at him wide-eyed in confused disbelief, they began to close in on the pair.

"Get back, *you goddamn scabs!* Get back, or I'll open you from stem to stern, I swear to Christ, *I will!*" William brandished both weapons in slow deliberate passes in front of him. From the corner of his eye he saw an arm move, saw a pistol—or was it a knife?—being unsheathed from a belt. Instinct took over and in a flash, William spun on his good foot and sent the amputation knife whizzing through the air. A scream from the target told William that the wickedly curved blade had found its mark, pinning the would-be assailant's forearm with a solid thunk to the mast behind the man. William heard a loud gasp from beside him.

"He's got the Devil's Hand!" a horrified sailor shouted.

"The Devil's Hand!" A second shout confirmed the observation. "Leave them be, the both!"

William looked down at his hands, and then understood. He had thrown the knife with his left hand. His webbed hand.

Superstition was a powerful force among men of the sea, William had come to realize, and the mere mention of the dark force was enough to sprawl the men backward on one another in a deep seated panic.

"What disorderly conduct plagues this crew?" A strange voice boomed out from behind the men.

"It's him, Captain Raleigh! It's him! He's got the Devil's Hand!"

"Do not spout such foolishness on board my vessel!" the merchant ship's captain warned. "Or are you intending to stir up the dangerous imaginations of those who can ill afford to carry more than a single thought in their heads at one time?"

"But Captain, it's true! And look how the two of them keep the cloven beastie! I saw it following that one myself!" The sailor pointed to John Robert. "It spotted him when he appeared over the side of the *Mary Jane* from the jolly boat, an' it come a' runnin' straight to him! Practically jumped into his arms, it did! 'Taint natural fer a dumb animal to cling to a man like that!"

"Natural behavior? Is that a topic in which you are well schooled?" the captain asked. "Well, tell me, then, is it natural, for grown and hardy men such as yourselves, men who tackle and win their fight daily with the sea and all of the possible deaths she has to offer you, is it at all *natural* for you to fear one small goat and a half-wit?"

Having had their manhood and egos called into question with the captain's veiled compliment of their courage, the *Mary Jane's* sailors muttered to themselves, but began to disperse to resume their duties. William felt like a small child all over again, wanting with all of his heart to hug his father in the sheer joy at finding him alive. Acutely aware of the scrutiny the two of them were under however, he restrained his initial impulse, and instead clapped his hand on his father's shoulder in a hearty greeting.

"I can't believe you're standing here in front of me!" William could not keep the smile off his face. "I also can't wait to hear how you managed to escape that cannon in the hold," he grinned at his father. "I know you'll try your best to tell me, and if I can't get the whole story pieced together directly from you, I just hope that someone will be able to fill in the rest for me."

That someone turned out to be a small but fervent admirer of John Robert.

Chapter Thirty-Seven

Between his father's grunts, semi-syllables, and many hand gestures, William was able to piece together parts of his father's story. From the time that William had struggled up the companionway with Mr. Lancaster, John Robert had continued to try to dislodge himself out from under the massive weight of the cannon. As the sea water had begun to flood in, the *HMS Argus* had slowly shifted on her side, with the cannon sliding further into and through the hole in the ship's side that it had made for itself.

William's interpretation of his father's story of his survival of the sinking fell apart however, when his father gestured that someone had put something under his arms and around his chest, and then apparently had left him there alone with the cannon and chest deep with the rising sea water.

"Da-ar!" his father pointed excitedly when the young boy—the powder monkey, Smith had called him—appeared on the deck.

"Hey! You there! Powder monkey!" William called to the boy. *What was his name?* William searched his memory. *Tommy! Yes, that's it. Tommy Jones.* "Tommy! What do you know of this man's rescue from the *Argus?*"

The boy approached William and his father uncertainly, his eyes downcast. "Sir?"

"Did you have something to do with this man's escape from the ship?" William tried to keep his voice friendly, tried to keep from sounding impatient, as the child's nervousness was apparent.

The boy shot a quick look up at John Robert, but remained silent.

"Well did you?" William could no longer keep the impatience out of his voice.

Tommy's shoulders hunched and a stifled sob escaped him. William blinked in confusion. Tears began to stream down the boy's cheeks and landed on the deck in great wet plops.

"What? What's wrong?" William crouched down and grabbed Tommy by the shoulders.

"Oh, please Sir!" the boy begged, his large brown eyes brimming with tears. "Please don' tell no one! I don' want no lashin' fer what I did but I couldn't leave him there to drown! I just couldn't!"

"Hey now," William soothed, "it's alright. What do you mean? Lashing for what? You did something, didn't you?"

The child nodded miserably, and gave a loud noisy snuffle of his runny nose. "I was down there, sent by Cap'n to rescue as much of the full ammo bags as I could carry 'afore she sank, when I see'd him trapped there." He sniffed again and inhaled a loud shuddering breath.

"And then?" William gently tipped the child's chin up with his hand to meet his own gaze. "What did you do?"

"I tossed the ammo outta' the waxy bags an' onto the floor an' blew them back up with me own breaths, then tied them all together as best I could. Then I wrapped them round him," he nodded at John Robert, and continued, "an' I hoped they'd float him up, after the cannon sucked him through the hole an' into the sea with it." He drew in another long shuddering breath and continued in explanation. "Them bags, they're special coated with somethin' to keep water from getting' in and wettin' the ammo powder. But I dinna' have time to pick up the ammo…." His lower lip quivered and his face crumpled again.

"Oh-h please! Please!" he sobbed anew, "don' tell no one 'bout the ammo! They'd whip me fer sure if they was to ever hear 'bout how I throwed it out an' left it like that! I lost it all!"

"Tommy? Tommy!" William said firmly, and then softened his voice. "That was a brave and gallant thing that you did. Do you hear me? It'll be our secret. Yours and mine." Tommy continued to sob with shuddering gasps. "And Tommy? Because you were truthful and brave enough to share your secret with me, I'll share one of mine with you." Tommy looked up at William, his tear-brimmed eyes wide.

"This man you rescued? He's my father. Now that'll be our secret."

Chapter Thirty-Eight

His preliminary intention of sharing the news of her betrothal with his daughter was lost in the chaos of rescuing the crew of the *HMS Argus*. Dr. Willoughby had anticipated that his head strong daughter would be initially resistant to the idea, and as he spent the next few days assessing the general health and specific injuries of the *Argus* survivors, he formulated a plan.

Tess had continued to be distant and marginally hostile towards him since the day he had caught her up in her atrociously concocted story about the marketplace. He was certain however, that she would come round to the idea of this marriage, after she had had time to consider the benefits of such a fortunate situation.

Edward Graham was a man of power and royal connections. Any wife of his would have a life of comfort and luxury. She would command nearly as much respect from the commoners around her as her husband. Edward was a handsome man in appearance and the fact that he appeared to be a decade older than Tess was of no consequence. He would need the advantages of age and experience to control such a wife as Tess. And best of all, wealthy in his own right, Edward Graham had not insisted on a wedding dowry of any size, declaring that Tess's beauty and family's good name would be gifts enough to keep him content.

And the ring.

Edward had casually added that he found the ring she wore to be quite attractive and probably of significant worth in itself.

Good riddance to it, the doctor thought. He was no more than fleetingly curious as to the real story of its acquisition, feeling only alarm at the thought of it and of the possibility of someone reporting it to have been stolen. *A gift from the Crone, indeed!*

Dr. Willoughby had, however, shared the details of Edward's request for Tess's hand in marriage with his wife. Elizabeth had remained poorly since they had sailed away from the Port of London, not venturing far from her bed except to make use of the chamber pot. The news of Tess's impending engagement, though, seemed to lift her spirits.

"Charles," she had sighed softy with a hint of a smile tugging upwards on the corners of her mouth. "It is a great relief to me to know that Tess's future has been decided–" A harsh bubbling cough interrupted the blossoming smile on her face, replacing it with a grimace as she held her linen handkerchief to her mouth in time to catch the froth of blood stained sputum. Her eyes were sunken and deeply rimmed with gray circles, and as she closed them her lashes lay softly on her cheeks. Cheeks that were pallid, but just now rosy colored from fever, belying her underlying poor health. Skin the color of the consumption, Dr. Willoughby noted with a twinge of alarm.

"It does gladden my heart …." Her voice faded away and she laid her head back on the pillow, drained with the effort of her cough.

Not much else gladdens your heart, Dr. Willoughby silently despaired. His medical knowledge and use of tonics had had no effect on her melancholy and it seemed to him that his wife was slipping away from him before his very eyes. He had even halved the dose of laudanum he was using in her tea–surely her nerves did not need any further calming at this point.

His daughter's state of mind was another thing.

Perhaps a drop of two of the nerve tonic in her tea would be just the thing to calm Tess down and restore her attitude to something nearer civility. He anticipated getting resistance from her when she was to be informed of her engagement. He even thought he knew what her specific objections would be. Edward would be too old. She did not know him well enough. She would not feel ready to leave her family and start one of her own. She had had no say in the matter. Yes, the excuses would be plenty.

His daughter's matrimony had been left too long. She'd become too headstrong already. A touch of the tonic would be just the thing.

Chapter Thirty-Nine

Tess was standing near the railing of the quarterdeck when her father's summons arrived.

Miss Willoughby?" a male voice softly inquired.

Tess turned towards the messenger, surprised that anyone would know her name. The tall, leanly muscled young man in worn breeches and a sleeveless white tunic stood a stride away from her. Tess's eyes flickered over his face and body. Light blue eyes blazed out from beneath a thick shock of sun bleached hair, his bangs having escaped from the bandana that held the rest of his hair in place. His skin was tanned to a deep golden brown, and his muscled arms folded across his broad chest. Pink licks of scars laced his upper arms.

Newly healed, Tess assessed, *and no older scars, so he's recent to this life of a sailor.*

"Miss?" A small grin appeared on his face. Tess blushed, suddenly aware of her bold gaze.

"Yes?"

"Excuse me, Miss, but Dr. Willoughby sent me to find you, with the message that you are to meet him in the officers' galley right away."

"He sent *you?*" Tess was confused.

As if they had a mind of their own, his eyes dipped momentarily, scanning over the curves of her dress's bodice before wandering back up onto her face. "Yes, Miss. I was helping him in the apothecary and he sent me to tell you that you are to wait for him there."

Helping my father? Recognition dawned on her. *Of course! He's the sailor who helped with the carpenter's amputation. What did he say his name was? William?* Tess felt a twinge of possessiveness towards her position as her father's aide.

William continued to smile at her and his nostrils flared ever so slightly. Tess stared back. *He's...is it possible that he's smelling me?* In a moment of pride, she hoped that her clothing had not taken on the stench of the ship's stale air in the tiny cabin that she shared with Cassie. She and Cassie had, at Mrs. Hanley's suggestion, rubbed the skin on their wrists and throats with either a dried stick of cinnamon or a tiny handful of crushed lavender each morning in a desperate attempt to counter the smell of wet mould and rotting fish that seemed to permeate everything aboard.

William studied her with those sky blue eyes, his lips stretching out in an approving smile. His bronzed skin glistened with a thin sheen of sweat in the morning's sunlight. She felt at once timid yet at the same time complimented by the intensity of his gaze and she squared her shoulders back in an unconscious gesture.

William's nostrils flickered again. Now she was sure of it. He *was* smelling her! Tess blushed and felt the heat of her blood coloring her cheeks. Men had looked at her before, even ogled her, but to be ... smelled? Somehow that seemed so personal. *So intimate. So ... attractive.*

"Your father, Miss. In the galley?" William spoke again, reminding her of his assignment and bringing her out of her private thoughts.

Not wishing to be seen as bowing to the whims of her father, Tess lingered. She allowed herself one quick sweep of her eyes down his sculptured torso, her gaze sliding down the front of his breeches before dropping to the wrappings around his foot.

"How is your ankle now, Mr. Taylor?"

His face looked startled. "Uh, it's on the mend, thank you."

"I see you are without a limp now. Mostly."

"Yes, Miss. Mostly." Her attention brought forth a shy grin from him; he was uncomfortable to be the topic of their conversation. There was an awkward moment of silence and he shifted his weight momentarily onto his wrapped foot and then just as quickly back to the uninjured side. "Begging your pardon Miss Willoughby, but your father–"

Tess lifted her eyes back up to his tanned face. He shot her a cocky grin as though he was enjoying her visual assessment. She felt her own cheeks turn scarlet as though he had been able to read her thoughts.

"May I inquire as to what it was that you were assisting Dr. Willoughby with?" she asked with as much dignity as she could muster.

His smile shrank to a tight pursing of his lips. His gaze shifted to a point in space past her shoulder.

"Well?" she pressed.

William cleared his throat and returned his stare to her. "Medications, Miss Willoughby."

"What medications?" Tess felt defensiveness rising. *That* had been *her* responsibility until now.

"Uh ... giving some of the boys a ration of mercury, Miss." His tight smile spread into a wide grin, anchored to each cheek by a small dimple. He glanced at his feet for a moment and then back up at her.

Tess blushed again. Mercury. Treatment for syphilis. So he had been helping her father while he checked the crew's private parts, looking for the telltale chancres. And when he found any, they would have administered a dose of mercury to the unfortunate man using a urethral syringe. Back home, Tess had seen the syringe lying on a shelf. And now, having spent several days on a ship in close contact with an almost entirely male population, she had seen more than just occasional glimpses of the men's private appendages as they blatantly lowered their trousers to relieve themselves along the pissdales and bowsprit. Only the females, she quickly came to realize, ever used a chamber pot.

Her father would have never have asked her to assist with the particular duty of treating genital diseases back in London, but she had heard moans and sometimes screams coming from behind the closed doors of her father's treatment room as he administered the mercury via the patient's penis with the wicked looking device. Not only would it have been absolutely unacceptable to Dr. Willoughby for a young female, especially his daughter, to participate in such a physical assessment and treatment procedure, but he would never have had so many patients to check at once. No wonder he had insisted upon this sailor's help.

"I see," Tess mumbled, embarrassed with the territory into which her questioning had suddenly taken them.

William cleared his throat. "I hope I haven't offended—" he began.

"Not at all, Mr. Taylor," Tess covered her discomfort with a forced smirk. "But now I suppose I must see what it is that my father desires of me." She turned and walked away two steps before pivoting to look back at him.

"Thank you, Sir, for your delivery to me of my father's message." Her smile blossomed into a genuine grin. "I have enjoyed our conversation."

"And I, too," he replied, the husky tone of his voice emphasizing the truth of his statement.

Chapter Forty

Pondering what her father was summoning her for, Tess played nervously with her ring, setting the silver band to spinning again in its polished golden track. A sudden vision of the ring being handed over to a waiting pair of hands flooded her mind. Tess worked her jaw open and closed in an effort to clear the maddening itch she felt tickling deep within her ears. Neither the thought of her ring being given away nor the itch in her ears had lessened as she knocked on the door of the officers' galley and entered the room. Finding herself alone she settled in one of the chairs to wait.

Moments later, she heard laughter. Polite business laughter. Her father's voice was joined by another male voice that she recognized as being Mr. Graham's. Fear gripped her chest at the thought of being in his presence and having him identify and accuse her as his assailant. Her breath came in quick shallow gasps and she felt her blood racing through her.

"Tess!" her father's voice boomed out as they entered the room. "It seems that you have caught Mr. Graham's eye."

Oh my God! Tess could hardly breathe. *He knows! He's recognized me!* She felt dizzy and the room began to spin, her pulse pounding hard in her temples. She barely heard what her father had to say next as she concentrated on staying upright in the chair.

"– And I have agreed. We shall have a snifter of this, the Captain's finest brandy, to seal the agreement." Her father held up a glass decanter containing clear amber liquid.

Agreement? To what? Am I going to jail? Both men were smiling. Even as much as she and her father had had recent disagreements, Tess did not think that the prospect of her being arrested would make her father look quite so happy. And Edward Graham was staring intensely at her, his mouth smiling politely, but his dark eyes hungry for her, roaming over her. His interest was unmistakable. *No jail, then what?*

Dr. Willoughby poured the glasses of brandy, and turning around to face the two of them, handed one carefully to Tess and another to Edward Graham. He raised his own glass, a look of satisfaction spreading on his face.

"Let us all drink!" her father commanded. Tess held her breath and gulped the fiery liquid down in a single swallow. Her father looked on in surprised amusement, then looked at Edward and smiled again.

"To your engagement!" he toasted.

"To us!" Edward raised his glass towards Tess.

Engagement? She was to be married? *To Edward Graham?* The brandy glass slipped from Tess's grasp and shattered on the floor. Her heart pounded furiously. She couldn't breathe at all. The room was spinning and a roar built in her head.

Good Lord! Married. To Edward Graham. To a man who she had seen first-hand was capable of grisly violence. She wasn't going to jail.

Just a different kind of prison, she thought desperately as unconsciousness overtook her, and she too, crashed to the floor.

Chapter Forty-One

Tess awoke, confused as to her whereabouts. She closed her eyes, and focusing her thoughts, tried to remember. *The engagement!* Her engagement. She felt nauseated and willed herself to slide back into the peacefulness of deep sleep, but it was not to be. She opened her eyes again and blinked to clear her vision.

Cassie's worried face swam into view.

"There you are! How are you feeling?" She swabbed Tess's brow with a cool wet cloth.

"What happened?" Tess's tongue felt thick and furry and a niggling headache snaked across her forehead.

"You fainted. Your father brought you back to our room. He said to give you this tea when you came to."

Tess smelled the spicy aroma rising from the cup of tepid liquid. "What's in it?"

Laudanum and some of Mrs. Hanley's tea leaves and cinnamon. They said it was to give you some rest and calm you, what with the news about you and Mr. Graham…." Cassie's voice trailed off and she looked as though she were about to cry.

Tess sipped the tea, feeling its warmth sooth the dryness in her throat. "So that's it, is it? Father would throw me away into the care of a murderer?"

"He doesn't believe us. There's no way to make him believe us." Cassie's brow crunched up with worry and she studied Tess's face, both of them sharing the fearful memory of the dying Crone. "What are you going to do?" she asked softly.

Tess finished her tea with a last swallow and looked into Cassie's anxious face. A warm buzz was creeping up her spine and she felt a feeling of calm wash over her. *What to do indeed?* She thought carefully for a moment and exhaled.

"I'll not marry," she said firmly. "Better to die by my own hand, than by his."

"I've been savin' this fer a very long time," Mrs. Hanley told Tess, as she handed her a small package of rolled ribbons. "It's not much, but who knows when a woman pretty as yerself will have nice things again in this new land. Go on. Take them. Fer yer weddin'. They'll bring good luck!" She beamed at Tess, her eyes floating with tears that threatened to spill down her cheeks at any moment. Her grandmother seemed genuinely delighted with the announcement of Tess's engagement.

Tess looked down at the ribbons that her grandmother offered as they lay in the woman's shaking hands. She took them, lingering a moment as her own hands touched her grandmother's work-worn skin.

Red ribbons. Shiny coils of crimson silk. Light as a feather, each one, but strong as a rope. A tiny item, but suddenly, the strands felt more dear to Tess than anything she had ever been given.

I will use these for something much happier than a forced wedding, she thought, no matter what her grandmother's intent was. Of that she was certain. Tess clasped the ribbons in her own hand and gathered the teary-eyed woman in a hug, feeling her own eyes well up with gratitude and guilt.

Where did she get these? Tess wondered. Such an item would have been very expensive to buy back in the market. Probably completely out of her grandmother's financial reach.

"Where—how did you get these?" Tess stammered.

Her grandmother grinned at her, obviously pleased at the reception of her gift.

"Do ya' like them? They're from China!" she proclaimed, as though she had personal knowledge of such a far off land.

"But they must have cost a fortune!"

"Aye, they did at that," she nodded, and puffed her chest out in pride. Then she whispered conspiratorially, "But there's rich folk, women with empty wombs, who was willin' to pay dearly fer the secret tinctures what allowed them to get with child." She hugged Tess tightly to her and kissed her cheek.

"After all," she continued, wiping her own cheeks with the back of one hand, "what worth was all their fortune to *them* if they couldna' bear any young? If they couldna' have any *family?*"

Chapter Forty-Two

Mrs. Hanley, unused to being idle, soon found ways to pass the days aboard the ship. Immediately after Tess's faint, the housekeeper insisted that Tess spend the next few days lying down. She herself, Mrs. Hanley announced, would assist Dr. Willoughby in looking after the patients in the sick bay, until Tess regained her strength. Cassie, she reasoned, with her strong aversion to the sights and sounds of Dr. Willoughby's surgical room, was more suited to looking after baby Charles and Mrs. Willoughby than the sick ones anyway.

Sick bay on the merchant ship was little more than a storage hold outfitted with four hammocks and two long low tables. Spirit lamps burning a sharp mixture of brandy and turpentine were allowed here under careful supervision during the daily inspection of the sailors' wounds. The fumes from the lamps' fuel helped to mask the thick gut-wrenching odor of decay that was a constant companion of the sick and injured. A thin curtain partitioned the room in half, the intent being that the sick and fevered men would lie on one side, and those with physical injuries on the other.

She had spent only one day in sick bay before Mrs. Hanley observed that two who were injured seemed to have their own personal attendants. A crew member, who went by the name of John Robert, whose hands and face had been badly burned in the *Argus's* fire and the carpenter whose lower leg had been amputated were both frequently visited by a small boy and a young sailor named Mr. Taylor. The boy was obviously malnourished and scratched shamelessly and furiously at his hairline, his armpits, and his crotch. Mrs. Hanley made a mental note to herself to ask the doctor's permission to douse the lad's cooties with full strength turpentine. The one they referred to as Mr. Taylor seemed to be in good health and was obviously adored by the younger boy.

"Don't scratch, Tommy," he warned. "You'll only make it worse." Tommy looked up at the older lad and grinned, then gritting his teeth, scratched with renewed vigor behind one of his ears. "You need a good scrubbing with the lye soap!" he chastised Tommy. "That's what my mother would have done with you, back home."

Mrs. Hanley wondered where 'home' had once been for either of them.

Since the burned man's hands were still wrapped in bandages, even though they were, by now, crusted over with dried purulent fluid, Mr. Taylor brought him his meals and patiently fed him three times each day. Each time he arrived with a meal, he knocked and waited to be let into the room by Mrs. Hanley, acknowledging her with a sharp nod of his head. *That young William Taylor has fine manners*, she thought as she watched him balance a full bowl and two slices of bread spread thickly with lard.

"It's fish chowder today," William explained to his waiting patient, "and better bread than we ever got on the *Argus*." John Robert smiled and grunted in reply. At least Mrs. Hanley *thought* he was smiling. It was hard to tell. The man's face had been deeply scorched by the fire and the scar tissue there was already tightening, as it began to shrink and cure, like a piece of wet leather drying in the sun. His eyelids pulled tightly across his eyeballs, giving him the appearance of someone permanently squinting; the corners of his mouth pulled back into an ugly scowl. His hair and eyebrows showed no sign of re-growth. The overall effect was one of a rather terrifying façade. Quite imposing it was, given the man's height and massive build.

"It's the finest of the fish piss passin' fer gruel, ya mean, don'cha? 'Course ya' do!" the carpenter chuckled from his hammock. Mr. Lancaster was one of the best natured men Mrs. Hanley had ever run across. It had been nearly two weeks since his surgery, and it was time to change his dressing. She hoped his jolly outlook would carry him through the removal of the stuck-on bandaging. The infection would have made the stump end very tender by now, and judging by the ripe odor emanating from it, it *was* infected, as nearly all wounds came to be.

"Mr. Taylor? Tommy?" Mrs. Hanley asked. "Would ya' be so kind as to help John Robert out into the fresh air after his meal is done?" She intended to give Mr. Lancaster as much privacy as she could, given their surroundings, when she revealed his leg stump to him for the first time.

Bringing a bucket of sea water to him, she set it on the floor in front of him. "Stick yer leg into the water fer awhile," she instructed him. "It'll loosen the wraps a wee bit." She opened a tall cupboard door and produced a part bottle of rum from within. "This here's meant to flush out the wound," she informed him as she tilted it to wet a strip of linen. "An' it might sting a wee bit."

"Hold on now!" Mr. Lancaster exclaimed. "Ya don' intent to pour that nectar on the wrong end of me, do ya'?" he asked in amazement. "'Cause if ya' was to ask me, I'd be tellin' ya' that it'd do a whole lot more good goin' in this end of me!" and he pointed to his open mouth.

Mrs. Hanley laughed at his earnest observation. He had a point. She looked at him for a moment and decided.

"I'll get a cup fer ya' then. Just stay put."

"Can I make another request of ya', if it's not too forward of me to think it?"

"An' that would be?" she asked warily.

"Bring two. I'd hate to be celebratin' the loss of me foot all alone."

Chapter Forty-Three

The knife felt strangely familiar. Its handle lay heavy and warm in William's hand. The strange double curved blade had, at the moment of its birth in the fires of a skilled but long-forgotten smith, been forged as an extension of the metal handle and now, as William's fingers curled around it, it nestled solidly in the palm of his hand.

A perfect fit.

It was unlike any skinning or hunting knife he had ever handled. Plain and darkened with a deep grey tarnish, it had been overlooked by the rest of the crew, bypassed in favor of the more ornate and lengthy weapons. William had found it at the bottom of the *Mary Jane's* arms chest.

Perhaps it had been considered by the others to be too small to be safely used in hand to hand combat, too dangerously diminutive to be pitched against a sailor' preferred weapon such as a cutlass or boarding axe, and thus it had been left behind. To William, however, it would be perfect in such a fight.

Perfect to be launched from a distance.

From a practiced hand.

Or from either hand, he smiled to himself. *Now to fashion a sheath for such a thing. Perhaps the bos'n will not miss a small amount of sail and thread.*

Lost in his thoughts of the logistics of obtaining materials for such a casing, William descended into the lower levels of the ship, intending to smuggle a small amount of cloth from the hold. His new weapon had a comfortable weight to it, its surface slick and smooth, its shaft feeling well balanced against the mass of its handle. Overcome with a totally impetuous desire to test its behavior in flight, William hurled his dagger, aiming for the corner of a wooden box stored in the shadows at the base of the galley wall. With a spontaneous flick of his wrist, he sent it spinning on a short trajectory path. It found its mark landing with a satisfying thud as the tip bit deeply into the box.

William stared in distress.

Only a hair's breadth away from his knife, a hand froze in mid-reach. A delicate hand that had come out of the shadow without warning, apparently seeking the same box. William sucked his breath in sharply as his eyes, now adjusted to the low light, came to rest on the blue ring, glowing ever so faintly even in the semidarkness.

God Almighty! What have I done!

He opened his mouth to utter an apology, an explanation, anything at all, but all that exited from his throat was a ragged breath.

Tess stepped out of the shadow and fixed him in her stare. William was sure she could hear the panic in the hammering rhythm of his own heartbeat. For a few tortuous heartbeats neither of them spoke, and then Tess took a deep breath.

"What were you aiming for?" she inquired, her voice steady and low.

"Miss Willoughby! I am so sorry! I didn't see anybody around and I didn't know that you were reaching for it! It was inexcusable and–"

"What was your target?" she cut in, her voice just as calm as William's was frantic.

"Uh … the corner of the box, Miss," and he nodded miserably in its general direction.

Tess peered down at the box and spoke out loud, though William was not sure that it was for his benefit at all.

"My gran–Mrs. Hanley requested that I bring some dried sprigs of mint to her for use against the malodorous air in sick bay." She grasped her ring with the fingers of her free hand, absentmindedly toying with it, or perhaps just hiding it from his eyes. William was not sure which.

"I had been momentarily confused about opening the box. In the dark I was not sure it was the one I sought, therefore I hesitated before reaching out."

She bent forward again, squatting beside the box, and ran her fingers along the knife blade and handle.

"Well Sir, it appears that you have found your intended mark indeed." She looked up at William and smiled. "No harm done at all then, as *I* was aiming for its latch. Do you often hit your mark dead on?"

"Nearly always," William sputtered, "But Miss, I am sick to think of what might have happened ...." His voice trailed away.

"What do you propose you do to make it up to me then?"

"Truthfully, I have no idea but I assure you that I am at your service, Miss! No request from you would go unanswered."

"None?" Tess's smile had been replaced by a stern look, desirous of his affirmation.

"I assure you that."

"Then ...." She stepped forward and drew herself up as tall as she could. The nearness of her once again made William's breath harsh. He stared into her eyes; even by lantern light they were as deeply green as the ocean they sailed upon. For a few powerful heartbeats they stood, their faces mere inches apart.

God provides the birds with food, but He does not drop it into their nests. Make what you can of your given opportunities.

Seemingly out of nowhere, Captain Crowell's words whispered inside William's head nudging, taunting, and suddenly he felt their hidden meaning open up to him.

Impetuously, he reached out, his hands resting on the slight swells of her hips, his fingers drawing her against him. There was no hesitation in those emerald eyes. William bent his head forward and lightly brushed Tess's lips with his own, then pulled back and searched her face. Her eyes were half closed, the contours of her face beautiful even in the shadows of the dim light. Her body pressed against him.

He kissed her again, this time tasting her lips, meeting the soft tip of her tongue with his own. His lips and tongue alternately licked and suckled her skin, trailing butterfly kisses gently down the front of her throat, the tip of his tongue stopping to swirl enticingly in the dip above her collarbone. Tess's lips parted as she tilted her head back and a soft moan escaped her. Her breath came in shallow waves as she drank in the sensations he was causing. Lost in a moment of lustful madness, William kissed her again, and felt her hands slide up around his neck. Her touch upon his skin was thrilling, so overpowering ... and *quite* wonderful.

She responded to him, leaning into him, caressing his face with her fingertips, feeling the short stubble on his skin, and then slowly outlining his cheekbones, drawing her fingers along to track the angle of his jaw. Her touch was electrifying and William groaned with the pleasure of it.

"What was it that you wanted to ask me?" he whispered softly, hopefully, nuzzling her neck just below her ear.

"Hmmm?" Tess softly exhaled. "I–I wanted to ask you ... to teach me ... to throw as you do. With a weapon of my own."

Chapter Forty-Four

Her words sent an instant chill through William, squelching the heat of the moment. He pulled away from her and his eyes widened. *Does she know what she asks of me?* To teach a woman to use a hand weapon, here on a ship would be a forbidden thing, he was sure of it. *Probably a lashing, or worse if I'm caught! It would have to be done in secret, and how would that look, if anyone discovered us together?* And then the reality of being together, of what they were doing–had just done–the reality of being together under these far more treacherous circumstances washed over him.

What in the bejeezes hell am I doing? he cursed himself. Not that he regretted having Tess in his arms. It was the sudden realization of the danger that his own actions had put her in, as well as himself that made him feel shaky and sick to his stomach.

And her already being betrothed! If her miserable fiancé were to catch us, we'd both be thrown overboard! How could I have put my own desires ahead of her safety? To have put her secure future into jeopardy? And now, to do as she asks? To teach her to throw?

William looked into Tess's face. It was full of steely resolve. He saw no hope for himself. If he didn't agree to her terms, and she were to tell anyone of his rash behavior, knife or otherwise, he would be severely punished, most likely ending in a long-drawn out and painful death. Of that he was certain.

He mulled over his options. There were only two. Refuse her and have his actions be revealed to the captain, and then his flesh and bone would be broken under the force of the lash. Or accept her terms, and after being caught with her, hope for nothing *worse* than his body being broken under the force of the lash ....

William stood unmoving, engulfed for a moment in the beauty of Tess's features. Her lashes, long and sultry, framed her eyes, and William was certain that he could smell a faint wisp of tonic tinged with cinnamon on her breath. The stern expression had left her face, replaced by a softer countenance. Her demeanor suggested more of an inquiry forthcoming now.

"Will you?" she asked and reached out to him. The facets of her ring's emeralds twinkled as they caught the smoky light. Her fingertips rested softly on the back of his hand, sending an exquisite sensation of sparks up his arm again.

Maybe some things are worth dying for ....

William leaned over and withdrew his knife from the lid of the spice box.

"Yes, of course," he heard himself say, while simultaneously a quiet voice in his head whispered a timid third option. *Maybe, if I'm very careful, I'll get to spend time with her and not get caught, I'll escape the captain's torture and death sentence, and—*

His gaze fell upon the deep gouge his blade had made in the wooden lid and froze there, just as Mrs. Hanley's generous bosom appeared next to Tess's shoulder, announcing the impending and enthusiastic arrival of the rest of her.

And Mrs. Hanley will strangle me on the spot.

Chapter Forty-Five

"What's keepin' you, child? Oh! Hullo, Mr. Taylor!"

Surprised by the sound of her grandmother's voice, Tess spun round, her skirts nearly knocking the woman over.

"Oh! You startled me!" Tess exclaimed, reaching out to steady her.

"Hah!" the effusive housekeeper grinned and patted her own ample rump. "The dark's truly a maid's friend then, if'n neither of you was able to see the size of me comin' at ya'!"

Dark enough to hide you perhaps, but light enough to show the fresh scar in your spice box thought Tess, her eyes following William's petrified line of sight.

"So did ya' get the mint sprigs?"

"Uh…no, we, that is, *I* was delayed just now …." Tess's voice trailed away as her thoughts scrounged madly about for an explanation.

"Eh? What's this?" Mrs. Hanley had spotted the gash in her trunk.

"It was me," William quickly confessed. "It was from where my knife landed."

Tess stared outright at him. *His courage is admirable, I'll say that for him! Outshone perhaps only by his honesty!* She touched her grandmother's arm and cut William's confession off.

"He threw his knife at something that was here only a moment ago!" Tess interjected. *Not really a lie,* she told herself. *My hand.*

Mrs. Hanley peered more closely at her precious small trunk. "Hmmph!" she snorted, "t'was probably a rat, I've no doubt!" She wrinkled up her nose in distaste. "Foul stinkin' brutes! An' so many of them, too! There's gettin' to be more an' more of them, the longer this damnable voyage takes! They're all over the place! Breedin' like—well, like rats!" She looked up at Tess and shook her head. "The doctor has diagnosed several cases of rat-bite fever in the men, too! An' us stuck on this floatin' hole, with nothin' much to help them with!"

She leaned in towards Tess and William and lowered her voice in a conspiratorial tone. "Mind, I've got a bit of roots an' such fer the cure, but just enough fer those of us who matter!"

She smiled at William and nodded, "So ya' go on an' keep tryin' to kill them, I say!" Turning to Tess, she added, "I'm thinkin' I'll mention it to Dr. Willoughby, that it would be some good fer ya', if ya' was to have a wee blade of yer own, for yer personal protection against such horrid, filthy creatures! If the doctor's in agreement, an' I don't see why he would object to such an obvious matter concernin' yer safety, perhaps Mr. Taylor here could arrange fer a dirk–lady-size ya' understand, now–an' would make sure that ya' knew how to use it without comin' to any harm of yerself."

Before Tess could recover from the shock of her grandmother's statement, the housekeeper examined the gash in her spice box once more.

"Looks like the first part of me letter," she announced, fingering the edge of the small straight cut. She looked up at William. "Would it be too much to ask, Mr. Taylor, if ya' could finish this into a proper 'H'? On account of that's me letter," she added with a wise nod of her head. "Or even maybe carve the whole thing fer me? Hanley?"

Tess noted William's hesitation was misread for an impending rejection, because her grandmother quickly added, "Perhaps I could exchange a service fer ya'? An' I wouldn't expect it to be done fer free, ya' understand?"

William continued to stare mutely at her.

"Perhaps, well…would ya' be needin' anythin' repaired or sewed up, like?" she asked hopefully.

William fingered the bare blade of his knife. A deal had been struck.

Chapter Forty-Six

Spurred on at the insistence of both captains now aboard the *Mary Jane*, surviving sailors, marines, and passengers alike fell into busy daily routines. Captain Raleigh lorded over those whose duties it was to sail his ship and therefore the men under him kept the vessel's decks, riggings and sail cloths clean and orderly.

Captain Crowell, with his military background, continued to be in charge of the ship's defenses. Almost all of the remaining men from the *Argus* now found themselves taking on training in weapons and warfare. The tall blond captain seemed outwardly as unperturbed and in control as ever, but inwardly, he despaired over the loss of the ammunition and guns that his own ship had carried. He himself had checked the stores on board this new ship, the *Mary Jane*, and had been alarmed at the relatively small amounts of gunpowder and cannonballs contained in the merchant ship's hold. Most of her cargo space was packed with boxes and casks; some were supplies for the ship's journey, but a large section was destined to be unloaded at Port Royal.

Only he and Captain Raleigh were aware of the contents and value of this cargo. Tea, fine cloth, tools with which to build, and weapons with which to defend oneself were packed within the many crates and barrels. Of much greater value was the stained glass; the dismantled pieces were being carried safely within barrels of molasses. Such beautiful glass pieces were intended to be fashioned into windows to adorn a new church that was to be built and dedicated to the King. As well, several crates contained ornate religious artifacts fashioned from precious metals and decorated with jewels; all had been blessed by the archbishop before their departure from London. Such items, back in England, would have been valuable enough there, but were precious enough to the British subjects already in the West Indies settlements that their arrival was eagerly awaited. Precious enough that the merchant ship had been assigned their naval escort.

And now, the effectiveness of such an escort had been destroyed, their defense lying scattered, encrusting on the ocean floor.

Nevertheless, routine and busyness kept the men occupied and prevented complacency and boredom from setting in among the crew. Captain Crowell was well aware that idleness, if allowed for too long, would result in the availability of both too much grog and pent-up energy among the crew. In the life of a sailor, such a combination was always a sure recipe for brooding and fighting among themselves. Therefore, even those with no previous aptitude for weaponry were assigned to artillery and fighting drills.

John Robert and William attended weapons practice, initially as a fulfillment of their duties upon the ship, and then as a way of showing off their skills to the others, reinforcing the impression that they were not to be challenged in any sort of confrontation. Both of them were given a wide berth by the hands on the *Mary Jane*, interacting with her seamen only when forced to.

William's keen eyesight would have ensured that he had the makings of an excellent powder marksman, had the marines and newly conscripted sailors-turned-infantrymen been actually allowed to fire powder shots at practice targets aboard. As it was, the scarce ammunition was being hoarded, to be kept for future use, should a real threat require it. The men went through the cleaning of their guns in minute physical detail, while the guns' loading and firing was done entirely in pantomime.

Target practice with knives was a different matter, however. Knives, as weapons, could be easily retrieved from the targets and reused. William quickly established dominance with both his accuracy and speed.

Because of his brawn, however, John Robert was chosen by the gun captain to be 'Number Two', the man in charge of positioning the cannon's gun barrel. Although all of the large cannons aboard the *Argus* had been lost with her sinking, those fitted upon the decks of the *Mary Jane* were 'four pounders'—heavy enough, with each weighing around eight hundred pounds—and it took several strong men to maneuver each forward into place.

During the drills, each six man gun crew competed against the others, moving as quickly as possible, rolling the huge iron cannons forward into their dockings and securing the wheeled trucks with breeching. These were massive ropes which were looped around the cascabels at the back end of the guns and in turn, were attached to the ship's sides, in an effort to limit the cannons' recoil when the great guns were fired.

John Robert's scarred face, slurred attempts at speech, and lurching gait provided ample fodder to feed the cruelty of such men–men who had been raised to survive in a world that had no mercy for any perceived weaknesses. He responded to their jeers and taunts with roars and frequent slams of his powerful fists against the sides of their heads, his frustration boiling over into physical actions. Nevertheless, reluctant admiration for John Robert grew among the gunners, as he quickly became adept at heaving the cannons into position.

No one on board could match his brute strength. The uncoordinated movements still plaguing him as a result of his head injury vanished with the intense efforts required to position the monstrously heavy guns. His reputation as a fierce and disfigured warrior spread among his shipmates, although none had actually seen him in any kind of real confrontation since the skirmish between him and Cook had occurred.

That event already felt like years ago to William.

He rarely thought of his mother and sister anymore, nor of the grisly find of his brother's body stiffened upon the ground. Sometimes memories of them threatened to invade his thoughts, but the pain that the recollection of them brought was still too acute for William to deal with. He wondered how his father dealt with such thoughts. Wondered if his father even had such thoughts.

His Da's lack of speech was nearly as frustrating for William as it was for his father. Many times when William ached to hear his Da's opinion about something, the big man's features would tighten and his brows would knit together in a fierce scowl, as he clearly understood the questions but could emit no intelligible answers. He often ground his teeth together in exasperation but most times spat out no more than a defeated grunt.

William stared into his father's face. The thickened ridges of scar tissue from the burns twisted in angry tangles across his cheeks, mouth, and forehead, leaving only those familiar blue eyes untouched. They stared back at William, full of unsaid emotions and thoughts. William's throat tightened as he read the unspoken plea in his father's eyes. How he yearned to have a conversation with his father again! If only there was a way to replace his Da's injured tissues ....

It was possible to substitute a man's missing limb with a wooden peg to walk on–Mr. Lancaster was learning to do just that with one that William had fashioned for him out of a scavenged piece of wood from the *Mary Jane's* carpentry supplies–or an iron hook to replace a man's grasp when fingers or hands were missing, but there was no substitute part, William noted forlornly, for a man's missing speech. Not even with hours of practice in vocalizing simple words with his Da' had they made any real progress.

More than anything, William wanted to ease his father's mounting inner anger and frustrated sadness. Wanted to pierce his lonely and silent world and forge a bridge back for him. But how to do that?

The answer came serendipitously one day, in the form of one small goat.

Chapter Forty-Seven

"Do ya ever watch that damned goat?"

William stood quietly behind two sailors and overheard them in conversation. "The way she watches the big goon, I mean?"

"Yeah," his fellow ship mate shook his head. "Never seen nothin' like it. Ya'd think she thought he'd birthed her himself!" and the two of them doubled over with coarse laughter.

For as large and fierce as John Robert seemed, his ongoing attachment to the doeling *was* entirely out of place. The burly man appeared larger than ever in comparison to the elfin kid who frolicked and trotted at his heels, behaving in much the same fashion as William had seen dogs do with their masters back in his village.

The way Lucas used to with—Stop it! he scolded himself. *Focus on what's here and now. You can't change what's happened.*

William could see that the tiny goat obviously appreciated his Da's reciprocal attention. *And why not?* Everything pleasurable in her life came from the man—food, water, clean stall, and grooming. In fact, since her rescue from the *Angus* fire, Gerta had imprinted on John Robert, as nearly as a goat could do. His Da's few distorted syllables were entirely acceptable to the little animal, and she responded to his grunts and snorts as easily as a young child would have obeyed a parent.

Gerta was sprightly, William had to admit, in spite of her progressively reduced amounts of feed. Provisions, this far into the journey, were becoming sparse for all aboard the ship, livestock included. William had come to realize that goats were the preferred animals to take along on such a journey as they consumed far less forage than cows and horses, and perhaps more importantly, especially to the one in charge of the livery shit pot, they produced significantly less volumes of liquid and solid waste than the larger animals did. Livestock waste management was always a concern on a ship.

Besides being more compact, goats usually provided a good source of milk for the crew on ocean voyages. Had she survived the fire, Gerta's nanny would have fulfilled that role, but Gerta herself, having never had offspring of her own, produced no milk. She had become useful in another way, however, perhaps in an even more important capacity.

Gerta predicted oncoming storms.

Sensitive to barometer changes or perhaps blessed with a keen sense of smell for rain, Gerta's behavior was as predictable as any of the familiar signs of oncoming inclement weather.

"Look! It's her 'fussy dance', Da'. Do you see that?" William laughed at the doeling's display. She stomped her delicate front hooves in a furious rhythm on the deck and punctuated the maneuver with a series of short snorts that sounded for all the world like a human sneezing. "Rain squall'll be coming up shortly, then," he remarked and checked the skies for telltale cloud masses developing anywhere along the horizon. "I'll tell the captain."

"Ya-ah..." his father replied as he scooped the small animal up, and set her up on the top of a large crate. Gerta loved to be on high surfaces and had climbed nearly every available solid surface on the ship.

William watched his father as the man produced a simple boar-hair brush from his waistband satchel and began to groom his young charge, patiently brushing the tangles out of her silky coal black coat until it shone. Such tenderness was in direct contrast to the gruff demeanor Da' showed toward crew members.

In her friskiness, Gerta attempted to rear up and butt her head against Da's stomach. John Robert instantly grabbed the goat's legs and flipped her onto her side, pinning her firmly to the crate top with one hand.

"Na-ah-agh!" he admonished her and waved the index finger of his other hand back and forth. The kid lay still, her eyes locked onto John Robert's hand. Slowly, he lifted his other hand from her chest and she jerked her head and neck up as though attempting to right herself.

"Na-ah-agh!" he repeated with another wave of his finger. Gerta lay back, perfectly still except for the impatient flicking of her tiny tail. His father grinned at William and then returned his attention to the goat.

"Wah-ap!" he commanded and curled his fingers into the palm of his hand. In a flash, the she-goat was back on her feet, calmly rubbing her head against his leg, as if to assure her keeper that she bid him no ill will at all for his discipline he had inflicted upon her. William gawked in amazement, stunned by a revelation.

Hand signals. Of course! It was the very answer William had been searching for.

Chapter Forty-Eight

The crowding aboard presented the happy opportunity for sailors to observe their female passengers more frequently and from a much closer vantage point than normally would have occurred. Encouraged by Captain Crowell, Smith began to pick up skills in navigation, and a lesson in learning how to use a backstaff provided William and Smith with the ideal cover. Holding the instrument up to shoulder level they took turns staring at the horizon through its slits. It was perfect luck that Tess and Cassie Willoughby often stood at the railing directly in the sightline between the backstaff and the ocean's distant edge. Navigation practice took on a whole new level of concentration at such times.

"Gawd, she's a beauty," Smith murmured under his breath. "Have ya' ever seen such beauty all in one place? What I wouldn't give to be able to touch her skin an' hair, just once."

"It'd be the last thing you touched," William countered good-naturedly. "Haven't you seen the doctor's collection of sharp—very sharp—cutting tools?"

"Just a wish, me boy, just a wish." Smith feigned looking at the horizon again.

"Didn't you hear? She's engaged."

Smith lowered the backstaff and cocked a questioning eyebrow. "Just who are ya' talkin' about?"

"Well, Tess, of course. She's beautiful alright but above anything either of us will ever amount to in life. On shore, the likes of us would never even be allowed in the same room as her."

"'Taint the engaged one what stirs me," Smith asserted and raised the backstaff again. "An' I'll look all I like. Just 'cause I'm poor don't mean I'm blind."

"Mr. Smith!" Captain Crowell's unmistakable voice rang out.

Smith snapped to attention. "Sir!"

"It is impressive to see you so diligently studying new found navigational skills. But perhaps it is time to change duties for awhile, lest you ... strain your eyes." Captain Crowell allowed a small smile to show. "And Mr. Taylor, I feel it would be in the best interest of all aboard to release some building tensions between the two crews. What think you if we were to have some song and dance tonight?"

"Yessir!" William replied stiffly.

"You have retained possession of your instrument?"

"I have, Sir!"

"Gather any who have musical abilities. From both sides. I shall have the event announced." The captain was about to turn away, when he added, "I myself am fond of the way the sun looks as it sets upon the horizon. But it is best not to stare too long at any one spot, lest one were to get burned ...."

No crew member from the *Mary Jane* would respond to William's inquiry as to the availability of a fiddler among them, the *Argus's* man having been one of the casualties. Their superstitious fear of his webbed digits was obvious. Few even acknowledged him.

Fine. It'll be just me and the drum then. And there'll be all the more rum for those of us having a bit of fun. The crew's apparent resentment of their new brethren from the *Argus* frustrated William. He stomped away from the men manning the afternoon watch. *Don't you realize we were along to offer protection to you, you useless buggering arse-lickin' sods?* He stopped in his tracks. *We? Gawd. I'm even thinking like a tar now.*

Chapter Forty-Nine

Edward Graham was not a patient man. There had been no event in his life so far for which he had been content to sit back and wait for it to happen. It was best to aggressively pursue what a man wanted in life. Waiting was a tactic of the cowardly, a tactic of those who were unsure of their goals, uncertain of themselves.

Edward was none of those. His ambitions were strong, scarcely hidden. He was a royal courtier to the Prince of Wales, who was, in turn, the man next in line to be King of the British Empire! And Edward intended to be First Advisor and the most valued consult to the royal position when that happened.

His plans had been coming along nicely, almost too good to be true, when Prince George had heard tell of a seer. Men of Parliament and of the court spoke of her. An old woman with powers of uncanny prophesy. Edward had been instructed to seek her out; and he had dutifully, if reluctantly, done so, armed with a list of inquiries from the Prince. Edward had been sent on such visits more and more frequently, and on several occasions the Prince had even acted on the old bat's advice, taking it over Edward's. Jealousy did not befit him, he knew—she was a commoner after all, a mere beggar—but he could not tame the rising urge to rid his world of the Crone each time her advice proved worthy and true.

However, her reassurances to the Prince on the appointment of Lord Chamberlain as godfather to the Prince's son had gone badly. Being banished by the King from the royal residence and forbidden to take the children—their own children!—with them to Leicester House was nearly unbearable to Prince George and his wife, Catherine. An intolerable outcome to them perhaps, but to Edward it was a stroke of extremely good luck.

He had nearly pissed himself in giddy anticipation when the Prince had ordered Edward to sever all ties with the Crone. It had been Edward's own idea to return to her miserable abode to exact retribution. The blame, after all, fell squarely on her shoulders. And besides, he had, by then, noticed her ring.

If she, upon hearing about her great misjudgment, could have been bullied into handing it over to him, well then, he would have had no intention of delivering it to anyone. He had been passed over on several occasions, his own council having been shamefully ignored in favor of that ragamuffin's, his ego sorely wounded each time.

The ring should have been his. It was the least he was owed. Who could have known the old hag would have been willing to put up such a fight to prevent him from having it? And then to have been attacked from behind and to have had to leave empty-handed with nothing but a serious head wound to show for his visit! He should have known that such unsavory quarters might be harboring thugs.

Thank God Charles Willoughby was a skilled doctor who also knew the value of discretion, especially within royal circles. He had asked only a minimal amount of questions regarding Edward's acquisition of the wound, and had not pressed for any further details. It had been the result of Edward's well-placed suggestion that the doctor had been offered the tempting position as the chief physician in the West Indies. The placement would seem like a gift from Edward, and yet it would relocate the doctor, along with his knowledge of the few details of Edward's attack, far from the ears of any court spies. Edward considered it to be a prudent suggestion. Just in case.

He had despaired of ever seeing the ring again. There had been a slight chance that it would surface again sometime in the future, a bobble on the hand of somebody's mistress or adorning the finger of an imported, politically-placed wife perhaps, but he doubted it. He had thought it was lost to him. And then! To have been assigned by the King himself to sail upon this wretched vessel, chosen to be the royal representative overseeing the ongoing rebuilding of Port Royal in Jamaica—why, it was as though he too, were being banished. The fact that Prince George had given his word to Edward that he would be sent for and returned to England just as soon as possible, had done nothing to lessen his despondency.

The night he had taken supper with the captain and the officers, however, was the night that he was catapulted back up to the very top of his world. He could not believe his eyes. The doctor's daughter. She wore the ring. *The very one!*

And now she was officially going to be his. She was young, well-educated, lovely to look at, and, her father had confidentially assured him, a virgin. Edward was delighted. She was the perfect package. She was his. Along with her ring. Soon to be *his* ring.

Edward paced impatiently on the open deck. The damned sun was getting hot and he longed to retreat into the shade of his cabin, but dared not, in case Tess should emerge from hers and he would miss her appearance. Prickly sweat tickled him along his hairline before rolling down his neck and soaking into his fine ruffled shirt.

How long is it going to take for her to wake up this time? He'd begun to look forward to their daily strolls around the deck together. And she was keeping him waiting longer than usual this time.

He'd kept his annoyance hidden from the doctor, that his betrothed had been drugged with an obviously large dose of laudanum in her celebratory glass of brandy, and that her daily drinks had continued to be laced with more of the same. Edward had wanted Tess to be awake, alert. The doctor had explained that in view of the fact that Tess and Edward had not met prior to the engagement, and had not had a chance to exchange even polite conversation, she would be understandably caught off guard by her engagement to him. The doctor had wanted her to receive and accept the news with a tranquil state of mind, easily produced by the tonic.

Edward had given some thought to this. Perhaps the doctor was right. Perhaps, if she were not so anxious, she would agree to marry him on the ship. He saw no advantage to waiting for a wedding blessing on land. Besides, he was keen to bed his new wife. To explore her lithe body with his own. To teach her things of pleasure. To feel her warm, firm flesh yielding under his hands…. He felt his own flesh firming as he thought of her.

His impatience was growing. In fact he was sure that the captain could and would perform the ceremony on board that very day, if the doctor were willing to have it so. Edward would do what he could to make it so.

He was so engrossed in his plans that he did not heed the sailing master's call for more sail, did not look to see where he stepped. A length of cable of woven hemp whipped by his head, snapping the tip of his ear as it was sucked up from its neat coil upon the deck by the newly freed canvas which boldly inflated in the tropical breezes high overhead.

Surprised by such movement in close proximity to his head, Edward instinctively ducked and whirled around, tripping over a crew member. The sailor had been one of many crouched down on hands and knees, all of them either scrubbing the decks with the abrasive surface of a holystone, or using a caulking mallet and iron to stuff the deck seams anew with oakum and tar. He fell heavily onto his back, pinning the sailor's arm and caulking iron beneath him.

Shock slammed into him and a fierce stab of pain tore through his flesh as the pointed tip of the caulking iron gored his flank. He laid on the deck, struggling to breathe, his body deeply impaled on the sharp edge of the fan-shaped tool. Its handle protruded just below his rib cage.

Horrified that their royal passenger had been injured on their shift—and likely mortally at that—the men on deck rushed to transport Edward into Dr. Willoughby's care.

Chapter Fifty

"Leave the blade where it rests!" Dr. Willoughby ordered, tearing Edward's fine shirt from his body in order to examine the punctured area. "Bring packing and wet tobacco. And I need a lamp. Immediately!" He squinted in the low light and palpated the area, but even without the clarity of a lantern, he knew that he needed to look no further.

Edward Graham was a dead man.

Or would be soon. It was only a choice of timing.

If the iron was to be removed, Edward would bleed out in a matter of a few heartbeats. His abdomen had already begun to swell from the bleeding within. If the iron were to be left in place until the bleeding clotted, his body cavity would most likely fill with putrification over the next couple of days, slowly poisoning all of his systems, painfully leading to a confused state of mind, then a coma, and then death. Which way to go to arrive at the same destination? It should be Edward's choice, he felt.

Bending close to Edward's face he saw that his patient was still conscious. *Damn it!* It was such an unpleasant thing, offering a man a choice of deaths. It would have been a much simpler thing to have withdrawn the iron if he had been unconscious and not capable of making that one last decision for himself. However, here they were, with Edward's dark eyes fixing on his own as he began to explain to Edward his options.

When he was through, Edward simply grunted, "Bring Tess to me."

✦

Tess arrived at her father's side looking bewildered and frightened. Her eyes widened when she saw Edward lying on his side upon the surgical table. Edward beckoned weakly to her.

"Come here." His voice was faint and she bent her face close enough to hear him. "Go to my cabin. Under the bed there is a small box that will be unlocked by this key I wear around my neck. Take it and open the box. Inside you will find a bronzed item shaped in the form of a small jeweled bird. Open the bird and place the ring you find within it on your fourth finger on your left hand and come back to me." He coughed weakly and his breathing became more labored.

"I will *not* wear your engagement ring!" Tess hissed into his ear, low enough that her father would not hear.

Sweat glistened on Edward's brow and he began to shake. Tess recognized the early signs of impending death. She had seen shock set in before, in other patients of her father's. Edward attempted to moisten his lips with his tongue.

"It is not ... not an engagement ring. Tess. I plead with you for my life. Take the key and get the ring. Put it on and return here."

"And why should I do that? Why do you want to have it here?"

Edward's eyes were as dark as sweet pools of molasses. He was pleading with her. He did not look threatening, did not look anything but resigned and sad and in need. *Why have I not noticed that about him before?* She was startled at her sudden feelings of compassion for him. His eyes searched hers, desperately raw with his need.

"Tess. The ring. It is the emerald spinner. Wear it next to your ring of blue tourmalines and the powers of both will be magnified." He hesitated in his explanation and took several quick shallow breaths, grimacing in pain with each one before continuing. "With their combined strength, you can save my life if you so choose. Spin the rings together and use your mind to will the bleeding to stop. Use your thoughts to keep the wound clean. But you must hurry." His next words were mere whispers.

"I will not survive without your help."

Chapter Fifty-One

A strange compulsion to do as Edward pleaded washed over Tess, although she could not identify even one logical reason as to why she should do anything to assist with the man's survival. It had been still early evening when, following Edward's instructions, Tess found the ring nestled within the belly of the palm-sized bronze bird, just as he had described.

She slipped it onto her fourth finger, barely registering its magnificent design and ran back to where Edward lay ominously still. As she watched, his chest had risen slightly with a shallow breath, and without opening his eyes, he addressed her.

"Spin them," he softly whispered the instruction. "The rings. Do you feel the attraction they have for each other?"

She did. There was an invisible pull, a surge of warm pulsing energy in her hand. Edward reached out, his own hand feebly grasping her wrist. "Spin them again!" he commanded, the desperation in his voice coming through even in his throaty whisper. Tess didn't move, confused and embarrassed that she was being drawn into such childish beliefs in magic.

"The decision is yours," he acknowledged when Tess hesitated, "but I have made mine." He looked at her, his voice as soft as velvet.

"I wish to live."

Dr. Willoughby wiped the sweat from his own brow. Although the medical cabin was always uncomfortably warm, only he knew that he had been perspiring more in nervous anticipation of removal of the iron from Edward's back than from the stifling air. In spite of the doctor's explanation of the outcome, Edward had decided to have the iron withdrawn.

Edward had also insisted in having a few private whispered exchanges of words with Tess before the removal. *That is to be expected.* She was, after all, the man's fiancée. The doctor had seen the ring from Edward that Tess had returned with and was impressed by so gracious and honorable a gesture.

Even if it is to be the man's last action of his life.

Tess had allowed Edward to hold her hand for a few moments and she had then gently placed both of her hands on the site of his wound, one of them directly around the blade handle, and the other, now adorned with the two rings on her outstretched fingers, slowly circled and hovered over the wound site. Her eyes were closed and her lips moved silently. Her father looked on in surprise.

I had no idea that she was so taken to prayer. I suppose her words would be as good as any for a Christian send-off.

The extra time Tess had spent ministering to Edward in this fashion had allowed the doctor to position an empty cask on the deck floor just below the table where Edward laid. It looked to be just large enough to hold the entire blood supply from an adult male. Dr. Willoughby supposed that there would have been some clotting by then but not enough to have made a real difference in the expected volume of an impending ex-sanguination.

It was time.

Dr. Willoughby sighed. There was no further reason to put off the inevitable. His daughter's secured future was about to literally bleed away before their very eyes.

He braced one hand against the lower edge of the back of Edward's chest, and pulled firmly on the iron's handle, withdrawing its blade slowly from the wound. It made a wet, sucking noise as it exited the wound's entrance. As had been expected, a burst of warm blood exploded from the puncture site, gushing over his hands, spilling down onto the table and splashing loudly into the empty cask below. And then, just as suddenly, it slowed to a trickle. The doctor stood dumbfounded, his eyebrows arched high in surprise.

What is happening? Where is the blood?

The wound still bled but no more than as if from a superficial slash of a knife. He checked the wound entrance carefully.

He must have bled out internally

But no, Edward Graham moaned, then sighed deeply, and stretched out both of his legs. *Hardly the posturing of a dead man!*

"Packing!" the doctor roared, recovering his wits. "I may be able to save this man's life yet!"

He flushed the wound with dark rum, and packed it with steamed tobacco and cotton. As a final administration to his patient, he dispensed a strong tincture of henbane for pain, pleased that Edward's breathing seemed to have become less labored. Throughout it all, Tess stayed, never taking her eyes off of Edward, except for brief glances during which she appeared to be studying the ring she had received from him. And then, as strains of a flute and fiddle had filtered into the room from the open deck, the doctor touched his daughter on her shoulder.

"Let him sleep for now, Tess. In the days ahead he may fester or he may heal. But he'll not die tonight. Let us get Cassie and Mrs. Hanley, and join the festivities. I'll have another stay on watch with him for now."

And with that, they had left Edward and joined the reverie of the night's music and dance.

Chapter Fifty-Two

William and Smith opened the evening with a foot-stomping jig. Smith kept time on makeshift hand drums—the side of a cask and an over turned bucket—while William led with the melody of his choice. It was a moderately bawdy song and before long several voices rose in chorus, and hands clapped along to the beat. The flute made only thin notes however, and just a few songs into the revelry, William realized the strains of a fiddle had arrived to fill in. An officer from the *Mary Jane* stepped forward with the instrument tucked under his chin and a bow in hand.

Now we have the makings of a real party. The officer took his cue from William and followed along, alternating from melody to harmony and back again. Once again under the guidance of a waxing moon overhead, with plenty of rum flowing freely in their veins, crew members gave in to the joyful trance of the music; it became invasive, soothing them and flowing over their rough edges, wearing away much of their harbored suspicions and hostile feelings.

Lit almost entirely by moonlight alone, faces took on two-toned shadings of silver highlights and dark shadows, making most individuals in the gathered crowd identifiable only by their shapes and movements. Even so, William noted that the two ships' crews began to mingle together. *Captain was right.* The man had a sense for such things. He was aloof, as an effective commander had to be, and a hard man to please, but William often found the captain's thoughts to be wise and insightful. William abruptly abandoned his consideration of the man when a silhouette appeared directly across from where he stood.

It was Tess.

Alluring as he found her in the golden light of day, by moonlight she was breathtaking. *Not so curvy as her darker sister, but plenty there to warm a body and cushion a fellow's bones,* he reckoned. Glancing down at

Smith he saw that he was not the only one to be distracted by the girls' arrival. His friend's drumming took on a noticeable flourish, its steady rhythm morphing into a furious and showy display, leaving William and the fiddler hard pressed to keep up. It filled the assembled men with a deep primal recollection, and many sprang to their feet, their arms and legs flapping wildly, their bodies spinning and dancing with boisterous abandonment.

Easily hidden in the merriment of the moment, William allowed himself a leisurely study of Tess. She was clapping her hands along in time, the rhythmic swish of her skirts giving proof of her hips swaying from side to side.

And she was smiling.

William was captivated. During her near constant companionship on the open deck by either Cassie, her father, or by Mr. Graham, he had not seen her show any emotion. Especially not towards him. In fact, day by day, her eyes had seemed increasingly glazed and vacant. But not now. Not tonight. He couldn't help but wonder what she would be like if she were unfettered by her station in life.

William scanned the bodies standing next to Tess. Cassie stood on her left, and sure enough, on her right stood Dr. Willoughby and Mrs. Hanley. Edward Graham seemed not to be in attendance for the moment. William had heard the man had suffered a serious wound earlier on. *Probably counting his riches lying down in his elegant cabin while he recovers.*

William noticed with satisfaction, the unmistakable outline of his father in the crowd. John Robert stood a full head taller than most of the others, and it was easy to see his head bobbing in time to the music as his feet shuffled in a half-time step dance.

The song ended with an explosive cheer from the crowd and just before the next tune could be started, a high pitched wail drifted above the sounds of the rum-soaked company. *The doctor's son.* William noted that the doctor quickly bowed his head to speak with Mrs. Hanley and then retreated in the direction of his family's cabin.

"Hey there!" a drunken voice greeted William a little too loudly. It was the *Mary Jane's* navigator, the man from whom Smith had been learning to plot and read the ship's charts. The man's breath was a fetid mix of rot, tobacco, and rum. Even in the dim light William could

166

see a thick rivulet of tobacco juice drool exiting from the corner of his mouth.

"What say ya' let me have a go on that pipe of yers?" the man slurred. Without bothering to wait for an answer, he grabbed the flute out of William's hands and held it up to his own slobbering mouth. Repulsed at the thought of ever putting it to his own lips again, William bade a silent and sudden good-bye to his only possession and made no attempt to retrieve it. Much to his surprise, the navigator could play and played reasonably well, given his state of inebriation.

"Keep it," William told the man with a false note of cheer in his voice. Seeing the look of surprise on the navigator's face, he clapped the man heartily on the back. "My gift to you."

"Mr. Taylor!"

William squinted to see the source of the call, although he recognized the voice. Mrs. Hanley waved a hand in a beckoning posture.

"I need yer help, young Sir," she explained, and grinning widely, she pointed to Mr. Lancaster. The carpenter had been sitting on a small box just behind her. A makeshift crutch lay across his lap.

"Help him up, if ya' would."

The craggy carpenter protested. "I don't need any help. Wasn't plannin' on gettin' up. Not goin' anywheres, was I? 'Course not. Not yet anyways."

"Help him to his feet, Mr. Taylor," Mrs. Hanley persisted, "an' catch him if he falls." She turned to look down at Mr. Lancaster and smiled. "We're havin' a dance, Sir. Right here, right now." Upon hearing this plan, the carpenter was stupefied.

"Wha-? Dance?" He looked truly astonished. "I've lost me buggerin' leg!" he sputtered. "An' you've lost yer mind, woman!"

"And it appears *you* have lost yer manners as well as yer foot!" she retorted. "A *lady* has asked ya' to dance. An' bein' as how you're so focused on yerself, it would be good practice fer yer balance. Well? Are ya' goin' to further insult me or are ya' risin' to dance?" She held out her hand to him. Mr. Lancaster stared up at her, his jaw sagging open in continued amazement.

"But it's not proper, a dance between a lady like yerself and plain ruffian the likes of me!"

"Nonsense, Mr. Lancaster. As carpenter, you're of Lieutenant rank, answering to the Captain, and I am house servant to the Doctor. None will object. Help him up, Mr. Taylor," she repeated firmly.

Supported from behind by William's hands on his shoulder blades, and the crutch under one arm, Mr. Lancaster stood and appeared confused as to where to place his free hand. Mrs. Hanley had obviously already thought it out.

"If ya' was to hold tight near my waist, there'd be less risk of ya' fallin' down."

Surprised and himself made shy by her boldness, he nevertheless complied, tentatively placing his calloused hand ever so lightly on the thin material of her dress.

"Ya' may hang on as is necessary fer yer safety, Mr. Lancaster," she instructed him. "You'll find I'm built quite sturdy after all."

William watched in amusement and couldn't decide. Was it fear of falling and making a fool of himself, or was Mr. Lancaster taking advantage of a situation that had literally been thrust into his hands? The carpenter had begun the dance with his hands barely in contact with Mrs. Hanley, and progressed to steadying himself by leaning heavily and comfortably into her shoulder and bosom. *And perhaps it's the rum,* thought William, *but she doesn't seem to mind.*

He caught Tess's eye and she smiled conspiratorially back at him, as if reading his own thoughts. *Now that I'm relieved of music duty, maybe I could dance.* He looked at the carpenter steadied in a warm embrace, then glanced at Tess. *What an opportunity! Only I'd never be allowed to dance with her.* He watched the carpenter swaying on his remaining foot while Mrs. Hanley steadied him. *Maybe if I was her patient? If only my own ankle sprain hadn't healed up so damned quickly!*

Chapter Fifty-Three

Edward's survival of his wound was nothing short of amazing to all on board. It was, everyone agreed, a testament to the remarkable skills of Dr. Willoughby. Tess had attempted to resume her place as the primary caregiver in sick bay, but Mrs. Hanley had insisted on continuing to personally carry out her rehabilitation routine with Mr. Lancaster.

"He's too heavy fer the likes of yerself, Tess," she scolded. "If he was to topple over, he'd squash ya' right flat! An' I've plenty of practice with tendin' to boils an' rashes an' such fer these other gents." She waved a hand in the general direction of the sick bay hammocks. "But that's another story altogether. Besides," she added with an approving nod of her head towards Edward's cabin, "it's only proper that ya' be lookin' after yer man in there." She grinned at Tess as she concluded the suggestion with another one of her familiar declarations, "There's always somethin' what comes from somethin'," and punctuated it with a wink.

Edward had been moved to the privacy and comfort of his own cabin the morning after his injury. Dr. Willoughby had determined that bleeding from the wound had all but stopped by then, and Edward seemed to be running only a slight fever.

Her father was relieved, almost overjoyed, it seemed to Tess, that her financial security and social position had been resurrected with Edward's escape from a shadowy death. At her father's insistence, Tess spent most of her daytime hours at Edward's bedside, occasionally assisting him with changing position in bed, taking a few steps around the room, and helping him with his meals. In between these activities, Edward slept, and at such times, Tess quietly reflected on her predicament.

Her discovery of the odd looking brand on his left upper chest had initially shocked her; its similarity to the shape of her own birthmark was eerie. Intuitively she knew there could be no coincidence. She stared at the delicate braided bands of sky-blue jewels already adorning her left hand and then studied the details of the new ring which nestled by its side.

The emerald spinner.

A broad band of gold inset with a spinning band of silver encircled her fourth finger. Within the silver band, which could be made to spin around in its golden track, were glistening emeralds, themselves secured within tiny clasps of gold fashioned into the shapes of oak leaves.

Edward had said the ring could heal. In the few days that it had adorned her fourth finger, the swelling in the knuckle of her sprained fifth finger seemed to have lessened. Her first ring, with the wavy strands of glowing blue jewels, now nestled comfortably around her finger without too much tightness at the joint.

Coincidence. Surely it was just a matter of time. It would have healed anyway. She studied the new ring.

Edward Graham had had a spinner ring! Tess recalled the Crone's words of warning about the power of such a ring used for the wrong reasons. In the hands of the wrong person.

And Edward Graham is certainly the wrong person! Tess sullenly admitted to herself that he hadn't actually killed the Crone–she had died from hitting her head on the ground when she fell off her stool.

Not fell. She was pushed. Had to have been. By either Edward or his companion on that day, she corrected herself. *And Edward attacked her, maiming her intentionally!* Tess felt a cold shiver rush up her spine as the unbidden image of the severed fingers flooded her mind.

Why then, did I save his life?

Tess realized with alarm that she already believed that she had done the impossible. Had she really influenced Edward's survival? She studied the rings again.

And if I did, then why?

He was a danger to her.

She did not love him. Could never love him.

And if he lived–and it certainly appeared that he was going to–she would have to marry him.

Had she sacrificed her future to save his? What had she seen of his inner being in those few seconds when he had pleaded with her to use the rings' powers to save him?

Remember the Crone. No matter what you saw momentarily in him, no matter how attractive he seems, he has proven himself to be a cold-blooded killer, she chided herself. The realization weighed heavily on her.

She searched her thoughts for a reason for her actions, grasping for any explanation. She held her hand up to the cabin's tiny window, as a beam of murky sunlight bored its way into the room through the pane, and marveled at the intricate construction of the rings' settings. In spite of the dullness of the light bathing them, their gems sparkled, staying true to their own colors.

Her thoughts wandered and for a moment Edward's face swam into her mind's eye. His eyes were darkened, black pits of danger and his hands seemed to be dripping blood. Abruptly repulsed, Tess felt dizzy and light-headed. As she felt herself falling backwards, Edward's image held out his hand, slick with blood, catching her own in mid-fall. Disgusted with this unbidden flight of fancy, she shook her head, confused.

Where on earth did I conjure up that little scenario from? The implied violence of it sickened her. *What was I thinking?*

Suddenly the room seemed too close, the air too stale. Seeing Edward's chest rise and fall, and hearing his soft snore, Tess carefully rose to her feet and tiptoed out of the room.

I need some fresh air out on the open deck. Perhaps now would be a good time for another lesson from William.

Chapter Fifty-Four

Thunk! The tiny knife had catapulted neatly three times, creating a shrill whistle as it sped unerringly towards its target. Its tip bit deeply into an old piece of board upon which a horde of rats had hastily been drawn with a lump of charcoal scavenged from the ember pan of the kitchen's galley hearth.

"Now you try it," William nodded towards Tess.

No matter how hard she wished for it to be successful, her throw continued to fall short of the charcoaled rats. Her knife twirled in a crazy, lopsided spin and skidded on the decking with a loud clatter. Increasingly embarrassed, Tess was grateful that her father had requested an order from both of the captains that crew were to avert their eyes during Tess's daily lesson. She could not ever remember having been so frustrated by an inability to gain a new skill.

"Bloody hell!" she hissed under her breath, not really caring how unladylike it sounded. She bent over and scooped up the disagreeable little weapon.

"You will obey me!" she commanded the knife, as though talking to an unruly servant. Today's practice fed her increasing tension. The tropical heat, crowded conditions, and progressive shortages of food and drink fueled a growing surliness inside.

William chuckled. Throwing had come naturally to him. Without any formal instruction and very little practice, his skill level had quickly become far greater than just the mild proficiency shown by his brother and friends back home.

"You need to hold it in your hand, just so," he advised her. "Feel the weight—really feel it—and adjust the power you give to it."

Tess held the knife, with her arm stiffly extended and quickly launched it underhand again. This time the knife flew straight and steady. Straight up, that is, before flipping one hundred and eighty degrees and quickly imbedding its pointed tip deep into the flooring of the deck at her feet.

William stared, completely at a loss. She had no feel for the tiny blade, no sense of its balancing point. None at all. He sighed. She needed a connection. A true feel for its potential. And that would require a slower concentration from Tess, centering on the ballistic feel of her weapon.

There was only one way to show her. Only one way for her to learn it.

Retrieving the dirk from its landing place in the plank, William held it in his hand.

"May I have your permission to help you?" he inquired.

A look of annoyance flashed across Tess's face. "Of course!" she retorted. "That's what you're supposed to be doing!"

"Then come here," he commanded and pointed to his feet.

A moment of defiance flared between them before she took a calming breath and stepped towards him.

"Do I have permission to guide your hand?" William thought it was best to be clear about that before he made physical contact with her.

Tess flushed, then visibly relaxed. "Yes, of course," she assured William. "Teach by whatever means are necessary." She stared into his clear blue eyes and took another step closer. A small smile tugged at her mouth. "Is this close enough?"

"Not quite," he replied, a tiny grin spreading across his own mouth. "Here, turn around and take your knife in your own hand." William reached around her from behind, encircling her with his arms, and enclosed his hand over hers holding the knife. This close, heat from her body seeped into his, encompassing him, and his heart hammered like thunder in his chest. Her scent hovered in front of him, filling his nostrils. *Mildly salty, a delicious womanly musk, and*, he thought, *a bit of … cinnamon?* He felt a heaviness grow in his groin. *Concentrate on the throw!* he chided himself, irritated with his body's unruly response to her presence.

"Hold it lightly," he said, "and now close your eyes. Just concentrate on the feel of it in your hand. Relax and breathe as I do."

Tess closed her eyes and leaned slightly back into William's body. He felt her shiver slightly at the physical connection, and hoped that she could feel his body heat radiating back to her through the thin linen tunic he wore. His chest expanded and fell with a perfect, even rhythm as his arms corralled her. She nestled her head back against him, just under his chin. He was surprised, then pleased, at how perfectly they seemed to mold into one another. *This is madness. She's in your arms in broad daylight!* He focused on her knife. The next throw would have to be perfect. To provide life-saving justification for this dangerous physical embrace.

For a brief moment she stood still, absolutely lost in the sensation that being this close again to William created. His nearness was exquisite in a way that she had never experienced, certainly had felt nothing even close to this when she was with Edward. Edward smelled of rancid tobacco and often of the sticky sweetness of brandy. William smelled of—what was it? Just himself and nothing else. She wanted to melt into him, wanted to turn and feel his lips on hers, to embrace him—the vision was so real that she felt dizzy and her own heart galloped in her chest.

Stop it! she scolded herself. *I am promised to Edward! To be even this close to William is probably suicidal for us both. Get it under control!*

She slowed her breath to match his and returned her concentration to her hand. William's hand felt warm and strong overtop of hers. She tried to slightly relax her hold on the knife's handle, letting the slow pressure of his fingers guide her grip upon it.

"That's better," his voice was husky yet soft in her ear. "Now open your eyes and focus on your target." He raised her arm and hand with his own and gently bounced it a time or two, as though re-determining its weight.

"Now!" he barked and flicked her arm and wrist in perfect symmetry with his own.

This time the blade twisted in three perfect circles before sinking directly into the middle of the target.

"There you are! Well done!" William cheered, reluctantly letting his half embrace of her go. His nostrils were still full of her scent. Tess stared at the target, her face shining. "Oh! That was good, wasn't it?" she squealed.

"Very good!" William cheered in agreement. He returned Tess's smile. Her excitement was contagious.

"Yes. Well done, my dear." A strong combination of sharp perspiration, tobacco, and brandy greeted them just as the words did.

Edward Graham.

"I see you take a great interest in your student, Mr. Taylor," Edward's voice dripped with hostile sarcasm. Edward slipped his arm around Tess's shoulders and clutched her tightly to him, nearly pulling her off her feet. "I appreciate your efforts, and I'm sure my *fiancé* does as well," he continued, hardening his grip around Tess's shoulders. "But there is no need to overstep your assignment. Do I make myself clear to you both?" His black eyes seemed to have no irises at all, only huge pupils, dark and deadly.

He seeks to own you. Be very careful, the silent mentor in Tess's head suddenly cautioned.

"Overstep?" Tess glared up at Edward, her belligerence resurfacing. *And when did you get well enough to come out here?* She silently pondered this, surprised at the strength in his grip. She shrugged her shoulders as if to loosen a disagreeable shawl but his hold on her only tightened. Edward stared down at her.

"You know how to *breathe,* surely," he taunted her. "And as you've hit your target," he scowled at William, "your lessons with my betrothed are done. Forever. At this time *I* have some lessons for her."

Chapter Fifty-Five

With their engagement being common knowledge, Edward had noticed that the doctor seemed unconcerned if Tess were occasionally alone with Edward in his quarters. Now, seated across from him at the small table in the privacy of his cabin, Tess held Edward securely in her gaze and launched her direct inquiry before he had a chance to start their conversation.

"Where did you obtain this ring?"

Momentary surprise flickered across his face as Tess's question hung in the air between them. She had barely spoken to him at all during his period of convalescence. Yet now …. *Her confidence has grown.*

Edward studied the lines of her face, trying to determine an answer that would contain an acceptable amount of detail. He had questions of his own to ask her and he doubted that Tess was any match for him in the area of obtaining information, even from a reluctant informant.

"You shall have your answer to that after you reply in kind. I should like very much to hear how you came to have the tourmaline ring in your possession. Blue tourmalines are very rare, you know." *What happened after I left the old woman's place?*

Tess pressed her lips together. She was nervous, Edward could tell. *She's fidgeting with the ring. She couldn't possibly know the power available to her ….*

"I have no story to tell," Tess began. "I acquired it in a simple boring fashion." She glanced down at the ring and then back up to Edward's face.

Edward's eyes locked onto hers, staring back intently at her. It seemed to him that Tess was choosing her words carefully

"It was a gift to me, a remnant from a brief but intense friendship." Tess lips lifted in a small smile. "A gift," she repeated. "Nothing more."

Edward's eyebrows arched slightly, briefly exposing his surprise at her words, and then his face resumed its neutral expression.

"Such a handsome ring as that is hardly a simple gift," he argued, "although I can believe that someone would easily find one so beautiful and clever as yourself to be worthy of such an endowment." His voice was smooth, too smooth, but Tess would not miss the underlying misdoubt in his statement.

"I am intrigued and wonder who it was that gave *you*, now my *fiancée*, such a priceless item, and in fact I believe the details of your complete story would be of great interest to me." There was no mistaking the challenge in his voice.

"And why would that be?" she charged in return.

He studied her face for a few silent moments as he again decided how much to reveal to her.

"I was briefly acquainted with it in the past," he began slowly, "and I had believed it to have been lost to its previous owner through an untimely sequence of events." He paused, then suddenly reached out, capturing her left hand with his own. Tess pulled back but her hand remained firmly caught in his grip. Ignoring her recoil, Edward drew his fingertips lightly across the surface of both rings. He pulled her closer to him and held her hand up, brushing it across his own cheek.

"Tell me, Tess, what do you know of the significance of these rings? Of their powers?"

Tess dropped her eyes to her lap. *What does she know? How did she get the ring? Get on with the telling of it!* Edward took a long calming breath. To rush her now would only make her defensive and wary. *Wait. Give her time.* She raised her eyes to meet his gaze and for long moments she and Edward stared at each other as though trying to outguess the other's next move in this mental game of chess. The creaks and groans of the ship, the muted shouts of the crew, and the cracks of the sails in the winds, punctuated the conversational silence between them.

"I think that you know more about them than I do," Tess finally spoke aloud.

Edward leaned across the table, closer still, his face continuing to be a mask, showing no hint of threat or anger.

"Tell me how you came into possession of the tourmaline ring," he urged her again, "and I will, in turn, tell you—nay, *teach* you—all that I know about them both."

Tess pulled her hand from Edward's grasp and let it fall protectively to her lap, buried amidst the folds of her skirt. She was nervously fingering the rings on her hand again, and he wondered what he could say to persuade her to use him as a confidante. *Why does she hesitate? What reason would she have to fear me?*

A slow look of calm and confidence settled over her and Edward knew success was forthcoming. She had made her decision. She wanted to know what he knew.

Needed to know.

Chapter Fifty-Six

Tess struggled to put her questions into some kind of logical order. *The rings' powers?* Yes. She was curious about that. *How did he come to have the healing emeralds?* That too, was a puzzle. But more importantly, she put one questions at the top of her list, above all the others.

What was it about them that had been worth killing for? Worth dying for?

It was what she knew about Edward and the tourmaline ring that had kept her silent to this point. It was what Edward knew about her and the tourmaline ring that urged her to begin speaking.

Tess casually splayed her left hand back up on the tabletop to focus Edward's attention on the rings. As she began her story, Tess slowly slipped her right hand down the outside of her skirts to her lower shin and noiselessly slipped the small dirk from its sheath fastened just above her ankle. She was grateful for William's lessons. The small knife's handle, fashioned out of polished bone, had come to feel as comfortable as an old friend's handshake. Familiar. Warm and smooth in her palm. She just wished it wasn't so headstrong in its flight path.

Best to be ready for anything. Just in case.

"The ring was given to me by an old woman," Tess began quietly, her eyes never leaving Edward's face. "With her dying breath, she gave it to me."

Edward's features tightened in confusion, then hardened in dawning recognition.

"The old seer? The one they called the Crone?" he asked unable to conceal the astonishment in his voice.

Oh my God! This is it! Tess thought, and she sucked in a large, shuddering breath. *I'm making my own confession to the executioner.*

"Yes," she blurted out. "That's the one!" Under the table, she squeezed the handle of the dirk in her hand, running the pad of her thumb lightly over the sharp edge of its blade, reassuring herself of its potential.

"I was there, in the back room, when you paid your last visit."

Edward's dark eyes blackened further in mounting anger. His eyebrows knotted together and his jaws clenched.

"You ... you were there?" he hissed.

Tess glared back, her own mouth silently set in a belligerent grimace, as her heart continued beating wildly against her chest wall.

Edward's simmering fury was palpable in the air.

"You!" he repeated, shaking his head slowly from side to side, as though he could not believe his own conclusion.

"You ... attacked me. It was ... you." It was a statement, no longer a question requiring any confirmation.

"You attacked *her!*" Tess spat out her own accusation. "How could you!" She shuddered with her own rage. "She was just an old woman. No threat to you!"

Edward snorted. "Do you have any idea of the value, of the *power* of the rings? Their ability to *corrupt* is *equal* to their ability to *promote!*" he snarled. "Yes, I know this first hand–even *I* was overcome with greed!

"My emerald ring was a poor fit on me and therefore not dependable for me. Weak in its supposed power to heal. Not even with certain– adjustments–that I made, was it satisfactory on me!" His hand slid over his upper left chest and he scowled. "And what need of the power *to heal* did I have anyway?

"But *hers!*" His eyes shone even in their strange blackness, sending a cold chill down Tess's spine. "Hers was the tourmaline spinner! Tourmaline! It was mined in the days of ancient peoples and a new supply of this gem has never been found since. Do you understand? So very rare! It becomes charged with power when it is exposed to heat–that is why, when it is handled, it seems to *glow!*

"Its power is that of prophesy. Now *that* would have been useful to me! Its assistance would have enabled me to guide those in high places, those with the power to change the course of history, to make certain choices!" His eyes narrowed as he continued. "I could have molded outcomes that would have affected governments, countries, whole populations!"

"You attacked an old, defenseless woman over a piece of jewelry, for your own personal gain!" Tess's accusation interrupted Edward's tirade. His brow furrowed in puzzlement.

"Personal gain? Perhaps, as a corollary. But can one as young, as sheltered as you, grasp the enormous consequences of having one's monarch choose to spend a larger portion of his country's taxes in areas that would strengthen its trading position? To be able to help him decide with a new level of certainty which wars would be worthy to fund and which would not? Or what about which decrees to make to keep the population satisfied and loyal, to avoid civil unrest? What price could you put on that?" He broke off from his rant and closed his eyes.

Tess hoped that he had a recollection of the tiny stone room, with the old woman's face floating tauntingly behind his closed eyelids. *Yes! Recall those horrid details. May they haunt you forever!*

Edward opened his eyes, but his stare was distant. "The ring's power *had* to be passed on. To one who could use it for the good of our country. *She* was the greedy one, using it to satisfy the curiosity of the pathetic rich, receiving only a few coins in exchange, squandering its power." He glowered at the memory and shook his head again.

"Even so, I never expected that she would go so far to keep it from me ... that she would cut her own fingers off!"

"What?" Tess gasped.

"Yes!" Edward's face snapped back towards Tess's. His voice shook, partly in revulsion and partly in morbid admiration. "The foolish old woman grabbed a blade and severed her own fingers! Right in front of me! She was about to throw them *and* the ring into her hearth's fire!" He glared at Tess, his chest heaving with the ferocity of the telling of the story.

"When I reached out to stop her, she twisted out of my grip and crashed backward onto the floor. And before I could help her, we were–I was–attacked from behind. He reached up and gingerly touched the dent on the back of his skull.

She cut her own fingers off? Tess contemplated this in shocked confusion. *She maimed herself? Then it was an accident!*

"I suppose you know the rest of my adventure." Edward's voice intruded into Tess's dazed thoughts. "Now it's your turn. How did she come to *give* you the ring?" His emphasis on the word 'give' revealed his

181

disbelief and suggested to her that he, like her father, assumed that she had stolen it.

"It's true!" Tess persisted. "She gave it—or rather, told me to find it and keep it. She insisted."

Tess hesitated as she saw skepticism cloud his eyes. She paused briefly then continued, delivering each of her next words with deliberate clarity.

"She called me ... a Quintspinner."

The uncertainty in Edward's eyes turned into incredulity.

"Wh-why ... why would she have done that?" He stumbled over his words, his calm façade of control shattering with this new revelation. His eyes widened even as his gaze upon her intensified.

"Because of this!" Tess retorted and angrily flipped back the heavy plait of hair from the side of her neck. At the same time, she pulled the high collar of her blouse down to her collarbone in one smooth movement.

Edward gaped at the exposed flesh of her neck. Ever so slowly, he reached out and touched her birthmark, softly rubbing his fingertips over it as if to assure himself that the mark was really there, that it was authentic and had not been painted on in some manner.

"A Quintspinner!" he marveled in a soft whisper.

Chapter Fifty-Seven

At once his demeanor changed, and his hand lingered upon her skin, his warm fingertips skimming lightly up along the curve of her jaw, then fluttering over the tip of her ear before delicately, slowly, descending back down over her cheekbone and finally tracing the curved outline of her lips.

In spite of her lingering distaste for the man Tess shivered under his touch. It was as if his fingertips had left a shower of delicious sparks trailing along her skin. *How could simple touch, even from him, feel so intense?* The Crone's words drifted back to her and she remembered something about the rings and the wearer's senses. Her breath quickened as he stood and stepped beside her, his fingers lacing through her hair, gripping it, and pulling her face against his.

"You *are* the one, Quintspinner," he murmured into her ear, his lips as soft and warm against her skin as his fingers had been. He slid his other hand across the back of her waist, and then down, cradling her curves with his hand. Goosebumps blossomed along Tess's arms and neck, and she shivered again in spite of the trapped heat of the room.

Edward's breathing, too, was raw. He pulled Tess tightly to him, and her arms reflexively braced against his shoulders.

The forgotten knife she had been holding clattered loudly onto the floorboards, bouncing dully upon the wooden surface. Instantly Edward sprang back in alarm, his instincts suddenly on guard, the moment of passion broken.

"What's this?" Bending to the floor, he scooped the small weapon up and looked questioningly into Tess's face. Tess was staring back at him with a mixture of defiance and fear. He hesitated only a moment before handing the knife back to Tess. Tess's arms remained still, hanging stiffly at her sides, her eyes locked on Edward's face.

For several heartbeats neither of them moved. Finally, Edward inhaled deeply and let out a sigh of resignation.

"You nearly killed me at the Crone's with your blow to my skull, and once again in sick bay when you hesitated so long in making your choice to heal me. I suppose that I could possibly survive a third attempt, should you be so inclined ..." and he motioned again for her to take the knife.

Tess took her own deep breath and slowly shook her head, her eyes never straying from his face.

"Well then, I'll leave it here, shall I? In case you should change your mind," he added with a wry smile as he laid the thin blade and handle on the edge of the table.

"Now where were we?" His eyes smoldered as he wrapped her once again in his arms.

Somewhere, dimly in her mind that was once again distracted by his velvety touch, three temporarily forgotten questions nudged to break free from her subconscious.

What do you know of this Spinner legend, Edward Graham? How did you come by your ring and having one, do you, an educated man, truly believe in the possibility of their powers? And her third silent inquiry: *how would being in William's arms compare to this?*

The words forming these questions were suffocated, snuffed out before they could be uttered, as Edward lowered his lips upon her own, his tongue delicately tracing the edge of her mouth. His own mouth moved against hers with some urgency and she felt herself responding as she kissed him back. His hands moved slowly over her shoulders, engaging gooseflesh once again with his light touch. Bracing her against his body with one hand, he cupped her breast with the other, and felt her nipple harden in response to his touch through the layers of the soft cloth of her bodice. Surprised and caught off guard at the boldness of his touch, Tess stiffened and gasped as he continued to explore her flesh. Her body began to shake—

The urgent pounding on the cabin's door made them both jump.

"Yes?" Edward called out, his word more of a harsh bark, not bothering to conceal his annoyance at the untimely interruption.

"Beggin' your pardon, Sir! So sorry for the intrusion!" The voice carried quite clearly through the door and Tess recognized it as that of William's. In spite of his words, he did not sound the least bit sorry.

William continued, "I am sent to say that Dr. Willoughby orders the presence of his daughter in their own stateroom immediately, Sir!"

My father? So he is keeping track of me. She couldn't help but feel that it was more likely to protect his own reputation, rather than out of concern for her, that he monitored her whereabouts.

Edward held Tess tightly against him for a miserable moment, then replied hoarsely, "She'll attend to her father's wishes momentarily then." He lowered his face to Tess's once more, grazing her ear with his lips and whispered, "Don't be long. I have much more to share with you."

To share? Do you mean information about the rings? Or ... something else? Tess wondered, blushing at the intensity of her own unleashed desire. She stepped towards the cabin's door, brushing past Edward's chest as she passed. Edward's arms shot out, encircling her shoulders and waist from behind, pulling her firmly back against his own chest. He nuzzled her neck briefly then whispered, his next words making her gasp.

"These rings—the tourmalines and the emeralds, and their powers— are only the beginning. There are others, you know."

Chapter Fifty-Eight

Sunlight shone through the murkiness of her parents' cabin window, setting off a faint sparkle in the rings upon her fingers. Tess stared at them. At times she forgot they were there; at others, like now, they drew her attention to them with their weight and shine.

What if the legend is true?

Had the emeralds really provided her with the ability to heal? And what about the thoughts she heard, and the daydreams she had? Were they nothing more than odd concurrences? Edward had survived a mortal wound. Coincidences were happening around her daily. Or was it that she just wanted it to be so? Her doubts and hopes ricocheted back and forth as she gazed at her mother propped up in the bed.

Her father's new insistence that she and Cassie begin daily walks with her mother around the ship's deck was irritating to her, especially since her mother was weakened not only by her ongoing physical ailments, but also from the nearly six weeks of self-imposed bed rest. Added to this was the fact that her mother was not the least bit inclined to accompany them on a foray outside her own cabin, and appeared ready to resist their attempts to dress her in suitable clothing.

"Mother! Both captains say that we shall be arriving at our destination within a few days," Tess explained in exasperation. "You have, at best, a week to recover enough strength to exit this ship and travel to our new home."

"How about wearing this one?" Cassie asked, holding up a crimson dress. "It always looks wonderful on you."

Elizabeth looked at them, both standing expectantly at her bedside. "Yes, perhaps tomorrow." She smiled apologetically. "I'm afraid that I'm a bit too tired today to fuss much with my appearance."

Motivation. I'm sure that she could do more if she felt strongly enough about something. Tess began to wonder if her mother felt as discontent as she did, having to uproot and move to a strange place to begin life all over again. Mired in her own misery, she had not considered that her mother might have been unhappy about such circumstances.

"Father says you must. And he says we are not to take 'no' for an answer from you," Tess replied. She threw back the sheets from her mother's bed as Cassie simultaneously lifted the woman into a full sitting position. Tess was till shocked at her mother's thinness. She looked to have barely enough flesh left on her limbs to stand up, let alone walk.

"Come on, Mum," she encouraged, with more sympathy this time. "We'll be with you the whole way." Watching Cassie expertly slip the nightgown from her mother's frail body while lowering the blood-red dress at the same time over her mother's arms and head, Tess touched the emerald spinner on her own hand. Her finger was maddeningly itchy by now.

What makes it feel so? Tess wondered. *It's almost as though it wants my attention. Well better my finger than my ear. At least I can rub the itch away.* And then another thought hit her—too crazy for her to seriously consider but too desperate not to take note of. *What if I could heal her? Like I healed Edward?* She thought her mother's cough would surely improve but what about the melancholy? As Cassie finished doing up the long procession of buttons on the back of the dress, Tess spun the emerald spinner, setting both rings in motion, and placed her hand over her mother's heart. Her mother looked up questioningly.

"I'm just checking your heart, Mother," Tess smiled and reassured her. "Father always says one's heart is a good indicator of the body's state." She thought she felt her mother's heartbeat quicken a little.

"Well, then, let's go!" Cassie had finished dressing her mother and now carefully assisted her to a standing position. "Hold her under her arm, not at the front of her chest," she admonished Tess. "You can't lift her or steady her to walk otherwise."

Tess reluctantly changed her contact with her mother's frame and helped her mother take a few feeble steps towards the doorway, supporting her under her arm. Cassie was right. She could not hold her mother this way and maintain contact over her mother's heart at the same time. She would have to perform the healing touch pattern that

Edward had instructed her in, at another time. *There will be plenty of time for that over the next week,* she reassured herself, and immediately a new itch, fiercer in intensity than the one under her blue spinner, began under the emerald band.

What is happening? The itch was almost unbearable. She had to find something to treat it with, some way to rid herself of it. *But how and with what?* She was anxious to return to Edward. Somehow, she felt, he would know what she should do about it. She was certain that he would have answers to questions that she had not yet even thought of.

"Have you stopped taking the tea with tonic that your father was having prepared for you?" Edward's question caught Tess off guard. He poured a small amount of brandy into the crystal goblet he had set before her. Tess noted that her father had seemed more relaxed about her being in Edward's presence, unchaperoned. It annoyed her to think of the amount of trust her father had in Edward.

"What business of that is yours?" she replied indignantly.

Edward sat across from her and raised his own glass of the amber liquid to his lips. *Stupid girl. The rings must be freely given to me preserve their powers or I would have removed them from you by now.* Through the vapors of time, his mother's words, further teachings to him in his childhood, came back to him, swirling in whispers as faint as ghostly impressions. *The power of a spinner ring cannot be used against a true Spinner,* he heard her long forgotten voice whisper in his head. *The ring's power can only be used to aid such a one. Cannot be used against ....* Edward considered this knowledge and decided to keep it to himself for now.

"One must be of sound mind to fully harness the power of the spinners." He pointed an accusing finger at her. "If your mind is dulled by the daily infusion of a tonic such as laudanum, it will most certainly make you deaf and dumb to the spinners' council."

In spite of her natural inclination to be defensive towards his words, Tess knew she was being instructed in an important first detail. Edward was right about the dulling effects on her thoughts. In fact, Cassie and Tess had had such an argument only that very morning, as Cassie had accused Tess of becoming complacent about everything.

"It's the damned tea! Don't you see yourself changing?" Cassie had shouted at her.

"Father says it's in my best interest—"

"And when did you stop standing up to him in times when you thought differently from him? I've never seen you to be such a–a ninny!"

"What's your worry then?" Tess had hissed at her. "I'm his daughter. I'm doing as I please!"

Cassie's eyes had widened at the thinly veiled insult. "Well aren't you just the bantam cock strutting on his own dunghill!" Cassie's words had stung and Tess had burned with the shame of her pointed statement.

Well it's true! Tess had thought haughtily. *I am the daughter they first chose,* and she had whirled around and left their shared cabin, slamming the door loudly behind her.

Laudanum was a general tonic used often and liberally for many conditions in a medical practice. She had come to enjoy–no, even to eagerly look forward to–the pleasant sensation of a wash of head-to-toe warming that the tonic always produced. It was soothing, calming, and, Tess slowly realized, addicting. Now Edward was on about the same thing. Her irritation with him was growing but she knew that annoying him would not get her the answers she sought. She tried another tactic.

"Tell me more about the spinners," she suggested. "And more about what you and the old woman both seem to think I am. What is a Quintspinner?"

"Further instruction will be wasted on you unless you are able to forgo the tonic," Edward replied calmly. "On each day that you arrive here clear of its influence, I will offer further knowledge to you. Otherwise, you will be lost to your great purpose in this life." He stared at Tess, making sure that she understood his resolve. "For today, I will offer the story of my own involvement, as such a tale is not of as great importance as the workings of the spinners themselves. But," he warned her again, "after today, no further tonic. And Tess, I *will* know."

"I'm the one with the tourmaline ring!" Tess retorted. "You don't have access to its power of prophecy!"

Edward snorted and shook his head in amusement. "The ring is not needed to know such a thing, my dear. Your own eyes, the very pupils which shrink in response to the tonic, would give you away."

Chapter Fifty-Nine

"My father was a scribe," Edward began, "summoned, by Princess Catherine of Braganza, from their home country of Portugal, soon after her wedding in England to Charles II. My mother came from a country further east of Portugal, its identity unknown to me; I had heard it said that she was a woman from a gypsy caravan, a woman who bewitched my father with her beauty and powers of persuasion. While in the royal court, my father was granted permission to have his wife reside there with him. She became pregnant soon after her arrival and barely survived after the difficult delivery of her children."

"Children? Do you mean she had more than one?" Tess was instantly intrigued by this possibility. "More than one at a single birth?" In all of the births she had attended with her father, no babies from a multiple birth had ever survived. Surviving twins were a rarity.

"Indeed. I have a brother, Thomas, and—"

"You have a brother?" Tess broke in. She could hardly contain her astonishment. "Where is he now? Is he still living?"

"I suppose that would be a slight possibility, although I have not had word from him in many years." Edward saw Tess's inquiring look and he continued before she could interrupt him again. "Thomas and I were very different from the start. Both of us were well schooled in several languages, both written and spoken, as well as in mathematics, history, philosophy, and a certain amount of warfare techniques. It was in the physical lessons that Thomas excelled and I failed miserably."

"What do you mean?" Tess asked.

"Although we were delivered from the same woman's loins, and we grew and thrived under much the same court tendencies and experiences, I found myself able to influence others by speech alone, and I was therefore trained as a scholar, groomed to be an effective emissary as a courtier for the British monarchy. Thomas, however, had different aptitudes and appetites ....." Edward's voice trailed away as if he were lost in long-forgotten memories.

Tess waited impatiently for Edward to go on. He continued to stare off into the distance.

"What happened to him?" she asked when she could stand his silence no longer.

Edward blinked and returned his gaze to her. "Thomas was brash. And cruel, I think. He abused his position of power in court from an early age, wielding harsh penalties upon his underlings for even the most menial of infractions, and often taking their women and daughters as he wished to slake his own lusts. We were still very young men when his reputation became known far and away, and his actions became openly resented by the commoners under his ownership and control." Edward paused and leaned forward.

"I was therefore not sorry to have my father gain an appointment for him as a captain of an exploring sea-going vessel and to have him delivered not only from the court, but from England itself. You see, his unfettered appetites for lust and cruelty provided his own demise when, after one particularly brutal rape of a young girl, forcibly done in front of her father, resulted in both the girl's death during the delivery of the resultant child, as well as that of her despondent father. Word of this event and its outcome spread among the farmers, the trades people, even among those living in court themselves, and my father feared Thomas might have hung for it. Especially if it had become known that Thomas carried the mark."

"The mark?"

"The very same as you have. The mark of a Quintspinner. His mark appeared under his arm and was therefore more easily hidden, although it would surely have been discovered if he had been held in any prison.

"It is carried down family lines. *He* was born with it and I ... was not," Edward finished bitterly. After a moment, he continued, "Just as well, I suppose, that he never gained the knowledge, never took the opportunities to travel to countries with much more ancient knowledge than ours ... never came into possession of a spinner ring as I did, and never became a *Spinner*."

Tess's head was reeling. Her chest felt tight and her breath came in shallow gasps. *Thomas's story! The details! They were identical to–*

Her thoughts were interrupted when Edward placed his hand on her arm and gently stroked her hand with his.

"So you see, our family received a letter from Thomas every few years, but he did not return to England in person, and eventually even the letters stopped. His present whereabouts is unknown to me and it is likely that he no longer survives." He sat back with a look of satisfaction on his face. "Now, I wish to hear the details of your family's background. The Quintspinner mark *is* a family inheritance, after all."

"I–I was adopted by the Willoughby's," Tess stuttered. "I am ... was ... an orphan." Waves of nausea washed over her. She jumped up from the wooden stool, sending it crashing over in her haste. "I have to go! I don't feel well!" she exclaimed and bolted for the door.

"You are ... *an orphan?*" Edward was clearly disappointed.

"Yes!" Tess affirmed as she ran from Edward's cabin. *And you are my uncle!*

Marriage arrangements between family members were commonly done, she knew. Among royals and upper class, marriage between blood relatives happened for reasons as diverse as preserving blood lines, securing political power and social status, or to gain wealth. But none of these mattered to Tess. It was time to confide in her grandmother.

The opportunity for that, however, was stolen from her.

Chapter Sixty

The warmth of the air as the *Mary Jane* sailed closer to her southern destination soothed tempers like udder balm spread on an open boil. Sunshine, splashing hot on their skin, filled the crew and passengers with a mellow sluggishness as the days passed. A pleasant laziness as such had seeped into them all when the cry from the foremast lookout struck a universal bolt of fear into each sailor.

"Ahoy! Sail ho! Ahoy!"

The lookout's voice brought everything to a sudden standstill as voices and activity alike froze. The silence was immediate and eerily complete as all eyes trained on the top hand perched in the sky overhead. Both captains appeared on deck.

"Where away, Sir?" Captain Raleigh bellowed.

"A glass! Bring me a glass!" Captain Crowell barked. Men scrambled and a telescoping spyglass was produced. "Where away is the sail?" he too shouted as he rushed to the railing of the foredeck.

"Larboard astern!" The muffled cry filtered down from the top hand. Larboard *astern*. An approach from behind. Tension gripped the crew as men strained to catch a glimpse of the sighted vessel. Larboard at this stage in their journey meant an open water approach. Perhaps it was only a merchant vessel like herself, loaded with goods for trade and headed for the islands. That was it, most likely ….

"How make you her in appearance?" Captain Raleigh shouted up.

The lookout hesitated a moment.

"You! Top mast! I ask you, what does she look like?" Captain Raleigh demanded.

"Sir … a frigate, Sir, I think, but …."

"You think? How is it that your damned eyes cannot tell us?"

"Sir!" the lookout hollered down, "She's a frigate, there were three masts, of that I am nearly certain, but … she's dropped back over the horizon. Her sail showed but only a moment, Sir!"

Captain Crowell held the glass perfectly level to his eye, his hips and knees bending with the roll of the ship. He stared through it for several heartbeats, scanning the complete horizon behind the *Mary Jane*. Captain Raleigh stood by his side, waiting for his assessment of the intruder.

"I see no sign of her," Captain Crowell finally spoke aloud. "Perhaps she has turned away, uncertain if we are pirates and therefore giving us wide berth."

"Ahoy aloft! See you any sail still?" Captain Raleigh yelled up to the top hand.

"No Sir! Nothing since first sighting!"

Collapsing the spyglass down, Captain Crowell handed it to the sailor next to him. "Captain Raleigh and I shall confer with regards to this," he informed the men. "It is for every man to keep a sharp eye. This close to the coast, we are within sailing distance of rogues who would mean us only great harm. For the present time, let us see some haste made through these waters." He concluded in a voice low enough that only those standing directly at his side could hear, "I think it is not by coincidence alone that we are followed in our path by a strange ship."

For the first time since the two crews had been forced into sharing the space of one ship, they felt a common concern strong enough to produce unquestioned co-operation among them. Those of the *Argus* marine division set about checking all available weaponry and ammunition supplies on board, while the men with the most sailing experience clambered up the riggings, furling enough canvas ahead of the winds to drive their ship onward. An extra lookout was ordered; now there was a man atop both the fore and main mastheads and several posted to the railings around the *Mary Jane's* perimeter.

In spite of all of these extra reassurances, Tess could not quell the building storm of anxiety that prickled inside of her. She had been avoiding Edward whenever she could since their family background chat, and it did not bother her to leave him wondering why. Now, however, he cornered her and she felt new dread as he began to speak to her. Much to her surprise, he did not refer to their most recent conversation.

"You must remove your rings and store them safely out of sight. Come to my room and I will show you a hiding place for them."

A ploy to get me back into his room! And even if it isn't, why should I remove the rings now after boldly wearing them for all this time?

"Here," Tess replied. "Take yours back if that's what you want. I shall keep mine."

"No!" Edward's tone seemed more insistent that it needed to be. "They must stay together. Let me store them within the secret compartment in my cabin."

"Why?"

"To keep them safe. To ensure that they remain yours."

"But everyone on board has seen me wearing them. No one could steal them from me now, or they would suffer the Captain's wrath."

Edward's dark eyes bore into Tess's and his jaw clenched as though holding back a furious retort.

"You are feeling perfectly comfortable wearing them then?" he asked cautiously.

"Of course!" Tess lied. The itch had intensified to a slow burning sensation over the past day and in fact she felt no sense of comfort at all. The building uneasiness she felt inside, was fueled in part, she was sure, by Edward's annoying presence.

Edward scanned her face as though trying to read her thoughts. Tess hoped that she was able to look impassive. Neither spoke for a long moment, and then the dangerous darkness of Edward's eyes lifted, and the firm line of his mouth curved upward into a gentle smile.

"Well, perhaps at least, I could show you the compartment?"

A small bank of drawers, their faces built flush with the cabin's wall, were situated at the foot of Edward's cot. Their surfaces were ornately decorated in geometric patterns, fashioned from many inlays of different woods, stained and lacquered to a glossy finish. The pulls on each drawer had each been carved into a small five pointed star.

"See here, Tess," Edward explained as he pulled the second drawer open. "It looks like an ordinary drawer. But things are seldom what they appear on the surface. Watch."

Holding onto two of the tiny star's points, Edward gave a sharp pull and the points lifted slightly away from the remaining three. Edward twisted the raised portion one half turn to the left. There was a soft click and then, to Tess's amazement, the entire drawer front slid off the boxed frame. Turning the drawer front over in his hand, Edward slid the back open, revealing a small hollow space concealed within.

Tess could not be sure but she thought she saw a momentary sparkle emitted from within the secret space.

I shouldn't be surprised that Edward would have even more valuables with him.

It made sense that he would hide such items. She wondered if all of the drawer faces contained such hidden spots.

"They would be safe in here," Edward simply stated.

A last effort to convince me to part with them. Well, the emeralds are his. But how would I ever get mine back from him?

"Here. Take yours back but you'll not have mine," she asserted, as she twisted and pulled on the emerald spinner. The ring did not budge. Edward noticed her effort and spoke.

"I doubt that you can remove only one. Now that they have been reunited, they will not be so easily parted."

"You may lose them by force, and lose not only the rings, if the vessel that shadows us proves to be hostile," he continued with a slight shrug of his shoulders.

Was he was speaking truthfully to her? After a long pause Tess reluctantly held out her hand towards him. *At least if I removed them both,* she hoped, *the damned itch and burning would stop.*

"Help me with their removal then," she said, deeply sighing in resignation.

Chapter Sixty-One

Smith and William found themselves on the mid watch together. Just after midnight the ship had entered into a fog bank and by now even the overhead carpet of stars was obliterated. The ocean was relatively calm and the *Mary Jane* rocked her way gently onward through the inky blackness.

"Eerie, ain't it?" Smith remarked. "Not bein' able to see any further than her bowsprit, I mean."

William squinted into darkness but could see nothing, could not even make out the usual rows of white foam on the cresting waves alongside.

"Yeah," he remarked to his friend, "it does feel funny–kinda' like being suddenly blind."

"Well," Smith reassured him, "it'll be dawn soon. The sun'll burn this off. You'll see."

Being devoid of one of his senses while on lookout duty left William feeling nervous however, and he strained to listen to the sounds of the ocean around them. His ears picked up the usual creaks and familiar groans of the ship's wooden structure, and the soft rustle of the canvases strung up high overhead–he had come to think of such noises as the ship's pulse and breathing–and then he thought he heard a faint new rhythm. As quickly as it had pricked his senses it was gone ....

William cocked his head and leaned over the railing trying in vain to see past the impenetrable wall of fog that enveloped them. "Did you hear anything?" he asked Smith in a low voice.

Smith too, leaned over the railing and listened. He shook his head and looked questioningly at William.

There it is again! A rhythmical splash, not unlike the ocean's melody, a soft regular swish as their ship sliced through its surface, but this sound lagged ever so slightly, as though it were a half a beat behind their own.

And then it hit him. At first it was just an uncertain whiff. A faint tendril of pernicious stench, full of human decay, rot, and unwashed flesh. His nostrils flared involuntarily and he swallowed back his stomach's attempt to empty.

William's heart began to pound so hard in his chest that it felt as though it was knocking the air right out of him. He whirled on Smith. "Sound the alarm!" he hissed.

"What? What's wrong?" Smith asked bewilderedly.

William's eyes were wide with panic. "Do you not smell that?"

Smith inhaled deeply then exhaled. "Smell what? I smell nothin'." He frowned, his deepening unease etching worry lines in his face. "C'mon Taylor, this isn't funny. You'll spook us all!"

William inhaled again. "Holy friggin' Christ!" he whispered, paralyzed. "They're here! There's a friggin' ship *right behind us*! I *smell* them."

N
W —◇— E
S

Captain Crowell stood beside William and peered into the moist gray curtain which still wrapped itself around their ship. He turned and stared into William's face. He himself smelled nothing, heard nothing out of the ordinary, but he had recognized the intense look of fear in another man's face many times in his life and at this moment, it was staring back at him.

"Mr. Smith! As smartly as you can!" the captain suddenly demanded. "Pass my commands thusly with speed to all, Mr. Smith: Stir yourselves, down to the last man. All hands on deck, clear for action. Show no lights. Man the larboard battery and open the ports. Make stealth in all that you do." He quickly returned his look to William. "And may we all be saved by your warning, Mr. Taylor. Although I have no proof of your claims, I'll not send luck away."

As he grasped the handle of the sword that hung from his scabbard, he added, "As for *your* orders, Mr. Taylor, I fear I have a desperate job ahead for you …."

Chapter Sixty-Two

William pounded on the Willoughby's cabin door, torn between waiting appropriately for the doctor to open it, and wanting to burst in, saving precious time, maybe even saving their lives. He did not have to make the choice as Dr. Willoughby wrenched the door open, snarling, "I'm coming! What in God's name is it?" He blinked uncomprehendingly at William standing there.

"We're under attack Sir! The Captain has ordered that the women be taken below and concealed."

"Under attack?" The doctor looked skeptical. "Under attack?" he repeated.

"Yessir! We're being overtaken from behind. There's little time, Sir! The women must be taken off deck immediately!"

William noted that the doctor continued to scowl, being unconvinced of any truth in William's words and gave a sudden push on the cabin's door to shut it.

William made a last frustrated attempt. Jamming his foot in the door jam, he shouted "Captain says they'll likely *die* if they stay on deck!"

"Take your dresses off!" William's face was flushed with embarrassment but his mouth was set in a grim line of determination.

"I beg your *pardon?*" Tess wondered if she had misheard.

"Dresses off! Put these on, all of you!" William tossed a smelly bundle of hastily gathered men's trousers and shirts at each of them.

"What's the meanin' of this, Mr. Taylor?" Mrs. Hanley's voice was strident with indignation.

"Begging your pardon Ma'am, but we're being closed upon by a hostile ship. There can be no good come of a vessel that sails so close to another. We'll soon be under attack and it will be safer for you if you were to be overlooked as part of the crew."

"But who would attack?" Tess's mother stepped forward. Tess was surprised to see her so steady. *Motivation. Even fear could be the right stuff.*

"Captain says the lookout yesterday couldn't be sure but he thought the sail he sighted was a frigate's, one that'd been made flush. With her top taken down like that, she'd travel faster than most could. We'd never be able to outrun them." William looked at his unwilling brood standing before him, and took a big breath before continuing.

"Captain says that flushing a vessel's a favorite thing of pirates to do. And he says another favorite thing of theirs is to torture and ra- uh, assault female captives." William nodded at the bundles lying at their feet. "Change your clothes now. Please. And hurry. It'll go better for you if we're boarded and they think you're just crew."

At that moment a high pitched wail drowned out his words and the milky sweet odor of baby poop filled the air around them.

"And what about my child?" Elizabeth glared at William challenging him for a solution.

Ma'am, you being the good doctor's wife—you must know of something to calm the child. Give him something to put him to sleep."

"We'll need to go back up on deck to change him. I'm sure you can smell the truth in that!" Mrs. Hanley snorted. William turned his gaze to Tess and Mrs. Hanley, and he was about to speak when a voice carried out of the gloom behind him.

"Captain's orders are fer all of ya' to stay down here. None of ya' goes back up on deck. Only us two." Smith pointed at William and himself.

"But what about his dirty nappy?" Mrs. Hanley pleaded. "What am I to do with that?"

Smith looked at William, whose embarrassed gaze dropped to the bucket Smith held. "Uh, well … it'd be best if you'd smear a bit of it on yerselves after you've changed outta' them dresses."

The women stood in shocked silence, their mouths agape.

"Well, it's either *his*, or that what comes from the chickens' enders what's gonna complete yer disguises." Tess and the women around her

stood as if frozen, not comprehending his intention. "See, it's desperate measures, ya' understand," he continued, as though working up to an apologetic explanation. "We have to make ya' as unattractive as possible, and fer some," he said, looking directly at Cassie, "that will be a difficult thing to do."

The baby's shrieks were growing in volume. Smith looked down at the bundle in Mrs. Hanley's arms, into the small purple face whose eyes were pinched shut but whose mouth was twisted open in a furious howl.

"Ya' have to quiet him! Ya just have to!"

He and William turned their backs on the women while they changed, all the while hastening the ladies' efforts with the procedure by issuing the threat of turning around to gather up the discarded dresses. With the women's garb almost complete, Smith nodded at the newly transformed crew members standing awkwardly before him. Holding up the shit pot and wooden spatula he quickly asked, "Now then, what's it gonna be? The wee lad's or the birds'?"

"You can't be serious!" Elizabeth gasped.

Smith simply held the bucket and spatula out towards her.

Elizabeth drew herself up as straight as her weakened state would permit and announced, "I shan't! I cannot—"

A strange tearing shriek cut off her words. It was followed almost immediately by a thunderous crack which caused the very floorboards under their feet to shake. William leapt up the stairs in the companionway far enough to see the cause.

"God help us all!" he yelled. "The main sail and mast are hit! They're down!"

"Forgive me, Miss!" Smith cried, and heaved the shitpot towards Cassie, its contents slurping over the edge and sloshing down the front of her shirt and breeches. He spun on his heel and emptied the dregs of the bucket onto Tess's shoulders before Cassie's outraged scream was finished.

"You've no choice now but to use the wee chigger's nappy!" Smith shouted at Mrs. Hanley and Elizabeth, as he scrambled up the ladder behind William. Looking back over his shoulder one last time, he screamed a warning, "Do it now!" before disappearing into the mayhem above.

Chapter Sixty-Three

The roar of the confusion which greeted their ears topside was deafening. William stared. All about him the crew's hours of tedious rehearsal were being put to the ultimate test. Men streamed about the deck, participants in a well choreographed battle dance. Voices screamed above the deafening blasts of the deadly cannons. Orders were trilled out on a shrill silver whistle, whose tones pierced through the hullabaloo of their voices.

Still present, the heavy fog was illuminated slightly by a faint pink glow that announced an imminent sunrise on the eastern horizon. William nose told him that not all the denseness of the air was fog however; there was a burning, acrid smell of ignited gunpowder in the thick clouds of smoke which belched from the mouths of their own cannons. The attack was clearly from their larboard side and although the attackers' vessel remained hidden from clear view, her position in the semi-darkness was given away as flashes of yellow and orange spat from her side.

The broken mast lay on the deck, its massive end splintered and entangled in a trap of fallen and chaotic mounds of rigging. Around the edge of the ship, men worked furiously at their battle stations, plunging their wetted sponge rods down the hot smoking barrels and then reloading the cannons with another round of deadly iron balls and links of chain shot. The gun captain charged up and down the deck, running from cannon to cannon, hammer and spikes in hand, wedging his beloved cannons' barrels into a variety of positions.

"Take out the bastards' sails an' riggin' with *this* beauty!" he roared, leaving the gun's barrel aiming high. "And send them all to hell with *these* darlin's!" he screamed as he drove a wedge under each of the barrels of the next three, leveling them to sight at a height even with the attackers' estimated broadside.

"Fer those aimed high, fire on the uproll!" he screeched. "An' fer those aimed low, fire at will! Let's blow those friggin' arse-lickers into holy kingdom come, me lads!"

The concussive blasts from the cannons' firings slammed hard into the men's bodies, and the great guns hurled themselves back against their restraining tackles, their carriages rolling with the recoil. Each time, the barrels were sponged again. The heat within them that had been produced by their artillery explosions sent clouds of steam sizzling upward, as the wet cloths wadded around the sponge rods made contact with their inner surfaces. William spun around, disoriented and not knowing how to help, not knowing where to start.

Powder monkeys, the smallest and youngest crew members, frantically raced up to the cannons from the ammunition room below, the gunpowder magazine being situated in the hold two decks beneath the guns. Tommy, and three other young boys not much older than him, delivered round after round of deadly armfuls of gunpowder cartridges which were wrapped in dampened coats and pieces of wet canvas to keep them from exploding prematurely. Two of these young sailors charged past William, then suddenly fell to the deck in a blast of flesh and blood as an incoming cannonball made a direct hit upon them. Instinctively, William dove to his knees and reached out for the boy nearest him.

"They're already dead to us!" the gunner bellowed. "Leave them and get yer ass up an' hand their cartridges over to the guns!" William scrambled to find the dropped ammunition, frantically searching along the deck which was now slippery with blood, vomit, and entrails.

Where is Smith?

"Load and stay steady, just the same now, boys!" the gun captain screamed, his voice straining to be heard above the fracas. "There's a wind a stirrin', but she'll do us no good—we've no sail left to hold her with. There's no choice but to outfight them bastardly scugs! Ready ... an' fire!"

Just then the gunner froze.

Out of the dark and mist came the other vessel, her bow rising menacingly, appearing above the *Mary Jane's* side like an evil specter about to swallow them

"Her bow's loaded with chase guns! She's showing no broadside fer us to hit!" he wailed.

William stared, unable to tear his eyes away as the ship advanced upon them, the cannons mounted on her bow continuing to fire high, shredding the *Mary Jane's* sails and riggings. Several cracks, sharp as gunfire and loud as the cannon fire itself split the air. Men aboard the *Mary Jane* screamed as they were crushed or impaled by the falling yard arms and debris crashing down from another broken mast. All around him, men and boys fell and shrieked in living agony, fell and died in silent relief.

At the last moment, when it seemed the *Mary Jane* was about to be fatally rammed, the enemy vessel slipped sideways in the mounting early morning wind and aligned herself parallel to the *Mary Jane*. William could see their attacker's name clearly now, painted on her side.

The Bloodhorn.

A black flag, emblazoned in the middle with a ruby-red powder horn that appeared to be dripping blood, flew from the top arm of the main mast.

As the two ships sailed so closely side by side, the cannons from both vessels were now being loaded with canister and grape shot. William could see that this type of ammunition was particularly destructive at such close range. When fired from the cannons, the bags of grape shot exploded with dozens of small iron balls, spraying the decks and everyone on them with cones of deadly tiny missiles. The canisters had been packed with broken bits of glass and shards of metal, with this content becoming equally destructive to human flesh and bone when discharged from the cannons.

Muffled as his hearing was from the roar of the great guns, the screams of the wounded still pierced William's ears. The bodies of those who had been killed outright, and any whose injuries were deemed on the spot to be mortal, were tossed overboard. Those who could be salvaged were dragged or staggered on their own, down to the deck below, to the waiting services of Dr. Willoughby.

An agonized scream in front of him broke through William's stupor and Tommy's small body flew back, smashing against his own. Two large splinters of wood pierced both the boy's right temple and cheek, having narrowly missed his eye socket. What remained of his ear hung in shreds from the side of his face. He lay ominously still, and whether he had died or had merely fainted with the shock of his wounds, William could not tell. He could not bring himself to throw the boy overboard and so scooping up the small broken and bleeding body, he staggered towards the ladder and open hatch of the deck below.

A deafening blast knocked him to the deck just short of the hatch. A searing pain ripped through his chest wall. Twisting sharply to avoid crushing Tommy with his own body weight as he fell, William slammed heavily onto his back. Lying on the deck, he sucked desperately for a breath. This effort was cut short by a fresh slash of pain and the best he could do was to suck in a shallow smoke-filled gasp.

Chrissakes! I've knocked the wind out of myself! Slightly dazed, he continued to assess that perhaps he had even broken his ribs, as he simply could not inhale.

Down to the Doctor! I've got to get Tommy down the hatch!

He struggled to rise up, clutching the still form to his chest. Dizzy with the exertion and feeling like Tommy's weight had inexplicably become too heavy to lift, William strained to support himself, rolling over onto his knees.

A scream involuntarily tore from his throat as he moved his left leg, emptying his lungs of what precious breath he had taken in. A blinding stab of white-hot pain burst through his leg. William stared at his lower limb, squinting in the darkness, through the smoke and floating ash. At the spot where his knee had been just moments before, there was now a dark tangle of flesh and cartilage.

My leg! I've lost my leg! He squinted and was relieved to see his limb was torn and bleeding, but its length was intact. *But I'll lose my friggin' life if I don't reach the Doc! Got to get moving!*

Gritting his teeth together against the pain, he sucked a small gasp in, and then hauled himself inch by inch towards the hatch, dragging Tommy's limp form along with him. Reaching the open hatch but unable to maneuver himself down the ladder, he pushed Tommy's body over the sill and then propelled himself head first to follow, landing with a sickening crash at the ladder's base on the deck below.

A wall of odor, a collection of human misery, hit him full on. Unlike the open deck, where the wind renewed the air around them, here, in the confines of the lower deck, the mixture of spilled body fluids, kerosene from the lamps, and pre-existing rot and mold was unlike anything William had ever experienced. Dr. Willoughby and three helpers gave his arrival no more than a glance, as they remained bent over several of the wounded, alternately trying to staunch bleeding and then flushing out wounds with any available liquids they could lay hands on.

"I have a boy here!" William cried, pushing himself up onto his hands.

"Tend to him yourself!" Dr. Willoughby snapped. "And then help me with this one. I cannot save this limb!"

William looked about for a place to drag Tommy to. Every square inch of the floorboards seemed to be full of wounded men.

"Over here. Lay him here!" one of the assistants shouted. William's face jerked up in surprise. It was Tess. She was hardly recognizable in the sailor's shirt and breeches, the front of which, besides being stained with the slosh of the shit pot, was now soaked with the blood of her wounded charges. He squinted only for a moment at the others who were helping the doctor and recognized them to be Mrs. Hanley and Cassie, their sailor's garb likewise stained.

"I'm sorry—I know that you're busy but I think—well, I'll be needing some help with moving him ...." William didn't realize that his voice was by now only a whisper. His shortness of breath was making it hard to stay focused; the screaming pain in his lower leg made his own ambulation impossible. He felt hands grab him under his arms as someone hauled him to one side of the room. Tommy's slim form slid along side of him, the boy's shirt clutched firmly in William's fist.

Lying beside Tommy, whose diminutive form was still unmoving in the corner of the crowded space, William took stock of the situation. Oblivious to his own smashed limb, he looked about for a piece of cloth, a rag, anything which he could use to press against Tommy's bleeding skull. Fighting off a new round of dizziness, he debated whether to remove the jagged wooden missiles himself. The boy's wound was bleeding heavily already and William had seen many wounds bleed a man to death when such projectiles had been removed.

At least, he reassured himself, *his blood is still flowing and that means he's still alive!* Finding no cloth available within reach, he struggled to tear pieces off his own shirt. "Here goes, my little man," he said softly, and grabbed the deeply imbedded wooden shards in Tommy's flesh, hardly noticing the small bleeding hole in his own bare chest wall.

A faint ringing in his ears threatened to drown out the sounds of the wounded men's suffering and a grey curtain began to cloud his sight. As he fought for another shallow breath, William's world of such despair disappeared, and he slipped into a heavier darkness, his fingers still curled around the piece of fractured wood.

Chapter Sixty-Four

To Captain Crowell, the scene on deck was one of absolute carnage and destruction but the fight's outcome was far from being decided.

"Prepare to be boarded!" he roared his command, and the marines readied their guns and swords. The invaders swung across the chasm between the two ships on long lines secured to their own ship's yard arms, their landings skidding them directly into slaughter where, often as not, they were met with the deep thrust of a sword or were mowed down in a volley of musket balls. Nevertheless, the pirates appeared to outnumber those aboard the *Mary Jane*.

And we had the advantage of surprise in our readiness for attack! We might have suffered complete annihilation, had it not been for the warning given to us by Mr. Taylor.

All around him, men screamed and cursed, fighting hand to hand. Swords parried and were thrust over and over into the relatively soft targets of human bellies; still others hacked desperately at limbs, sometimes severing, sometimes only tearing open fierce gashes. Sailors from both ships fought and fell, their bodies trampled by those still standing.

It was common lore that pirates rarely fought so fiercely, depending instead on an early surrender by their intended victims. Such surrender would normally be brought on by the sheer terror invoked by the pirates' reputations and appearances.

I doubt that they expected to be challenged by naval troops aboard a merchant ship such as this! Captain Crowell slashed at the wall of intruders storming towards him.

At that moment, his eyes came to rest on a horrific struggle happening to his left. A young marine—the captain could not place the fellow's name at that instant—was being held, his arms pinned to his sides by one man, while being fatally run through from the front by another's cutlass. The captain stared, his shock turning quickly to acute despair, not wanting to believe what he was seeing. The young man's death was no different than that of dozens of others occurring all around him but for one detail.

The marine's two assailants were crew members of the *Mary Jane*.

Chapter Sixty-Five

Looking around, Captain Crowell realized with a sinking heart that a mutiny had begun.

Without the manpower of the *Mary Jane's* crew fighting alongside the *Argus's* marines and sailors, his few remaining men stood barely a chance. With the men of the *Mary Jane* actively siding with the pirates, all would be lost. Neither victory nor escape was now possible. Further fighting would be folly; the pitiful concept of fighting to the last man would bring no badges of courage; there would be no survivors left alive to tell the tale of a courageous fight to the end. He was certain that his own life would not be spared either way. Looking desperately about him, he realized with absolute certainty what had to happen now.

Captain Crowell gave one last order. Strike the white bunting.

As the white flag climbed up the remaining mast, gun blasts and cannon fire alike ceased. A few moments of near silence ensued, punctuated only by the continued screams and moans of the wounded and dying, before a resounding cheer from the victors was heard.

Captain Crowell stood tall, showing no hint of cowardice as he held out his sword, laying it flat in his hands before him, as he waited for the conquering captain to identify himself. He dimly wondered if it would be Captain Raleigh.

It was not.

A large pirate, his long black hair braided in several thin strands decorated with beads and reaching to the waistband of his topcoat, stepped forward and bowed with an exaggerated curtsey. In one hand he brandished a long bloodstained cutlass, and in the other he held a severed head by a handful of it hair. Grimly, Captain Crowell realized that Captain Raleigh, or part of him, had, in fact, come to attend the merchant ship's surrender.

"Buenos Dias! May I introduce myself?" the pirate captain began, his speech thickened with a Spanish accent. "It is my pleasure to share my acquaintance with you. I am Carlos Crisanto, present leader of these fine men." He motioned with his cutlass towards the gathering circle of pirates and *Mary Jane* crew members. "And you are Captain–?"

"Captain Crowell, of the *HMS Argus*, British Naval escort to the merchant ship upon whose deck you now stand, the *Mary Jane*." He looked at the man standing before him, trying to judge how best to plead leniency for his surviving men. He continued in a voice that was clear and steady. "It is with sadness but immediacy and total surrender that I defer and offer control of this vessel to you."

A broad smile broke out across the pirate's face–the naval-trained captain had judged him well–and then Carlos suddenly extended his head back and let out a feral howl into the sky. Captain Crowell's brow creased in surprise for a split second before he resumed his impassioned look. *The man is insane!* He forced himself to meet the pirate's eyes as the howl died away in Carlos's throat.

Carlos Crisanto was grinning again. "Round up the prisoners! I want them all brought before me. Pronto!"

It was apparent that not all of the *Mary Jane's* crew had been involved in the treasonous partnership. A few of her crew were pushed forward and shoved to their knees before the pirate leader. One of these Captain Crowell recognized as being the man who had come into possession of William Taylor's flute. As the fellow had since proven himself capable of playing it and there seemed to have been no animosity between him and its former owner, the captain had not inquired as to the details of the transfer of ownership; he had assumed it had been a consensual exchange. No matter now. A name to a face at this point was useless.

All in all, there were just a half dozen *Mary Jane* crew members who were brought forward as prisoners. The rest of the captives were from the *Argus's* original roster. There was Seaman Smith–perhaps his newly acquired navigational skills would confer some worth on his life–and the mute and disfigured Taylor whose size and strength alone would be valued by the pirates ....

So few of us left! Captain Crowell was dismayed. He wondered how many were alive but too badly wounded to have been brought before the pirate leader. *And what of the passengers? The Willoughby's and their daughters and housekeeper … and what has become of the royal courtier, Edward Graham?* As though conjured up by his merely thinking of them, a ruckus in the companionway announced their arrival on deck, each of them roughly spurred up the ladder by the prodding tip of a pirate's cutlass.

Captain Crowell tried not to stare at the disheveled appearance of the strange captives as they emerged from the lower deck. Had it not been for his own order to dress the women in sailor's clothing, he would not have guessed their sex. Blinking and frowning with uncertainty in the brightening light of the early morning, the three of them stood by Dr. Willoughby, their faces dirty and blood-streaked. Their tunics and breeches had darkened to a deep wet crimson. Blood dripped slowly from the ragged hems of their garments, the droplets landing with loud, rhythmical splats upon the deck.

Three of them! Where is the doctor's wife? And his child?

"Found these tendin' to the wounded, on the deck below, Captain," a pirate announced as he stepped forward from behind them. A stained scarf covered this man's head and large golden hoops swung from his earlobes. He wore a bandoleer, stretched across his bare chest, its makeshift pockets laden with small satchels of shot and short daggers. His breeches were torn in several places and held loosely around his waist by a strand of fraying rope. A tattoo of indiscernible design splashed across his shoulders and rose up one side of his neck, ending just under his chin.

As Captain Crowell scanned the pirate crew he thought that the man's garb could have been a standard issue for the crew of *The Bloodhorn*. All of them seemed to be dressed in a bizarre fashion—most wore head scarves or feathered hats, and several had adorned themselves with bright poufs of cloth wrapped around their torsos and hips. All were heavily armed; knives, canisters of musket shot, and pistols were either attached to a chest band or tucked into the waist band of their trousers.

"Well," Carlos smiled his maniacal grin again, "let's have a look at them. Take their clothes off, starting with these ones. The sight of so much blood on them disgusts me." At this, the pirates doubled over with gales of laughter, and whether it was in gleeful anticipation of stripping their prisoners naked, or in true appreciation of their captain's attempt of a humorous understatement, Captain Crowell was not sure.

Dear God in heaven! He silently prayed, *Spare the women this humiliation! Please!*

"Carlos!"

A voice rang out, cutting through the laughter.

"Hold off!" Carlos held up one hand and peered into their group, trying to place the source of the voice. "Who calls my name?"

"We found one more in this cabin. This one's high and mighty, too! Real educated like!"

In the cabin? It has to be Elizabeth Willoughby! Captain Crowell closed his eyes for a moment and thought, *she must have disobeyed the order I gave the family to disguise and conceal themselves, and made her way back to her room. The woman had practically hibernated in the room for the entire voyage and now—*

His thoughts were interrupted by Carlos's voice. The giddy tone in his voice had suddenly been replaced by an impatient snarl.

"Well? Don't keep me waiting! I have a body count to get on with after all!"

Captain Crowell held his breath, awaited Elizabeth's entrance, and began to pray again for merciful and quick deaths for the survivors, although he knew that it was much more likely that prolonged and horrific torture awaited them all. He shuddered, anticipating the endless ravages about to be endured. Death's release for them from the hands of the pirates would be welcomed.

"Get the hell out there or our captain'll skin ya' alive!" the unseen pirates yelled at their newest prisoner. Emerging from the cabin's shadows, Edward James stepped forward and strode directly towards Carlos Crisanto.

Captain Crowell exhaled softly, finally aware that he had been holding his breath. *Not Mrs. Willoughby! Edward Graham. The man has courage, I'll grant him that . . . .*

Chapter Sixty-Six

"Carlos, you old swabby sea dog!"

Instant recognition spread over Carlos's face. "Eduardo!" he exclaimed, grinning from ear to ear.

"May I be the first to congratulate you on a job well done?" Edward glanced around while greeting the pirate with a welcoming hug and hearty back slap. "Even if it was bit messier than I was led to believe your technique would be!"

The prisoners and pirate crew alike stood gaping at the two men. The depth of Edward's treachery was beyond comprehension for Tess. She stared at him, a pyre of burning hatred towards him igniting and building inside her, as she listened to their conversation.

"Is she everything you thought she'd be?" Edward was asking.

"That I cannot say, Eduardo, until her cargo proves to be all that you have promised me," Carlos responded, clapping Edward on the back.

"I trust that you will be more than satisfied. I personally itemized and witnessed the packing as well as the loading of it all in London, and you, my friend, and all of your crew," he added, looking around at the fierce men surrounding them, "you will all soon be very rich men!" Looking directly at Carlos, he continued, "You *do* have a certain item for me?"

Carlos's eyebrows knitted together and he shook his head, causing the beads and shells in his braids to clack against one another.

"I do not understand that you would want something so badly that you are willing to exchange all of this for only one thing, but ... yes, I do have it." He reached deep into the side pocket of his trousers and withdrew a small leather pouch, handing it to Edward.

"To you, Eduardo, from Evangelina," Carlos solemnly offered.

Edward's eyes gleamed as he fumbled with the knotted drawstring at the mouth of the pouch. When he managed to untie it, he carefully withdrew its contents. It was a small brass box, no bigger than the brass bird that Tess had first retrieved the emerald spinner from. The entire box had been dipped in wax and a seal imprint had been applied to each of its six tiny sides. Clutching the small box to his chest with both hands, Edward sank to his knees.

"Evangelina!" he shouted up to the sky. "For this, I will forever love you!"

Tess watched, stunned beyond belief. Impossibly, in that single gesture, Edward's disloyal behavior had sunk to an even lower level and his treachery had just risen to a new height.

Her surprise and outrage was no less than that of her father's, however.

"You bloody scheming bastard! You barbarian!" Dr. Willoughby roared. His face was purpled with fury and he hurled himself towards Edward who was still kneeling on the deck. A half dozen pairs of hands shot out, clutching him, bringing his lunge to a complete stop in midair. As though crazed by this sudden confinement, he continued to scream, "You traitor! Taking sides with the likes of this–this murdering, son of a whore!"

Tess's disbelief at Edward's behavior had now shifted to her father's. She had never heard him utter a single profanity in front of her before. In spite of their present danger, she felt a small spark of joy. She had never seen her father react so passionately to anything.

Her attention returned to the fierce pirate captain and Edward, and she watched as Edward's eyes narrowed. His voice was cold and deliberate. "Are you addressing *me*, Sir? A fellow gentleman?"

"You are *not* a gentleman!" Dr. Willoughby roared. "You are worse than a common rogue! You are scum! How dare you disgrace the honor of–"

Tess could not believe her ears. *He's outraged! He's defending my honor! My honor! He's–*

"– your King and country!" the doctor spat out.

King and country? Tess was stunned. *Whose honor? Not mine ....* A slow, suffocating sadness filled her chest and Tess felt utterly spent. As she blinked back her gathering tears, she dared to glance at her grandmother's face. Her grandmother was staring straight ahead, her jaw clenched tightly shut.

Carlos drew his saber and stepped forward, its point piercing the skin on Dr. Willoughby's chest. The doctor's eyes bulged in outrage as much as in fear, and a thin trickle of blood spilled down the front of his shirt.

"I will not let your slurs towards *me* go unanswered, Sir," Carlos growled ominously. "Do you have anything to say which might redeem yourself?"

"Carlos," Edward interjected and placed a restraining hand on his friend's arm, "this man is not a man of war, and in fact, saved my life in London–"

Carlos turned to look at Edward but did not lower his blade. "He has spoken vile accusations, and his insults reach beyond my forgiveness, yet you tell me that you owe your life to this man?"

"I do," Edward conceded.

Carlos slowly returned his gaze to the doctor.

"What am I to do then?" He stared at the doctor and a small smile began to spread across his mouth, his murderous demeanor melting away before their very eyes.

The man is truly demented! Tess shuddered at the change in the pirate leader. *It's as though he's possessed by more than one personality!* She stood rooted to the spot, terrified that the slightest movement would set him off again.

It was obvious to her that she was not alone in her fear. Not one sailor so much as shuffled his feet. They all seemed mesmerized by the drama unfolding before them. Carlos's eyes began to sparkle with a maniacal gleam again.

"Yes!" he shouted gleefully. "This situation provides me with the opportunity to show you just how much of a gentleman I am!" He sheathed his saber with great flourish.

"I shall spare your life!" he announced cheerfully, his grin fully blossomed.

"You see? Your mouth might have cost you your life, but I am not the–what was it you accused me of being?–oh yes, a murdering, son of a whore, wasn't it?" The smile dropped from his lips. He closed his eyes for a moment and when they opened, they glittered with a dangerous fury. He drew in a deep breath, and then slowly exhaled.

"Call me what you will, but my mother made her living the only way she could." Nodding to the burly man holding one of the doctor's arm, Carlos directed, "He may live but he'll utter no further insults. Take his tongue!"

Chapter Sixty-Seven

Thrown to the deck, his arms and legs pinned down by the pirates, Dr. Willoughby writhed helplessly and a guttural screech exploded from his mouth as they pried it open. Tess's scream was lost in the melee as the flash of a dagger's blade appeared over her father's face. Above it all, a shrieking wail pierced through the roar of adult voices.

"Hold on!" Carlos commanded. His brow was gathered in confusion. "What *is* that offensive squeal?" The intended tongue mutilation came to a temporary halt as all eyes locked onto a disheveled looking pirate who pushed his way through the crowd with his outstretched arms offering a squirming, squalling package.

"It's a milksop, Sir! Found him in with the chickens. But it's not a normal lookin' sucklin'. Have a gander at this!"

Carlos peered into the blankets without touching the bundle. His nose wrinkled up in disgust and his look of confusion was quickly replaced by one of suspicion.

"A suckling? Where is the mother?" he roared. "There is *a woman* on board! Show yourself!" His head swiveled from side to side, his eyes sweeping over those who stood before him. "I swear I will strip and whip each of you until I find her!" With a sudden bellow, he grabbed the baby, holding him upside down by one scrawny leg. Swiftly he slashed the child's thigh with a small hand dirk, turning the babe's cry into a shriek of pain. Tess cried out, her own wail going unheard as just then, with a murderous howl, her mother broke through the wall of bodies and launched herself in a ferocious attack on Carlos. She was wearing her dress, having changed back into it once again, and her hair flowed loose and long behind her. Maternal instinct exploded.

Tearing dementedly at Carlos's face and eyes with her bare hands, Elizabeth Willoughby slashed at him with unbridled fury. Caught off

218

guard, he attempted to protect himself with his free hand, while he continued to hold the dangling baby with the other.

The baby's screaming had intensified momentarily with the burn of the knife wound, but his screams suddenly lapsed into a choking gasp that always heralded his seizures. His small body stiffened and spasmed, his distended head bobbing violently at the end of his fragile neck. The seizures swept over the baby's body in fierce waves, magnified in their strength by the increased pressure on his brain in the inverted position.

And then, just as suddenly as they had started, the paroxysms stopped. Elizabeth abruptly ended her attack on Carlos and directed her attention towards her child. The infant dangled from Carlos's hand, his tiny body hanging ominously still. Elizabeth tore her son from Carlos's grasp and cradled the baby to her chest, collapsing down onto the deck.

A grievous keening escaped from her lips as she stared into her son's sightless eyes, his tiny pouty lips already turning a dusky blue in early death.

"You've blinded me, you bitch!" Carlos clutched at his face, his hands suddenly free. Reaching down, he yanked Elizabeth roughly to her feet and threw her against the deck railing. A momentary flurry of activity broke out as Captain Crowell and a few others from the *Argus* crew lunged towards the woman in a useless gesture of assistance, their attempts to help her cut short by the restraining strength of the pirates around them.

"Is it dead?" Carlos sneered, clutching the side of his face that bled freely where his eye socket and cheek hung open in dripping strips of torn flesh. "Extending your misery and pain is going to provide me with such great pleasure!" he laughed viciously, "and I *always* get what I want!"

"When I am finished with you," he continued his threat, "you will be begging me to let you join your abomination of a son in death!" He slowly advanced upon Elizabeth with deliberate steps. Struggling to her feet, she clutched the tiny corpse to her chest, backing up firmly against the railing, until retreat was no longer possible.

"It is *you* who are the abomination!" Elizabeth spat the words out loudly and clearly. "And I will take from you, all possibility of such a pleasure."

Carlos hesitated a moment, surprised by the strength and conviction in her words.

"You will have no choice in what happens to you!" he snarled.

"You are … so very wrong," Elizabeth taunted, and smiling as confidently as Tess had ever seen her mother smile, Elizabeth catapulted herself soundlessly backwards over the railing into the waiting ocean depths below.

Chapter Sixty-Eight

"No-o-o-o!"

It was as close to the sound of a man's soul breaking as any could imagine.

Although Dr. Willoughby had remained firmly pinned to the deck, he had managed to twist his face towards his wife's last words and had seen her feet disappear from his view. Enraged with the strength of one who has nothing left to live for, he tore himself from the grasps of those holding him down and launched himself at Carlos, his hands throttling the pirate's neck.

Carlos's eyes bulged, at first with surprise and then with ensuing strangulation, as the doctor's deadly grip crushed inward on his windpipe, its rings of cartilage beneath his fingers yielding and snapping under the force of such pressure. Things had happened so fast that for a heartbeat or two, no one moved, no one comprehended what was happening.

Suddenly Dr. Willoughby gave a soft grunt and released his grip on Carlos's neck. Both men collapsed simultaneously to their knees, Carlos grasping his mutilated face and crushed windpipe, and Dr. Willoughby clutching his abdomen. A large dagger hilt protruded between his hands.

Looking down at the weapon, his mouth opened and closed though no words came out, as the shock of his injury sank in. Lifting his eyes up to scan the faces of those gathered around him, Dr. Willoughby locked his gaze for a few moments on the horrified faces of Mrs. Hanley, then Cassie, and finally on Tess.

His face crumbled in grief and his eyes filled with unspoken emotion, full of longing for words that had never been said, and of regret, too late, for the ones that had. He slowly returned his gaze to Mrs. Hanley's face which was now streaked with tears, their pathways having washed small ruts down her cheeks through the blood and soot and odorous muck that caked her skin.

"Take care of my girls, won't you?" he pleaded out loud to her, his voice cracking with emotion, and then grasping the dagger's bloody handle, he gave a fierce tug and watched as the blood pumped from his body, his life's force splashing onto the deck at his knees, watched until his eyes became sightless and he collapsed down into the already gelling pool of his own blood.

"*Girls?*" The word had not escaped Carlos's notice. "What *girls?*" he wheezed, his voice already strident with the swelling of his bruised vocal cords.

"*Father!*" Cassie and Tess screamed out in unison, and heedless of their disguises, threw themselves upon his lifeless body.

"Eduardo!" Carlos beckoned while casting a glance about with his remaining eye. "You have *more* women on board? Just how many surprises do you have for me?"

Rushing forward, Edward grabbed Tess by her arm and hauled her to her feet. "What in the hell are you doing in this filthy garb?" he demanded, his face screwing up in disgust. Spinning around, he addressed Carlos. "This is Tess Willoughby. My fiancée. And," he hesitated for a moment as he peered at the other sailor lying prostrate across the doctor's body, "I believe this is her house servant. This one is called Cassie."

"She's my *sister!*" Tess spat the words out at both him and Carlos.

"Attractive as she is, it's obvious that you don't share one drop of blood with her!" Edward retorted. "And *bloodlines* are the only thing that matter."

"Bloodlines!" Tess's loathing for Edward surfaced, numbing her grief. You think *bloodlines* are important? Then you should know that your brother–"

Tess's words were choked off as Edward quickly smothered her mouth with his hand, snarling at her. "I will not tolerate insubordination from you or any other. Do I make myself clear?" She saw the familiar blackness fill his eyes, and she froze under his grip.

"That one is merely a servant," Edward reiterated to Carlos, "and there should be a garrulous housekeeper somewhere ...."

"She is *careless?* This housekeeper? Why do you tell me this?" Carlos's brow furrowed in confusion.

"Garrulous! Garrulous! Not *careless*," Edward laughed brashly. "Can you not hear out of your ears? Or has your command of the English language deteriorated in all of this time? "

"I can speak as well as you!" Carlos retorted in a wheezy gasp, "and it is my eye and throat that need help, not my ears! Which one is el medico?"

"That one." Edward pointed at the doctor's body.

Alarm spread over Carlos's face as the realization sunk in.

"You see, Carlos, your hotheaded temper will be the death of you yet!" Edward chuckled and shook his head. "But don't despair, my friend, as my fiancée here has learned well from her father before his untimely passing. She herself brought me back from the brink of death."

Now it was Carlos's turn to laugh. His swollen throat made it sound more like the hiss of a serpent than a chuckle. "Another rescue from the doorway of death? How many times do you get to visit it and talk your way back before you are to be shown in?"

"Ah ha! That, perhaps, is the question we would all like to have answered for ourselves, wouldn't we?" Edward smiled. "And with such help from Evangelina," he murmured, brandishing the brass box still in his palm, "I may have all of the outcomes that I could ever want!"

Jerking roughly on Tess's arm, he scowled at her, while speaking in general to all those present, and to Carlos specifically. "So now, if we may be allowed to exit from this welcoming party, I shall ready my fiancée to return to the sick bay with the *proper tools* ... and much cleaner attire." He grasped her tightly to him and began to walk towards the companionway, before turning around once more.

"Oh yes, Carlos. One more thing. The others–" He nodded his head in the direction of the remaining captives. "Do with them what you will. My gift to you."

Chapter Sixty-Nine

Tess found herself alone with Edward in his cabin and once again she struck out offensively. "Who is Evangelina? And what was it that she sent to you, delivered by that– that *monster* up there?"

Tess's questions hung sharply in the air between them. Edward laughed and replied mockingly, "Do I detect a tone of jealousy? Could it be that my bride-to-be is already madly in love with me and objects to hearing another woman's name on my lips?"

"You flatter yourself!" Tess spat angrily. "No woman who knew you—*really knew you* and the kind of person you are—would ever have anything to do with you! She must be desperate, insane even, to have any interest in you!" she seethed.

At this accusation, Edward's eyes narrowed and his jaw clenched as he bent over to open the secret drawer in his cabin.

"Evangelina … is … my sister, if you must know," he stated nonchalantly as he manipulated the small star knob on the drawer front. "We were not just twins you see, my brother and I, but two of a surviving set of triplets. She, the girl child, shortly after being weaned, was sent back to be nurtured by my mother's people, whilst Thomas and I were raised in the London court, with the appropriate court training as befit us."

"A sister?" Tess was momentarily struck dumb by this revelation.

"Yes. And now married to Carlos," he added with an amused smile.

"*Married* to him? Is such insanity a *family* trait then?" Tess's anger had returned and her tone was scathing.

"You are brave and foolish all at once, to aggravate me so, Tess," Edward sighed, "and I warn you now that when *we* are married, I will break your high spiritedness down into proper submission, suitable for a wife. It can only go badly for you if you continue to insist on such insubordination." He turned around to face her and held out his hand. "Put these on."

Edward was giving the rings back to her. "You will need them to heal Carlos. The blue of the tourmalines will produce strong intuition–clarity to see possible outcomes, and the emeralds, as before, will ensure the success of your treatment choices."

Outraged at Edward's assumption, Tess shrieked "He killed my father!" and then her voice broke and trembled. "He killed my father ... I will not lift a finger to save him."

"You *will* do so because *I* wish it to be so," Edward whispered calmly, stepping so close to her that she could feel his heart beating as he clutched her to his chest. She stiffened at his touch and attempted to pull her face away from him as his lips brushed her earlobe. "And if I am kept happy," he continued, his voice soft and dangerous, "and if Carlos is kept alive of course, it may go better for your housekeeper and servant." Tess's own heart thudded in alarm at this spoken threat.

Edward's hand brushed her hair, tucking a loose strand behind her ear. Out of the corner of her eye, she saw a gleam of gold on blood-red, reflecting the lantern's dim glow.

A ring! He's wearing a new ring! Her thoughts were whirling inside her head, coming together almost faster than she could recognize the details within them. *Where did he get it? Is that what was in the box from—what was the wretched woman's name? Eveline? No ... Evangelina. That's it! His sister.*

And without needing to ask, Tess suddenly knew that the ring was what the sealed brass box sealed had contained. And she knew with certainty why Edward wore it, knew what the ring must be. Another spinner.

What is its power?

She glanced at the band encircling his little finger, surprised to see that it had fit. Edward continued to whisper words into her ear but Tess was no longer listening. The presence of the new spinner made her acutely aware of the high pitched hum starting in her ear, drowning out Edward's instructions or further threats. Tess did not know what he was saying nor did she care. She was only aware that she felt compelled to set her own rings into motion.

"Why have you done this to us? To me?" she pleaded. "Is this wretched ring you're wearing worth it?"

Edward glared at her. "It was my mother's."

Your mother's! Tess felt as though she had been punched. *My blood grandmother! The gypsy who bewitched your father!*

She swallowed hard and then met Edward's stare with her own. "I shall return to sick bay. There are many there needing help, and therefore I must have Cassie and my gran—my housekeeper—there with me."

"That may not be possible," Edward hesitated.

"Why not?"

"Carlos will likely have disposed of them in one way or another by now."

A bolt of red-hot anger shot through her, shattering the wall of numbness she had sought refuge behind. Rising up on her tiptoes, until Edward's eyes were level with her own, Tess leaned in against him, her lips only an inch away from his. His eyes momentarily widened with surprise at her boldness and she saw a flicker of uncertainty sweep across them.

She locked him in her gaze and spoke, slowly and deliberately projecting her words at him as though each were a poisonous dart. "If he has harmed them ... then he too will die. I will see to that even if it is to be my last act upon this earth. The fever and pus from his wound will enter his head, tunneling deeper, festering inside and I will gladly stand by and do nothing to relieve it. I can assure you that it will be a slow and *very* painful death for him."

For a moment Edward did nothing, continuing to stare back at her. Then as suddenly as a serpent's strike, he lashed out with both hands, squeezing Tess's face between his hands. With one hand, he grasped a thick handful of her hair, savagely jerking her head back, exposing her throat to him. With the backside of his other fist, he slammed his ruby ring into the centre of her forehead. Tess cried out with the slash of pain as the gemstone cracked into her forehead. She was barely aware of Edward's next words to her.

"You *will* do as I bid! *This* is the ring of persuasion! *A posse ad esse! Ave! Adsum! You will!*" he chanted in a commanding low voice, his words rising and falling in a strange rhythm. Although she struggled uselessly against his painful grip, he continued undaunted, focusing on the ring as he ground it harder into her forehead, further splitting her skin. *"Fiat! Fiat!* You *will* carry out my commands! *Factum est! You will do ... as ... I ... bid!"* he finished in a dangerous snarl, his chest heaving with the exertion of holding her prisoner to him.

"I will not!" she screamed at him, the pulse in her extended throat bounding furiously.

Edward froze, looking completely frustrated at what he was hearing. Tess felt a rush of momentary exhilaration. She was denying his bidding. Denying his ruby spinner's power of complete persuasion. He had even used some sort of ancient commands.

She felt his hold on her falter. Pushing with all of her strength, she broke free of his grip. The unleashed force of her struggles sent her flying back and she crashed into the wall behind her. Dazed, she slid down the wall and her hand brushed against her leg. She gasped; the outline of her forgotten dirk still strapped to her calf was plain to her touch. Its sheath was firmly held in place, tied to her leg just below her knee by her grandmother's gift of the red strands of silken ribbons. She fumbled at the ragged hem of the sailor's dungarees that she still wore, frantically grasping along and up the inside edge of the frayed trouser leg for her knife's familiar handle.

Recovering, Edward lunged towards her, his hands outstretched as though he meant to strangle her. The blood from his ring's laceration of her forehead had already begun to dry in a crimson rivulet down the backside of his hand. To Tess, it served as evidence of his foiled attempt to harness the ruby ring's power. Edward gave a howl of disillusioned rage, and launched himself towards her, springing like a lion coming in for its kill.

The cold blade drove deep into the bottom tip of his lung, stopping only when its hilt lodged between two ribs. Gripping it steadfastly with both hands in front of her, Tess had hardly felt the jerk on the handle, as the razor sharp blade had sliced through the layers of his chest wall: gristle, muscle, and finally soft frothy lung.

As he collapsed on top of her, Tess saw the look of rage upon his face turn to shock. He had choreographed his own impalement upon the tiny but deadly blade. Kicking and squirming to get out from under his weight, Tess pushed him off of her, panicking that he would continue his attack at any moment. Still grasping her knife, she withdrew its blade from his body. Her legs shook as she pulled herself up into standing and looked down at his crumpled form. Each intake of his breath rasped harshly in her ears.

Dear God! The implication of what she had just done washed over her. *How will I ever convince Carlos to keep Cassie and Grandmother unharmed, without Edward's obvious influence on him?* And dimly she also realized that Edward's protection of *her*, his shielding of her, from the spontaneous violence of the mad pirate captain, was also now just as surely lost.

Closing her eyes, and slowing her own stricken breathing, she searched her mind for possible solutions.

"The blue of the tourmalines will produce strong intuition— clarity to see possible outcomes…do not question, do not think—just believe!" Tess jumped as a voice rang in her ears. She stared down at Edward, her chest full of fear, her concentration broken. Edward remained unmoving, sliding into unconsciousness. Each of his raspy breaths was filling with wet gurgles.

Intuition. Prophesy. These were the supposed powers of her beautiful blue ring. *What had Edward called its gems? Tourmaline. Blue tourmaline.* Tess spun the ring, its silver band gliding smoothly and soundlessly around her finger in its golden track. Closing her eyes once more, she listened intently, trying to get past the familiar high pitched hum in her ears.

How can we be spared? What will convince these pirates?

As she filled her head with these two thoughts, a warmth and brightness splayed across her closed eyelids. Surprised, Tess opened her eyes. A beam of sunshine shone through the window of Edward's cabin wall, announcing the arrival of the day's sunlight. The narrow sunbeam splashed across the floor, across Edward, and climbed up the front of Tess, teasing her with its sudden brilliance. From the corner of her eye, she saw a radiant flush of scarlet on the floor, sparkling in the sunbeam's path.

The ruby spinner.

Feeling like a common thief, Tess suddenly bent down and removed the ring from Edward's little finger, sliding it onto her own index finger.

It was a perfect fit. The thin gold band was adorned by two sets of four vanes, shaped like those on a windmill. One set of four sat directly over top of the other, and both were centered on the band by a ruby the size of Tess's little fingernail. Eight miniature arms in total. Each vane was outlined with scarlet shards of rubies, and each set of four spun around the central gem, one set spinning to the left, the other to the right. One could not be spun without the other joining in the movement.

I might be able to use these rings as payment to Carlos in return for sparing us. She opened the cabin door, forcing herself to step over its threshold. With a final glance back at Edward's body still lying motionless on the cabin's floor behind her, she hurried out onto the main deck beyond.

Chapter Seventy

Although she had been gone only a short time with Edward, a roll call of sorts was already in progression. As was often done, captured crew men were being given the chance —the *grand offer*—to join the pirate's crew. Those refusing to 'join the company' of their own free will were sorted into a small group to one side; Captain Crowell was among them, as were several of his surviving lieutenants. Those signing on with their new crew had been grouped to the other side of the pirate captain.

These newest recruits had seen the logic in Carlos's offer. To refuse to join would result in them being thrown overboard to briefly endure a death by drowning or more gruesomely, to be torn apart by the frenzy of sharks already attracted to the boats' perimeters by the bodies of the grievously injured or battle dead. If their sea skills were deemed useful, however, those refusing would become enslaved aboard either the *Bloodhorn* or the *Mary Jane*.

It was already apparent that the pirates intended to repair the broken merchant ship and claim her as their newest prize. Mr. Lancaster, as the knowledgeable and experienced carpenter on board the *Mary Jane*, had already been deemed worthy enough to be kept alive for the time being. The carpenter had claimed that, himself having only one foot, he had effectively and necessarily been aided by a young sailor by the name of William Taylor, and who, he assured the pirates—if he could be found and still lived—had shown himself to be a worthy apprentice and would no doubt be of excellent service to them.

John Robert's immense size and strength had also impressed the pirates, and his physical attributes had secured him a probationary trial of time. With the masts being as damaged as they had been, all knew that there was much back-breaking lifting ahead of them, and a man of his build would certainly be put to good use.

In spite of there being a duplication of their positions, Carlos, with the approval of his men, announced loudly that he had decided to keep Captain Crowell alive, reasoning that if the *Bloodhorn* should become engaged in a future encounter with a British naval war ship, the blond captain could be used as an effective hostage to be ransomed off in exchange for a get-away for the *Bloodhorn* and her crew, should things go badly. It was assumed that there would eventually be another ship dispatched from England when the *Argus* and the *Mary Jane* with her precious cargo failed to show up at Port Royal as expected. Furthermore, when the *Mary Jane's* cargo of gold and silver currency, spices, ammunition, stained glass, and fine timbers was sold or traded ashore by the pirates and became recognized, the hunt for the pirates would intensify.

Yes, it was agreed, a high profile hostage could be useful.

The fate of the Mary Jane's lieutenants refusing to join the pirates' roster was given no further discussion; as Tess watched from the edge of the companionway, the men were systematically run through with a cutlass and their still writhing bodies were tossed overboard.

Her silent appearance behind them went unnoticed as the men's attention was focused on the prisoners. Tess scanned the backs of the men in front of her, desperate to find Cassie and her grandmother. It took only a second to discover them. Tess's stomach lurched; both women stood side by side, their hands tied behind their backs and their tunics ripped open to their waists. Cassie's shoulders heaved uncontrollably as she sobbed but Tess's grandmother stood absolutely still, her face betraying no emotion.

"And of those wishing to join of their own free will, only fair and just treatment, as well as a portion of the spoils gained here, awaits them, provided they live by the following." Carlos began to read the pirate's charter of rules to his newest recruits. The abrasive tone of the words from his injured throat made it hard to hear him and all listened attentively. "Above all, Brethren shall vow not to conceal any plunder, nor steal from any other aboard. If any man do so rob another, he shall be shown no quarter, but shall have his nose and ears slit from his person and shall be cast ashore to live or die as he pleases.

"Secondly, none shall strike another while on board the ship, but every quarrel–"

"Carlos!" Tess's voice rang out. The effect was immediate. All heads swiveled in her direction. The sudden silence was unnerving. The sound of her own frightened breaths seemed painfully loud to her.

Carlos stared at her, his uninjured eye resting upon her and sending a cold chill down her spine. He waited for her to speak again. Tess's mouth was dry and her tongue stuck to the roof of her mouth. Her head buzzed. It was several heartbeats before she could utter her next words.

"I have come to strike a bargain with you, on Edward's behalf. Let us be. Take your treasures but leave all of us unharmed, and in return I will let you live."

Stunned by her own words she thought, *Dear God! What am I saying? That is not the bargain I had intended to offer!* She had voiced aloud the whispered thoughts in her head.

Carlos's eyebrows arched in surprise. Then he began to chuckle, his surprise at her challenge turning to glee as a wicked smile spread lopsidedly across his face. The sound of the laughter that exited from his injured throat set the hairs on Tess's arms on end—it was a series of high pitched, screechy whistles and gasps, unlike anything Tess had heard coming from a human being's mouth. His injuries had to be painful, yet Carlos hardly seemed to be taking notice of them.

"A deal?" he squawked. "You offer my life for yours?"

"Your life, if you spare us *all*."

Carlos stepped forward, his putrid breath causing Tess to choke back her revulsion.

"And if I refuse …?"

He was calling her bluff. If she showed any fear or hesitation, Carlos would win. Speaking clearly, with a bravado that she did not feel, she asserted, "Then you will die slowly but most certainly, of your pustulant wounds. As will all of your injured crew. A fitting end for you, perhaps, but not one, I am thinking, that you will want to be remembered for." The man's arrogance suddenly seemed as blatantly apparent to her as his rotting breath.

Carlos seemed to consider this for a moment and then inquired, "So what are your terms?" His voice was light with amusement—this woman, claimed as she was by Eduardo, greatly intrigued him. Few men had ever stood up to him, and never before had a woman shown such courage in his presence.

"First, untie my sister and grandmother and let them be covered. A *gentleman* such as you should not tolerate such immodest treatment of women."

Carlos still grinned at her. "And then?"

"And then they will be allowed to help me in the sick bay, to tend to the injured, yourself included, to save those that we can." She felt a flicker of hope as the pirate captain continued to stare at her. She had his attention. "And allow the *Mary Jane's* crew to repair her," she continued, her words picking up speed, "and finally, when this has been done, you will agree to board your own vessel, taking only your desired items from our cargo in the hold, and you will sail away from us."

The ruby spinner had set up a fierce itch around her index finger and Tess had been unaware up to now, that she had set all the rings into motion, nervously spinning them, so intent had she been upon her deal with Carlos. She laid the fingers of her right hand across them, stopping their movement, and rubbed furiously at the itch. At the same time, Carlos's countenance suddenly changed.

You will survive this by reason, the by-now familiar whispers in her head announced. Wishful thinking or not, Tess found the thought reassuring.

"Now here is my counter offer to you," the pirate smiled. "I will set the women free. One will help you, and one will accompany me on board the *Bloodhorn*."

"No! That's not–" Tess interjected.

"Yes it is!" Carlos countered just as quickly. "I shall take your servant back with me," and he swung his gaze towards Cassie, his intent unmistaken in his visual assessment of her half naked body, "for ... collateral." His eyes lingered on her for a moment longer before he returned his gaze to Tess.

"She's not going with you! You cannot take her!" Tess argued shrilly.

"Oh, but I can, and I will. However, as to those not wishing to formally join with us, I shall spare them for now, providing of course, that each proves to have skills worthy of the food and water it will take to keep them alive."

"And what would your wife–*Evangelina*–think of you, taking another woman onto your ship?" Tess spluttered, desperate to appeal once again to Carlos's self judgment as being a man of good conduct and manners.

"Ah, Edward wasted no time in his explanations to you, did he?" Carlos stepped back and tucked his chin in, the gesture a haughty one. "Evangelina is just that! A wife. A wonderful wife, but one who I am with no more than one return visit per year. She is not a mistress. She is *a wife*," he emphasized. "Intimacy does not factor in so much to marriage. I love her neither more nor less for that." He sighed, registering Tess's look of outrage. "You are young. It is known to all worthy women that a man has needs." His gaze hardened and he glared at Tess.

"Your servant will be transported over to the *Bloodhorn*," he said with an air of finality. "And now that our negotiations have finished, you must uphold your end of the bargain."

"Release the women!" he barked, his voice intended to be commanding, but producing only a raucous rasp. His chest was heaving with the exertion of drawing breath through his bruised vocal cords; their swelling was persistently narrowing his windpipe.

"Ferry the servant back over to my quarters, and send the large one to sick bay with this one." Turning to Tess, he threatened, "Your servant will come to no harm, as long as my vision and voice are returned to me."

Breathing hard, he grabbed her by her upper arm. He seemed to be using this grip to support himself upright as much as to steer her towards the open hatch which led down to sick bay. He stumbled, nearly pulling Tess off her feet. Recovering, he stood still for a moment, swaying slightly as he attempted to catch his breath. His next words were slurred as the lack of air began to dull his abilities.

"Where's Eduardo, hmmm? Wha' have you done with him?" he asked as he brought her hand up to his lips. Too late, Tess realized the gesture exposed her rings; their gems sparkled fiercely in the early morning sun. Carlos stared at her hand and grasped it hard, holding it close to his face. "Ah, Eduardo adorns you ver' nicely I see. It's a good thing for you, I think, that you are already spoken for by him, or ...." He shrugged and the corner of his mouth lifted in a lecherous sneer. Even as his voice gave out, his unspoken intent was plain. Tess fervently hoped Carlos had loyalty enough to the Brethren's code that her rings would be safe from theft by any aboard. *He did declare 'no stealing', and he thinks I'm Edward's possession ....*

A horrible realization swept over Tess, that her unintentional protector lay quietly bleeding to death in the cabin across from where they stood. Without him, without his influence, these human predators would show her no mercy. Of that, she was certain. And in that moment, her triage of the wounded suddenly rearranged in order of importance. Not to save their lives, but to save her own.

Chapter Seventy-One

William wasn't sure which of his senses brought him back to the brink of consciousness first—the fecal smell of hot bowels and blood, the dissonance of the cries of the still-conscious wounded, the burning thirst in his throat, or the firm and warm pressure of someone's hands over his lower rib cage.

His eyelids were sticky and dry, and they fluttered as he attempted to open them. He blinked to clear his vision and a familiar face swam into view, hovering over him, with sweet lips moving in an almost inaudible murmur.

Tess!

A spreading, pleasant warmth was moving through him, emanating from her hands which she had placed front to back on his lower chest wall. William struggled to remember what had happened. The brutal recollection of the battle and of his attempted rescue of Tommy came back in broken bits of detail. He lifted his head and attempted to locate the young boy. He recalled having dragged the unconscious youngster alongside him, wedging the small boy's body between the ship's wall and his own, intending to shield him from being trod upon by those moving about in such a packed space. William turned to look at the wall.

The spot beside him was empty.

Feeling both confusion and panic rising in him, he attempted to sit up. Another pair of hands at his shoulders held him firmly in place.

"There, there now, Mr. Taylor. Lay there, still as a mouse fer a wee bit longer, won'cha?" Mrs. Hanley's voice was less soothing than he supposed she meant for it to sound, as the extra volume to be heard over the background noises gave her words a harsh edge. "The wee lad's alright, don'cha know? He's been sittin' back in the corner waitin' fer ya' to wake.

Fell asleep himself, waitin' fer ya', and it's best he be left awhile. Now hold yerself still so's Tess can finish her work on ya'."

Having tended to William's chest wound, Tess offered a weak smile to him and moved on to the next moaning form. Mrs. Hanley placed a moist poultice over his torn chest wall, and a wispy sweet scent of the crushed leaves of Agrimony drifted over William's face. She bent close to him as she dressed his wound with strips of linen and whispered, "I was savin' this and the Comfrey in case of the rat-bite fever but it seems that ya' might not have lived on long enough to be needin' it fer that." She shrugged and then continued, "I hated to think that it would be there in my trunk, all tucked in nice an' cozy with the cinnamon an' dried spices, with me maybe gone yonder to meet me husband an' daughter, an' it endin' up bein' used an' wasted on the likes of these scum!" She scowled and her thick brows knitted together as she chatted aloud.

"I don't know what's come over my Tess," she said shaking her head, "that she saw fit to tend to the wounds of that scoundrel, Mr. Edward, an' that—that *ogre* what calls himself captain now. Not with decent men like yerself needin' the help. Lord knows, there's no shortage of ya' in here." She moved down to his knee and sponged the wound there reasonably clear of blood, then picked out remnants of the imbedded grapeshot.

"What's become of my Da' and Captain Crowell and Smith and—?"

"Easy now, they're all up on the main deck—none of them worse fer wear neither. Your Da's a mighty man, talk or no talk, an' even pirates understand how valuable a man like that can be. Already he's been forced into helpin' make repairs to the railings an' decks an' such. Mr. Lancaster, bein' the fine carpenter that he is, was spared as well, once they found out his abilities at boat buildin', an' yer friend, Mr. Smith, well, I'm sorry to be the one to have to tell you, but …." She breathed in and out deeply before continuing. "But, he was one of the first to sign on as a new recruit fer these damned pirates."

William took in this news in astonished silence. He had known his friend to be one who judged things in life with a calm acceptance, but Smith had shown himself to be a loyal ally on many occasions. To even consider that he would so easily change sides was unthinkable.

"I need some fresh air," he announced, intending to find out Smith's whereabouts for himself.

"You'd be safer stayin' put," Mrs. Hanley admonished, and then looking around her at the grim collection of the wounded men, most in various stages of dying, she reconsidered. "But maybe some air up top would do us all some good." She handed William a long piece of wood to use as a makeshift crutch. "Best ya' try them stairs while the laudanum an' lard in them poultices is still workin' good."

Gritting his teeth against the residual pain, William struggled to his feet and hopped towards the ladder's base. Slowly, one rung at a time, he hauled himself up and out of the sickbay hellhole and slithered out of the hatch onto the deck above. Although the *Mary Jane* prisoners were already hard at work scrubbing with holy stones and rinsing the wooden planking with buckets of sea water, the deck was still slippery with the bodily wreckage spilled during the battle. William blinked in the sunlight and searched for familiar faces. The pirates seemed to be lounging in supervisory capacities while the captured sailors were doing the cleaning up and starting to repair the battle's damage to the *Mary Jane*.

Smith was nowhere to be seen. Mrs. Hanley had been telling the truth, then.

William leaned on his crutch, confused as to what to do. He was breathing hard from his exertion in exiting the deck below, and his chest ached, as did his knee. He would not be able to kneel with the others, cleaning the scum and plugging holes in the floorboards.

"Can ya' sit?" a familiar voice asked him quietly from behind. "Course ya' can. Just plunk yer arse down on this crate an' use yer knife to carve somethin' out of this broken piece of mast here."

William swung his head around in the direction of Mr. Lancaster's voice. "What—what should I carve?" he asked bewildered.

Mr. Lancaster shrugged. "Somethin' that sorta' looks like a yard arm, I be thinkin'. Anythin' to make them freebootin' vermin think yer doin' somethin' worthwhile."

Chapter Seventy-Two

As the morning sun climbed overhead, so too, did the air temperature rise. Tess overheard snippets of conversations between the seasoned sailors, complaints that the ships were caught in the doldrums alley.

"Tis a common thing of it, fer the winds of these West Indies to abandon both good ships an' bad, fer hours an' even days. We're stranded, an' at the mercy of the ocean's pull."

Hearing this, Tess groaned. Today of all days, there would be no refreshing wind to carry the battle stench away from any of the ships' decks.

The air in sick bay was thick with the heavy odor of ripe flesh wounds and body fluids already undergoing early rot. She had set all three of the rings to spinning, and had felt an immediate warmth flush through her hand. The strange but mild heat sensation had continued to crawl up her arm and across her torso into her other arm and hand.

As she had done with Edward's first injury, she closed her eyes and palpated the areas around the wounds, visualizing them as being healed, while repeating such whispered commands as *Stop bleeding! Pain be gone. Restore and heal.* After a few minutes of such attention, she and Mrs. Hanley set about to washing, stitching and dressing the wounds. Those requiring amputations were moved apart, to the far side of the room, the bleeding from their crushed and torn limbs controlled for the moment, with tourniquets fashioned from dirty strips of cloth and frayed lengths of hemp.

By the time she had tended to the dozens of injuries, the sun had passed its zenith and Tess was dizzy with exhaustion. An angry growl from her stomach reminded her that she had not eaten since supper the night before, and slim pickings that meal had been. Distantly she wondered if anyone had thought to prepare any food at all. Wondered if any of the pirates could even cook. It wouldn't have surprised her to have learned that they ate and drank nearly nothing else besides salted pork and copious amounts of grog, except when they came across food supplies on any captured ships under their control. Unfortunately, *this* ship's inhabitants had already been at near starvation rations, due to the doubling up of people and the loss of the *Argus's* stores. Their own food supplies were scant.

Ignoring her body's demand for sustenance, she wearily climbed back up to the main deck and squinted in the searing brightness of the clear day. With some trepidation, she entered Edward's cabin.

Here is where she had elected to have Edward stay for treatment, and at Carlos's own insistence, she had treated the pirate captain in here as well. There was no doubt that these two men would not have been pleased to have been placed among the other wounded crew. Tess glanced around the room, her eyes slowly adjusting to the relative dimness of the cabin's interior.

Carlos had appeared only slight surprised upon his discovery of Edward's frame lying face down on the cabin's floor, and had looked even more perplexed after crew members had lifted Edward onto the bunk, to see that the front of Edward's shirt and trousers were soggy and dark with blood.

However, Tess supposed, living life as Carlos and all other pirates did, conferred a sort of immunity to any shock at encountering severe injuries or episodes of a violent nature. Sickness and death were constant companions. Seeing only a simple shrug of his shoulders, Tess felt a wash of hope. She had been spared having to give any immediate explanation, as Carlos's curiosity about Edward's plight had apparently already taken second place to his concern regarding his own injuries and his impatience to have them tended to.

Carlos was no longer in the cabin. Tess presumed he had left to resume his control over the two ships. Only Edward remained, lying completely still on his bunk. Tess had mixed emotions as she watched his chest rise and fall with a steady, even rhythm.

Her smoldering anger burst to the surface first, stripping her thoughts of all civility. *Looks like the bastard won't be dying after all!*

And then calmer logic settled over her like a cool cloth. *I'm safe from the others while he lives … but what will he say, when he wakes up? How much will he tell of how he became wounded? Perhaps it would be better if he remained unconscious.* Tess formulated a plan in her head—she had access to medical tinctures and powders to accomplish just that.

Seeing that Edward was much as she had left him before going to tend to the others in sick bay, Tess stumbled back out into the blinding brilliance of the afternoon sun, frantically scanning the deck for Cassie. She was nowhere to be seen.

All around Tess men worked at clearing and repairing the battle's damage to the ship. Although the pirate's respect for human life was almost negligible, in comparison, the value they placed on material goods was almost unbelievable to Tess. All scraps of wood, cloth and iron were salvaged and sorted into piles according to size.

Standing a head above the rest of the men, John Robert had been assigned to handle and sort the largest and heavier pieces. Sweat glistened on his torso but such glands upon his head and neck had long ago been damaged in the *Argus* fire. Still, the giant of a man toiled as ably as any of the others. The captive men's ongoing participation was being reinforced by the liberal use of a cat-o-nine-tails by yet another pirate who applied his weapon indiscriminately to the prisoners' backs and shoulders.

A frightened bleat pierced the air and John Robert froze in mid stance, clutching a large piece of broken mast to his chest. The voice of a *Bloodhorn* crew member cackled with glee.

"Looky here, mates! A wee kid—she'll make as tender a' stew as you buggers could hope fer!" and he held Gerta in the air suspended by her two front legs, her body dangling and her hind limbs furiously kicking in mid air. "Someone give me a hanger to skin her with, quick, afore she kicks the shit outta' me!" he laughed as he lowered his arms to waist level, allowing her back legs to touch the deck.

The attack happened with lightening speed.

The jagged piece of mast tore through the air as straight and true as if it had been a giant arrow released from a powerful bow. The barbed tip buried itself deep into the intended target of Gerta's tormentor, impaling him through his midsection and narrowly missing the kid's head. Suddenly free, Gerta charged towards the only safety she knew, skidding into John Robert's shins before standing perfectly still at his feet, as though sensing that the grave danger for her was not yet over.

Picking Gerta up and tucking her securely under one arm, John Robert advanced on the dying pirate. Gently setting the small goat down, he squatted beside the body. Gathering the man up in his arms, in one fluid motion, John Robert stood up, heaved the body over the side rail, and bent back down tenderly scooping Gerta up in his arms.

The whip wielding buffer lurched toward John Robert, fury blazing in his eyes.

"Ya' stupid, deformed godfersaken sonofabitch!" he cursed. "While Carlos is on the *Bloodhorn*, I'm bloody well in charge here! An' if ya' ever, *ever* wastes so much as another *sliver* of salvage wood again, I'll whip the very skin off yer back an' then I'll send ya' overboard to retrieve it! Do ya' understand that, ya' big dumb shit?" He wound the strands of his whip up in his hands and shook it menacingly at John Robert.

To the pirate's shock, John Robert's hand shot out, enclosing the buffer's own fist. There was a sickening crunch of bone and the man shrieked with blinding pain, as his knuckles fractured under the pressure of John Robert's viselike grip. Pulling him closer, John Robert stared intently into the pirate's eyes, as though passing an unspoken warning of his own back to the man.

"Ya ...," John Robert nodded toward Gerta. "Yo-o-o unnerstan?" he slurred.

"The damned goat is yers! I get it!" the man gasped in pain, sinking to his knees.

"Ya!" John Robert exclaimed, his lopsided grin sealing the agreement, as he released his grip. Turning around, his eyes opened wide in surprise.

"Wee-um!" and his grin broadened as he sighted his son. Only a few paces away, William had propped himself upright on the crutch with one hand, his knife poised to throw with the other.

"Ooh-ah!" John Robert exhaled softly, holding out a fist which he opened and closed with each syllable.

Smiling in spite of the tension in the men around him, William repeated the gesture, uttering the same strange word. "Ooh-ah!"

Throughout this struggle, Tess had watched, standing frozen to the spot as the scene had played out before them all. Momentarily distracted from her quest to find Cassie, she watched in amazement as William and his father appeared to communicate in an eccentric mixture of sounds and subtle hand gestures.

The open-close movement of their fists. It looks like ... a miniature hug ... yes! That's it! The unspoken gesture was in fact, she could see, loaded with meaning for the father and son.

The details of the brutal deaths of her own parents suddenly crashed into her thoughts and, caught off guard, Tess could no longer ignore the fierce pain in her chest as the belated terror of it all ripped through her. Deep grief locked tightly away until now broke free, as caustic to her innards as fire on raw skin. Struggling to control her gasping cries and feeling as though she might suffocate in doing so, Tess heard a strangled sob burst from her throat and she collapsed onto her knees, not having the strength to stand any longer. No longer caring about anything, she curled into a protective ball, sobbing uncontrollably, as the men nearest to her looked on in surprise.

She was barely aware of being lifted and carried back to her parents' former cabin where she grieved until the tears would flow no more. Utterly exhausted, she sank into a deep dreamless sleep.

Chapter Seventy-Three

It was ever so faint but the delicious aroma of garlic and onions drifted past her nose and Tess reflexively inhaled. Sorely roused, her empty guts growled and sloshed about in protest. Slowly she surfaced from the security of sleep

My parents' cabin.

She had returned to the waking nightmare of the ship. She tried to sink back into blissful unconsciousness but gnawing hunger tugged at her, insisting that she waken and be present.

"Tess?" A voice hissed from somewhere in the semidarkness.

At once Tess's heart hammered in her chest, putting her on full alert. She blinked hard, focusing on the voice, and fought to clear the grogginess from her sleep-filled mind. She groped frantically along her leg, searching for the familiar dirk handle. It was there, lying warm and smooth along her calf. She withdrew it from its sheath and held her breath as a shadow appeared across the doorway.

Someone had let themselves into the cabin.

He stood halfway in the doorway and whispered her name again.

"Tess?"

Tess peered at the silhouette and tightened her grip on the knife. Her palm was clammy and the handle felt slippery in her grasp. Frightened as she was, there was something familiar about the voice.

"–William?" she inquired. Neither of them had given much thought to the familiarity they had both fallen into, their mere acquaintance status having been accelerated by the force of the tension of their situation.

"Begging your pardon, but Mrs. Hanley sent me to fetch you to the galley. She needs some help."

Wearily Tess pushed herself up from the narrow cot and stood, nearly toppling over as she did so. In a flash William dropped his crutch and wedged his good leg against the wooden frame of the cot. His arms shot out and steadied her as her bruised knees creaked in protest of bearing her weight.

William's arms were strong, offering solid support; his touch and his nearness were more than comforting. Her stomach tightened as butterfly flutters flickered their way through her. She leaned into him, pressing against his chest as though thrown by the ship's roll, and his arms reflexively tightened around her. She could feel his heart thudding softly from within the depths of his chest. His breath was husky and warm against her ear and as he exhaled against her skin, she felt a smoldering heat climb up her neck and sweep across her cheeks. For a long moment neither of them moved, preferring to pretend to the other that their stance together was purely accidental.

As they climbed down to the middle deck, the mouth watering smells grew stronger and Tess realized that they were coming from the two large iron pots hung over the galley's fire. Her grandmother bustled around the heavy wooden table, alternating her efforts between rolling out dough and stirring the contents of the pots. She tucked a greasy strand of hair that fell into her eyes, behind one ear and stared at Tess.

"Why, you've not even changed outta' that filthy sailor's garb!" She clucked her tongue in disapproval. "Clean yerself up a bit an' then give me a hand here!" Tess grabbed an apron hanging on a protruding nail in the wall beside her.

"What are you doing?" she asked, watching her grandmother incredulously. The woman seemed to have no end of stamina.

"Makin' myself *needed*." She looked pointedly at Tess and continued. "That devil captain made it quite clear that only those he found useful would be spared. You've showed them you're a healer, and I'm provin' that I can cook. An' there's no point to be savin' all these wonderful spices an' such fer our new life that's never goin' to happen, is there? So sprinkle a little cinnamon on the dough there." Turning to William she ordered, "an' some sugar, if any's left, from stores if you please, Mr. Taylor. An' if any gives you grief, tell them it's fer their own supper. Yer leg's well enough to get you there and back?" William nodded and caught Tess's eye. His gaze held her as securely as his arms had moments ago. He gave her a wan smile before reluctantly hobbling back towards the open companionway.

"What's in the pots?" Tess asked, her mouth watering.

"That one's a hearty meat soup fer the devil captain an' his own crew. Nothin' will impress them more than full bellies."

"What's in it? Where did you find ingredients? It smells wonderful!"

"Don't it just? There's nothin' that some dried onions and garlic can't make turn tasty."

"But ... I thought there was only salted fish left in the galley stores," Tess persisted.

"True enough. That's what's in the next pot. Fer us." Her grandmother continued stirring the pots with a wooden ladle in each, not looking at Tess as she did so.

"You're giving the meat soup to *the pirates* and we get left-over rancid fish?" Tess asked in disbelief.

"Just make the cinnamon buns an' be leavin' the soups to me," Mrs. Hanley countered firmly and she poked at the fire's embers, coaxing a little more heat out of the flames.

"I don't understand! Where did you find meat—real meat—and then why would you prepare it for those *vultures!*" Tess kneaded the dough roughly and continued to gripe to herself loudly enough that she did not pay heed to the faint smile that crept across her grandmother's face, nor did she hear her grandmother's soft explanation.

"Well, you see, child, even a snake'll often eat its own ... an' it seemed a shame to throw away all them lost limbs ...."

As violent as they were, members of pirate society operated by offering democratic votes on nearly every decision concerning the crew. Later that night, amid much praise and admiration for such tasty fare, Mrs. Hanley and Tess were voted to be the permanent cooks aboard the *Mary Jane* by a vote count of forty-seven to one.

The only dissenting voice came from the *Bloodhorn's* cook—a filthy looking man with grimy hands and blackened fingernails nearly as dirty as his bare feet—who insisted on two details: that Mrs. Hanley's remaining precious spices be divided in half between the two ships, so that he would have access to some for the fare he prepared aboard the *Bloodhorn*, and that Mrs. Hanley be ferried over to the *Bloodhorn* every second weekend to allow him an evening off from his own cooking duties, and whatever meal that was to be prepared on that night, was to be served to him as well.

Chapter Seventy-Four

Life aboard the *Mary Jane* now was fraught with an increasing amount of tension and fatigue. Tess continued to tend to the wounded, her success rate earning her begrudged admiration from some and fearful respect from others.

"She's uncanny, she is," a skeletal looking pirate stated, unaware that Tess stood just mere feet away from his post at the helm. It had taken no skill at all for Tess to have judged such a skinny man's innards to be infested with worms and to have treated him with a strong tonic of Boneset that was both emetic and purgative.

"Maybe so, but it ain't right to have any woman on board. Especially a witchy one. That's just sheer foolishness, letting the Devil's handmaid bunk along with us," his shipmate retorted.

"Ha, you've a split tongue today, Cabe. I seen ya' sittin' there, meek as a blind pup, lettin' her sew ya' up. An' ya' didn't look too upset to be having her hands upon ya' then!"

"Still, this ship'll be cursed and damned with her on it. You just wait an' see if it ain't."

"Is that a wash of yellow I see in yer eyes?"

"Oh, say you so now, you chunk of worm's meat! I warrant you yerself don't have the balls to rid us of her."

"Aye, you've pegged that right, for any bucko who was of such a mind would suffer, her being under the protection of Captain's brother-in law, never mind the Devil's as well!"

Tess shifted her weight and stepped away, intending to return to the companionway. The creak in the floorboards underfoot drew the pirates' attention.

"Hell-fire! She appears out of nowhere! Upon my life, she's an imp of Satan, that one!" The fear in the man's voice was palpable. Tess was not quite out of ear shot when she heard, "She'll have us scuttled and sunk, mark me!"

For the time being, Tess did not mind having such a reputation. Such fears seemed to confer a temporary protection for her from what would otherwise have surely been brutal treatment from them.

She had also been successful so far in keeping Edward from rising from his sick bed. During the times that he was awake, she fed him a thin gruel laced with enough laudanum to ensure he would slide back into uneasy dreams. Often he called out, but his words were slurred and incomprehensible. It was only when he attempted to hold his mug on his own for the first time, and spilled its contents that Tess took further notice of his overall condition.

Looking closely she noted that one half of his face seemed to have sagged. She had just assumed that his mouth had turned down in a scowl at her presence but now upon closer inspection she observed that his eyelid was also heavy, giving him the appearance of one who was half asleep.

You are safe for now, the strange voice in her head interrupted.

Could it be? Excitement built with the thought flitting in her head. Attempting to draw him into a brief conversation confirmed her discovery.

It was a common belated occurrence with many whose injuries left them bedridden. Edward had been robbed of strength of movement on one side of his body, and more importantly, robbed of his power of speech.

The story of their scuffle could not, would not, be told. She breathed a sigh of relief. It was one less thing to plague her. She would no longer have to keep such a rigorous schedule for Edward's laudanum ministration. As soon as that thought vanished, it was replaced by a familiar jolt of panic.

Can't speak. Can't move. All very well for now but what if he dies? What will happen to me—to all of us then? Once again Tess felt her safety slipping away. Anxiety gripped her chest. She needed to talk to her grandmother.

It was also time to tell Edward's other story—the one of which even he was unaware of its significance—to her grandmother. Upon hearing it, would her grandmother reach the same conclusion that Tess had? For what reasons had these strange circumstances brought her and Edward together, not only as a couple betrothed, but as uncle and niece? Tess thought her grandmother would be sure to have an opinion on that. Later that afternoon, Tess joined her grandmother, standing in the blistering heat of the fire which crackled before them in the galley's hearth.

Unlike her normally cheery self, Mrs. Hanley listened somberly to the details, and then sat silently brooding over their significance.

"It had to be him. There could not be two of the same with that mark you carry," she finally said, "but why?" She sat without speaking for another long time before continuing. "There's always somethin' what comes from somethin' …."

Tess could tell the woman was lost in her thoughts, distant but still painful memories of everything and everyone who had been taken from her so many years ago. She gently laid her hand on her grandmother's arm. "Are you alright?"

"'Course I am," her grandmother replied. Tess couldn't help but notice the new similarity to Mr. Lancaster's speech pattern. "I was just thinkin' about all the changes what happened to us an' wonderin' why? Why was my little one attacked, I'm wonderin', and then it comes to me—it was so's I could have you. An' why did we end up on this journey, mixed up with the likes of Edward Graham? An' that, too, brings us the answer—it's so's he could fill ya' in on yer family tree, an' give ya' details on yer destiny with them rings … who else would have known such stuff?" Her grandmother nodded her head as if in complete agreement with herself. "Always somethin' comes from somethin' …" she repeated.

"So do I tell Edward about this or not?" Tess had been pondering this for awhile.

Her grandmother's eyebrows pulled together in quick thought. "I think not. An engagement with the man can always be undone. A family blood tie cannot."

Chapter Seventy-Five

At the end of the first week, under heavy supervision, William and Mr. Lancaster were rowed over to the *Bloodhorn* to assess her damage from the battle and to oversee any needed repairs. Besides being on the lookout for Cassie, William wondered about the plight of Captain Crowell and of Tommy, both of whom had been forcibly removed to the *Bloodhorn*.

Arriving on the pirate ship for the first visit of several that they would make, William was distressed to see a sailor squatted on the open deck, chained by one ankle to the main mast and dressed only in tattered remains of his former *Mary Jane* uniform. William recognized him as the officer to whom he had given his flute. The man seemed not to recognize William. In fact he seemed to have lost all sense of reality, as he clutched the well worn flute to his bare chest and rocked himself back and forth. His shoulders bore the evidence of numerous burns and vicious whippings. Some of the ravaging gashes were new–still open, bleeding and weeping–and some had barely scabbed over. His frame was already painfully thin and his eyes had a hollow starved look about them.

"Ha ha! You like our music monkey?" Carlos's voice rang out. Already his vocal cords seemed to be healing. His voice was strong again. "He tried to escape– only once, mind you–and had to be taught a lesson." He lashed out at the man's shoulder with a short quirt. Fresh slashes split the taut skin across the tortured man's shoulders, and he cried out in agony. Carlos snorted in disgust at the man's show of pain. "If we had had another decent musician, we might not have needed to keep this one alive." William shuddered at the thought that had he not given up his flute, it might have been *him* chained to the mast, enduring the daily floggings from this demented captain.

"Play!" Carlos roared at the chained sailor. "Play for our guests!"

The flute's notes were as sweet and clear as William remembered they could be, but the sailor's melody was a haunting one. It was entirely fitting, William realized with a bolt of recognition.

A simple English funeral largo.

Because of the need for so many supplies to be brought back on board from shore, Carlos decreed that two jolly boats were to be made over, one to be in working shape for each of the mother ships. It was obvious that this would require that the two remaining, more heavily damaged boats be dismantled and their lumber be reused in the repairs.

William's knee injury had left him with a pronounced limp as the joint did not yet fully bend. Squatting down in the more crowded spaces inside decks was not an easy task; even Carlos had seen the practicality of assigning the jolly boat repairs on the open deck to William, while Mr. Lancaster would be responsible for all remaining main ship repairs.

Returning from their first visit to the *Bloodhorn*, Mr. Lancaster murmured to William, "Them boats is the only way off the main ships. If a man could gradually store up a few essentials in, say … a secret compartment what was built into the jolly's wall …"

William frowned. "I don't think I understand. What–"

"'Course ya' do," the old carpenter continued softly, looking straight ahead. "The opportunity's there–nearly's landed in yer nest, hasn't it? 'Course it has! But ya' got to be brave and tricky enough to make such a situation work fer ya' …."

Nest? Captain Crowell's cryptic proverb came back to William.

The wily carpenter was on to something! The chance was there. But was William willing to act upon it? That night as he lay sleepless in his hammock, his tormented mind alternated between composing a list of things that he would need to survive if they ever made it to a shore, and presenting the unbidden picture of an agonized, tortured soul–the result of a failed escape–chained to a mast, dying a little bit at a time, while playing out the miserable remainder of his abbreviated future.

Chapter Seventy-Six

If life as a passenger on a merchant ship had been unfamiliar and boringly repetitive, life as a prisoner on a pirate ship for Tess was continually unnerving and full of dreadful apprehension. Skirmishes with other vessels took place on a regular basis and it fell to her to continue to mend the crews after such assaults.

Carlos and his two crews overtook, pilfered, and on occasion, destroyed any smaller vessels within their sights. Having no destination to call home, the *Bloodhorn* spent all of her time cruising the warm shallow waters of the islands, pursuing merchant ships laden with riches—coins, sugar, coffee, tobacco, rot-resistant cedar wood—that had been intended to be sent back to European ports.

Such ships and their crews were generally easy prey, unfortunate enough to be using the same waterways, but usually intelligent enough to give up all of their cargo without much of a struggle, in exchange for their lives being spared. Resistance from their quarry was rare. The pirates' fierce appearances and reputation for barbaric and merciless treatment of those who gave resistance continued to be all that was needed to subdue the overtaken vessels.

There came the day, however, that a lucky merchant ship outran the *Bloodhorn*. The *Bloodhorn's* outer skin had become roughened and thickened in places with barnacles, and slimy in others with the weedy growth of the tropical waters, increasing the drag, making her slow and difficult to steer. It was time to careen her.

The ships were sailed into the privacy of a cay of a small island, and for the first time since the pirates' attack on them, those crew members and prisoners of the *Mary Jane* who had resided aboard the *Bloodhorn*, were rowed over to the merchant ship.

"That's likely so none can escape on land," Tess's grandmother had observed. "He's a careful scumbag, that Captain. Wily as they come, but still a scumbag."

Tess awaited the arrival of the *Bloodhorn's* jolly boat with a mixture of excitement and fear. She had grilled William for details about Cassie on each of his returns from the *Bloodhorn*, but he had not seen Cassie on the open deck even once. His only news had been that Captain Crowell was a chained prisoner and Tommy had been forced to become a cabin boy to Captain Carlos. Tess played nervously with her rings and tried to focus on the broken bits of images which flickered through her thoughts.

Cassie is alive.

Tess felt certain of that, but an uncomfortable wariness flooded her thoughts of her sister. Was Cassie sick or injured? What had these months of Carlos's treatment done to her? Tess's unease grew.

And why should things be right? she chided herself. William's description of the horrid treatment of the flute player had continued to haunt her.

More ominously, Cassie had been Carlos's captive for nearly three months.

Tess shielded her eyes against the glare of the sun and squinted in the direction of the oncoming yawl. Captain Crowell's fair hair was easy enough to distinguish. There had been no encounter with another navy warship in which his usefulness as a captive to ransom would be proven, yet still the pirates had kept him alive. Tess skimmed past the faces of the others in the small boat and gasped.

There. At the stern of the jolly boat. Cassie's black hair hung loosely down, like a thick cape over her shoulders and back. She sat upright, her spine stiff, and her mouth was set in a determined flat line.

"Cassie!" Tess cried, as Cassie was helped over the railing onto the *Mary Jane's* deck. She hugged her sister firmly to her, and felt Cassie's arms automatically encircle her. Cassie made no sound but clung fiercely to Tess and buried her face in Tess's neck and hair. Silent shudders rocked her frame and Tess felt her neck become wet with Cassie's tears. "Oh God, Cass, I have worried about you!" Tess pulled back from Cassie and tried to see her face but Cassie clung to her even more determinedly.

"Are you alright?" Tess whispered into her sister's ear. "How have you been treated?"

Even as the words left her mouth, Tess's hands slid down to her sister's shoulders and froze over top of a softly thickened weal on Cassie's right shoulder. Tess pulled her hand away and stared.

"Oh my God, Cass," she whispered hoarsely. "What had he done to you?"

Under the inquiring touch of Tess's fingertips, an angry raised mound of fresh and tender scar tissue stood out. Clearly it was a miniature form of the powder horn depicted on the pirates' flag.

"He—he *branded* you?" Tess gasped.

A brand. Carlos's brand.

Burned deeply into the soft flesh of Cassie's shoulder, it marked Cassie forever as his own.

Tess swallowed hard as sudden waves of nausea threatened to expel a rush of bitter bile. Anger deeper than any she had ever known cascaded over her in a hot rush.

"*That bastard!*" she seethed. Looking into Cassie's tear filled eyes, and seeing the intense anguish there, she clasped her sister hard to her chest once more. "He *will* pay for *whatever* he has done to you!"

"No-o-o," Cassie softly moaned. "He will kill you if you try anything." Her eyes pleaded with Tess. "Save yourself if you can." She laid her own hand gently over her branded tissue. Her voice was barely a whisper.

"I am doomed."

Chapter Seventy-Seven

Tess watched from the railing of the main deck of the *Mary Jane*.

"Aye, 'twill take at least a day fer each side, it will," Mr. Lancaster explained. "First they'll take her guns ashore, but before they can do that, they'll be building earth mounds fer them." To transport the heavy cannons to shore and then mount them on the hastily built mounds seemed like a lot of extra trouble to Tess.

"That's in case we're discovered and put under attack," Mr. Lancaster explained. "Can't be takin' a chance of being attacked and no guns now, can they? Course they can't." Hope brightened Tess's face.

"If another ship came along now we could be rescued!" she exclaimed.

"Be careful what ya' wish fer," the carpenter shook his head. "Any oncoming craft would see only two pirate ships, now that her flag's been replaced." He pointed up to the mast where a makeshift flag nearly identical to the *Bloodhorn's* fluttered. "Watch now," he suggested, pointing to the beached *Bloodhorn*.

The ship listed hard as the sailors winched her over onto her side. "Now they'll set to scraping barnacles off her bottom and her sides up to the water line," the carpenter continued. "An' next they'll be patchin' up any holes and gouges before they smear her whole body with a thick new layer of pitch and tallow. Helps to repel them water chiggers. The same work done to the other side, an' she'll be good as new."

Mr. Lancaster just can't help himself, Tess noted. *He's a sailor through and through and he's fascinated by ships more than anything else in the world. Even one commanded by buccaneers.* The thought of the pirates brought her attention back to their own ship. She stared at Cassie's silhouette at the bow of the *Mary Jane*.

At least, Carlos is feeding her. Unlike the chained sailor who was being starved to death. Tess had not seen that sailor among the rest of the captives who had been transported over to the *Mary Jane. Perhaps the wretched man has already died and has been mercifully released from his misery. It was lucky for William that he was not the one who ended up having to play the flute for the demented captain.* She shuddered at the thought of Cassie having to return to the *Bloodhorn.*

Two precious days, maybe three, were all that they were going to have together. Tess cherished each minute she spent with Cassie, becoming highly resentful whenever she was required to leave her sister's side to tend to the onslaught of sailors' fresh wounds, boils, and fevers.

At Tess's insistence, Cassie accompanied her to the sick bay, but she sat motionless on the medicine trunk while Tess worked, moving only to stand when Tess required an item from the chest. Cassie's former dislike of medical procedures seemed to have disintegrated into total disinterest. She sat, staring at a point in the air, occasionally glancing at Tess and peering into the chest with only minimal interest when it was opened.

In fact, during the entire careening time, Cassie remained silent and mostly unresponsive, no matter how hard Tess tried to cheer her. It was as though the weight of a heavy veil of sadness pinned her down and made even the simple act of conversation too much to bear. Only when Mrs. Hanley gathered Cassie into her arms, and rocked her gently back and forth as though she were a small child to be taken care of, humming a soft lullaby as she did so, did Cassie seem to relax, and the look of fear melted from her face. At such times, Mrs. Hanley combed her fingers gently through Cassie's tangled locks, smoothing and detangling the long wavy strands, and finally braiding them into a long thick plait secured at its end with a strip of slightly tattered red ribbon.

For Tess, the careening days passed by with the speed of an oncoming storm. All too soon, the captives were loaded back into the jolly boat and rowed back across to the newly righted *Bloodhorn.* Cassie had been among the first of the two boatloads to have been transported back. She and Tess and her grandmother had clung desperately to her one last time on the *Mary Jane's* deck, eventually requiring the strength of two sailors to wrench them apart.

"Cassie!" Mrs. Hanley's and Tess's sobs blended together, their voices each a high pitched wail, as their throats constricted with despair. Just as she had on the way over, Cassie now sat on the return trip, with her spine stiff and her face set forward. For her to have looked back would have been unbearable. Aboard the *Mary Jane*, Tess and her grandmother watched, sinking into grief-stricken silence, their souls having been emptied of tears. Neither one had words of consolation to offer to the other.

As Cassie was roughly hauled up and over the *Bloodhorn's* railing, she abruptly twisted out of the pirate's grasp and turned back towards the *Mary Jane*, suddenly raising both outstretched arms and hands towards the *Mary Jane*. Instinctively, Tess raised her own, opening and closing her fist as she had seen William and John Robert do.

Ooh- ah.

The nonsense syllables filled Tess's head and she mentally tried to project their intended message of love across the watery gap to Cassie. The fist gesture had shifted the tourmaline band and as it began its slow spin around her finger, Tess was filled with a cold sense of dread and new understanding.

Cassie's wave to them had not only been one of love. It had been a final goodbye.

Tess turned towards her grandmother, her head pounding, and grabbed the older woman's arm. "Something's horribly wrong! I feel it! With Cassie, I mean. She's in danger! I just know it! She's been gripped with a horrible melancholy and she's—"

"She's with child, I believe," Mrs. Hanley announced quietly, her voice still thick with emotion. Her eyes were swollen and red-rimmed, the outward signs of the heartbreak that she too, felt with Cassie's departure.

"*What?*" The pronouncement jolted Tess with its content but even more shocking was the sudden comprehension that it offered. Cassie's figure had not been the result of adequate nourishment but rather it was the outline of the swollen breasts and early bloating of a pregnancy!

Bolting from the spot, Tess flew down the ladder to the deck below and sprinted as quickly as the cramped space would allow, into the sick bay area. After her parents' deaths, she had had her father's medicine chest moved from under their bed to this more convenient placement. Throwing back its lid, Tess scanned through the contents.

Her father's trunk. The sturdy case contained not only the tools of his trade—scalpels, needles, scissors, syringes and catheters—but also a relatively extensive pharmacopeia. Within it lay leather bags and pouches of many common herbs as well as a supply of the more rare, potent, and even lethal plants. Back in London, the various leaves, stems, flowers and roots had been dried and ground up, flaked or powdered, to maximize their stored volume within the limited storage scenario of a long ocean voyage. The resulting collections were concentrated many times beyond their normal efficacy.

Not content with her visual inventory, Tess dropped to her knees and scrabbled through the trunk's contents.

"Oh dear God!" she cried aloud, frantically tossing the sacks and satchels aside as she began her mental inventory.

Laudanum. There had been several bags of powdered opium which, when reconstituted with alcohol, became the laudanum tincture. Its use covered everything from cough suppression to fever relief, from menstrual cramps to depression to chest pain. Tess wasn't sure if any was missing.

Thoroughwort. Also called Boneset. She had used this on the emaciated sailor to successfully rid him of his parasitical worms.

Agrimony. It was useful in wound healing, and effective in shrinking warts and some tumors of the skin, while moderately useful to staunch internal bleeding.

Bittervetch. If chewed, it would relieve the desire for food or drink, a useful thing in dire times of starvation.

Soapwort. Her father would have used this for old venereal complaints when the mercury had failed.

One by one she identified the botanies, praying that she was wrong in her review, yet continuing to search until the trunk had been completely emptied, not wanting to believe her findings and hoping that she had overlooked its missing contents.

She had not.

Dazed by her discovery, she was vaguely aware that her name was being called. Breathing deeply and attempting to control her mounting panic, she spun the tourmaline ring. She squeezed her eyes shut in an effort to block out the caller and focus inward on what her ring was trying to tell her.

"Tess-s-s!" The voice cracked but was insistent, breaking up her concentration. There were heavy uneven footsteps on the ladder now.

Tess whirled around in annoyance as the intruder's shadow blanketed over her, then stood still in shock at the sight confronting her.

There, at the bottom of the ladder, with his eyes boring into her stood Edward. Tess immediately regretted having given up on his drugged gruel. He had appeared to be so weakened that it had no longer seemed necessary. Too late, she realized that Edward was a man of great determination. He had roused himself from the cot in his cabin and had somehow managed to find her here on the lower deck.

So! His movement has come back. More importantly, she wondered how much speech, if any, had returned.

A rush of garbled syllables from Edward's mouth confirmed that his recovery had not been a full one. Her name seemed to be the only word he could enunciate clearly. It was with some degree of satisfaction that Tess realized that for now at least, Edward was locked in a lonely prison of sorts–not unlike the one John Robert had endured all these months until he and William had been able to work out their system of hand signals.

"What do you want?" she inquired.

There was another string of unintelligible sounds.

"You are making no sense at all," Tess said pointedly. Pushing past him, she added, "If you'll excuse me, I have important matters to attend to–" Edward's hand shot out and grabbed her arm. She was astonished by the strength of his grip. He brought her hand up to his face and tilted his head.

The rings! His rings!

The three rings nestled around her fingers as comfortably as though she had worn them forever. Quite often she even forgot that she was wearing them at all.

Edward had not. He tugged now at the ruby ring, even as she reflexively closed her fingers into a fist. She needn't have worried; just as they had once before, the reunited rings resisted any attempt to be removed individually. Tess could feel the strange invisible pull–the magnetic draw–that they had for one another. So too, could Edward, as he threw her hand down in apparent frustration.

"You see?" Tess hissed. "Nothing wants to be with you–not even a ring." Edward's gaze flickered, his eyes full of uncertainty. Tess was not sure if he understood everything that was being said to him, but if he did, she thought he must be wondering as she was, if without speech, the ring would ever be of any use to him personally.

She was not anxious to find out.

Chapter Seventy-Eight

Carlos found women quite disturbing.

In his experience, they were often shrill—incapable of silence in the face of danger—and of no use at all for the demands of brute strength that his world of sailing and fighting demanded. And as for their hidden inner charms, well, Carlos had often noticed that, pleasant as the destination was, an intimate coupling with a woman was more likely to be a source of disease for a man than would be a brief encounter with a cabin boy or powder monkey.

And the women always expected something in return—money, love, presents ….

However, he was greatly intrigued by his newest captive. Cassie's toffee colored skin and thick tresses were attractive, true enough, and Carlos had intended to use her a time or two for his own pleasure—her soft inviting curves would be a welcome change from the hard buttocks of his sailors—before selling her for a handsome profit to a plantation overseer.

It had been a long time since he had lain with Evangelina—just over a year, he estimated—and although his wife was always accommodating, he found his couplings with her to be barely satisfying. Nor were the slave women he had plundered from other ships—starved and filthy things by the time they reached his part of the world—any more useful to him.

The healer woman's servant was different. She was curvaceous and attractive, and had all of her teeth. She differed from the other women in another way, as Carlos had found out the first time he had tried to mount her.

This one fought.

He had stripped his tunic and breeches off and was swishing one last rinsing mouthful of wine around in his mouth when she had attacked.

Grabbing anything within her reach, she had swung at him, clubbing him ferociously about his head and shoulders. Initially caught off guard, Carlos had thrown his hands up to his face in a reflexive defense of her fury, warding off the heavy candlestick blows with his forearms. She had been, however, no match for his strength and determination, and he had quickly disarmed her, pinning her beneath him. He had marveled that she continued to struggle even so—and had been further amazed at how exciting he had found this to be. He had not thought it possible to become any further aroused until he made one more discovery.

Cassie was untouched. A virgin.

Carlos could hardly believe it. She would not be infecting him with any women's foul smelling diseases or chancers, and lying under him, still she fought and silently struggled. Carlos was delighted.

He had never enjoyed himself more.

From then on, he had kept Cassie exclusively as his own, and his *Bloodhorn* brand would mark her as such to all.

Keeping her constantly tethered to the foot of his cot, Carlos had expected Cassie to become resigned to her circumstances, but each time he had advanced on her she had met him with renewed feral resistance, attacking him like a cornered jaguar, biting him and clawing at him with her nails.

Her resistance was thrilling. It made sex freshly exhilarating and at the end of each day, he hungered intensely for his new plaything awaiting him in his cabin.

And so, the day after her return to the *Bloodhorn*, when Cassie's eyes had suddenly rolled back into her head and she had begun to convulse underneath him, it had been with much distress verging on hidden terror that he had sent for immediate help from Tess.

It had not escaped Carlos's notice that one new recruit—the navigator called Smith—had shown a barely concealed admiration for Cassie, and so, expecting that the intensity of the young sailor's interest in her would speed him along, Carlos had chosen Smith to captain a return boat over to the *Mary Jane*. His assessment had been correct, for Smith had frantically urged his three fellow mates onward, setting a wicked pace by rowing like a frenzied madman himself.

Chapter Seventy-Nine

Directly upon arriving on the *Bloodhorn*, Tess was quickly ushered into Carlos's quarters where she found Cassie on the floor, only semi-conscious and still lying on her back where Carlos had left her. His only concession to Cassie's predicament had been to pull the thin linen tunic that she wore back down over her body.

Tess noted that Cassie's fingertips were pale and waxy looking, but her fingernails were blood-stained–apparently she had fought him fiercely even during this last time. Small flecks of foamy blood-streaked saliva clung to the corners of Cassie's mouth and a pool of vomit collared her head. Tess knelt low and sniffed, her nostrils twitching with the acrid scent of bile. How she wished she had William's ability to smell! He seemed able to pick out even the faintest differences in scents. Closing her eyes, she focused on the odor.

There! A small whiff of mint. And ever so faintly, a sweetness. Her worst suspicions confirmed, and without requiring further proof, Tess set about rousing Cassie as best she could.

The odors had offered proof that Cassie had ingested dried Pennyroyal, a powerful abortificant. Its distinctive minty smell was still present both on her breath and in her spewed stomach contents. Tess was guessing that the sweet odor was Blue Cohosh, often used in combination with the first herb to induce deliveries. She had brewed the two into teas on several occasions back in London for her father, whenever a fetus had obviously died before a pregnancy had come to term, and it had been necessary to have it expelled from its poor mother's womb. Unofficially, as well, such a mixture had often been sought after by many others, wishing to terminate the evidence of illicit affairs.

Her father had been very explicit in his teachings to her. The teas could be flavored with the addition of peppermint or cinnamon to make the concoction more palatable without diluting its strength. Either herb, if taken in a concentrated oil form however, was known to be commonly fatal, inducing splitting headache and extreme nausea, before convulsions and massive hemorrhaging set in. There was no way to know for sure, the effective strength of the dried contents.

Whether it was out of nervous habit or because her belief in the rings grew stronger the more that she focused on them, Tess spun the rings and listened to the thoughts filling her head. Confidence in the accuracy of her assessment of this situation flowed through her.

Cassie had had access to neither of those flavorings and had apparently washed the dried herbs down with only a few mouthfuls of rancid wine. The frailty of a newly pregnant woman's constitution had tipped the scale in favor of Cassie's survival. Not all of the herbs had been absorbed, Tess grimly noted. She fervently hoped that little enough had been digested to be ineffective at starting a life threatening uterine bleed.

From the time that Tess had entered his cabin, Carlos had not shown any interest in her assessment of Cassie. In fact, he had not entered the cabin at all, refusing to show, in front of his crew, any further concern for his captive. Smith, however, had remained hovering in the cabin's doorway, and at Tess's beckoning, he rushed in at once, and knelt at Cassie's side. His jaw was clenched hard with tension and he searched Tess's face for answers to his unspoken questions.

"She is pregnant. With Carlos's child." Tess's words sounded harsh, even to her.

Smith's work-worn fingers balled up into tight fists of fury and he turned his face towards Tess "I couldn't protect her ..." he moaned softly before his voice faced away.

Tess stared. His own face was desperately stricken, with lines deeply drawn by a mixture of frustrated anger and grief.

It was the face of a young man about to lose someone most precious.

In a moment of startling clarity, Tess understood his motivation.

He loves her! He 'joined' the crew to be here on this ship, to be near her! His actions were so plain! How could we have not figured that out?

"Is she—is she dead, then?" he stumbled.

"No," Tess replied quickly, wanting to reassure him, to reassure herself. "She tried to rid herself of his child, and she has taken herbs to that effect, I think."

Confusion spread across his brow and a low breath escaped his lips. "She'll live?"

"I'm not sure how much she took–" Tess's words died in her throat as she stared at the thin tunic that Cassie wore. A small but bright red patch had seeped into the material at the junction of Cassie's legs.

Oh dear God!

It had started.

The antidote! While still aboard the *Mary Jane*, Tess had followed her hunch and had filled a medicine bag with anticipated needs–needle, sutures, packing–and had grabbed several pouches containing dried products known to staunch bleeding, as well as a pouch containing a small amount of clean water with which to mix them. There was no time now to properly prepare and steep the tea–she would have to rouse Cassie as best she could and spoon the cold mixture down her throat.

"Help me sit her up," she instructed Smith. As the young sailor held Cassie steady against his own chest, Tess spooned the watery mixture past Cassie's lips, firmly stroking her sister's throat to bring on reflexive swallowing. When she was satisfied that enough of the medicinal liquid had been ingested, Tess sat back and looked at Smith. The effectiveness of her antidote preparation would become apparent shortly.

"That's it. Now we wait. Tess saw that Smith nodded nearly imperceptibly at her words. He had seen Tess's treatment of the sick before and seemed to have full confidence in her regimens. Tess saw no reason to burden him now with her nagging fear.

There was one more item missing from the trunk, besides the Pennyroyal and Blue Cohosh. What has Cassie done with it? Where is the Monkshood? Hurriedly she reviewed what she knew of it.

The root of the deadly Monkshood plant was by far, the most potent to be found in any pharmacological collection. Many exotic cultures used the root's juices as a powerful and fatal arrow poison. The mere contact of abraded flesh with the juice, she had been told, could bring on death due to a paralytic action on the respiratory centre. Nevertheless, physicians cautiously used it in drastically minute quantities for its therapeutic effects of producing pain-relieving numbness and its ability to slow the pulse in those suffering heart palpitations.

Where is it, damn it! Tess scanned the room; its contents were few and rather stark. *Surely she hasn't swallowed that fatal preparation as well?*

"I am doomed" she had said ....

Tess felt Cassie's throat.

The pulse there was sluggish and faint. Not nearly as fast as she would have expected nor as strong as she would have liked.

Tess's own heart hammered in her chest. If Cassie had taken even a relatively small amount of the Monkshood, there would be no saving her. On the other hand, a slow pulse produced from any other reason would mean less bleeding ....

If only I knew for sure! Tess realized that her uncertainty would have no effect on her actions either way. She had done all that she could to counteract the effect of the Pennyroyal and Blue Cohosh, and there was no antidote at all for Monkshood.

Wait! There was *one thing more* ....

The healing emeralds would have to do the rest. And the ruby spinner—supposedly able to influence people's actions—would it be able to influence desired outcomes? Tess started the rings in motion, and laying one hand on the crown of Cassie's head and the other on her sister's abdomen, she began to focus on Cassie's face, quietly intoning her words of healing, while trying to ignore her own building feelings of despair.

Chapter Eighty

The shouts from the deck of the *Bloodhorn* blasted Tess out of her meditation at Cassie's side. The cabin's door flew open as a pirate burst through. The man was as intimidating as any of the crew but Tess detected a strip of fear in his voice as he grabbed for her, shouting, "You! Healer! Get out here now! It's Carlos!"

Caught in his grip, with no choice but to stumble out after him, Tess realized that she was trembling herself. Not knowing if the man's fear was *because of* Carlos or *for* Carlos, she panicked for several heartbeats, confused as to why she had been summoned.

What has happened?

She was unable to see past the grime encrusted backs of the unwashed men in front of her, but realized that they had gathered around something. Or someone. Lying on the deck.

Carlos?

"Make way, ya' dung-souled buggers!" Tess's escort bellowed as he pushed his way through, dragging her along behind him. The crowd of sailors parted and stepped back, giving Tess a first glimpse of a body lying crumpled on the deck. Warily she stepped forward and peered at the man lying at her feet. Tess gasped a sharp intake of breath as the shock of what she was seeing coursed through her.

Carlos lay face up, still and helpless, his body paralyzed.

Monkshood! That is the only explanation! But how could he have been exposed to it?

His respirations failing, Carlos struggled as each breath became slower and shallower. Tess could only watch as the paralytic effects of the Monkshood quickly and surely ravaged his central nervous system.

Hers eyes drifted over Carlos's torso and riveted on the dozens of fresh and deep scratches crisscrossing his chest. The memory of Cassie's blood-stained fingernails slammed back into Tess's head.

That's it! Cassie had used them as the only weapons she had available. A certainty of the events flooded Tess's thoughts. Cassie had tipped her fingernails with the powdered monkshood root, probably having reconstituted it with a few drops of wine, and the poisonous chemicals had quickly entered Carlos's system, starting their deadly work at the moment of the very first tearing of his skin with her nails.

Cassie had to have been exposed to the chemicals as well then! And yet she had shown no respiratory difficulties when Tess had been with her in the cabin.

Satisfaction washed over Tess as she realized that the horror of a death by Monkshood poisoning was that the person's thought centre remained totally unaffected by the plant's chemicals, with consciousness and intelligence remaining normal until the victim's last breath.

Tess bent forward and pretended to be examining Carlos's breath and pulse. She whispered to him, "Has revenge ever been so sweet to you as it is to me?"

Eyes of madness, glowing like embers in a fire and glittering with hatred stared back at her. Tess met the malevolent glare, and watched without fear, as evil in human form took its last breath. Carlos's chest rose slightly, fell one last time, and then rose no more. The eyes, once so full of malice, slowly glazed over and stared sightlessly out of their sockets.

"He is dead," Tess announced simply. "I need to return to my other patient."

"Why should we keep either one of you alive now?" snarled one of the pirates, lunging forward. He pointed the tip of his cutlass at Tess's breast.

Weary and once again emotionally drained from the ferocity of the change in circumstances that her life had taken, Tess drew herself up as tall as she could and, slowly spinning the rings once more, she glared unflinchingly back at the man. At once she knew what she had to say to make him believe. Holding him steadily in her gaze, her tone scathing and sounding as threateningly as she could manage, she replied, "You need me to keep *you* alive. I am the only healer here. And Cassie carries

Carlos's child. Without me, they will both die as well. It may already be too late as you have kept me far too long from her." Stepping confidently towards the cabin, she turned and played further on the superstitions of these men of the sea.

"In fact, if she and the child *do* die," she barked in a voice that carried to the ears of every man there, "the same curse that killed Carlos will fall onto the heads of the rest of you." There was a loud murmur among them but none barred her way as she hurried back into the cabin.

There, much as she had left them, were Cassie, her head now cradled in Smith's lap, and Samuel Smith, his hand tenderly stroking her cheeks. Cassie's chest moved rhythmically with shallow but even breaths.

How could she have escaped the effects of the Monkshood?

Examining Cassie's fingers more closely, Tess discovered her answer. Cassie's fingertips, waxy and pale, really *were* waxy and pale.

Clever! Tess smiled in spite of her worry.

Her sister had dipped her fingertips into molten candle wax, before applying the powdered sludge to them, in a desperate gamble. She had depended on the wax to provide her with enough of a protective barrier to the fatal preparation's effects.

It had worked.

Chapter Eighty-One

Unfortunately not even their fear of rousing the wrath of a witchy woman would bring the pirate crew to the agreement to have Cassie transferred back to the *Mary Jane*. Cassie had soon regained consciousness and the best that Tess could demand for her was that Cassie be allowed to recover for a few days in the confines of Carlos's cabin, while the crew decided what to do with her and her unborn child, following Carlos's demise.

New and more pressing business—the choice of a new captain was to be voted on by the pirates before any other decisions could be made—had bought Cassie only forty-eight hours of precious time. As such, Tess was to be allowed to be rowed over from the *Mary Jane* for only one more visit.

"We *have* to devise an escape plan!" Tess pleaded to her grandmother upon returning to the *Mary Jane*.

Her grandmother's eyebrows raised in surprise. "Escape to *where*? To the open waters? To the shorelines of these unknown lands? How can that be any better than stayin' put?"

"They will kill us all eventually. I feel it." Under the pressure of her grandmother's continued stare, she added, "My ring tells me this." She paused for a moment. "It's true we don't know what islands we're sailing past, but if we could reach one, surely we could get help. Officials in Port Royal were expecting our family." She saw her grandmother's features soften and her head nodded ever so slightly at Tess's reasoning.

"I'll have to take the details back in two days' time. It's the only chance we'll have to get a message to Cassie!" Tess continued. "Gram, what are we going *to do*?" She fell silent as her grandmother pursed her lips together in grim thought, staring off into space as she considered Tess's plea.

"There are so many of them … there'll be only one chance for escape." Her grandmother's voice trailed away as they both shuddered to think of what fate awaited them if they were to fail in their attempt. "We need to change the odds in our favor … but how and when?" Her grandmother's brows knitted together in deep thought.

A nighttime escape under the cover of darkness seemed to be their best choice. Lookouts would be less likely to see them and musket balls would be less likely to find their targets in the dark. Confronting the sailors on the evening watch would be out of the question, however. Stealth and absolute secrecy seemed to be their only option. But how to escape from a ship where there was virtually no privacy? In the warm air of these West Indies, the men frequently slept shoulder to shoulder on the open deck, preferring its hard surface to the dank air of the quarters below.

It was improbable that the women would survive in the open sea—swimming skills were questionable—so the need for items to keep them afloat was without question. They would be needing casks, barrels or a boat. That detail was paramount to the success of such an attempt. And any of these items would require the co-operation of a man—one at least—to help hoist them overboard into the sea. Mrs. Hanley shook her head as the problematic details piled up, reducing the probability of escape to nearly impossible.

"We'll probably die, if we try to leave … you know that, darlin', don'cha'?" Her grandmother's voice was soft and sad as she took Tess's face between her hands and gently tilted it to meet her gaze.

"Gram, being without Cassie, and living in fear for our lives like we do now, without even trying for freedom, is already a kind of death of its own …." Tess blinked back the hot tears that threatened to spill from her eyes. She was filled with a cold sense of hopelessness as her grandmother slowly looked around at the filth that caked everything. The stench of rot and mold was persistent everywhere.

Her grandmother slowly exhaled and as she shifted her weight, her bare heel crunched and slid on the rodent scat that seemed to be underfoot everywhere. She brushed the revolting gritty particles off the soles of her feet, then sucked in a large determined breath and suddenly smiled at Tess.

"I believe I've stumbled onto an idea," she beamed.

Chapter Eighty-Two

Two days later, Tess filled her medicine satchel with the necessary supplies and climbed down the hempen ladder into the waiting jolly boat that bobbed alongside the *Mary Jane*. The short trip between the two ships passed without incident, although Tess was stiff with tension in anticipation of seeing Cassie.

Her sister lay quietly upon the narrow cot, and a small sickly smile tugged upwards at the corners of Cassie's mouth as Tess entered the cabin.

"Cassie." The word hung heavily in the air between them and for a moment, Tess did not know if she was welcome or not. She had foiled Cassie's plans, had undone the effects of the stolen herbs, and even though Cassie's life had been spared, so too, had the unborn child's.

Carlos's child.

"Tess!" Cassie sobbed the name and held out her arms. Tess rushed into them and clasped Cassie to her. For several long moments, they clung to one another, neither knowing what to say.

"I still carry his child …." Cassie's face was tightly drawn and she searched Tess's eyes, searching for something–whether it was for confirmation of her statement or for forgiveness or even acceptance of her actions, Tess was not sure. Her eyes never left Cassie's face.

"You're still with child," she nodded, "but it's your child now. Yours alone. *Only yours*," she emphasized.

"Carlos–"

"Is dead," Tess confirmed.

Upon hearing this, Cassie's eyes filled with tears but she too nodded, and as they spilled down her cheeks, relief spread in a silent slip of a smile across her lips.

Realizing that no one had informed Cassie about the chain of events that had come to pass over the past two days, Tess read the lingering fear in Cassie's eyes, as she spoke to her about the choosing by the crew of a new pirate leader and of the pirates' insistence that this be Tess's last visit.

"But we have a plan," Tess rushed on. "I am going to see if they will let Tommy in here for a moment." She crossed quickly to the door of the cabin and summoned the nearest sailor.

"I need assistance in here," she stated. "As it concerns womanly things for *Carlos's* captive, it would be appropriate that I assisted by the young child, Tommy, rather than defile both her modesty and your *captain's* memory, by the presence of any grownup gentleman." Tess hoped respect for Carlos was still strong enough to influence the sailor. To her surprise and relief, he raised no objection, and quickly returned with a frightened looking Tommy in tow.

"Tommy, I'm glad that you were available." Tess hoped her tone was reassuring to the boy as well as to the sailor. "I need your help only for a moment," and she ushered the boy into the cabin before following him in and closing the door tightly behind her.

"What duties did I summon you from?" Tess inquired, her voice as casual as she could make it.

"Pumpin' the bilge," the small boy mumbled. His eyes were downcast but shot furtive glances at both Cassie and the closed door of the cabin.

"Ah! Well, that is a very important duty indeed," Tess affirmed, now noticing the ripe smell of the putrefying fluids which sloshed around in the belly of the ship. The odor was wafting off the tattered slips of cloth that passed for the stained breeches cinched up around Tommy's tiny waist. "You are keeping this ship afloat then."

Tommy glanced at Tess, unsure if she was complimenting him or accusing him of assisting the enemy.

"You are a brave young man," she continued, "to be put in charge of such a thing. Is it horrible? Down in the bottom, I mean?"

"It's kinda' scary, I guess. I don't like being in water but it's not so bad if ya' can stand on the cork," Tommy offered. His eyes flickered around the room, his discomfort at being interrogated about his duties plainly apparent.

"Cork?"

"Yes ma'am. This ship's from Portugal."

Portugal? That explained Carlos's accent.

Tommy rushed on. "'Her hold's filled with it. Cap'n Carlos was planning on sellin' it in the colonies here in the West Indies. Fer ship-buildin' with hulls what won't rot, an' fer stoppin' up fancy bottles an' such."

"I see," Tess replied, even though she did not. Tommy's extended answer had revealed to her, however, that he had relaxed a bit, if only slightly. She smiled at him and motioned to him with a wave of her hand. "Well, Tommy, I have another, even more important duty for you.

"Kneel on the cot behind Cassie and support her shoulders," Tess instructed the bewildered boy. Tommy did as he was told, but looked suspiciously at Tess, any relaxation that had occurred within their brief conversation having quickly vanished.

"That's just for looks," Tess whispered to both of them, "in case any of them should break in here. Now here's the plan ...."

Quickly she outlined the essential details. For the rest of the day, Tommy was to capture and kill as many rats as he could without raising any suspicion.

"I imagine that there are a few of them in the hold, right? Lodge a small iron ball from the ammunition stores into each rodent's mouth to weigh it down and drop the carcasses into the rum barrels. Do not drink any of the contents from these barrels," she warned, but from the disgusted look on Tommy's young face, her warning was unnecessary. "Serve as much of the rum to as many of the pirates as you can tonight. We'll do the same to the crew on the *Mary Jane*." Confusion clouded both Cassie's and Tommy's faces.

"If you can drop enough of them in each barrel, the rats' bodies will infect whoever drinks from those barrels. Within two days the symptoms will be showing," she explained. "By midnight the night after next, just after the change of lookout from First Shift to Graveyard, most of the crew will hopefully be sickened with the rate-bite fever. That's the time we'll all make good our escape over the railings." Ignoring their looks of disbelief and shock, Tess continued. "If, on that night, you cannot escape in the jolly boat, then jump over the side with something that will keep you afloat."

Tommy and Cassie continued to stare, their raised eyebrows relaying their extreme uncertainty.

"Spread the word to those few you trust and any you want to come with you." She looked meaningfully at Cassie.

"Put this on." She held out the ruby spinner. Only then did Cassie see that Tess wore only the original sparkling blue tourmalines.

"The rings have an attraction for each other. I can take them off my fingers together and then force them apart, but each one seems to have a very strong draw towards the others." She slipped the rubies onto Cassie's finger. "If we come to be separated, maybe they'll help us find one another. And if not … maybe their value will serve other purposes." Tess did not want to spend any energy on the thought of this second outcome. She set her mouth in a determined line.

"We have only one shot at this. Our lives with the pirates will come to an end two nights from now. One way or another."

Chapter Eighty-Three

The plan's details seemed to be falling easily into place. *Too easily*, thought Tess. She had come to expect the unexpected. Since her brother's untimely birth–*Good Lord, that feels like a lifetime ago*, she sadly reflected– nothing seemed to have gone according to plan. However, select barrels had been infected with the sick rats' remains, courtesy of William's keen eye and deadly aim with a knife, and Tess had spread word of the proposed escape to John Robert as well as to Mr. Lancaster.

She smiled to herself as she recalled her grandmother's request. It had been the only time in Tess's life that the woman had ever shown a scrap of embarrassment, yet she had shyly announced to Tess that, in her opinion, Mr. Lancaster's presence would be desperately needed, both in the boat as well as on the shore to resurrect some sort of eventual shelter. He was, she pointed out to Tess, one of the few who could be trusted. Her grandmother's cheeks had burned crimson with an adolescent's blush but she had grinned when Tess had agreed with her assessment of the man. In her own case, Tess realized that she had assumed from the beginning, that William would be accompanying her. William had been delighted to be included, and had already played an integral part in setting the escape plan in motion.

That left only Edward to deal with.

Not really, Tess reminded herself. She had played the part of the doting fiancée, delivering a large goblet of the infected wine and several refills to Edward in his cabin.

Right now, he's probably sleeping it off, but by later tonight he'll be burning up with the onset of the fever. She hoped his case would be a severe one. The infection would bring on vomiting, joint and back pain, headache and disabling muscle cramps. Her grandmother had expected most of the crew to be incapacitated by the abrupt onset of these symptoms, making the escape far less likely to be challenged. Already the sailors on the First Dog watch had taken to their hammocks early, claiming to be unwell and unable to complete their shift, which normally stretched until the evening meal was to be served.

William and John Robert had taken the sick sailors' places. Tess watched Gerta scampering and playfully head butting John Robert as he stood watch along the forecastle railing. The spirited she-goat seldom ventured so close to the railings, having, as all goats did, an intense dislike of being wet, whether it was from a rain storm or from the spray that splashed and misted over the ship's sides. The forecastle deck was high enough however, to be out of reach of the splash of the oncoming waves as they were split by the ship's massive keel.

Tess smiled when she thought of the young goat's continued devotion to the large man. The two were nearly inseparable. In the doeling's world, he was her herd mate.

John Robert reached down and scratched her between her shoulders, sending her tail into a flicking frenzy of pleasure. Impatiently, she butted the leg of her giant caretaker again, demanding more of his attention, her best efforts hardly registering against the enormous thigh. She was rewarded by another delicious scratch, which seemed to satisfy her for the moment, as she then happily bounded off down the stairs and galloped out onto the main deck. Suddenly skidding to a halt, the silken haired kid delicately sniffed the air, as if deciding in which new direction to next explore.

Tess returned her gaze to the ropes holding the jolly boat to the *Mary Jane's* side. She tried to be casual about her visual attention to the boat's details, not wanting to arouse any suspicions. She allowed herself to breathe several deep and relaxed sighs of relief.

The crews on both ships had been infected by now. She had managed to give one ring to Cassie, the other to her grandmother to wear. She had sewn her father's microscope's lens into a second layer in her bodice—it was the only item remaining to her as a family heirloom of sorts, although of what use it would come to be, she couldn't imagine. She just felt an aching need to have something of her parents'—something to focus her memories of them on. Her dirk lay alongside her ankle, its sheath securely tied to her calf by her grandmother's precious red ribbons.

Yes, everything was proceeding as planned.

But then Gerta began to sneeze.

Chapter Eighty-Four

Every year, the summer's sun-drenched heated air, laid in an invisible layer over the waters surrounding the West Indies. It cooked the sea's top layer into an evaporating highway that rose straight up into the upper atmosphere. Meeting the cooler temperatures there and influenced by the agitating winds, water droplets condensed into a pinwheel of thickening clouds, turbulence begetting turbulence. Because of such geography, this was the birthplace of some of the most vicious tropical storms and hurricanes on earth.

The powerful storm had started out as a small wisp, a combination of moderate winds and water, south of the tropical island chain, but as always, it built upon itself by the hour, the storm's churning winds creating a vacuum in its centre, sucking up more of the sea, twisting itself faster and faster as it travelled. Such storms arrived without much warning, and all ships, under normal circumstances and regardless of their sizes or destinations, would use any lead time afforded to them to sail around the storm cell, giving it as wide a berth as possible.

Under normal circumstances. Unfortunately, the *Mary Jane* and the *Bloodhorn* were presently caught up in very abnormal circumstances.

The two ships shared crew and sailing intentions, therefore independent decisions were rarely made. As well, the crews had not yet come to a definite choice of captain to replace Carlos—bickering, petty jealousies, and split loyalties had hampered such a decision—and a mysterious illness had swept over nearly all aboard, leaving very few fit enough to reef let alone furl the enormous sails, even had there been anyone in charge to give such definite orders.

As it was, the pirates aboard the *Mary Jane* put no stock in the prophetic temper tantrums of one diminutive goat, and any such protective lead time was therefore forfeited. By the time clear sight was lost in the dwindling twilight of the evening, and the singular lookout spotted the heady bulge of the ominous cloud formation on the horizon, the ships were squarely in the storm's pathway.

Darkness at such latitude arrives rather suddenly, quickly extinguishing the fiery tails of the setting sun. For those aboard the two ships, evening's cloak slipped over them before the power of the impending storm could be fully realized.

Had they been able to see more than the massive cloud's tip building just beyond their horizon, the captives' escape plan might have been postponed.

Had those on the *Mary Jane* had any way of communicating with Cassie and the others on the *Bloodhorn*, the escape plan might have been postponed.

Had there been a longer window of opportunity which was determined by the sickness that simultaneously affected both crews, the escape plan might have been postponed.

And had Tess heeded the insistent worried thoughts that flooded her mind along with the fierce itch that had returned to her finger beneath her tourmaline ring, the escape plan might have been postponed ….

As it was, none of these came to pass, and Tess, William, John Robert, Mrs. Hanley, and Mr. Lancaster met as arranged, at the side of the *Mary Jane* where the jolly boat was lashed. In fact, they were grateful for the presence of the building winds and rougher seas, as it demanded the full attention of those freshly posted on the Graveyard watch. Among their group, only John Robert seemed to be distracted—Gerta had gone missing, hiding out somewhere in anticipation of the squall.

The oncoming storm first announced its imminent arrival with swelling seas—angry, froth-capped waves roared towards them with unnerving speed—and the winds propelling these white caps shrieked through the masts and riggings, creating an ungodly whistle.

"On deck! All hands on deck!" The urgent cry went out just as the first of many towering waves smashed over the main deck's railings. A cold green tidal wave of salt water, thigh deep, swept across the deck, sucking any loose items along with it into the sea as it exited on the far side of the deck.

Fear began to cloud Tess's mind. She had thought of nothing else these past two days except what it would be like to be free and back on land. She had spun her crystal blue ring and reflected on the tantalizing thoughts of life ashore. At times she swore that she could smell the sweet perfumes of the tropical flowers that surely awaited them there. Daydreams of what she hoped lay ahead had filled her with fresh faith and courage. But now, to leave the big ship seemed suicidal. It had weathered many storms and survived. There was still water, some food, and a scant supply of medicines aboard. Surely the small boat would be immediately swamped in the tossing seas. Creatures lurking beneath the watery surface would feed on them. She would never see Cassie again.

Cassie!

Tess peered across the chasm of boiling sea but the *Bloodhorn* was hidden behind a curtain of heavy rain that had begun to fall. There would be, as there always was during rough seas, a 'lights out' standing order. She closed her eyes, habitually spun her tiniest ring, and concentrated her thoughts on Cassie, welcoming the intuitive impressions into her consciousness.

If they did not escape, Cassie's demise seemed certain. She would die slowly and horribly at the hands of the remaining pirates. At least with their escape attempt, there was an infinitesimal chance of living, of surviving this hellish adventure. Tess wondered if Cassie and Smith and Tommy would be able to break loose from the *Bloodhorn*. Given the storm, would they even try?

Uncertain as to whether they should continue, Tess spun back towards William just in time to see her grandmother's face disappear over the railing as William and John Robert, played out a rope, lowering her down into the pitching jolly boat and into the waiting arms of Mr. Lancaster already in the lowered yawl. A hot surge of adrenaline coursed through her.

Don't think it to death. Just believe! Shutting out all logic and letting her intuition wash over her, Tess knew their escape had to be attempted. *Besides, the decision has already been made.*

As a fresh wave crashed over the railing and tugged at her feet, Tess's chest tightened in a renewed burst of fear and she stared wild-eyed at William. Lashed by the rain and sea water, his long blond curls were now pasted to his face, and he squinted back at her. He was grinning.

"What's to smile about? Have you lost your senses?" Tess yelled in disbelief.

William shrugged and replied, his blue eyes piercing her heart with his sincerity, "No one gets outta' life alive—and if it's my time there's no one I'd rather take the journey with—" The smile suddenly dropped from his face and he screamed, "*Tess! Jump!*" and he lunged for her.

"What?—What do you mean? What are you *doing?*" Tess screeched in alarm.

"I smell *him!*" William cried. "It's *Edward*! Jump! *Now!*"

Chapter Eighty-Five

Out of the shadows behind her, a pair of hands shot out. At the same moment, William shoved Tess hard against the railing, just out of reach—too hard—and with arms and legs flailing, she toppled over the edge and plunged down the side of the ship.

Instead of their intended target, the hands closed around William, one of them clamping firmly around his neck and the other jamming the barrel of a pistol against his temple. Strengthened anew by his failure to apprehend his destined victim, Edward lurched forward, shoving William along in front of him, as he peered over the edge from where Tess had disappeared.

A deep throaty growl tore through the howl of the wind. Edward's head snapped back to the deck and his eyes fixed in surprise on John Robert. The giant's lips were curled back in a dangerous snarl and his eyes glowed with hatred as he slowly advanced upon Edward and his prisoner.

"S-stop!" Edward's mouth still drooped but his speech, although slurred, was clear enough. "Or … else I'll … kill hi-im!" As if to emphasize his threat, Edward shifted his grip on the pistol, straightening his hold on the barrel until it was aimed perfectly perpendicular to William's skull.

John Robert froze in his advance, his eyes locked on the two bodies in front of him. At their feet, nests of floating ropes snarled their ankles while torrents of sea water swirled and tore at their legs, attempting to pry them loose from where they stood. The salt and sea minerals in the spray scalded their nostrils and throats, and half blinded them all. John Robert's lids had no eyelashes to protect his eyes but still he glared unflinchingly as Edward blinked and squinted against the burn of the sea water.

"Trade!" Edward demanded. "You have hi-i-im. I wan' Tess. For me!" Edward shouted. "Bring her up or I kill hi-i-im."

Ever so slowly John Robert raised his arms, as an unarmed man would do, never taking his eyes off of his son and the deathly barrel pressed to William's head. Almost imperceptibly he flexed his index finger and wrist.

Responding immediately to her master's signal and without a heartbeat of hesitation, Gerta launched herself off the high ground of the quarterdeck's railing behind Edward, where she had sought refuge from the ocean's invasion of the main deck. Sharp pointy hooves and all thirty pounds of her smashed into Edward's head and shoulders from behind. In the same split second, John Robert charged at William, ripping him from Edward's grasp. The momentum of this maneuver freed William, spinning him over the railing, as the roar of the pistol blasted beside him.

Instinctively, Edward grabbed Gerta by one hind leg and in a roar of rage, flung her up and over the edge of the ship.

"No–o–oh!" John Robert screamed and grasped for them both as William's and the tiny goat's limbs entangled and they dropped from sight. His fingers snapped shut on thin air. One of his arms dangled uselessly at his side, the pistol's ball having blasted its way through his shoulder, but the huge man whirled on the spot, his remaining arm smashing into Edward's skull with the fury and power of a launched boulder. It was Edward's turn to scream as his skull bones snapped, cracked, and caved under the pressure of the blow.

Collapsing backwards, Edward was overcome with instantaneous dizziness and nausea, and through his fading sight, he registered John Robert's shape hovering over top of him. From behind him, the blurred forms of two pirates swam briefly into view, and John Robert's form suddenly sank to the deck beside him. Edward closed his salt-burned eyes and drifted into unconsciousness.

John Robert had been thwarted in his attempt to strangle Edward. The musket ball had shattered his right arm and shoulder at the socket, leaving it hanging heavily and useless at his side. Sharp shards of bone pierced through the muscles and skin; exposed and torn tendons flapped in the fury of the gale around him. He knew that he was not likely to survive this wound. He also knew that his great strength had been the only thing that he had had that was of any value to those around him.

Except to William.

He hoped that his strength had been a worthy asset to William, both to protect him with and to pass on to him, but John Robert also trusted that his own courage and life as it had been lived, would be an inspiration to his youngest son, to help him through future quests. For always, he knew, life offered unending struggles and choices.

John Robert had been provided with many experiences. He had known the love of a woman of his own choosing, had been blessed with both a daughter and sons, and had been given the opportunity these past months to bond with William in a way that had brought them closer than either of them could ever have imagined. It had been one last wild ride together.

William's adventures were not yet done, John Robert realized, even as his own was coming to an end. There would be dangerous trials ahead, and his heart ached fiercely as only a parent's can for their child, even as a new, acute pain ripped through his chest as the tip of the pirate's broadsword thrust from behind pierced his body. John Robert looked down in mild surprise—he had not heard the pirates' approach above the scream of the wind—and then he simply acknowledged to himself that he was a lucky man once more. This second wound would only hasten his release from his disfigured body.

He slumped to the deck and the icy waves which surged across the deck engulfed him and carried him with them, extinguishing the fiery pain in his wounds. The shriek of the storm was silenced as he drifted beneath the ocean's surface; invisible currents tugged at him, spiraling him down, deeper into their depths. Its cold was comforting.

There were only a few moments of unpleasant air hunger before he slipped into hypoxia, before his mermaids arrived to take John Robert home with them.

Chapter Eighty-Six

Aboard the *Bloodhorn*, men lay half-mad with raging thirsts, their tongues thickened and black from rat-bite fever and dehydration. Some struggled to their feet and staggered out onto deck, where, seasoned sailors that they were, they recognized their predicament. Although the sudden miserable illness had them all feeling like they were going to die, the approaching storm was far more likely to mete out that ending.

The wind had whipped the ocean's surface into a furious topography of towering foam-capped mountains which rose above the bow and rails, cresting ominously for a second before breaking into a freefall crash onto the deck below. Sea water cascaded off the quarter deck above and invaded every level of the *Bloodhorn* below; salt water torrents roared through the peripheries of battened-down hatchways and rushed through every available crack in the decking, coming to a dangerous final pooling in the bilge hold below, turning it into an almost certain deathtrap for those sent to man the pump there. It was therefore no surprise to anyone that Samuel Smith, little Tommy Jones, and the former captain Crowell found themselves all to be deemed dispensable in this way by the pirate crew, and ordered to do continuous shifts with the pump.

It was a great surprise, however, to all in this small group, to be joined in this watery graveyard in the ship's bowels, by a slender sailor with a woolen Monmouth cap upon his head. He seemed to nearly disappear in the remnants of a too-large topcoat and britches, both of which had been hitched fast around the sailor's waist with a long strip of material. It was only when a severe roll of the ship suddenly threw them all tumbling and smashing up against the hull's walls, with their arms flying wildly to steady themselves, that Smith's jaw dropped open in astonishment. The strange sailor's arms flew up overhead, stretching the topcoat's fold out long enough for Smith to glimpse a flash of red ribbon tied around the sailor's waist.

Cassie had joined them.

It was Tommy who noticed that the strange bundles which had once been stacked in an orderly fashion on top of the gravelly layer of ballast, now floated upon the surface of the rising water level in the bilge compartment. The long and narrow bales of Portuguese cork bark were both naturally buoyant and rot resistant. It took only a few moments of hurried discussion to hatch a backup escape plan to fortify that of stealing the *Bloodhorn's* yawl. They would lash some cork sheaves to the narrow rails of the yawl, in an effort to increase the small boat's chance of remaining afloat in the clutches of the storm. Captain Crowell was offered an invitation to join their escape expedition.

"A captain does not desert a floundering ship," he declared upon considering their invite. "However, it would seem that I have been demoted these past weeks and therefore," he grinned and offered his hand forward in a handshake sealing the deal, "although it does go against my officer's nature, I am under no compunction to stay aboard this vessel. I suggest we make hast to abandon her before the storm's full wrath is upon her."

Topside, the sickened and storm battered crew clung for their lives to the ratlines and yardarms as they fought to control their sails' canvasses in the shrieking winds. They took no notice of the group of four nor of the long items that each clutched tightly, the four having hauled the strange cargo out of the hatch opening and over towards the rail where the jolly boat was fastened to the *Bloodhorn*.

Just as they arrived at the side railing, a thunderous crack behind them pierced through the sounds of the storm.

"*Look out!*" Captain Crowell's screamed words of warning were lost, ripped from his lips by the fury of the gales, and he sprang forward towards his three shipmates. His violent push into Smith and Tommy sent them flying into Cassie, and in a domino effect, all three crashed into the railing, just as a piece of broken mast smashed heavily onto the deck beside them.

Scrambling to their feet, they were sickened to see the side of the jolly boat crushed and broken by the mast's massive weight. Shock gave way to raw horror as they saw, at the mast's middle, the captain lying face down on the deck, pinned beneath the giant piece of wood. It took the combined strength of all three to lift the jagged timber off of him. He gritted his teeth against the pain, and his face twisted in agony as they rolled him face up.

"C'mon, Captain!" Smith yelled, as he attempted to hoist the captain to his feet. The captain's body sagged, a dead weight in his arms. Smith shouted desperately, still tugging upwards under the man's armpits, "Up and into the boat with ya'!"

"Save yourselves!" Captain Crowell's tone had once again taken on the hard edge of a commander. "The jolly's too badly damaged," he grunted between clenched teeth. "Clasp fast to the cork oak and leap into the sea. I have seen it float when all else sinks. It's your only hope! Go!"

"But we can't leave ya', Sir!" screamed Smith trying to be heard above the roar of the storm.

"Go! Now! While you still have the chance!" He cut off any further objections with a somber announcement. "My back is broken. I cannot move my legs," Captain Crowell was announcing his own death in the most simplest of terms. "It seems that it was not in my destiny to leave this vessel after all ...."

"Do something!" Cassie sobbed. "We can't just leave him!"

"He's as good as dead if his back's broke!" Smith countered, ignoring Cassie's pleading. "The most I can do is make it quick fer him." He brandished a small blade and knelt beside his captain.

Captain Crowell nodded in immediate understanding, his eyes unflinchingly locked on Smith's face.

"You have my gratitude, Mr. Smith."

"No, wait! You can't!" Cassie screamed and, grabbing Smith's arm with all of her might, she wrenched it backwards.

"It's a final help to the Captain, don'cha see?" Smith shouted, struggling to loosen his arm from her grip. "Fer God's sake, woman! Let me do this fer the man!"

At that moment the sea took matters out of his hands, as a wall of water crashed over the deck again, sweeping them off their feet, and carrying them all through the break in the railing.

Chapter Eight-Seven

Aboard the *Mary Jane*, sailors staggered from their bunks and hammocks, and groped their way to the main deck, struggling to climb up the rat lines which vibrated and hummed fiercely in the grip of the howling gales. The lines threatened to shake them loose and send them spiraling to their deaths below. The sails, already reefed, still offered too much resistance to the oncoming blasts and men climbed and clung, desperate to make their way up to the heavy sheets of canvas, risking their lives in an effort to lash the escaping edges that flapped like great wings, securely to the yardarms.

Far below them, on the pitching surface of the sea, the jolly boat heaved and dropped, then rose and reared. Suddenly free of its mooring line to the *Mary Jane*, it began spinning and bobbing at her side like a cork caught in a river's angry eddy. The wild sea had been whipped into great white frothy peaks alternating with dark troughs and the small boat slipped her nose nearly vertically downwards before she suddenly bucked backwards on the uplift. Her occupants hung on precariously, desperate to prevent being thrown over her sides.

"William!" Tess shrieked as his plummeting body hit the cresting water, piercing its surface and sinking under. Seconds later, his head broke the surface, only an arm's length from the boat, and he gasped and kicked his face clear of the water. Even in the darkness Tess could see that William held one arm bent at a peculiar angle.

My God! Tess panicked. *His arm is broken! He'll drown right in front of me!*

"Help me!" he pleaded and kicked furiously again, raising himself a few inches higher in the water.

"Grab hold!" Mr. Lancaster held an oar out to him, battling to stay within the tossing boat himself. Against the bottomless blackness of the ocean, it was nearly impossible to even see William.

"Take her!" William gasped, groping blindly with one hand for the end of the oar offered to him, just as a wave threatened to suck him out of reach.

"What?" The howl of the storm and the crash of the waves as they battered against the *Mary Jane* made it impossible to hear clearly if at all. "Take what?" Mr. Lancaster shouted, and then demanded, "Hang on with *both hands*, boy!" as he began to haul the length of the oar back towards the boat. Over head brilliant stabs of lightening sizzled and flared, the boom of its deafening thunder arriving almost simultaneously.

Drawn to the craft's side, William coughed and retched on a mouthful of sea water. "Gerta!" he shouted. "Take her!" And from within the crook of his bent arm, Tess could see a small muzzle, the whites of the terrified goat's eyes glinting in the light of the heavenly flame as the lightening crackled overhead.

All three of them reflexively reached out, grabbing at William and Gerta, but their combined weight on one side threatened to capsize the small boat. Clutching Gerta to her bosom, Mrs. Hanley immediately pushed back to the opposite side, counterbalancing the rescue efforts of Tess and Mr. Lancaster. Mr. Lancaster seized William by a handful of hair and Tess reached out, grabbing William's outstretched hand. Together, they held him fast to the side of the boat, as a wave lifted William's body up with its fresh surge over the craft's edge. In a synchronized effort, they half pulled, half floated William over the top edge into the boat.

"Da'!" William struggled for breath as he lay on the bottom of the dory, almost totally immersed in water that was collecting there at an alarming rate. Sitting up, William looked around wildly. It was only then that any of them realized just how far they had become separated from the *Mary Jane*. Illuminated by another sheet of lightning, the stern of the great ship was barely visible to them.

"Da'!" William bellowed, scanning across the mountainous seas. "Da'!"

"Yer Da' dinna make it off!" Mr. Lancaster's voice was desperately strident, laboring with the effort to be heard above the storm, and strained with fear and grief for their situation. Prying open a small hatch to a secret compartment behind a second wall that William had built into the boat's side, he reached inside and withdrew an armful of tin tankards, thrusting one into each pair of hands.

"Bail!" he ordered. "By God, this dammed sea has not yet claimed us! We must survive this night's storm!"

Powered by both wind and waves, their boat was driven onward in the direction of a waiting land mass which lay guarded by the deadly ragged teeth of its protective reef. In spite of their most frantic efforts, water poured over the edges and continued to engulf them waist high. For nearly an hour they bailed, their arms becoming heavy and slow with fatigue, their muscles numb from the lashing cold of the wind and water.

Lightening crackled overhead again setting the gems in Tess's ring to glow. Staring at them, she felt a sense of grim satisfaction. *At least I foiled Edward in his quest for the rings. For all of his fine training and wealth, he is just a common pirate in a gentleman's disguise.* Tess's thoughts began to drift, her body too chilled and her mind too tired to be frightened any more.

The anticipated warmth of Port Royal in Jamaica played like a daydream in her head. There were strange animals and brightly colored birds there, her father had told her, with the land being covered by a carpet of green lushness, the likes of which she could not even begin to imagine. As her father had talked about it, and had spoken about their new home-to-be, with its palm trees, soft sands, and gentle turquoise waters, it had been the sunshine and the pleasure of the warm seas that Tess had been looking forward to the most ....

Dimly aware of her present surroundings, she was not alarmed but only vaguely annoyed when the water-laden boat gave way beneath them, spilling them out into the icy clutches of the roiling water.

A crushing wave broke over them, pounding down upon them, sucking each of them deeper into its plexus. *It's supposed to be warm!* she thought sullenly as she sank.

Chapter Eighty-Eight

Many ships, great and small, met their deaths when pitted against the enormous power of seas churned by such devil winds. Often capsizing on the open water or being driven into and torn asunder by the ragged reefs which lined the shorelines, the great vessels and their weighty treasures of gold, silver, ivory, jewels, and human cargo frequently sank. Any bits of wrecks which washed ashore were quickly scavenged and salvaged by the island inhabitants who regularly scoured the beaches in the aftermath of such storms.

On this particular morning, those brought to the water's edge by the potential opportunity of finding useable items—canvas or wood scraps, perhaps even a surviving cask of rum or two—crept in silence not wishing to be seen, darting among the predawn shadows of the lush vegetation. Between this and the ocean's edge, a stretch of fine powdery sand had been blown into finger dunes pointing inland. Palm trees rose above the more dense undergrowth, their fronds rustling in the remaining breezes. The sun had not yet risen above the horizon, although a pink hue heralded its arrival.

A bare foot nudged at a mound half buried in the storm-strewn sand, sending a stream of young land crabs scuttling out from beneath the mound. The mound remained unresponsive. The only movement came from the flush of the waves which rocked it from side to side. Reaching down, a pair of hands rolled the mound over and the owner of the bare foot stepped back in surprise.

Barely aware that someone had rolled her over, Tess sucked in a large shuddering breath and momentarily sank back into the safety of unconscious exhaustion. An incessant tugging at her finger roused her—the grip was rough and strong and the pain was intensely acute. Her finger's joints felt like they were going to dislocate.

Edward! Her heart pounded frantically. *He survived!* A voice screamed in her head. *He's trying to steal my ring!*

Too numb to cry out, she curled her fingers into a fist and attempted to pull her hand out of the strange grasp but her fingers were pried open and splayed out upon a piece of exposed sandstone. She blinked and tried to clear her vision. Shafts of the early morning sun streaked over the horizon and scalded her salt-scalded eyes. Through her watery vision Tess saw the flash of a knife blade and realized, *My God! He's going to cut my finger off to get the ring!*

A scream strangled in her throat just as a familiar voice rang out.

"Leave her alone, you son of a bitch! If you even touch her, I will kill you!"

For just a split second, the grip on Tess's hand let go and she twisted away, pulling her hand free and rolling onto her stomach before struggling onto her knees. Looking up, she saw William, a pistol held steadily in either hand and both leveled at her attacker. Looking back she was stunned to see, not Edward, but a man, in tattered dungarees, with skin as black as charcoal. He held a broad-bladed machete in one hand and even from his knees, stared steadily at William, as though gauging the threat.

Shadows in the underbrush behind William suddenly merged into human forms as three more people stepped forward, their skin colors an artist's mixed palette of gilded browns to inky sable. Steadily they advanced on Tess and William, encircling them in an ever tightening ring. Outnumbered, William held the pistols at arm's length and slowly turned on the spot, pivoting around on his damaged and stiffened knee.

"When I say so, you run!" he whispered to Tess out of the corner of his mouth.

"Where did you get the guns?" Tess softly inquired.

"I got two blades as well," he replied softly. "They're from the false compartment in the boat's wall. It was the sturdiest section." William continued in a hushed tone. "It survived and washed up on shore alongside me just beyond that spit of land over there."

"Jacko!" A high pitched voice barked out the name. The man with the machete jumped to his feet. One of the islanders stepped forward, and staring at Tess, advanced towards them, with a stride that was purposeful and fearless. As the stranger stepped closer, only two strides away, Tess gasped.

From this close distance, she was clearly a woman, her form wrapped in a ragged and sun-bleached caftan. Glancing at William and staring briefly down the barrels of the pistols, the woman then brazenly reached out and touched Tess's neck.

"Erzulie?"

The foreign syllables in the woman's question hung in the air between them, but it was not her boldness that had made Tess gasp. There, imbedded into the slight curve of the woman's shoulder muscle, was the raised scar of the *Bloodhorn* brand.

"Erzulie?" the woman asked again, impatience creeping into her voice.

Tess frowned and pulled the woman's hand away from her neck where it had rested on her birthmark. Now it was the strange woman's turn to gasp as daybreak's climbing light glinted off the blue tourmalines in Tess's ring. Her eyes narrowed and she stared at Tess.

"Come."

The command from the woman, in English, startled Tess and she raised a questioning brow at William, who still stood at her side, both pistols raised. He looked around warily but then simply shrugged. His eyes met Tess's and then regarded the woman's as he nodded.

"Lead on then," he consented.

Chapter Eighty-Nine

In single file, they walked back into the jungle, retracing one set of foot prints in the sand. Even these were whisked away with a palm frond by the last man in the procession. To the casual eye there were no remaining signs of a human presence upon the beach. It took only several steps past the vegetation's edge for them to be swallowed up by the dense rain forest.

One of the men led the way, his steps quick and surely placed, yet nearly soundless upon the forest's floor. Underfoot, a thick, wet carpet of leaves dampened their footfalls.

They trudged through the undergrowth, dodging curtains of ropey vines and pushing through sun-flecked walls of enormous heart-shaped leaves and spiky fronds. Moss coated tree trunks sprouted webs of twisted roots, anchoring them down to the jungle floor, while their leafy crowns stretched overhead and blended into a lacey canopy. A thick green wrap of living velvet coated everything around them—rocks, tree trunks, and the entwining strands which fell from dizzying heights overhead.

All around there was a discordant orchestra of sounds—twitters and shrieks, whistles and clucks—and from time to time there were flashes of brilliant yellows, oranges, and reds, but mostly this strange world was a quilt of endless shades of greens, soft and dappled with thin shafts of tropical sunlight.

The increasing burn in their leg muscles indicated that they were climbing all the while. William's stiff knee caused him to struggle as the ground underfoot became steeper. At one point, he lost his footing and began to pitch backwards but Tess struck out with her hand, barely grasping the front of his threadbare tunic, as she counterbalanced his sprawl. Sheepishly he regained his balance, remarking, "Thanks for that."

Pulling him close to her, Tess responded, whispering into his ear in a way that raised gooseflesh on his arms, "Were you falling for me?" Besides being embarrassed at tripping and being rescued by Tess, her attempt at humor under the circumstances left William annoyed. He grunted and continued on past her.

In fact, William had been concentrating on the body language of those around them, rather than watching his footing. He noted the way they walked in a semi-crouch, their eyes never still, constantly scanning as their heads slowly swiveled from side to side. They stepped silently, moved silently, with no conversation between them.

He recognized the signs.

They are afraid of something, William thought. *But what? There could be all kinds of predators in this place, but surely we would be smelled by them no matter how silently we traveled ... what are they afraid of?*

The hairs on William's neck bristled as he felt the imaginary eyes of unseen watchers on his back. He, too, began to glance furtively around him as they traveled. The tension in their small group was palpable. Surveying the jungle to his side, William miscalculated a step and caught his toes on a fallen branch, which sent him sprawling face first. The others recoiled at the unexpected movement as if he had discharged his gun among them.

William lay shame-faced in the jungle mulch for only a few seconds but it was long enough. His nostrils were filled with a scent that was completely out of place and set off alarm bells in his head. The odor was familiar yet screamed of danger.

It was a pungent mixture of horse shit and blood and ... the odor of wet dog.

A fraction of intense homesickness stabbed through William as he tried to decipher the scents. The heme scent was faint, older, but still metallic. The manure was relatively fresh, and the dog ....

Jacko had reached down and was pulling William to his feet when William spotted the slight impression in the leafy trail bed. Someone with boots on had stepped in this very spot. Recently. Someone with a dog.

A tracker. Most likely a fierce and skilled hunter whose tracking abilities would be rivaled only by the amount of cruelty and violence that such a job required to be successful.

His discovery did not escape his captor's notice. Instantly crouching beside William, Jacko squinted at the impression and then back at William, as if trying to anticipate William's next reaction.

William, too, was making an instantaneous decision. To cry out for help and bolt now into the care of this unknown hunter, or to stay with known opponents. Which was going to be the lesser danger? Leaving Tess behind was out of the question—even if he were to manage to escape, Tess would be killed. That was a certainty. William could sense their new captors' strong drive for self-preservation; it was deeply steeped in primal fear and fueled by their instinct to survive at all costs. Any hint of escape by either William or Tess would be construed as a fatal threat. As well, the open hostility shown towards them upon their discovery on the beach had left little hope that this was a sympathetic search party. Yet he and Tess had not been harmed so far .... *Maroons! These people have to be Maroons!*

He had often heard the sailors talk about bounty money there for the taking, by rounding up ex-slaves on the islands and returning them to their owners. Resulting riches or not, the sale of human flesh was repugnant to him.

William quickly made his decision.

"Horseman," William whispered to Jacko who had remained crouched beside him. "And blood. With a dog." He saw the man's eyes widen in understanding and momentarily flash with fear, and then, just as quickly, Jacko issued a short bird-like warble. Simultaneously, his companions dropped to the ground, pulling Tess down with them and disappearing from sight. For long moments no one moved while the rhythm of the jungle filled in the silence around them. William's back and legs ached with the tension of lying so still when every cell in his body screamed for him to get up and run. His level of anxiety was magnified with the mounting fear of their discovery. He lay face down for what seemed like several minutes and began to wonder if the danger had somehow passed them by.

And then he noticed it.

An audibly steady rhythm. Mouth-breathing. By one who was perhaps overdressed, laboring to breathe in this humidity and heat. By one who wore boots.

Nodding his head ever so slightly in the direction of the sound, William squared his gaze on Jacko lying beside him. Acknowledging the intent of William's message with a head nod of his own, the man suddenly slithered backwards on his stomach, disappearing into the foliage.

What the hell? Where is he going? Oh my God, he thought bitterly, *he's gone. The bastard is saving his own skin and leaving us here to be slaughtered!*

A wash of terror swept over William and he could hear the quickening pulse of his blood as it coursed through his veins. He fought to keep his own breathing quiet and under control but survival instincts kicked in and he rolled off the path, slight as it was, and under the fronds of a giant fern. The faint tremor of footfalls reverberated against his cheek as he lay pressed against the ground. He lifted his head as high as he dared, scanning the area where he had lain just moments before.

A harsh sniffing sound filled his ears. The excited huffing rhythm brought back a flash of memory of a time when Lucas had hunted alongside William. The intense snuffling pattern was the same. *The dog! It's hunting us!*

A low menacing growl rumbled close to the ground. William froze as his eyes stared into the animal's. It was close enough that William could smell the carnivore's hot, foul breath. Its lips were pulled back over slavering fangs in a menacing snarl and the dog sank into a low crouch–a familiar posture that screamed of an imminent attack. William's heart thudded painfully; he could smell his own fear. He hoped the end would come quickly. The animal looked savage and strong enough to make that happen.

A pair of khaki trousers materialized on the trail behind the dog. The hunter advanced another step forward and then slowly sank down onto one knee beside his hound, sighting down the barrel of his musket which he held ready.

A flicker of surprise flashed across the man's face as his eyes locked onto William's. William was only partially camouflaged by the fern fronds, and for a moment the man seemed uncertain of what he saw. The tracker's hound had no such misgivings however, and with a rumbling snarl, launched itself, leaping onto William, fangs bared, aiming for a throat hold. Reflexively, the dagger handles were in William's hands before he could even think about saving himself and the jungle's clamor was split by one long howl, as the dog slammed into William's chest, the force of the attack driving the knives' lengths into its neck and chest. The dog quivered, and was still.

With his gun still aimed directly at William, the tracker hesitated, not immediately comprehending his animal's demise. The moment of hesitation proved to be fatal. A hand shot out from behind, covering the man's mouth and a rusty blade sliced across his throat, unleashing a spray of blood. The hunter's eyes rolled back in his head, and with no more than a single gurgle, he collapsed, revealing Jacko standing behind.

Rolling out from beneath the dog's body, William watched as Jacko quickly stripped the body of every piece of clothing as well as the weapons before bending over and pulling the man's stained boots off. There, stuck between the heel and sole of one, was a wedge of horse manure.

"Slave catcher!" Jacko's eyes narrowed and his voice trembled as he spat out the hated words. He landed a vicious kick to the corpse's face, and then, tying the boots' laces together before slinging them over his shoulder, he called to the only woman in their group. "Mambo!" He handed the machete to her as he picked up the hunter's long barreled shotgun. Holding the heavy blunderbuss to his chest, he simply pointed uphill.

"We go."

Chapter Ninety

They had stopped for a brief drink from a stream whose edge they appeared to have been following. Tess sat quietly, her back resting against a mossy tree trunk. Her mind spun with an increasing sense of dread. Where were they being taken to? *What* were they being taken to? Spinning the fine tourmaline gold and silver braid around her finger, she begged her frantic thoughts to settle into some semblance of order.

She inhaled the tropical fragrances hanging in the humid air and closed her eyes, willing herself to relax. The scent here was captivating– moist and earthy mulch mixed with heavy floral tones–and she could almost taste the air's sweetness on her tongue. The slow slide into meditation was momentarily intoxicating and she was caught off guard by the intensity of an unexpected vision. Its content caused her to startle and she choked on a panicked cry of surprise in her throat.

"What is it?" William's worried eyes were drawn tightly with renewed tension.

Tess blinked, confused as what had seemed so real inside her head only a heartbeat ago.

"I had thoughts of–a battle of sorts…" The idea sounded so stupid out loud that she let her words die away. "Just starting to dream, I guess." She looked up at William and saw that her words had not been convincing.

"A battle?" His forehead creased in further worry and his nostrils flared slightly, as though he were picking up on the scent of her building anxiety.

The image had been only a fragment but there had been flickers of fighting. Of blood. Screams of pain. Most frightening of all, she thought that the screams had been hers.

Tess shook her head as though clearing her mind of the thoughts. "Just too tired, I guess." She smiled wanly at William. "I must have started to doze off. It was just a bad dream." *More like a waking nightmare,* she told herself.

Jacko and Mambo openly stared at her and then, glancing at each other and sharing an unspoken thought, jumped to their feet.

"We go! Now!" Jacko hissed the order through clenched teeth and he spun around, sending Mambo vaulting past him up the streamside trail with an urgent shove to her back.

The attack happened without further warning.

Before the rest of their small group could stumble to their feet, the air around them roared with the deafening blasts of musket fire. Giant philodendron leaves exploded, then shuddered and fluttered to the ground, shredded to pieces. Clouds of gunpowder smoke billowed through ragged holes that had been blasted in the thick leafy curtains.

Through her confusion and fear, Tess had not quite risen from her seat at the base of the tree, and panic-stricken, she dove under the thick foliage at her feet, scrambling to tuck her legs under the low boughs. Her own scream was lost among those filling her ears—the howls of the maroons as the musket balls hit, tearing away flesh and shattering bones. Their vocal misery was punctuated with the cheers of the slave hunters as their ammunition felled their quarry.

Dear God! The vision—the nightmare—it's coming to life! Curled into a tight ball, Tess watched, paralyzed, as Jacko pivoted and leapt after Mambo, following her fleeing form into the jungle's thick cover. Before he could take a second stride, however, he seemed to rise straight up in the air, his body stiffening as his left buttock burst open with a spray of blood and muscle. He fell with a sickening thud and did not move from where he lay.

The bloody onslaught was over in mere minutes. Tess remained frozen in her spot, hidden from the attackers for the moment, praying that they did not have another tracking dog along.

William! Silently she shrieked his name. Was he alive or not? *Please, please,* she begged silently, *let him be alive!* She hadn't seen him since the first volley of musket balls had sent everyone sprawling.

"Fer Chrissakes, ya' buggerin' bloodthirsty idiots!" a voice snarled. "Ya' was supposed to capture them, not kill them! How the hell is a dead one gonna' lead us to their goddamn camp? Hmm? Ya' tell me that!" A small wiry man stepped into view and kicked at the body lying at his feet. "See if any of these sonsabitches still lives!" he ordered, and from where she lay, Tess counted three more pairs of legs stepping past her. A remaining hunting party of four.

That's why they'd been able to surround us!

The men moved noisily around, slicing into the flesh of the downed bodies with heavy cutlasses, waiting to see if the pain of fresh wounds roused any of them. It did not. When they came to Jacko's body, Wiry Man himself plunged his blade into Jacko's uninjured thigh. A strangled wail made them all jump.

"Ah ha!" Wiry Man snorted with glee. "We have a live one!" and as if to convince himself, or perhaps just for the cruelty of it, twisted his knife blade a half turn in the new wound. Jacko screamed in agony.

Suddenly Wiry Man toppled forward, falling with all of his weight upon Jacko, who shrieked again with renewed pain from the pressure on his injuries. The three other slave catchers gawked at their boss lying crumpled on top of the wounded slave. For a moment they stood dumbly, not comprehending, and then with a strangled gurgle, one of them staggered forward, falling heavily face first into the jungle matting at his feet.

"Fer Chrissakes! What the hell–?" one of the two still standing on his feet blurted out before stumbling back from his fallen companion's body. "Oh shit!" he bellowed, pointing alternatively at a dark object protruding from the back of each of the fallen men's necks. From behind the thin veil of foliage, Tess squinted at the bodies. Even from where she was, she recognized the blade handles of William's daggers.

He's alive! Oh my God–he's alive! For a split second Tess felt an immense jolt of relief before she slid back down into her cold pool of terror. The two remaining hunters dropped instinctively into a protective crouch and their heads swiveled wildly as they searched for the source of the weapons.

Use the guns you have, William! Use them now! Tess sent out a silent plea of desperation. These men were trackers–trained to spot even the most insignificant signs of their prey–and she knew her ragged breathing was going to give her away at any moment. She had no sooner registered that thought when one of the men suddenly twisted and sprang out of his crouch, smashing into her with a heavy crash. A calloused hand muffled her scream and at the same time forced her head back. She felt the burn of the sharp edge of his hunting knife as it sliced into her skin just below the corner of her jaw. Her world spinning in terror, Tess's vision clouded and she felt herself blacking out. She prayed the faint would overtake her before he cut any further.

Surprise slowed the slave catcher's hand. The only thing dark about his victim's skin was a strange mark trailing down the side of her neck. The rest of her skin was a creamy tan. Shock crackled though him as he realized that he had nearly killed a white woman. And with all of the runaways dead or dying, how could he have blamed it on anyone else?

"Stop right now, you bastard, or I swear it'll be the last thing you do in this life. Drop. The. Knife." William's voice seemed so far away, yet it was clearly his. Tess blinked and tried to clear her pounding head. She focused on his voice. It was calm. Commanding. And coldly threatening. As the blade at her neck was withdrawn, Tess clasped at the slash in her skin with her own hands, trying to staunch the bleeding.

"You. Slowly stand up and step away from the lady. And you–don't even so much as twitch or I'll blow you both away."

Tess peered at the scene before her. Her attacker was kneeling on the ground in front of William; the other hunter stood a few feet away, his hands raised shoulder high in submission. William held a pistol in each hand. One set of barrels was pressed firmly against the back of the kneeling man's head, the other gun pointed squarely at the standing hunter's chest.

"Easy now! We meant you folks no harm." The standing man gave a limp smile and issued a nervous laugh. "We've no fight at all with you. T'was only them runaway darkies we was followin' anyhows. We had no way of knowin' they'd taken white folk prisoners." He glanced at Tess and his eyes traced the trickles of blood that dripped from her wound as they ran down the front of her dress and clotted there in the material. "Yer Missus' is needing a kerchief, looks like," he nodded at William. "I've got just the thing in my chest pocket, if you'll allow …." Without waiting for permission from William, he slowly lowered his hand into the pocket of the lanyard strapped diagonally across his chest.

The dark glint of the tiny Queen Anne pistol looked nothing like the promised kerchief as the man withdrew it and in a flash, had it leveled at William. A broad toothless grin spread over the man's face. "Now we is about even in surprises, ain't we?"

William froze, with only his eyes flicking from Tess, who stared determinedly at her assailant still kneeling head down in front of her, and then back to the small but lethal weapon pointed directly at him. He slowly raised his eyes from the muzzle of the gun to the man's face, and his eyebrows arched.

"Not quite." William's gaze never faltered as the swoosh of the machete struck the man's ears, its blade biting into the side of his neck and slicing through. Mambo stood behind the headless body as it toppled forward, her chest heaving with the exertion of the heavy blade's swing.

Tess's simultaneous attack on the hunter still bowed at William's feet attracted his attention though. Unsheathing the small dirk that had travelled all this way securely attached to her lower leg by the strength of her grandmother's red ribbons, Tess lunged up from her squatted position and drove the blade deep into the man's chest. The blade was minute in comparison to the machete but days of tending to fatal chest wounds aboard the *Mary Jane* had given Tess perfect anatomical understanding. A human heart was not hard to hit if one knew just where to aim.

Chapter Ninety-One

Again the slave catcher's bodies were stripped of all clothing and weapons, and their nude corpses were dragged away from the stream's edge into the jungle's undergrowth.

"Shouldn't we bury them or something?" William asked.

Mambo shook her head. "De jungle spirits, dey hungry. Dey feast tonight."

Tying a pistol and a powder horn to the sash at her waist, and slipping both the machete and a smaller dagger into leather sheaths taken from the hunters, Mambo held William and Tess in her gaze, before striking off into the foliage. She was expected to return with help to transport both Jacko and Tess to the village. She would, William knew, return with assistance for Jacko, even if she didn't care about Tess's or his own survival. He had seen how tenderly the woman had cared for the wounded man. *Her mate,* William corrected himself. Their relationship was apparent to him now. Being moved had been excruciatingly painful for Jacko, but he now lay on a bed of soft leaves gathered by Mambo. He was mercifully unconscious.

Mambo had packed his hip and leg wounds with a sticky mat of colorful crushed leaves and sap before she dressed them with strips of cloth torn from Tess's dress. William, too, had carefully wrapped Tess's neck wound, accepting Mambo's offer of a poultice of the strange jungle plant mixture to lay overtop of the gaping laceration.

If only Tess hadn't given that emerald ring to her grandmother! William despaired. Tess may still not have been fully convinced of its ability to promote healing but often enough William had watched her use it nonetheless, among the sick and injured, and incredulous as the notion of its power seemed to be, he was, by now, unable to dismiss the possibility. *And the blue one —it warned her of the attack on us! She knew!*

It was all so weird. The logical portion of his brain still resisted, and had done so since Tess had tried to explain the rings to him, but a deeper knowing tugged at him. *How else could any of this be explained?* he wondered. *Maybe there was some truth seeded in all legends. Maybe we aren't supposed to, aren't even able to, figure it all out.* His head was cramping with the doubts and questions that filled it. He sighed and decided he would probably never know how or even if, it was the rings that had worked. *And really does it matter?* he mused, looking down at Tess who rested quietly beside him. For now, life's sweetest moments were also the unexpected ones.

After what seemed an eternity, Mambo returned with only two others, making it plain that Tess and William would walk. They were going to transport Jacko on a narrow stretcher constructed of thin branches woven into a fishnet. The flexibility of the device made portaging through the jungle's maze possible where something less supple would have rendered passage impossible.

The tropical vegetation had blended into a forest of tall trees and stony crevasses when their small group traveling in single file stopped at the foot of a smooth vertical cliff. The stream they had been following seemed to gush out from the foot of its rocky face, which was dressed with a thick and tangled veil of hanging plants. Pulling this living curtain aside, the leader of the group stepped into a small opening in the rock and was swallowed up in its darkness. Those in front of William and Tess followed him.

Tess, however, stood riveted at the stream's side, feeling quite uncertain. She stood swaying slightly, her earlier wooziness having been replaced by a general deep fatigue. She sensed William's nearness and knew he was standing close behind her. She'd noticed that sometime during the climb, he had stuck the pistols into the belt of rope that he wore around his waist. He was directly behind her now, his presence reassuring, his muscled body warm against hers. She flushed at his touch.

"Do you have the guns ready?" she whispered over her shoulder. The uncertainty of what they were walking into unnerved her.

There was a moment of silence before William answered.

"Wouldn't do any good," he replied.

"Why not?"

He lifted his shoulders in a careless shrug and a soft chuckle shook in his chest. "Uh, the pistols and shot survived the seawater ... but the gunpowder didn't." He quickly added, "But only you and I have to know *that* little detail."

Tess twirled around and searched his face. "But then—back when we were attacked— it was all *a ruse?*"

"Well, the pistols made a good enough impression though, didn't they? That's all that matters." William gave a wry smile and nodded toward the waiting aperture. "Let's not keep our hosts waiting."

As she stepped into the cave's opening, Tess's finger began to itch under her ring and she felt the odd sensation of a soft yet invisible pull around her.

One of the other rings!

Surely that was the pull that she felt. Her pulse quickened and she stumbled on through the rough tunnel, heading toward a shaft of light that glowed up ahead. William kept pace behind her, his hand remaining in light contact at her waist.

Breaking out of the tunnel's end, and stepping into the filtered sunlight, they stood still, amazed at the sight before them. A small collection of thatched huts, barely visible in the camouflage of the surroundings, were tucked back along the perimeter of an ill-defined clearing.

They had been brought to their captives' secret encampment. They were standing at the edge of a village of the Maroons.

The sailors' stories burst into Tess's thoughts. Such places were rumored to be scattered throughout the islands, founded by groups of escaped slaves whose treatment by their white owners had been so vicious that they chose to face starvation and possibly death, rather than remain in captivity. Recaptured runaways were always branded and whipped; often the males were castrated and the women brutally raped. Once in awhile one would be dismembered, or hung, or burned alive as a warning to the other slaves. Tess shook her head as if to clear it of such nightmarish images. The village's occupants had every reason to be hostile to any white people that they encountered. Their need for revenge was raw and primal.

The Maroons' continued survival in these villages depended on complete secrecy of their whereabouts. Tess knew, now that they were here, they would not be allowed to leave alive. And the deep anger with which most of this scavenging party looked at them suggested that staying alive was not a likely option.

With fear building in her chest again, Tess began to twist her silver and gold gem studded bands, begging to be given some insight but all that she felt was the strange invisible pull. It was growing stronger.

As they were prodded down the tortuous path towards the clearing's center, Tess lurched to a sudden stop, causing those behind her to collide in a chain reaction. She blinked in disbelief at what she saw before her. Stepping out of one of the huts, into the bright sunlit clearing, was a form so familiar that it took Tess's breath away.

Cassie.

Chapter Ninety-Two

Tess stood shoulder to shoulder to Cassie in the doorway of one of the huts. Inside, William and Smith compared details of their escape from the ships, and their rescue, such as it was, by the scouting parties of the maroons. Neither one dwelled on the unknown fates of the missing ones–Mrs. Hanley, Mr. Lancaster, and Tommy–nor of the ones left behind–Captain Crowell from the *Bloodhorn*, and John Robert and Edward from the *Mary Jane*.

The two young men spoke quietly, both of them realizing that their own fates were no better, that in less than a day, they had gone from being prisoners of the pirates to prisoners of this band of hostile runaways. William listened calmly to the details of Smith's recall of his and Cassie's ordeal.

"We both was sickened with our bellies heavin' up sea water hard, an' not too sure we was thankful to still be alive in that condition, ya' understand," Smith recalled, with a wry smile. "But alive we was, with me caught by my trouser rope in between them giant sandstones just out aways, and her tossed up on the shore." His face clouded as he added, "There was no sign of young Tommy."

"Anyways, soon enough there comes these maroons and they haul poor Cassie to her feet, none too gently, with her still retchin'. Served them right that she puked all over them, she did." He grinned at the memory. "Then the woman, the one called Mambo, gets all tense when she sees Cassie's arm. Seems that she'd spent some time with that bloody Carlos herself, and wouldn't ya' know it, she's got his brand on her arm too, and didn't get it in an agreeable fashion neither. When she saw that on Cassie's arm, I could hear her holler 'Bloodhorn!' all the way out in the waves where I was still tied down to them stones. An' there was no mistakin' the hate in her voice, lemme tell ya'."

"An' then they waded out to me, where I was gettin' a touch worried bein' as the tide was risin'. They sliced me free and hauled me in an' just as I was thinkin' this might be a piece of luck, be buggered if they don't force me to my knees and was goin' to chop my head off, execution style, I kid you not!"

"Yet here you are. What happened?" William asked.

"The man with the machete saw his back," Cassie interjected.

"Nah," Smith countered.

"Yes, that was what saved you," Cassie insisted. "He saw that mesh of scars all over you and decided that you had had just as many or maybe more whippings than him. And when he hesitated in his swing, I threw myself on top."

"And that changed his mind?" William was skeptical.

"It was what she was yellin', as she did so," Smith explained. "There she was, plasterin' herself all over me an' screamin', 'He helped to kill Carlos! He helped!' An' *that* was what made the difference," he nodded and beamed at Cassie.

"You helped?" Tess was confused. She had seen Carlos die. "How?"

Smith grinned at her. "That's exactly what Mambo asked, too." He looked at Cassie, letting her deliver the answer.

"He brought me a candle."

Chapter Ninety-Three

The branded woman who showed such fascination with Tess's ring came to speak in private to Tess and Cassie. She was fluent enough in English and from her they learned that she and Cassie had shared abuse at the hands of the same despised man and that it was indeed the matching brand that ensured Cassie's refuge here. The white sailor who had been found with Cassie, however, was another matter.

White people had to be eliminated, Mambo explained, especially any who knew of the village's location. The continued freedom of the escaped slaves living there depended upon it and any details of the maroons' existence had to be kept concealed from their former white owners.

"If dey capture us, dey kill us and hang de bodies on tall posts all around till dey be rotted. All white people be silenced. We stay secret from dem." She glanced at Cassie in an apologetic way, then reached out and palpated Cassie's brand once again. She seemed lost in thought for a few moments before she looked up and regarded Cassie's dark eyes with her own.

"Dis devil man. He is really dead?"

Tess and Cassie both nodded in confirmation. Their captor sighed and grasped their hands together in her own powerful grip. The silence was almost unbearable as she struggled with her decision. Then, with a lightening flick of her other hand, she slashed across their palms, splitting them open with a shard of stone. Holding their hands together, dripping with the welling blood, she commanded, "Look. Inside we are de same. All de same …."

Her voice trailed away and a low hum vibrated in her throat. She cast a glance skyward and then continued. "Devil man dead. Den we be on de same side." She squinted at Cassie and hissed, "Dat man wit' you done a great favor." Her eyes flickered between Cassie and Tess. "Maybe we let both your men live. For now."

Four white captives. Her decision was a difficult one. She was a former member of the Ashanti of Western Africa, and now the group's Mambo, a priestess who was skilled and knowledgeable in communing with the spirits. Astonishingly to her, Tess's birthmark closely resembled Erzulie's mark–Erzulie, the spirit of the powerful earth mother and one who was capable of prophesy, especially in dreams. Mambo decided that, initiated or not, Tess was clearly Erzulie's choice, and therefore Tess's safety was indisputable.

The young white man who had been with her at the shore was also unusual. It had not escaped Mambo's notice that he bore webbing between his fingers. *Is this a sign that he belongs to the gods of the sea?* The villagers depended on the generosity of the sea's deities to provide them with their much needed source of protein. *If he is harmed, will the gods be angered?* It was best not to risk it.

How is it that so many strange persons should be delivered into her care, Mambo wondered. She sighed. *The gods are complicated.*

The spinning rings were another matter. The rings' gems were phenomenal in their own right, but many pieces of beautiful and priceless jewelry abounded, brought back from exotic and far-away lands to this area. These islands were, after all, home to most of the world's treasure-seeking pirates. Pieces were bought, traded, stolen, and flaunted on a regular basis.

But these rings were unlike any others. When Cassie returned the ruby spinner to Tess, Mambo noticed that the rings clung to each other. The spinning of the rings was a quality that no others possessed. Such items were sure to be coveted; they could bring unbelievable value in trade. The conversation with Mambo had nearly come to an end before Tess had an opportunity to explain that her grandmother and companion were missing.

"I have to search for them. Even if," she swallowed hard, "even if they have washed up on shore"

"Not possible for you to go," Mambo flatly stated.

It was not until Tess explained that her grandmother was in possession of a third ring, also a bejeweled spinner, that Mambo reversed her decision. She agreed to send out a small, unobtrusive search party to learn of their whereabouts if they still lived.

"Dat be easy if dey be dead, harder if dey live and are hidin', harder still if dey already been found by others," she cautioned. "Somet'ing must be sent along, in case payment for dem is needed," she continued, eying Tess's rings.

For a moment Tess was torn—the rings were just beautiful trinkets. Perhaps all the abilities that she thought she had been given by them were only imagination and coincidence. On the other hand, she had *felt* their power—had *seen* the results with her own eyes. She couldn't part with them—and as she nervously twisted them on her fingers, she instantly knew that she *must not* part with them. Yet Mambo stood, insisting on a valuable item for her grandmother's ransom. Tess closed her eyes and quieted her rising panic. Blanking out the fear, she realized what she must do.

"I have another thing of great value," Tess countered, tearing open the seam on the side of her bodice and reaching in. She withdrew a flattened, highly polished round plate of glass. "This can be used to show you tiny things that you didn't know existed. I am certain that there is no other like it here," and she dropped the microscope's lens into Mambo's waiting hand.

The polished disc nestled in the woman's palm as though it had been waiting all this time to settle into such a perfect fit.

Chapter Ninety-Four

Night was falling quickly as the villagers prepared for a ceremony. A large center pole fashioned from a tree trunk had been erected, its end tamped into a deep and narrow pit dug into the earth. Drums and rattles had been strewn in a wide circle about the pole, and the women were placing offering baskets of fruits and vegetables in strategic places around those.

The ceremony took place as the moon hit her vertex in the sky. Every member of this colony participated, taking turns drumming, singing, and dancing. The drums' sonorous voices reverberated off the cliffs' walls and pounded against the participants' chests, blending with the rhythm of their own life forces coursing through their bodies. The songs were sung in a foreign tongue, but the melodies and harmonies were hypnotically engaging. The shipwreck survivors felt themselves being drawn into the pageantry, compelled to dance and sing as joyously, as fervently and as unfettered as those around them.

"This reminds me of the night I saw you playing your flute on board the *Mary Jane*," Tess yelled breathlessly and she and William danced around the pole, following the patterned footsteps of the celebrating villagers.

"Me too," William replied. "I'd always hoped to get another chance at this."

"At what?" Tess teased.

"Dancing by your side. Only the first time, I was wishing that I was still hurt, so that I could have leaned into your arms, and now I'm wishing that I wasn't, so that I could take you into mine," William answered. Tess could feel herself blush at his honest reply, flushing with pleasure at his bluntness. She made a mental note to herself to do a healing session with William's knee in the morning.

All around them the drums and rattles and chants reached a dizzying pitch. It seemed impossible that the entire island would not be able to hear the festivities. Tess hoped that her grandmother could hear the rhythm, wherever she was.

She is still alive. I know it. I feel it in my heart … and I feel it with my ring.

Tess could not bring herself to consider any other possibility. The scouts would be leaving in a few hours, traveling in the safety of the early morning's moonlit shadows. They would look, they would inquire among those that they could make safe contact with, and they would search again. *They have to be successful. They just have to.*

Several dancers had fallen to the ground, some out of exhaustion and some in apparent trances, and it was then that Tess noticed Cassie crouched at the foot of one of the huts. Her shoulders shook as she buried her face in her hands.

"Cass …?" Tess approached her sister gently. "Cass, what's wrong?"

Cassie lifted her tear stained face up to Tess. "The baby. I felt it move. Oh my God, I felt it move!" she cried.

"That's good, Cass. That's what babies do—they kick and flip and turn," Tess floundered, not knowing what to say to ease Cassie's distress. "Feeling your baby move … is a good thing," she reiterated.

"It just makes it all so real," Cassie wept. "I am defiled. I carry another man's child." She looked at Tess and sobbed, "Who would ever want me now?"

Before Tess could reply, they were startled by a quick movement beside them.

"I would," Samuel Smith spoke, his voice tender as he stepped out of the depth of the shadows. "With all of my heart."

Chapter Ninety-Five

The searchers were expected to return within seven days. It was with much surprise then, that the lookouts ballyhooed their return just before noon of the third day. The returning scouts explained, with some annoyance, that they would have arrived even sooner if the found man's leg had been intact, but with one foot missing, he had had to be carried for much of the trip.

The white woman and man had been easily located. A covert inquiry had been made to a group of sugar mill workers at the nearest plantation situated at the foot of the island's mountains. Yes, the mill workers had easily confided, a pair matching the description had been recovered from the shoreline directly to the east of the plantation's edge. The two white people had been brought back to the plantation by the owners in fact, to work as a carpenter and a seamstress in the big house, when they had recovered well enough.

"Did you use the lens—the polished glass—to buy their freedom?" Tess impatiently asked the leader of the returning troupe.

"No," the long-haired caramel-skinned man replied, shaking his head in either disgust or disbelief—Tess was not sure which—as he looked back at the two new arrivals who were still struggling in their descent down the hillside.

"No, dat woman," he frowned and snorted, as though unable to believe his own words. "Dat round glass she use to buy dat black goat!"

Word of the shipwreck had spread rapidly among the island's inhabitants, and news regarding it had been brought back by the scouting party.

"I heard the plantation owner telling his wife not to worry. He told her that one of Carlos Crisanto's ships had capsized, whilst the other had been blown onto the reef of another island altogether," Tess's grandmother informed Tess and the others.

"Which ship sunk?" William pressed her for details.

"Didn't hear that. Don't know if they knew themselves. All that I heard after that was that the cargoes of both was probably lost forever. An' no mention of our poor little Tommy either, bless his soul." She dabbed at her eyes. "It's a past wiped clean. Just the six of us left." She looked at each of them. "We was brought together fer a reason, ya' know. Always somethin' comes from somethin' don'cha know?"

Relief at having found her grandmother soothed Tess's immediate worries, yet she woke each morning from sweet dreams that filled her head only to have them replaced with the pain of remembered losses, burning like an incision that was being slowly peeled open. *Grief is the price we pay for the gift of love* ... She wondered what balm could heal such an ache, as she busied herself with the daily chores, focusing on the exhausting business of tribal health care.

Within the first few weeks, Tess quickly established herself as one whose healing abilities surpassed even Mambo's. With the aid of the emeralds once again encircling her fourth finger, her advice and treatment were credited with Jacko's ongoing recovery.

Slowly others sought her out. Wounds and fevers, boils and babies—all were potential life threatening conditions in the tropics—and the Maroons therefore had nothing to lose in seeking Tess's help. Her knowledge and assessments were a good complement to Mambo's potions and botanical ingredients.

Cassie assisted with the weeding of the small gardens and tiny fields, while Mrs. Hanley made wonderful broths and mashes out of the measly food supplies available to the village's inhabitants. Shortly after her liberation from the plantation's big house, she had mysteriously been able to produce a moderate supply of tasty herbs and spices from numerous pockets sewn within the tattered folds of her skirt.

The three men quickly proved their usefulness as they expertly reinforced the camp's ramshackle living quarters with pieces of wooden debris recently scavenged from the shoreline. The village's huts which had been hastily erected to begin with, now boasted sturdy frames upon which heavily camouflaged surfaces, woven with fronds and vines, provided comfortable shelter from the daily tropical downpours as well as from the winds that affected the camp situated so high above the mainland.

Nevertheless, it was plain to all, that accommodating six extra people imposed a new strain on the existing living space.

It was Smith who arrived at an unexpected solution of sorts. He felt, however, a need to confer with William before putting his plan into place.

✦

Tess and Cassie sat side by side, taking a break from tending the meager plants which grew in tidy rows at the side of the camp. Both of them were weary in the midday heat. Cassie seemed resigned to her changing body and even smiled as she held a hand over her expanding girth, feeling her baby's strengthening kicks.

As Cassie wondered out loud where Smith and William had wandered off to, Tess idly spun her rings, thinking that she should probably remove them if she was going to do daily physical labor with her hands. Both of them nodded a polite greeting when Mambo strolled past and without warning, an absurd thought struck Tess, as clear as any event in her life.

"So where do you think they got to anyway?" Cassie was asking.

Tess, oblivious to Cassie's question, stared at the retreating silhouette of Mambo and her heart began to race in her chest. It was then that she realized that she was still spinning her rings. Fidgeting with them was becoming an obsessive habit. Quickly she squelched their movements, holding them still. The series of a few insistent pictures continued to play over and over in her head.

"Tess?" Cassie's gentle tug on her arm brought Tess out of her jumble of thoughts.

"Cass," Tess replied in a wary tone, "I've just had a vision—at least that's what I think it was—and I think we'd better get prepared."

It was only a few heart-stopping minutes before William and Smith reappeared around the corner of one of the huts. The Mambo stood behind them and watched as they made their way back up the path. They stopped just short of Tess and Cassie, their faces creased with worry.

Tess's heart pounded furiously and she felt the familiar vise-like grip of apprehension encircling her. She wasn't sure if she could suffer through any more uncertainty, any more change in her life. Bathed in such thoughts, her anxiety began to build, crushing her as William began to speak.

"Uh, I was wondering if—if—" William stuttered shyly and glanced nervously at Smith who stood completely tongue-tied but who stared at the rings adorning Tess's hand.

My God! Tess was momentarily confused. It had not escaped her notice that the rings remained the objects of many envious glances and outright stares. *Was I wrong? Don't tell me that they're going to ask to use the rings to ransom our freedom! They might be the way to our freedom—but free to go where?* Protectively, she nestled one hand over the rings on her fingers. A clear picture flashed in her mind at that moment and she inhaled deeply, her heart pounding.

William tried again. "We talked to Mambo and she …." William stopped and licked his lips, his mouth having suddenly gone dry.

Tess glanced at Cassie who looked no less anxious. In fact Cassie was visibly swaying, overcome with a dizziness that threatened to fell her. As Tess's own apprehension exploded, Cassie began to crumple. Her collapse broke Smith out of his stupor and he threw himself forward, catching her in mid-fall. Clutching her to his chest, he lifted a panic-filled face towards Tess.

"Wha—what's wrong with her?" he stammered.

"Nothing she won't recover from," Tess replied, more convinced than ever that the vision had somehow been a truthful glimpse into the near future.

Gathered in Smith's arms, Cassie stirred and her eyes fluttered. She stared up at his face, her eyebrows raised in surprise, but she made no effort to move.

William continued to look from Smith and Cassie back to Tess and appeared as though he truly regretted having started this dialogue, and that he might consider fainting himself.

"Would you please speak your intended thoughts and spare us all any further anguish?" Tess demanded. She had not intended for her words to have sounded quite so harsh and for a moment she empathized with his discomfort. Tentatively William reached out for her hand and taking a breath, struggled to find his next words. Tess could stand it no longer.

"Oh for goodness sakes!" she exploded impatiently. "Yes! From both of us! We'll give it serious consideration."

Three pairs of eyes locked onto her in astonishment.

"Yes to what?" Cassie inquired, freeing herself from Smith's arms and stumbling to her feet.

It was Tess's turn to become overtaken with sudden embarrassment. *What if the vision was wrong? What if it was only my imagination?*

A matching pair of face-splitting grins chased away the initial looks of shock on the faces of both William and Smith.

"You'll agree to think about it?" William voiced his proposal aloud, his voice tight with hope.

Tess regarded Cassie, whose brows were gathered together in complete incomprehension.

"Yes to what? Tess! Surely you aren't going to give up your rings!" Cassie's accusation hung in the air.

"My rings?" Now it was Tess's brows that pulled together in confusion. "Of course not!" She studied her sister's worried face. And then it hit her.

Of course Cassie doesn't understand—can't understand what's only been thought of and not yet said out loud! The vision had been right. The rings really did have the powers. *I just have to learn to focus on their messages to me. To trust in myself, in my inner knowledge.* It was becoming easier. The rings were a part of her new future now and for the first time since having left London, Tess felt the cloak of sadness slipping off her shoulders. Change did not always have to be foreboding. She understood that now. Perhaps she had little control of what was to come, but she had full control over how she chose to respond. The realization left her speechless and a little lightheaded with the tingle of a faint but growing joy.

"We'll build two more huts then," Smith was announcing simply, having found his voice at last. "The Mambo's agreed to do a ceremony of sorts," he added, "if you'd be in agreement with makin' do with the local customs …."

"Ceremony?" Understanding slowly replaced the confusion in Cassie's face and she gasped and blushed at the same time.

"Are you asking for my hand, Samuel?" she asked Smith unable to hide the incredulity in her voice.

"I'd like yer hand, yer heart, and … yup, I am," Smith concluded, his attempt at a romantic reply petering out.

Tess stared at William, who stood before her, still lost for words. Shyly he raised one hand and made a fist then spread his fingers out.

Ooh-ah. It was a choked whisper. He had barely mouthed the syllables out loud but there they were. Slowly reaching out to meet William's outstretched palm with her own, Tess marveled at the strength and size of his hand compared to her own. His fingers curled and grasped hers, his touch as warm as the smile that was spreading across his face.

"It won't matter who gives the blessings, will it? No matter how the ceremony's done?" William asked, swallowing thickly.

Tentatively leaning forward, she touched her lips softly to William's. As he wrapped his arms around her, pressing his mouth to hers, she felt him tasting her, inhaling her delicious scent, responding to her sweet breath upon his skin. Her lips lingered a moment longer upon his before she broke away, her voice full of promise.

"Our hearts will know the right words."

Chapter Ninety-Six

Finding Mr. Lancaster resting in the cool shade of an overhanging bough, Tess squatted down to examine him. She had stopped by to treat his stump, as the tender skin covering the end of his amputation had been torn open by the reef when he had been swept ashore during the storm. Mambo had given a salve to Tess and she applied it carefully to his stump's ragged wound. The carpenter scowled and grunted in discomfort, and then suddenly screeched, "Hold off! That burns like the flames of Hell, an' I'd rather snuff it from the pus than to have ya' burn me leg off a wee bit at a time!" His eyes bulged with indignation.

"Shush now, an' hold still," Mrs. Hanley scolded him and then added, "It'll heal ya' an' I want ya' to be in good enough form to dance with me at our weddin'."

"What?" Tess asked in astonishment. She looked at her grandmother and then at her patient who suddenly stared at his bleeding stump with a freshly found intense interest.

"*Your* wedding? Whose idea was–?"

Tess's incredulous inquiry was cut short by a cough and another grunt from Mr. Lancaster. He glanced at Tess for only a moment before dropping his gaze to study his leg once more.

"Your Gram, well, ya' know how she feels about things happenin' in three's–fer good luck an' all–an' it seemed an alright thing to do …." His voice trailed away and he shrugged his broad shoulders as though that was all the explanation in the world that was needed.

Tess looked at her grandmother who was grinning broadly, her news having been officially revealed.

"Can you use the ring, darlin'? To help his leg heal up quick, I mean."

"Gram," Tess began, examining the three rings upon her fingers. *Their brilliance in the tropical sunlight is remarkable. Almost like a rainbow of colors upon my hand.* "Do you really believe the story about these rings and why they were made in the first place?" Even as she asked aloud, her thoughts took a different direction. *Perhaps the leg really would benefit from a meditation and the glow of the emeralds, too.* The wound upon her own neck was nothing more than a thin purple scar now, and William's limp had certainly cleared since she had treated him.

Her grandmother looked at Tess in surprise. "Why, what's not to believe?"

"It just seems so ... incredible," Tess muttered.

"Darlin', it's the strengths of beliefs what makes the world 'round ya' real, don'cha know? 'Course ya' do," her grandmother clucked, and looked warmly at Mr. Lancaster.

"But, she called me a "Quintspinner"," Tess replied. "The Crone—she called me a 'Quintspinner' and ... well ... *quint* means five ...." Tess's voiced trailed away. "And all I have are *three* rings."

"Why, that just means life is not finished with ya' yet, me darlin'" her grandmother cut in, nodding her head in her usual sagely way. "Yer only better'n halfway through yer own quest now, isn't that so? An' in the meantime, ye've found someone very special to spend it with, haven't ya'?" she added, then quietly murmured, "as have I." She gripped Mr. Lancaster's hand in her own, beaming at the craggy carpenter who sat blushing furiously at her side. "There's always somethin' what comes from somethin'," she added softly to herself, nodding in confirmation.

"No, me darlin'," her grandmother continued happily out loud, "maybe there'll be more– 'Quintspinner' sorta' promises ya' two more, don't it?–an' maybe you'll just have to practice with what you've got 'til then, learnin' what they can do fer ya', an' all that. Three's a good number after all, ya' know."

Tess stared into her grandmother's eyes, so like her own—she could see that now—and waited, expecting to be retold the details of the magic of numbers. Instead her grandmother reached out and cradled her face, the sun-wrinkled fingers still tender and soft upon Tess's skin.

"I was always afraid, ya' know," the older woman continued calmly, "that my life was gonna' be lived too carefully to have anythin' worth tellin' about." She looked into Tess's eyes, her own shining with love for her granddaughter. Tess smiled back at her. As always, her grandmother had a way of seeing things in a positive light.

Before Tess could say anything in return, her grandmother carried on. "Three rings, maybe four, an'," she sighed, "maybe, just maybe, all five'll come to ya', when the time is right an' maybe each will have its own adventures attached. Who knows?"

Her grandmother bent forward and kissed Tess softly on the forehead, then giving her an impish grin and gathering her up in a loving bear-hug, she chuckled, "But that's another story altogether ...."

The End

LaVergne, TN USA
24 October 2010

202067LV00003B/35/P